SHOCKING HEAVEN

A room 103 Novel

**Eve & Jax's
Story**

By D H Sidebottom

Karen
with love
DHSidebottom

SHOCKING HEAVEN

Copyright © 2013

By D H Sidebottom

Contents

PART 1

PROLOGUE

Eve grumbled as shouting stirred her from her dreams. She rubbed her sore eyes, pulling her soft pink duvet further up to her chin as she tried to drag herself back to the pleasant dream she was having of Frankie, the boy she had the hots for at school.

She recognised her Dad's voice but she struggled to identify the other man's, it didn't sound the least bit friendly.

Being used to these moments, Eve shut her mind off and closed her eyes. The shouting stopped yet the voices seemed to be getting closer, in fact bang outside her bedroom door.

Suddenly all the hairs on Eve's body stood up as goose bumps erupted and she shivered, her internal alarms blaring loudly although she couldn't understand why.

Her breathing hitched when she heard the voices outside her door. She strained to listen but she couldn't ascertain what was been said.

She swallowed heavily when she heard her door handle squeak and squeezed her eyes shut, feigning sleep.

"Eve?" Her dad whispered but Eve remained silent.

"Mmm, not bad," the other man said as her dad sighed heavily.

"Please don't hurt her," he whispered.

Eve couldn't help opening her eyes to look at both men. "Dad?" she asked in a whisper as she took in his distraught expression. He looked away from her, sucking on his lips as he shook his head slightly.

Eve shuddered as she saw the other man's leer. "Eve, hi." He smiled as he approached and plonked his large body beside her on the bed. She scrambled up the bed as the man reached up and stroked her cheek with the back of his hand. "Hi, Eve." He smiled again and Eve gulped at his intimate touch. "We're gonna have a bit of fun pretty girl," he smirked and Eve's eyes widened.

She looked to her father. "Dad?" she pleaded, asking him to take him away.

She didn't like him, he gave her the creeps and she scuttled further into her headboard when his hand stroked down her neck.

There was only Frankie that had ever looked at her like this man was looking at her. Even at thirteen Eve understood the look of lust in a man's eyes and she was now frightened.

When his hand continued towards her small breasts she turned to her father. "Dad?" she choked out. Why the hell was he stood immobile when this man was touching places nobody had ever touched before?

"You're very pretty, Eve." The man smiled at her before he turned to her dad. "Deal," he stated simply. Her Dad sighed as if relieved, but his pained expression turned to Eve.

"I'm so sorry, Princess." He gulped and Eve frowned.

"Dad, what's going on?" she asked but he turned away and headed out of her door, quietly closing it behind him, leaving her alone with this creepy man.

Eve shot off her bed as the man's hand grasped her breast roughly. "What are you doing?" she stuttered as she backed her body against her wall.

"Get back here, Eve," the man said but Eve shook her head rapidly.

"You need to get out of my room," she said, pulling courage from somewhere, she had no idea where.

"Don't make me come to you, Eve or you will regret it," he demanded.

Eve trembled at the man's authority. She shook her head and made a sprint towards her door but she wasn't fast enough as the man's giant hand grabbed her hair and yanked her backwards, flinging her back on the bed. "Now keep still you little bitch," he growled as he climbed beside her.

Oh God, why was he touching her legs under her nightie?

"Dad!" she shouted but his hand came over her mouth.

Eve shook her head rapidly as tears rolled down her cheeks. "Please don't," she rasped but his hand got higher and higher. "Noooo......."

CHAPTER 1

"You sure they're okay here?" Mom asked. I smiled my acknowledgement with a nod. She smiled faintly before placing the boxes on the floor and took another look around my room.

"You think you'll be okay here, Eve?" she asked, no more than a whisper and I could hear the pain in her voice.

I smiled softly and nodded. "I think so," but added a shrug.

We both stood silent as Mom came to terms with my departure. I could feel her tears and despair from across the room and I made my way towards her.

Not sure what to say I just smiled again. She nodded and sucked in her lips, desperately trying to control her emotions. Dragging in an unsteady breath she palmed my cheek. "Eve," she whispered and I felt a tear escape at her turmoil.

"It's gonna be okay, Mom."

She nodded determinedly, "Of course." A tight smile pulled at her lips. "You have Cam and Aaron will be here in a few days." I nodded again.

This was so difficult. I hated to leave her. She needed me. She needed all of us after... after Dad's death.

And now we, all three of her children, were at university. Spreading our wings and leaving her behind... alone.

Mom swallowed heavily and grasped my hands, her sweaty palms sliding in mine. "Eve." Her face tightened as she struggled with her words, "It's... it's time to be free Eve, and live. Make sure you live. For me..." I fought the lump in my throat and nodded. Simply nodded. No words were there for what she needed to hear.

She rested her lips on my forehead. "Spread your wings, Angel. Your past is gone... left behind. Gone. Now it's your time to flourish."

She pulled away, nodded once and left, without looking back.

I sank down on my bare bed, my blurred vision concentrating on the swirls in the pattern of the threadbare carpet, as I heard her engine purr.

I was still sat in the silence as the familiar sound disappeared.

Alone, free... I sure as hell didn't feel free.

***

A soft tap stirred me from my dark thoughts and I looked up, confused at how dark it now was.

How long had I been sat here?

"E?" a voice came from behind the door. I blinked. Another tap snapped me conscious and I made my way to the door. "E? You in there?"

"Yeah," I answered quietly before I pulled open my door.

Cam beamed at me, his bright wide smile already lifting my spirits and I instantly relaxed. He entered without an invite and I chuckled as he scowled, his open thoughts on my room displayed in his curled lip. "Christ, E. It's a bit…"

I shrugged as he turned to look at me, "It's fine."

I shook my head at him and he regarded me seriously, "How was Mom?"

I exhaled a breath then sucked it back in through my teeth, "Rough but…"

Cam's face clouded and he shrugged, "She'll live. It'll do her good… some alone time. She gave us enough of it!"

I scowled at him. "Don't, Cam."

He snorted but moved on. "Anyway, you'll be at mine more than here so…" He shrugged as he took another grimace at my room. I agreed with him… it was shite!

"It is a bit… cold." I admitted and he chuckled low.

"Cold?" he repeated with wide eyes.

I giggled. "Fucking shit would be better but cold sounds more…humane!" I rectified.

He flung his head back and laughed, "Damn right, E. Shit is still being lenient."

I slapped his arm. "Hey, this is my home for the next year, try and be… optimistic," I scolded and his brows lifted.

"Optimistic would be calling it derelict," he scoffed but I shrugged.

"It'll be okay when I've put up some stuff and Luce will be here soon. I'm sure she'll work some magic." I smiled, more to myself than my brother as I let my gaze roam around the barren room. I gave a slight grimace but nodded my head firmly; endorsing my thoughts to myself, rather than Cam.

"Listen. Party at mine tonight, 9 O'clock. I can introduce you to everyone. Bring Luce." He grinned as he passed me his address on a piece of paper and waggled his eyebrows.

I smiled back and nodded. "Sure, although I do know where you live, Cam." I frowned at the piece of paper. "Gonna go to the digs bar first and see if they have any jobs going before all the others arrive."

He nodded, rubbing my arm. "Good idea. The address is so you get it right if you need to get a taxi. You've only been once!" He tipped his head towards the door. "Gonna go, catch up with the guy's. Settle back in before lectures start."

He stalked across the room, making his way to leave but turned back with a dark expression. "Listen, E." He swallowed roughly.

I nodded as I gave him a sad smile. "I know, Cam. It's okay." I shrugged. It had to be.

He smiled and sighed but nodded in return. "Yeah."

✳✳✳

The 'Z' Bar was temporarily being used as a registration office for Fresher's and as I entered through the door, the noise was deafening, the scent of sweaty bodies and beer permeating the air.

I squinted, already feeling the beginnings of a headache, and worked my way over to the bar, squeezing myself expertly between the mob already waiting to be served.

The dishevelled tall blonde girl situated behind the worn slab of wood, lifted her tired eyebrows at me, "What can I get ya' honey?"

Giving her my best smile, I leaned towards her. "I'm looking for a job."

She seemed to sag in both appreciation and relief. "You got any experience?" She asked as she glared at a lad that hammered his fist on the bar. "Wait!" she barked.

I nodded, "Two years waitressing but I practically lived in a pub so..."

She didn't give me time to finish. Tilting her chin to her side of the bar she grinned wickedly. "Come on. Let's see how you hang on with this lot."

I blinked, "Now?"

She nodded slowly. "Yep, sugar... Now!" she confirmed then disappeared to the other side of the bar to serve the hammering guy.

Shrugging, I tapped the boy beside me. He turned and lifted his eyebrows in query. "Help me over and I'll serve you first."

He grinned and I suddenly found his hands around my waist as he hoisted me up. Luckily for me he was a big guy and luckily for him I was tiny.

I winked back at him as I dropped over the other side. "What can I get you?"

He grinned at me, "VK Blue." I nodded and turned, scouring the low fridges that ran the length of the back wall behind the bar.

Locating the blue bottle and popping the cap, I placed it on the bar in front of him with a smile. He handed me a note but I shook my head, "On me."

He smiled his thanks. "What's ya' name?" he asked as his eyes flicked over my body.

"Eve." I answered as I wrote the amount I owed for his drink on the back of my hand.

He nodded and then grinned slyly, "As in forbidden fruit?"

I winked at him. "The very same!"

***

Walking through my dorm room door after three hours of serving drunken teenagers, I flopped exhaustedly onto my still unmade bed.

Smiling to myself I was already happy with the outcome of the day. I had moved out; fair enough into a shithole, landed a job I could do and would enjoy. I'd been tipped well by numerous lads and finally gained my freedom... or what I hoped would result in my freedom.

Lucy's loud tones echoed through the thin walls and I grinned at the sound. I loved my best friend.

"You tell all the boys 'No'
Makes you feel good, yeah

*I know you're out of my league
But that won't scare me away, oh no."*

Leaving my room, I made my way towards the kitchen where I could hear Luce singing *Emile Sande's, 'Beneath your beautiful'.*

She was stood against the cooker, undoubtedly destroying some innocent, once edible food, singing loudly. I joined in behind her, prompting her to turn and grin at me as I took over.

*"You've carried on so long,
You couldn't stop if you tried it
You've built your wall so high
That no one could climb it
But I'm gonna try."*

"E! Your voice eats some serious shit girl. It's husky and sexy enough to land you in a band," she declared loudly, always open and brutally honest was Luce. She hugged me, squashing me enough for one of my ribs to complain, "You're here!"

I scanned my own body. "Well, I think it's me Luce but you never know, aliens and all that..."

Rolling her eyes she walked back over to the cooker as a girl glided in. Her bright pink spiky hair, skinny frame and pale skin made her look ill but she smiled widely at us, "Hey girls." Holding out her hand I took the offering and smiled back at her. "Kaylee Miller," She introduced.

"Eve, but people call me E and this is Luce," I returned her introduction as we surveyed each other.

She seemed to accept us both when she nodded. "Anybody else here yet?" she asked as her eyes scanned over the room. Her lip curled when she spotted Luce's bright orange concoction. She flicked me a disgusted grimace and I nodded in agreement with a cringe.

"No, there's a lad coming in today but the rest aren't joining us while Sunday," Luce revealed as she turned back to us.

"What ya' cooking, Luce?" I held my breath, waiting for the dreaded information.

"Well…" she paused and cocked her head at the pan, "it's kinda a mix of veg soup, bacon and sausage… so sausage casserole." She shrugged as though it would be expected that, of course it was a sausage casserole.

Kaylee and I nodded slowly. "Uh-huh," I acknowledged before she turned back round to guard her fodder.

"Ladies." A deep voice sounded from behind us. I jumped and we all spun round.

He was tall, in fact he was huge and I silently wondered if he was a basketball player. His light brown hair was messy but it gave him that cute boy next door look and his smile was wide and filled his whole face.

"Hi." I smiled and walked over to him, holding out my hand in greeting, "E."

He frowned. "E?" His eyes perused every inch of me.

"Short for Eve."

"Ahh," he accepted before he turned to the others, his gaze stalling on Luce before returning to me. "Gavin White."

I smiled and nodded, "Welcome to Huntsman Block, Gavin White."

Returning the smile he stalked over to Luce and peered into the pan, "What the hell?"

Kaylee shot me a horrified look and I cringed.

Luce glared.

Gavin grimaced.

"Looks really... good," he backtracked quickly but Luce wasn't convinced.

"Wanna try?" She pursed her lips and narrowed her eyes on him as she offered some on a spoon.

He held up his hands in front of him as if to ward off evil spirits, which may have been released from the fumes of Lucy's concoction. "Thanks but I gotta... unpack." He retreated swiftly and disappeared through the door.

We all exchanged glances and Luce sucked in her cheeks; a sign of her temper.

"Well I'm starving," I placated as I silently cursed myself for my softness.

Kaylee nodded as if sensing Lucy's hurt feelings too. "Me too. How long until it's ready?"

I gave her a grateful smile as Luce turned back to her meal. "About five minutes," she answered and we both swallowed in apprehension.

"That's good then... Hey, party at Cam's tonight," I informed her, trying to shift the mood.

It worked. She grinned widely. "Goody. I can't wait to meet his housemates. They're supposed to be in a rock band."

I nodded. "Yeah. I think so. You wanna join us Kaylee?"

Kaylee grinned gratefully, "God, yes. Hot rock group?"

I chuckled and confirmed with a nod. "Then you can definitely count me in," she beamed but it swiftly fell when Luce placed a bowl of her unique cuisine in front of us both.

"Wow," we both breathed together.

CHAPTER 2

The door vibrated under my fist. The music was loud and the party was in full swing as the door opened and a grinning Cam greeted us. "E." His eyes widened when he spotted Kaylee.

"Hey." I rolled my eyes at his obvious appreciation. His face swung back to me and I tipped my chin towards the hallway. He frowned but then realisation sank in and he moved aside to let us in.

His eyes tracked Kaylee as she pressed passed him.

The music was pumping a rock track as bodies filled every corner of the small house. Cam took my hand and led us straight through into the kitchen.

People stood around and the table housed a shot competition. I caught Cam's wink as he tipped his head towards the game and I nodded slyly.

"Guy's. This is my little sis, E." Everybody turned to look at me. I shrank a little under the scrutiny.

A guy with the purest white spiky hair I had ever seen stood and stalked over to us. His bright blue eyes twinkled as he perused my body and his grin widened. His short sleeved T-shirt revealed both arms full of tattoos. I noticed how they reached up his neck and continued onto his face. I knew instinctively that he had a full bodied tattoo.

"Nice," he murmured as his eyes continued their inspection. "How ya' doing, Spanner?" His rough voice made me smile and he grinned back.

"Spanner?" I queried as Cam snorted beside me and I frowned.

"Yeah, Spanner... you tighten my nuts, sweetheart" he revealed with a smirk. Luce giggled beside me.

My eyebrows rose and I shook my head in confusion. I didn't think I warranted this much appreciation. I knew I wasn't ugly, just normal really. My wavy brown waist length hair was my best feature and I loved the deep red strip that decorated my fringe but I was tiny, all of 5 foot 2 inches with breasts that echoed my size... small. My tiny waist flowed out to wide hips and, in my opinion, a larger than average bottom.

"E, meet Romeo, lead Guitarist of Room 103." Cam's voice sliced my thoughts.

Romeo held out his hand and I hesitantly gripped it. "Real names Daniel Wolfe, but everyone calls me Romeo... you can call me anything you want," he revealed with a wink.

I instantly thought that his name was very appropriate for his personality, as another man approached us. "And this here is Ethan Hart AKA Boss, drummer and manager of Room 103. "Boss, meet E, Cam's little sister," Romeo introduced.

I flicked my eyes over Boss quickly. He looked normal enough. His long blonde hair was pulled into a pony at the nape of his neck and from what I could see he only sported one single tattoo beneath his ear, *'Room 103'*.

As soon as he opened his mouth I realised looks can be deceiving.

"Sweetness, Fuck!" he growled as he cupped his crotch and my eyes widened at his greeting.

Cam coughed faintly. "Boss!" he warned.

Boss flung his head back and laughed loudly. I realised he was high. "Simmer, Cam. You never said your sister was a fucking walking wet dream."

What did I say to that?

Luce nudged me and I eyed her apprehensively. Her eyes were full of humour but mine didn't reflect hers. Boss gave me the shivers and I swiftly placed my hand on Cam's forearm before he floored Boss, giving him a slight shake of my head.

"Fuck, Boss! Leave the poor girl alone, you'll scare the shit out of her." I spun round at the voice and was met with a face full of piercings, sparkly blue eyes and a close shaven head.

"Chase Donnelly, bass guitar, but everyone calls me Bulk." I smiled in appreciation for the diversion from Boss, he winked as though he could read my thoughts.

"Bulk?" I asked as I regarded all his piercings. He was decorated with 2 eyebrow bars, 3 lip rings, at least 8 studs in each ear, and a few in his nose with some dermal piercings on his neck.

Boss snorted beside me, "You sure you wanna know the answer to that question, baby?"

I nodded faintly, now comprehending why they called him 'Bulk'...obviously a reference to his man parts. Bulk winked and surveyed the room with a frown, "Where's Jax?" They all rotated their heads and then shrugged, together as one. I fought the smile as I took in their simultaneous motions.

"Most likely fucking!" Boss declared before sitting at the table then patted the chair beside him. "Come on, E. Let's get you naked or pissed," he smirked and I pursed my lips.

Hesitantly sitting beside him I shuffled my chair a little further away. He grinned and nudged his closer, giving me a sly grin. Rolling my eyes I smiled at the rest of the game players.

"Flip, sip or strip," Boss declared. I nodded. "You know how to play, hot stuff?"

"Sure," I nodded and smiled when I felt Cam's hands settle on my shoulders and squeeze.

Boss gestured to the other three people sat at the table, "Greg, Harvey and Jess."

They each smiled at me. I returned my own before Boss slapped the coin in the middle of the table, "Youngest goes first."

All eyes rolled to me and I shrugged and nodded.

"Call" Jess shouted as I flipped the coin.

"Heads."

Boss chuckled when it landed on tails, "Sip or strip, baby!"

Giving him a coy look I tipped back the shot, slamming the glass down as I passed him the coin. "Call," I said as he chose heads. It was tails.

"Sip or strip, baby" I winked.

He side huddled me. "I think I like you" he smirked.

The game continued until Boss and Greg were slaughtered and donning only boxers. Harvey had already passed out under the table and Jess was well on her way with just underwear. I was sat in jeans and my bra, untouched by the alcohol.

"Winner!" Boss declared as he raised my arm in the air. The room exploded in applause and I chuckled before the kitchen door flung open with a bang and a tall slim girl burst in.

Her manic eyes scanned the room and dropped onto Boss. "Sort him the fuck out," she raged, her face tight with her rage.

Boss flung his head back and laughed heartily. "Fuck Fran, you should know him by now." He shrugged, completely disregarding her argument.

Fran growled at him, "I'm fucking done!"

Boss shrugged again as she stormed through the outside door, slamming it loudly behind her.

"Oops," a husky voice spoke behind us, we all turned to look.

He was hot. Oh God, he was very hot! His deep green eyes landed on mine before they fell to my chest, widening in appreciation as he spotted the single dermal piercing I had in the centre of my breastbone. His lips curled upwards before he shifted his gaze back to my face.

He was topless, just wearing faded blue jeans hung low on his hips and I caught my breath at his physique. He had muscles where they should be on a man; strong pecs and defined abs with strong arms. His right nipple was pierced and his right arm was sleeved with ink. Just above each hip displayed a wing tattoo beside his man trial but it was his face that held me.

He was stunning. His short spiked black hair flattered his strong facial features, from his sharp eyes to his slightly stubbled square chin. His chiselled cheekbones screamed masculinity and even his straight nose fitted the image.

He was pure rock star. But once again, don't judge a book by its cover!

"Babe!" was all he said, his gravelly tone sending a shiver up my spine. His cocky eyebrows lifted high on his face as his eyes roamed back over me, coming to a halt on my bra covered breasts.

I had been eye-fucked plenty of times in my short 18 years, but I had never been eye-fucked like this before... hard and brutal against an imaginary wall, at a thousand powerful thrusts per second. I nearly orgasmed just from the sensation he pounded into me from those stern green eyes.

Christ!

"Jax, this is my sister, E." Cam introduced before leaning into his ear. "I'll warn you once, out of bounds!" Jax swung his eyes to Cam with a sly grin. "I mean it, Jax. She doesn't need your shit, man," Cam defended. I bristled slightly at Cam's warning. I could handle myself. I'd been doing it long before now.

Jax held up his hands in defence. "Sure." But he flicked his gaze back on me, his lips twitching with humour. His cockiness twinkled through his eyes and I decided I didn't like him. Just like that!

I diverted my gaze back to the table and downed another shot. "Hell Hot stuff, where the hell are you putting them?" Boss asked as he swung his arm over my shoulder and pulled me close.

I winked. "Stuff doesn't touch me… immune," I disclosed with a wry smile.

He laughed loudly and squeezed me tight, "Fuck baby, you could have warned us."

I scrunched up my nose and shoulder bumped him, "Where's the fun in that?"

"My turn," Kaylee announced. I shifted out of the chair for her to take over.

As I turned I saw Jax still eyeing me. His gaze dropped to my chest as I pulled my T-shirt back on and I cocked my head at him apologetically. He beamed at me before winking and disappeared from the room.

A few hours later, Kaylee had mysteriously disappeared with Cam, Luce was slumped in a corner of the sofa unconscious and Boss had finally decided I wasn't going to relent and give him the blow job he'd been asking for, for the last hour. So swiping another bottle of beer, I took myself and it out into the fresh air.

The weed inside the house was making me slightly light headed and I was struggling to focus.

I leant onto the railing of the decking and appreciated Cam's house for the first time. It was a stark contrast to my dorm. Boasting six bedrooms, the detached Georgian house still sported some of its original features complete with exquisite cornices, sash windows and panelled rooms. The furnishings were sparse but then again it was occupied by six males and I didn't think they would value lots of decorative items.

My dorm however had crumbling plaster, cold rooms and threadbare carpets with a thin coating of what can only be described as 'stained, off-white' painted walls. I chuckled to myself as I compared the two, their similarities were worlds apart.

A sound from down the garden caught my attention. I focussed my eyes to the darkness. My breath caught when I spotted the source of the noise.

Jax was sat on the garden bench with a redhead straddled across his lap, her body wildly bobbing up and down while her head rested against his shoulder as she tried to muffle her moans of pleasure.

My eyes found Jax's and I inhaled deeply as his dark gaze held me, his eyes penetrating straight through me whilst refusing to release me as erotic hedonism blazed in his tight features.

His teeth sank into his bottom lip and his eyes fired wildly as he climaxed all while continuing to hold me hostage with his eyes. A cocky smile appeared on his face as he winked at me.

I gasped when I finally pulled away and turned back to the house without giving him another glance.

I pulled heavily on my beer when I found the safety of the kitchen.

What the hell had happened? I was all too aware with the way Jax had looked at me as he orgasmed that he was connecting with me. His desire for me all too evident on his face.

I just hoped mine wasn't displayed as brightly as his had been.

I couldn't quite understand how I felt. Yes, desire had been one of the feelings but then again disgust had filtered through somewhere. Shock? Hell yes, but there was something else, something I refused to accept.

Jealousy.

CHAPTER 3

The week passed all too quickly; most of it filled with inductions, tours and meet and greets at uni, some of it consumed by shifts at 'Z Bar' and a little of it finally decorating my room with Luce's artwork.

I enjoyed her art. It was a mixture of traditional but with a contemporary twist.

My room now displayed a large beach scene that completely covered the back wall. Its tranquil scene radiated serenity but stood in the centre of the sand was me, well a rock version of me, stood on a mini stage. My long hair was mused sexily, my make-up wild and shocking, my body modelled tight leather trousers and bustier as I rocked out, a mic stand before me as I played guitar. I adored it.

The smaller wall of my room hung a painting of Luce and I, both of us happily grinning widely but the background was filled with an array of clouds, the whole effect made it look like we were floating. I loved it.

Luce had made me drape electric blue fairy lights around the ceiling and the small wall above my bed exhibited my pride and joy. My 1959 Gibson Les Paul Custom Guitar signed by the Riff Lord himself, Slash.

It was my most prized possession, and probably worth more than my life.

***

Saturday night my shift at 'Z' started fairly quiet until the resident band strolled in at 9:30.

Room 103 played every Saturday night and I soon discovered how popular they were. Trish, the bar attendant who was working with me that night had already warned me that when the band played, so did the students...hard!

Each band member approached the bar and when Boss spotted me he grinned widely, drum rolled loudly on the bar with his palms, vaulted over it, lifted me high and gave me a full on snog. The crowd cheered as he stood on the bar and whistled loudly.

"Fuck guy's! I'm dedicating tonight's show to this fucking hot babe here." He grinned wickedly at me before turning back to the crowd. "Who thinks she should initiate her employment in Z with a FUCKING BODY SHOT?"

The room exploded in applause, whoops and whistles as I rolled my eyes.

Boss beamed and gestured to the bar with a tilt of his chin. "Everybody give it up for E!" he yelled as I climbed up, and then turned to Trish. "Hit it, Trish," he shouted as *Def Leppards 'Pour some sugar on me'* filled the room at a deafening level. The mass of students went wild.

As I lay down on the bar, Trish brought over the items needed and the crowd parted as Jax appeared before me with a wicked smile.

"Boss?" I asked as I glared at him.

He shook his head slowly, "Me, babe."

Trish nudged me. I nodded my confirmation as she placed the shot glass between my cleavage, one I had managed to produce by squeezing my boobs together with my arms.

Luckily my work uniform consisted of a tight black V neck T-shirt so I didn't have to remove any item of clothing.

Jax held my eyes with his as he gripped the hem of my shirt and gathered it teasingly slowly under my breasts. His eyes flicked over my stomach before he quickly dipped down, running his tongue slowly around my navel.

My breath caught in my throat at the sensation. As if sensing my reaction, his eyes looked up at me and darkened. Wow, they were almost black and I gasped.

Quickly diverting my gaze as Trish filled the glass with tequila, she gently held the wedge of lime for me to take between my teeth, Jax poured the salt on the wet section of skin.

The crowd erupted in a chant. "Body Shot, Body Shot, Body Shot!" as Jax unhurriedly licked the salt in one continuous swipe of his tongue. I closed my eyes and swallowed heavily as desire soared through me.

Fight it E!

Jax's lips and tongue unhurriedly ventured up over my rib cage and when he hit my shirt he rose up, placed his lips and teeth around the glass and flung his head back, swilling the alcohol back in one.

The crowd approved raucously then started stamping their feet in synchronized rhythm as Jax whipped away the glass before leaning down and wrapping his lips around the lime. His eyes seized mine intensely as he sucked on the lime and mimicked a kissing motion. My breathing deepened as I stared right back at him, the feeling of his warm breath wisping over me didn't help the arousal situation.

I frowned when he continued to suck on the lime. Nobody could withstand it that long.

Eventually he pulled away, gave me a knicker combusting smile as the throng applauded rowdily and held his hand out to me. I smiled faintly but shook my head in amusement and placed my hand in his. A sensation shot through me and I shivered at his touch. Jax frowned deeply and then narrowed his eyes on me.

I lowered my face as he helped me down off the bar. As I turned to pull my shirt down his hand wrapped around my arm, stopping my movement. I started to turn around to him but he held me still. I gasped as his fingertip delicately ran along the tattoo at the base of my back.

His mouth rested beside my ear and I closed my eyes, holding my breath at his intimacy. "If you're going through hell, keep going," he whispered, reading the words from my ink.

"Winston Churchill," I informed him softly. I really didn't like the sensation of his mouth so close to me and I turned my head away.

"Fucking E, babe... all fucking E," his gruff voice rumbled beside me.

I shivered and closed my eyes before spinning round. He was nowhere to be seen.

Disappeared.

I blinked. Shrugging I turned back round to the bar and got back to work.

For the next half hour the band set up their kit as I was snowed under with orders but I couldn't help noticing the horde of girls already surrounding the guy's, especially Jax, who I was surprised to discover was the lead vocal in the group. He flirted right back with each and every one, devouring each in a full on kiss.

Not sure how to take his brazen behaviour, I shrugged and left him to it but not before I caught him looking at me through each kiss, spinning the girls around so their backs were to me and his eyes were on me, every single time.

Cam, Luce and Kaylee came in about twenty minutes later and perched on bar stools to keep me company as Room 103 started to play.

I was mesmerized.

They were fucking awesome!

Jax's gruff voice held each note perfectly as he worked the song, drew you in and made you feel it. Brought you to edge with him and engulfed you in the emotion of each and every word. I was amazed when he starting singing high notes, stunned that his hoarse voice could manage to reach that level.

"Okay, guy's and babes," Jax's voice boomed through the room after several songs. "We all have the need to fuck right?"

The crowd erupted wildly in agreement.

"Then let's create some fucking *ALLURE!!!*"

The room screamed with approval at the song choice.

"But first I wanna dedicate it!"

I had never heard so many words flow from Jax's mouth; it was usually 'Yeah' or 'Babe'... Hell! That's all I'd managed to generate from him.

"Hell, yeah!" Romeo shouted from the edge of the stage.

Jax's gaze swooped straight to me and I cringed at the attention, highly aware that Cam was watching with narrow eyes. "This one's for E. She makes me fuckin' hard boys."

I rolled my eyes as all the male heads in the room rotated towards me and cheered their approval.

Cam growled.

Luce whooped.

Kaylee whistled.

Boss shouted, "Fuck yeah!"

Romeo opened with a small melody on guitar as Boss got the beat going with the drums. I was surprised to discover it was a slower one than the others played tonight, but still a rock song in its own right.

Then Jax came in and I was utterly mesmerized as his eyes never left my face throughout the whole song, his voice soft and serene.

"My Father always said
She's just a girl, a hot-blooded woman
An invitation to pandemonium
Break it down boy, the Allure's just emotion."

The room then joined in with the chorus, every single person swaying with each word.

"The attractions temptation
Too much pull baby,
The Chemistry's insane
The hunger insatiable,
I need you, the desires too strong
I feel you, your caress damn bliss."

A small riff from Romeo again, much to the delight of all the females in the room as they all screamed and reached out to him.

"My mother always said,
It should be love, a deep seated hold,
An acceptance of real adoration
Break it down boy, the Allure's pure rapture."

I admit I was tapping my foot and swaying my hips slightly behind the bar as my hand drummed the beat against my thigh; I wouldn't admit it to Jax though. I just held his gaze nonchalantly.

The group and the room erupted into the chorus again before Romeo and Bulk played a long riff, each displaying their own unique playing skills. I welcomed their performance, both of them expertly lashing their instruments with vigour before Jax came back again.

> *"But you, you always said,*
> *It's gonna be prime, an intense affair*
> *An encounter, yielding to our lust*
> *Break it down boy, the Allure's just an urge."*

His eyes darkened as his voice growled the last lines and I bit into my bottom lip savagely.

> *"But me, I always say*
> *Break it down boy, the Allure's fucking E,*
> *Just fucking E."*

The crowd erupted in screams but Jax remained still, his eyes piercing my own. I narrowed mine, well aware he had changed the last words. Finally he tipped his head in acknowledgment and winked as a self-satisfied grin lifted his lips before he turned back to the rest of the band.

Cam peered at me with high brows and I shrugged, "Fool!"

He nodded at my description and I gave him a coy smile. "Damn fool," he reiterated and I clicked my tongue.

"Don't worry. No intentions at all. I'm here to live not love," I placated and he nodded.

***

The band packed up, the room emptied and soon it was just staff, friends and the band... along with their choice of girl for the night... Jax had chosen two, who were currently both attached to his neck!

"Come and sit down, hot stuff." Boss patted the chair beside him and I held up a finger.

"Two mins."

Filling up a round of shots and placing them on a tray, I approached the table and sited the drinks in the middle of the party. "Toast!" I announced as I took a seat and everyone grabbed a drink. "To freedom, friends and..."

"...Fucking!" Boss finished with a cheeky grin.

"...and fucking." I shrugged with a lift of my glass. I was going with fame but what the hell! "Freedom, friends and fucking," everybody chimed.

Boss elbowed me with a twinkle in his eye. "About the fucking?"

I laughed heartily at his efforts. "Well I do have something Bulk and Romeo might want a peek at in my room, you're very welcome to join us Boss."

Everybody's heads spun round to look at me.

"Fuck, Spanner," Romeo declared and I smiled at his pet name for me. He pushed his hook-up for the night off his knee and onto the floor, before walking round to me and plonking himself on my lap, settling his arm around my shoulders as he planted a big kiss on my cheek.

I felt quite sorry for the girl as everyone laughed but she stood up, shook herself off and joined another girl on Bulk's knee.

Whatever!

"Babe?" Jax growled from across the table. There it was again! Did I not warrant more than a single word? Did he think I was too dumb to comprehend more than three?

I raised my eyebrows at him as Luce shouted, "Party at ours!"

"Hell yeah," the room shouted.

Fuck!!!

CHAPTER 4

"Holy Fuck, E!" Bulk dropped onto my bed heavily as his knees gave way. Romeo started to hyperventilate and Jax gave me the usual "Fuck, Babe!" Boss just stared.

"Signed by the Riff Lord himself," I stated proudly as we all gazed at my baby.

Boss came to stand beside me, his head cocked as he stared at the guitar, "Gibson?"

I nodded. "1959 Les Paul Gibson Custom," I revealed as Bulk's head swivelled round to mine.

"Can I touch her?" he breathed.

"Be gentle with her." I smiled in pleasure. It was good to finally share my treasure with someone who appreciated it.

Bulk ran his finger over the dedication as he read the words. *Welcome to the Jungle E... Slash.* " He sighed deeply. "Fucking wow, just fuck! I bet she feels fucking awesome under the tip man." I gathered he was talking to himself not me when he said 'man'.

"Black Beauty," Jax whispered knowledgeably and I regarded him respectfully. He turned and smiled at me; a proper soft smile and my heart clenched at the sight.

I nodded slowly. "Yeah, Black Beauty," I repeated softly.

"Where the hell did you get her, E?" Romeo asked and I winked at him.

"Connections."

He nodded humbly, still speechless and wide-eyed. I looked around the room, grinning at the realisation that I'd managed to bring four grown men to their knees.

"Come on Jax, baby." Jax's girl tugged at his arm, obviously bored with a guitar. "They have spare rooms here," she told him excitedly.

Jax shot her a glare, "The fuck?" It wasn't just me that got simple words then!

She shrugged at him. "Empty bed," she reiterated as though that explained everything.

"Not here!" He shot me a look and I turned away quickly.

"Well it's better than your fucking car again, or a fucking bench or a fucking sofa or even the fucking floor!" Miss Eager declared. Jax growled at her.

"Then go home!" Simple see!

Miss Eager glared at him before spinning on her heels and left the room.

"You're such a romantic, Jax." Boss scoffed, "Why the fuck don't you ever let 'em in your bed?"

Jax shrugged but shook his head before turning and leaving. All three guys shook their heads at Jax's behaviour, and to be honest I did wonder the same thing. That's what beds were for after all... well that and sleeping.

"TEQUILA!" Luce shouted as she downed a shot and flipped the glass on the table. Romeo mirrored her action and soon we were all counting their shots as they rallied, each trying to finish as many as possible before the timer on the cooker pinged.

Laughing I made my way over to the couch in the corner, knowing Luce would be on her back in about fifteen minutes.

Cam settled beside me. I noticed Jax take a step back, retreating from his steps towards me now that Cam had taken his place.

"You okay, E?" He shoulder nudged me and I smiled at him.

"Yeah."

He nodded and pursed his lips as he slid his index finger back and forth over them. I recognised the familiar action as he argued with himself whether to tell me something and I narrowed my eyes on him, "Hit me!"

He sighed heavily, "Aaron rang me."

The hairs on the nape of my neck rose as my veins tingled. I closed my eyes in preparation, "What's she done?"

He remained silent for a while. "Cameron!" I persisted anxiously. He grimaced and looked at me, his expression sad and dark. Sucking on my lips I exhaled heavily. "Please tell me she didn't?"

His eyes closed in confirmation and I huffed with a sharp shake of my head. "Fuck!" I thundered before standing and glaring at him. "Get – Him – The – Hell - Out – Of – There - Now!"

Cam grabbed my hand, "Easy E, he'll be here Monday."

"Fuck Monday," I growled. "Get him here Cam, please."

He shook his head. "E... I... can't..." He rubbed his eyes with his thumb and forefinger.

I pulled my hand from his forcibly and swallowed back the lump as I shook my head wildly. "Please Cam," I pleaded again, tears welling in my eyes.

"Fuck E, there's no way I'm going back there!" he ground through his clenched teeth as he tightened his fists, his knuckles white at the pressure.

"We can't just leave him, Cam. I'm not there anymore! She'll... he'll... he'll..." I snapped my mouth shut as I realised everybody was staring at us.

"E?" Luce came over to me, worry etched on her face. I turned away from her, refusing to look into her eyes. "E!" she demanded as she gripped my arm. She tugged at her hair as tears dripped down her cheeks, "God E! We need to get to him!"

I took her hand, "We can't, Luce. We can't get there."

Her face crumbled and I pulled her in tight. "He'll be here Monday," I whispered in her ear as I saw everyone regarding us curiously.

Jax took a step towards me; his eyes narrow as he studied me. "Okay, babe?"

I sighed at his meagre conversational skills but smiled gently. "Yeah," I whispered as I led Luce to the sofa and crouched in front of her.

"I need to ring him." She looked at me and I nodded.

"Soon. Give it an hour."

She nodded. "But I... I'm in love with him, E."

I grinned as I cupped her face, "I know, Luce."

Her eyes widened as she regarded me and I laughed faintly. "I'm not blind. I see how you look at him, hun. Hell, he looks at you like a starving man at a feast. It's quite simple really and hey, he's my twin so he's fucking handsome." I winked.

A sob broke free from her throat and she smiled through her tears before turning to Cam "Please, Cam."

"God damn it! I CAN'T FUCKING DO IT!" he screamed at Luce. I flinched as he slammed the door on his way out.

Shaking my head sadly, I exhaled heavily and looked at Luce. "How much cash you got on you?"

She stared at me and when she realised what I was going to do, she shot up and scrambled through her bag for her purse. "About £24.37," she divulged with a curl to her lip as she counted up eagerly. I nodded and held out my hand to her as I sighed wearily. She placed it in my palm and smiled gratefully at me. "Thank you" she whispered.

"E!" she shouted as I reached the door. Her eyes said it all but she voiced her thoughts as I turned back to her. "Be careful."

I forced a smile on my face and gave her a simple nod before slowly walking to my room to grab my bag.

Quietly closing my door behind me, I palmed the wall and rested my forehead on it. Christ! Could I do this? I had hoped I would never have to return back there. Especially now I knew Mom was struggling with Aaron and mines departure.

"Fuck!" I slammed the wall and pushed back, pulling in a determined breath and slipped into my jacket before grabbing my bag off the floor.

I turned round and slammed straight into Jax, his hard chest providing a wall for my face.

"Christ," I murmured as I stepped back. "Do you know how to knock?"

He cocked his head as his eyes roamed over me, "Going somewhere, babe?" Honoured, I got three full words!

"I have to do something," I told him as I tried to step around him.

"Something?" His eyebrows lifted in suspicion and I scowled at him.

"Yes, something." I retraced my steps, attempting to escape again but he stood firm in front of the door.

"I'll take you, babe."

I stared at him but then shivered as my brain clicked back into place. "No... thank you, I'm good, I'm okay." I smiled tightly and gestured to the door with my chin, asking silently to be freed.

His eyes narrowed. "If I offer something, accept it and just say Thank you Jax," he stated resolutely, his husky voice making me shudder.

I blinked, rapidly I might add. Not sure if I was stunned at his authority or the fact that he had actually spoke an entire sentence. My mouth fell open at his dominancy. "Well... that's really not a good idea," I urged.

A low growl rumbled in his throat and I winced. "Babe..."

I cringed. "But I have to go to Chesterfield, it's in Derbyshire," I explained, hoping the trek would change his mind.

"I know where fucking Chesterfield is."

"But haven't you had a drink?" I tried anything to change his mind.

"Two shots, babe."

I nodded, "Oh..."

"No Oh... wait here while I get my wheels," he ordered.

"Okay," I squeaked. He nodded once and left. What the Hell?

I dropped onto my bed, mesmerised by what had just transpired. How the hell had he just took control over me like that? I was dumbfounded by my own submission. I was not relishing a two hour drive with a man that couldn't string together more than a few words.

"Oh God, E." I moaned as I rested my head in my hands.

My door opened thirty minutes later, no knock I might add, and I glanced nervously at Jax. He held out his hand to me, "Babe." I placed my hand in his hesitantly and he pulled me up off the bed. Wrapping his fingers around mine firmly so I couldn't escape he regarded me, "Ready?"

I sighed and frowned slightly. "I have to ask something first." I swallowed as my nerves surfaced.

His stare pierced my soul but he nodded, encouraging me to go on. "Well... whatever goes off tonight... well I need you to, well to kind of..." I stuttered as my hands trembled.

"Spit it out, babe."

I sucked on my lips and took a hefty breath. "Well, you need to stay out of it," I pressed, my nerves already shattered. His eyes narrowed fiercely and I cringed as he glowered at me.

He didn't speak, just pulled me through the building and out into the car park.

"Holy shit."

A solitary car was parked outside my residential block. My mouth dropped as my gaze landed on it. It was no ordinary car... Oh no! It was a BMW series 6 Gran Coupe, in shiny black no less and it was absolutely - fucking - gorgeous.

Jax pulled me across to the passenger side and after releasing the lock, held open the door for me. His eyebrows lifted when I stood immobile, gawping at his 'wheels'... Hell, no one should call this car 'wheels' it warranted something... more!

"You getting in?"

I nodded slowly and sank into its soft plushness. I jolted when the door slammed shut behind me, the noise reminding me to breathe. Jax slid in beside me as my gaze roamed the pure luxury encompassing us then a thought occurred to me. How the hell could he afford a car like this?

"It is yours, isn't it?" I asked hesitantly. If he had hot-wired it I would beat him to a pulp. His brows lifted again as he ignited the engine... oh the perfect engine. My mouth drooled at the sound of her growling to life.

"Babe, I may be many things but I aint no fucking joy-rider," he growled. I think I had offended him.

"No," I stated simply with a small shake of my head.

I jerked when I felt his breath on the side of my cheek. "By the way, in answer to your earlier statement... if someone tonight does something I don't like, then I will let them know that I don't like it."

I slowly turned my head to look at him. He was approximately an inch from me. His warm breath tickled my nose he was that close. His deep eyes shifted down to my mouth then back up as he held my stare, "You hear me, babe?"

I nodded vigorously and mumbled something incoherent. A smile lifted his lips before he retreated and swung us out of the student village.

CHAPTER 5

The man of not so many words was quiet for the first part of our journey and when my head was ready to explode with the silence, I reached across the dash and flicked a button for the stereo.

"IPod," Jax informed me as he pointed to the device sat between us in the console.

I smiled at the thought of rummaging through his playlists, wondering what genre of music he preferred. I nodded in appreciation as I scrolled through. His tastes were very eclectic and ranged from AC/DC all the way through to the Carpenters. I giggled as I stared at 'Close to you'.

He glanced at me. "Close to you?" I smirked.

A scowl pulled his face, "Fucking ace, babe."

I nodded and bit my cheek against the urge to laugh and clicked a *Pink* playlist. Her new song *'Just give me a reason'* with *Nate Reuss* blasted through the speakers and I smiled. I loved this track and after a while I couldn't help the words leaving my mouth as I tapped the rhythm onto my thigh.

> *"Just give me a reason*
> *Just a little bit's enough*
> *Just a second we're not broken just bent*
> *And we can learn to love again*
> *It's in the stars*
> *It's been written in the scars on our hearts*
> *We're not broken just bent*

And we can learn to love again."

I kept my gaze out of the window and when Jax came in with Nate's part I smiled and turned to him.

"I'm sorry I don't understand where all of this is coming from
I thought that we were fine
Oh we had everything
Your head is running wild again
My dear we still have everything
And it's all in your mind
Yeah but this is happening
You've been having real bad dreams
Oh, oh
You used to lie so close to me
Oh, oh."

Then we sang together, both grinning at each other like fools.

"There's nothing more than empty sheets
Between our love, our love, oh our love, our love..."'

We finished the track and Jax chuckled. "Fucking top voice, babe."
I smiled proudly at his compliment. "Back at ya'."
He laughed loudly. "Yeah," he said simply.

Pulling my phone from my bag I braced myself as I dialled Aaron's number and turned my body into the door, trying to hide my conversation from Jax. Aaron answered after a couple of rings. "E," he whispered.

I cringed at the roughness of his voice. "You okay, Aaron?" He was silent for a while then mumbled a confirmation.

I stole a quick glance at Jax before I asked the next question. He was tapping his thigh to the beat of the track spilling from the stereo and didn't seem to be paying attention to my discussion.

"How many?"

The sound of Aaron sucking air through his teeth made me swallow heavily. "About eight," he divulged and I hissed at his answer.

"You safe, Aaron?" I closed my eyes in preparation.

"Yeah E, at the moment."

I nodded and sighed thankfully. "Listen, I'm on my way with a friend and should be about an hour. Pack your stuff. You're stopping with Luce until Monday."

"Luce?" I could hear the question in his voice.

"Yeah, Luce. I don't think she'll complain do you?" I smiled. "We'll be as quick as we can, Aaron."

He moaned low, "Christ E, you shouldn't come here, not tonight."

I snorted. "Aaron, I've managed eighteen fucking years. I'm sure I can manage another ten minutes. Be ready!"

Terminating the call before he could argue further I slipped my phone back into my bag and diverted my attention out of the window.

"Clue me in, E." Jax's low voice slipped across the darkness of the car.

I swallowed. "I can't, not really."

"Babe?"

I knew I had to give him something; he was helping me out after all. "Just... just trouble with my Mom. We're going to pick up my brother."

He nodded and ran his teeth across his lower lip and I watched his tongue sweep across, soothing the plump flesh.

We were both quiet for a while and when we passed a sign for Derbyshire Jax's voice made me jump. "You born here, babe?"

I nodded and shivered. His eyes caught the involuntary action and a frown developed on his face.

"Where are you from?" I asked, realising I knew absolutely nothing about him.

"Sheffield."

"Oh, not far then." I smiled, don't know why.

He nodded, "Yeah."

It was like drawing blood from a stone... hard bloody work!

"Family?" I asked, trying to encourage any kind of conversation but he just shook his head once. Fair enough.

I pursed my lips and picked up his iPod, scrolling back through his playlist just for something to do.

I swallowed heavily as we entered my hometown.

"Where to, babe?" Jax asked eventually. I instructed him as we drove through the quiet town until we pulled up outside my former home.

Jax whistled as he took in the opulent house. "Nice."

I shrugged. "Looks can be deceiving," I mumbled as I dialled Aaron's number. He tipped his head and narrowed his eyes on me but didn't say anything to my words.

"Back door," I informed Aaron as he answered.

Taking a deep breath I opened my door and turned to Jax. "I'll be as quick as I can," I said quietly. My nerves frayed as my hands shook. Turning sharply I shook my head at Jax as he exited the car. "No, stay here!" I warned but he snorted.

"Might be trouble," he offered as his head tipped in the direction of my house.

Light was blaring from the windows and music could be heard playing loudly. I bit into my bottom lip and braced myself. "Please, Jax."

He lifted his eyebrows and his expression said it all... Not a chance! I sighed in resignation as humiliation surged through me. Could I take him in, knowing what was happening behind the walls? I didn't have any choice when Jax started walking up the long gravel drive.

"Round the back," I whispered to him. He nodded but didn't acknowledge any other way.

We crept around the outer wall, through the large metal gates at the side of the house and into the back garden. As we passed the utility room window I tapped on it lightly. Jax frowned, "Babe?"

I winced when his loud growl filled the silence. I immediately put a finger up to my lips to shush him but he had other ideas. "What the fuck's going on?"

Scowling at him, I repeated my motion and put my finger against his lips this time. His eyes softened immediately and his fingers curled around my single one. "I won't let anyone hurt you, E" he said gently. Well hell!

I smiled faintly in appreciation. He nodded once as light flooded from the back door before Aaron's head appeared round the edge.

His grin lit my heart. "E," he whispered softly. My grin grew into a beam. Aaron's eyes shifted to Jax as he exited the doorway with a few bags. "Okay?" Aaron mouthed, knowing the rules of remaining mute. I lifted a thumb in response as Jax moved forwards and took some of Aaron's bags.

Aaron tipped his head towards Jax with his eyebrows high, a silent question of 'who the hell is he?' I smiled and nodded, reassuring him that he was a friend as Jax made his way quietly back to the car.

Aaron picked up the remaining bags as I followed behind him, closing each of the gates quietly on our getaway, my nerves making my legs tremble.

I nearly made it. God! So close.

She opened the front double doors as I scurried down the driveway to catch up with the boys, my heart stuttering as she called out my name.

"EVE?"

I closed my eyes and stumbled to a stop halfway to freedom. "EVE!" she repeated. I turned slowly and swallowed my fear.

"Mom." I took a glance behind me, grateful that Aaron and Jax had made it back to the car safely.

"What the Hell, Eve?" Her words were slurred, her face slack as she wobbled towards me. I grit my teeth severely, listening to them crack under the pressure.

Her whole body was bent nearly double as she braced herself on her knees. I cringed as I took in her appearance. She wore only a see-through pink negligée, her hair was wild and her make-up was shovelled on with the aid of a trowel.

My heart froze to a stop as I saw him exit the doors behind her.

Shit!

I started to back up slowly. "Fuck... no!" I stammered to myself as I shook my head wildly. "Don't do this, Mom!" She didn't hear me, she couldn't.

He carried on coming and my lungs began closing down. My head felt light at the sight of him and I was struggling to move. Damn it E... Run!

He sneered at me, an ugly lift of his arrogant lips as he stalked over to me. My legs were wobbling and I had started panting.

His fingers curled around my arm as he leant in. I closed my eyes, swallowing back the nausea at his touch. I was silently begging for Aaron to stay in the car but I knew he would come back for me after he realised I wasn't coming. I wanted him to stay put... needed him to!

"Hello, pretty girl," he breathed in my ear. His rank breath flooded my senses and I stared at my Mom, pleading with my eyes. She smiled that fucking smile of hers! The one I always wanted to wipe off her once beautiful face.

His hand started tugging at my arm and I wedged my heels into the gravel. "No!"

He barked out a laugh, "Now we know better than that, Eve."

Refusing to open my eyes a small sob erupted from my throat. "No!" I reiterated. Not sure where the courage came from but I fed from it. "You need to let go," I choked out, no more than a whisper but still proud of my bravery.

"Open your eyes and look at me bitch." I winced at his rage but shook my head in defiance.

"No."

Yelping when his hand grabbed my hair, I curled my fingers round his, striving for some relief against the pain. "Please don't," I begged this time, my nerve had took the last train out of here, along with my mother who had conveniently disappeared.

"Shit!" I heard Aaron behind me and I flinched.

"Get back in the car, Aaron," I shouted to him but I could hear the crunch of the gravel getting louder as the hold in my hair tightened. "Aaron go back to the car *NOW*!"

"Remove the fucking hand before mine wraps around your fucking throat arsehole," Jax growled at the back of me. My eyes flew open and I stood stock still, embarrassment coursing through me.

"Jax," Aaron whispered with a warning, all too aware of what Keith was capable of.

Keith scoffed.

Jax growled.

I whimpered.

"Think you're hard lad?" Keith snarled at Jax. Jax laughed loudly.

I blinked as Keith was ripped from my side and floored in one fluid motion.

"Fuck!" Aaron whispered.

I just blinked... again!

Jax grabbed my hand and pulled as I stared at an unconscious Keith laid out on the gravel, his nose splattered across his face, "Now, babe!"

I nodded, more to myself as my knees buckled and I crumpled to the floor. Jax swept down and scooped me up, holding me close against him as he strolled back to the car. "It's okay," he whispered softly.

"Thank you," I whispered, not sure what else to say. He looked down at me; a small smile lifted his lips as he nodded once and my heart fluttered involuntary. Well Hell!

Aaron climbed in the rear of the car before Jax settled me down into the passenger seat beside him and pulled off. I never looked back.

CHAPTER 6

Monday morning rolled around all too fast. First day of classes and lectures had me exhausted before my shift at Z even started.

Jax hadn't mentioned or even asked about what happened Saturday night and I was grateful of his discretion. Aaron and Luce kept everyone up Sunday night with their loud love-making. Shiver.

Aaron moved into his own dorm across the village on Monday morning and we all breathed a sigh of relief hoping for some sleep tonight. Sunday brought the arrival of the rest of our dorm mates.

Josh White was a blonde haired quiet guy. He had informed me he was studying English language with creative writing the same as I was. We both welcomed each other as study partners and I was pleased to have a familiar face to accompany me to classes.

Austin Pearce, well I couldn't quite work him out. He seemed moody. One minute laughing and joking with the rest of us but then he seemed to withdraw and retreat into himself. Gavin kept shifting his eyes between Austin and me, both of us shrugging in puzzlement.

✳✳✳

After language studies Monday afternoon, Josh and I found ourselves in the campus Starbucks. "I'll get 'em," Josh declared as he nodded towards a table in the corner. After giving him my order I settled in a seat where he'd directed and pulled my phone from my bag, noticing three missed calls from my Mom.

Checking Josh was still in the queue I quickly dialled her number, cursing myself for being subservient.

"Eve?" Her voice was strained and rough causing a slight pang of guilt to surface.

"Yeah Mom, it's me." Her sob tore through me and my teeth sank into my bottom lip, "You okay?" Knowing it was a stupid question, I asked it anyway.

"Not really."

I nodded, well aware she couldn't see me. "Eve…" Another sob broke free. "I'm so sorry Eve, I…" I could taste her guilt and I squeezed my eyes shut against it.

The familiar intense pressure was building and I was struggling to contain it as I listened to her guilty cries. I couldn't deal with it now; I wouldn't be able to fight the urge to obliterate it, the pure craving of release I so needed.

"Mom, please… I, I can't do this now."

I heard her gasp and forced back the tears as my blood started tingling. The shiver racked its way through my whole body and I clenched my fist, desperately trying to push the longing back down as I concentrated on the wall clock behind the counter, forcing my eyes to track the movement of the second hand.

My hands were shaking violently and my eyes blurred.

Fuck!

Quickly ending the call with my mother I dialled Cam before it was too late. He answered after the second ring, "Hey."

Shaking my head wildly, his voice became distorted. "Cam." My voice was no more than a rasp.

"Shit, E! Where are you?"

I dropped the phone as the trembles ravaged me. I closed my eyes, my whole body screaming with the need for liberation, the pressure developing to an extreme level as though it would explode any second.

I noticed Josh squat down beside me, his face and voice a blur as he picked up my phone and spoke into it.

I covered my ears and tried to control my breathing. In, out, in, out...

You don't need it E, you don't need it, you don't need it! Over and over until it was all I heard.

Strong arms wrapped around me before I felt myself being carried out of the shop. Jax's scent permeated my brain as I was placed into a car and my body jerked violently. My tears and the strain clogged my throat, my fingernails dug deeply into my palms.

Cam's voice filtered through the haze as his hands took hold of mine, gently prizing my fingers open. "You don't need it E, you don't need it."

Yes Cam, I've been telling myself that for the last half an hour for god's sake!

***

I came to a while later, locked in Cam's arms as he rocked me back and forth.

"Cam."

"Hey." His face appeared before me, his smile soft and tender, "You good?" I checked myself and nodded slightly. "Good girl." He kissed my forehead gently, "Well done."

I smiled at the pride in his voice and I'll admit I felt proud of myself for not giving in to the craving.

"Eleven weeks now, E." I nodded in acknowledgement as I pushed myself up and took in my surroundings. We were at Cam's.

"What time is it? I need to get to work."

"Six." Jax's voice sounded from the doorway and I spun round, a blush creeping up from my neck and filling my face as his eyes skimmed over me. "Okay, E?"

I nodded, just nodded. He returned the motion, "You need a lift? I looked at him in puzzlement. "Work, babe!"

"Oh, nah, that's okay?" I fidgeted nervously, highly ashamed that he had witnessed my earlier behaviour.

His head cocked to one side. "...Yes thank you Jax!" he encouraged with a lift of his eyebrows, referring to our conversation Saturday night.

A small smile lifted my lips. "Yes thank you, Jax," I rephrased. He smiled and winked before turning towards the kitchen and returned with his keys. His head nudged to the door, a gesture we should leave now.

"E," Cam's hand settled on my arm. "You think you should go in tonight?"

I smiled back at him, trying to reassure him with a simple gesture. "I'm okay." He frowned but nodded.

"I'm not late," I growled at Jax, who was currently trying to display how fast his car could move. He glanced at me with a puzzled expression. "Slow down," I encouraged quietly. He shrugged but lifted his foot off the accelerator slightly.

"You get many?" he suddenly asked and I shrugged.

"Clue me in, babe," I retorted cheekily.

"Panic attacks babe," he clarified, either disregarding my sassy imitation or it didn't register. "Cam said... panic attack."

I gave him a bewildered glance before I realised Cam had covered for me again. "Oh." I shifted my gaze out of the window, "A few."

Silence filled the car for a few moments as he pulled up in front of Z Bar. I turned to him with a forced smile, "Thanks."

His fingers curled around my arm as I went to open the door, my eyes rose to his and he floored me with his intense look. Locking on, he held me immobile for a few moments before he spoke and I closed my eyes in horror.

"My father used to have a problem. Had terrible cravings E, racked his whole body when the tremors started. Couldn't breathe." His rough tones filtered through the dense heat of the car.

I pulled my bottom lip behind my teeth and swallowed heavily. I needed to get out of the car, the air was rapidly disappearing but he refused to release his hold.

"I know it's not drugs babe, so what is it?"

I shook my head, keeping my eyes closed tightly. I couldn't see him so he couldn't see me, that's how it works right?

"Please," I begged on a hoarse whisper.

After a heartbeat his fingers relaxed their hold on my arm but they grasped my jaw and he turned my face towards his. I could feel his breath breeze across my cheek.

"Open your eyes, E." His voice was no more than a low rough growl and the emotion in those four words stole my breath. I did as he asked and opened them, gasping as I found his near black iris's.

"Life is what we're given to live, E. Own it, use it, work it, babe. Make it what you want it to be."

I frowned at him. His eyes tracked his thumb as he brushed it across my bottom lip, releasing it from my teeth as he did so. "Don't bite your lip, babe. Makes me wanna do things to you that I think maybe you don't want me to do... yet."

A breath I didn't realise I'd been holding escaped my lungs in a swift gush, he smirked as he pulled back.

I practically fell out of the car, my heels not very supportive of my unsteady legs as I struggled to walk into the bar.

"Hey, E," Rachel, the afternoon bar attendant greeted.

She frowned and tipped her head, "You okay, girl?"

Shaking myself off, I nodded and smiled. "Yeah, just tired."

She nodded in agreement, "Yeah, first day of classes is always hard."

Nodding in agreement I noticed Austin sat at a solitary table at the back of the room. "How long's he been here?" I asked Rach as I indicated who I meant with a tip of my head.

"Good few hours. To be honest he's giving me the creeps. Keeps staring at me. Makes me appreciate how busy it is tonight."

I nodded in agreement as I scanned the room, "God, where did they all come from?" Each and every table in the room was occupied and I smiled brightly as I caught the members of Room 103 sat at their usual table in the corner.

"Spanner!" Romeo shouted in greeting. I lifted my hand and grinned.

Boss bounced up, his ever present energy feeding the room "Get us a beer, hot stuff."

I was already on it, popping the cap off his regular beverage. He grinned as I passed it him and handed me the cash, "Keep the change, baby."

Fran appeared beside him and I noticed his slight stiffness on her approach. "Fran," he greeted blandly.

She tipped her head and smiled at him "Where's Jax?"

"Home," was all he said. She nodded and left. I ignored the slight clench in my chest now I knew where she was headed.

"I take it she's not your favourite person?"

I chuckled as he faked a gag. "Fuck no, can't stand the bitch. Shark with tits!"

I laughed loudly at his description and he grinned at me. "That's better hot stuff; you seem a bit down tonight."

I scrunched up my nose and shook my head, "I'm good."

He nodded then reached across the bar and planted a tender kiss on my cheek. I regarded him with warm bewilderment. He just shrugged, a slight red tinge on his neck, and beamed at me happily then returned to the others. He was growing on me.

***

Walking across the village after my shift, I was chuckling to myself when a group of drunken lads were rocketing down the driveway on a shop storage cage singing what seemed to be a football chant, when a hand gripped my shoulder. Squealing loudly I spun round to stumble upon Austin. Jeez this guy was weird.

"You okay, love?" One of the drunken lads shouted. I raised my hand in confirmation, smiling at his chivalry.

"Walking back?" he asked. I frowned at the question. It was pretty obvious where I was headed but I gave him a smile and nod, just to be polite.

"How you settling in, Austin?"

He shrugged and pulled a grimace. "Okay, I suppose."

He seemed to be a bit of a loner. I had never seen him with any friends or come to think of it... anybody. "Next time you're on your own in the bar, grab a stool and talk to me," I suggested.

He looked at me and smiled at my offer. I noticed the faint glimmer in his eyes and I felt a little sad for him. "It's hard isn't it?" He nodded, understanding what I was talking about. "I'm lucky really. I have Luce and my brothers so..."

"I just... miss..." He didn't finish, looked as though he couldn't and I rested a hand on his arm.

"You left a special someone behind?"

His face tightened severely as his eyes darkened. "Not someone worth a fuck!"

His abrupt change of mood prickled at my senses. He seemed to immediately be angry and the fury he was radiating made my alarm bells ring.

"Fucking bitch doesn't deserve to reside in my fucked up head," he actually spat as he snarled. Okay!

"Right," I nodded; thankful we had reached our dorm.

His face spun round to me so quickly I actually thought it was going to snap his neck, his eyes narrowed and I noticed his knuckles were tight against his clenched fist. "You know you shouldn't really be out alone E, some real bad people about..."

His tone sent a shiver down my spine. I didn't know whether to take his statement as a warning or advice. I just nodded, simply nodded. Oh, and I may have involuntary wet my knickers!

CHAPTER 7

The week passed in a blur of lectures and ever mounting essays and as my shift Saturday night came around, I was lagging. We were packed out again, the atmosphere in the crowd reached fever pitch by the time Room 103 began their performance. Trish and I were struggling to keep up with the demand.

Austin had took my word literally and perched on one of the stools but as the night progressed it grew busier. The less I managed to talk to him, the more his demeanour seemed to grow darker. Trish kept shooting me a concerned look as Austin refused to remove his stern glare from me. I just continued giving him apologetic smiles, hoping to mollify him but I grew anxious as he drank more and seethed a little more.

"How we all doing?" Jax's voice filled the room, "We fucking good?"

The crowd roared in reply and Jax nodded. "I want to change tonight's sequence a little." The horde cheered their approval and I cringed when Jax's face rotated to mine with a shrewd grin. Oh Shit!

"I have a little something to share with you all." I started to back away, my intuition telling me that I wasn't going to like what he was going to do.

"I had the pleasure of spending a few hours in E's company and you know what guy's..."

"WHAT?" the mass chanted.

Jax beamed widely and pointed his finger at me. All heads rotated in my direction "...That fucking girl... CAN FUCKING SING!"

I groaned.

The crowd cheered.

Trish whistled.

"E! Get that hot little ass up here, babe."

I shook my head and glared at him. His lips lifted into a mischievous grin as he stomped his foot on the floor and began a chant.

"E, E, E, E, E....." The room joined in. The walls appeared to vibrate with the din.

I soon found myself swooped up by Romeo and hoisted up onto the small stage. Jax walked over to me and took my hand in his, pulling me into the centre of the platform as the crowd roared with excitement.

"Just give me a reason?" Jax whispered in my ear, his eyes bright and hopeful. Giving him a slight shrug, Bulk thrust his mic into my hand and I nervously stared out at the mass of people. Oh God!

I had never sung in front of an audience before and I gulped away the nausea as my stomach groaned with nerves. Jax's hand squeezed mine and I gazed up at him, he smiled with a small nod. As the music started I swung round and noticed Bulk had whipped out a keyboard from somewhere.

I closed my eyes and took a deep breath before I came in on time.

"Right from the start,

You were a thief you stole my heart,
And I your willing victim…"

I opened my eyes.

"I let you see the parts of me,
That weren't all that pretty,
And with every touch you fixed them…"

I relaxed and began to rock my hips to the beat.

"Now you've been talking in your sleep,
Oh, Oh
Things you never say to me,
Oh, Oh
Tell me that you've had enough,
Of our love, our love…"

Emotion from the song coursed through me and my voice steadied out as I continued and gave it my all. The crowd rocked out, whistling and joining in with the words. When Jax came in he locked my gaze and connected with me as he sang.

By the time the track peaked, we were both singing to each other with so much passion that I struggled to hold the pitch and all too soon it was my lines that finished the song.

"Oh we can learn to love again,
Oh we can learn to love again,
Oh, oh
That we're not broken just bent,

And we can learn to love again..."

The room was silent when I came to a close. I cringed at the quiet but Jax was grinning widely. Then... the whole of Z Bar erupted in what I can only explain as pandemonium. The air pulsated, the walls shook and the mass of students approved with a roar of whistles, whoops and chants of "E, E, E, E..."

Pure undiluted energy surged through me. I felt alive... utterly and powerfully euphoric. I turned to Jax, he was laughing and whistling with the throng. I launched myself at him, wrapping my legs around his waist and my arms around his neck; he caught me and spun me round.

"Fucking ace, babe."

His mouth crashed down on mine as he took me in a kiss so passionate and intense that I never even resisted and I kissed him back with as much vigour and hunger. Electricity coursed through me as he deepened his caress and raided my mouth with his tongue, sweeping it over my top teeth as he explored me.

A moan rumbled up my throat as his large hand palmed the nape of my neck and pulled me further in, devouring me thoroughly. A groan of his own erupted into my mouth. I pulled away suddenly, anxious of the desire swelling in the pit of my stomach.

A coy smile radiated his face, "Epic kiss, E."

I snorted at his choice of words, then smiled, then grinned, then laughed, a full on hearty laugh. "You have such a way with words, Jax." I winked and jumped off the stage, struggling to get through the throng of people wanting to compliment or congratulate me.

"Boyfriend?" Austin asked with a growl and a tip of his head towards Jax when I took my place back behind the bar. He was really quite scary, something about him was disturbing me wildly.

Shaking my head at his question I took the order from the girl next to him. I recognised her from my stylistics class, "Melissa right?"

She nodded and grinned. "E!" She smiled with recollection as she pointed her finger at me. I smiled and returned her nod with my own. "V and redbull."

She glanced at Austin as she gave me her order, I shivered when his eyes scanned the whole of her body. She seemed to nudge towards him and I wasn't sure if I was grateful she was diverting his attention from me or if I was worried for her. There was just something about him that... Oh give it up E; he's probably a great bloke when you got to know him!

Boss sank onto a stool and rested his chin in his hands on the bar, his eyes tracking every move I made. I smiled to myself when he remained silent but continued with his eye stalking. Eventually relenting, I went over to him. "Can I get you something, Boss?"

His wide smile made me chuckle. I was really warming to him. He was like a cheeky big brother and I knew instinctively that underneath all his innuendo that is exactly how he saw me, not saying he would refuse a roll in the sack if I offered though.

"Hot stuff... party at mine. You up for it?"

I lifted a shoulder, "I dunno Boss, I'm knackered."

Romeo settled onto the stool beside him. "Fucking awesome performance, Spanner." I smiled my thanks as I popped the caps on their beers and passed them across the counter. "Seriously, you ought to duet one of our songs with Jax. Crowd would love it."

I shook my head at his offer. "Nah, I'm good but thanks." He pursed his lips but hunched his shoulders in resignation.

"I'm trying to convince her to after-party at ours," Boss nudged Romeo. I rolled my eyes.

"Boss, you go on ahead and if after my shift I discover some hidden energy then I will come over," I relented marginally.

He squinted at me, "Promise?" Huffing in frustration I made a cross over my heart with my finger and nodded before heading to the other side of the bar. I cocked my head to the side when I realised Austin and Melissa had disappeared. Must have pulled!

By 2am I was officially worn out and in no mood for a party. My feet ached, my back pulled and my head was pounding, so instead of partying I made my way back to my dorm texting Cam that I wouldn't make it after all.

He text back to let me know that Luce and Kaylee were at his and that the guys were having a barbeque tomorrow afternoon and Boss wouldn't take no for an answer. Replying that I would be there, I entered my dorm and changed into the G N' R T-shirt that I always slept in then fell into bed.

BANG BANG BANG
A muffled, "Please stop."
BANG BANG BANG
"Take it bitch!"
BANG BANG BANG

What the hell?
Jolting upright and rubbing my eyes, I frowned at the sounds coming from the room next to mine.

BANG BANG BANG
"I Ca...can't..."
BANG BANG BANG
"I said fucking take it..."

I froze as I listened to what was unfolding through the wall, my breath held in my lungs as I frantically tried to work out what was happening.

"Please... Stop... Austin..."
"FUCK!!"
BANG BANG

Then I heard a faint crying.
SHIT!

I flung myself out of bed and into the hallway, relieved to see a sleepy Gavin also struggling to make out what was going off in Austin's room.
"E!" he whispered and I nodded.
"I don't like the sound of it!"

He nodded in agreement then tiptoed over to Austin's door, resting his ear against the wood to listen. His eyes widened before he pulled back and knocked on the door, "Austin! That you man?"

I held my breath as I waited for a reply but all was quiet. Gavin knocked again as I noticed Josh's door open before he appeared in the hallway, sporting just boxers. Quickly diverting my gaze back to Gavin I cringed as Austin shouted, "Fuck off, Gav!"

"I don't like this," Gavin murmured before placing his hand on the door handle. His eyebrows lifted at me in query whether he should open or not. I nodded, worried for Melissa.

Slowly pushing open the door I fought with myself whether I wanted to look inside or not but relented and peeked in. Wish I hadn't!

Melissa was tied to Austin's bed on her stomach. Austin was taking her anally, she was crying as he took her so hard his headboard was banging against the wall.

"Fuck!" Josh breathed behind me.

I stepped back, not wanting to see anymore and letting the guy's handle it.

"Christ, Austin!" Gavin growled.

"Fuck!" I heard Austin say as Melissa continued to whimper.

The guy's entered the room and I stood immobile in the hallway until Melissa appeared naked and crying. Placing an arm around her shoulder I led her into my room and shut the door before retrieving a T-shirt from my drawer and passing it to her. She was silent, just hiccupping as she slipped it on.

"You okay, hun?" I whispered. Why do you always ask that question when it's pretty obvious the person isn't alright?

Her wide eyes found mine and I cringed at the horror behind them. Settling myself beside her on the bed I placed my hand on her thigh. "Do you want me to phone the police?"

She shook her head. "No I... I consented but..." She sucked on her lips as another sob wrenched from her throat. "I... he got a little..."

"Rough?" I finished for her. She looked at me and nodded frantically. "Did you ask him to stop?" She nodded again. "Then I really think you should report it," I encouraged but she shook her head again.

"No I... I can't."

I really didn't like where she was heading with this. "Why don't you let me ring them and just see what they say?" She seemed to think it over for a while before giving me a small nod. Smiling I squeezed her thigh as I reached for my phone.

CHAPTER 8

Melissa and I climbed out of the police car and thanked the officer who had brought us home late the next morning.

"Do you want to come in for a drink?" I offered her then frowned when I saw Jax leaning against his car watching me with narrow eyes. He pushed off and strolled towards us.

Melissa shook her head, "I just wanna go home and flake."

I nodded sympathetically and pulled her in for a hug. She held me tight against her for a long while. I sucked in my lips as I felt a shudder rack her exhausted body, grateful that Jax had come to a stop, realising it was a private moment.

I squeezed her once more and watched her walk away, dragging her feet in desolation.

"Babe?"

I turned to face Jax. "Austin." He frowned at my simple answer. "Austin kind of... got a bit rough with her. Been at the cop shop all night."

"The fuck?"

I nodded at his simple statement, "Yeah, knew there was something about him. He gives me the creeps."

"What did the law say?"

I huffed. "Not a lot. I don't think they've even pulled him in yet. Cos' she consented they say it's her word against his, it doesn't help that there's no bruising. But... we'll see."

He pulled out a cigarette and lit it, blowing out a deep lung full of smoke he turned back to me, "He still living here, babe?"

I nodded and sighed as a quiver took my body. Jax's eyes were narrow, "The fuck you stay here, E!"

I squinted at his words. I really ought to get this man on a stage when I wanted a proper conversation with him, it was the only place he extended his vocabulary. "It's not that easy, Jax," I told him as I took a step towards my dorm.

His hand closed round my arm, "You're staying at mine, babe."

I laughed then... loudly I might add. His face halted me immediately and I swallowed heavily. Oops!

"Jax, there is no way I'm leaving Luce and Kaylee here with him. I'll be fine."

He cocked his head and his eyes darkened. "...Yes, thank you Jax."

I rolled my eyes at his familiar quote. "Not this time Jax. Did you want something anyway?"

He growled at my refusal, "Yeah."

My eyebrows rose as I waited for an explanation but he continued to glare at me, "Jax?" I urged him.

He inhaled loudly. "Picking you up for the barbeque, babe!" he revealed eventually.

I nodded in realisation but sighed, "I really just wanna sleep Jax, and I'm knackered."

But he shook his head slowly. "You're coming!" I pouted heavily but he shook his head again, "You can nap in my bed."

My eyes widened at his words but he continued to stare at me, his eyes dark and intense, daring me to argue. Rolling my eyes I shook my head in exasperation, "Fine, gimme ten minutes."

He nodded once and went to climb back in his car whilst I entered my dorm.

After freshening up and changing I climbed in beside Jax. "Ready?"

Leaning my head against the headrest and closing my eyes I mumbled a reply and smiled to myself as I felt the engine purr to life.

***

I woke a while later and shot up, trying to recognise where I was. The room was dark but some sunlight was managing to filter through the blinds, lighting the room enough for me to take a look around.

The walls were a deep slate grey; a huge flat-screen TV donned one wall whilst a stereo the size of Mars was perched on the floor underneath it with a pile of CD's teetered precariously beside it.

A huge photo of a young teenage girl hung from the left wall, she was really pretty; long black hair fluttered in the air around her face and a huge smile lifted her features as she winked at the camera. There was something about her that looked familiar, although I couldn't place it.

Swinging my legs out of the bed, my eyes widened when I realised I only wore a T-shirt over my underwear, and it definitely wasn't my T-shirt. I didn't own a Room 103 shirt. I scanned the room for my clothes and found them folded on a chair. Pulling on my jeans, leaving the T-shirt in place and retrieving a band from my jeans pocket, I pulled my hair into a high twist and went in search of people.

Stepping onto the rear decking I found everyone on the garden below, drinking, eating and singing loudly. I smiled as Cam's voice filtered across to me... that boy really shouldn't be allowed to damage anymore eardrums.

"Spanner!" Romeo smiled up at me from directly below. I leaned over the railing and beamed down at him. "Nice of you to join us, E." Chuckling I made my way down the wooden steps at the side of the decking and into the throng of people.

Arms circled my waist as someone hoisted me up and swung me around. "Boss!" I yelled.

His tongue swept my bare neck, tracing the ink that ran across the nape of my neck, "Nice ink, E." I waited for him to add another comment about my tattoos, just to see if it was him that undressed me but he seemed to just be referring to the one on my neck.

"You never fail until you stop trying," Jax's voice whispered across the bare skin of my neck as he

recited the quote I brandished. I nodded faintly. "And I love the stars, babe." He added wickedly.

I closed my eyes and sighed before I spun round, "You know you didn't have to undress me Jax, I would have been fine sleeping in clothes."

His mischievous grin lit his face before he leaned into my ear. "All those pretty little stars, all the way up the outside of your leg, from your toes to your..." I flinched and bit my bottom lip. "...hip and across your pelvis to your..." I was struggling to breathe as his warm breath excited me in places that shouldn't be excited. It amazed me how he knew so many words. "...forbidden fruit." He finished finally.

I released the breath I was holding with a slight groan but he hadn't finished... oh no!

"Fucking hot, babe. Made me wanna kiss each and every one of those sexy little tats." Another groan rumbled deep. "All the way up, just to see where they finish."

I decided to play him at his own game so I whispered back, "They finish with a Christina piercing and another little surprise."

He growled deeply, his fingers curling around the back of my neck as he pulled me in for a smouldering kiss; a dominating, controlling kiss that made my toes curl and the pit of my belly throb. A kiss that my heart refused to beat through.

"Love surprises, babe."

Shooting him a smirk of my own I walked away, leaving him watching the sway of my hips as I made my way over to Luce and Kaylee, swiping up a bottle of beer from the huge ice filled oil drum as I passed.

"E, what the hell happened last night?" Luce asked as I joined them.

Filling her in I noticed more people came to join our conversation, all of them wanting to hear the latest gossip.

"I knew he was weird" Kaylee shivered. I nodded in agreement.

"He walked me back from work the other night and he kind of got a bit... dark when I asked about his girlfriend, then he seemed to warn me without warning me if you know what I mean?"

"Fuck, E." Cam hissed behind me. I blinked at him. "Don't fucking be alone with him again."

"I'm usually in the bar every night, hot stuff. I'll start walking you back," Boss proposed and my heart swelled at his protectiveness.

"You're really quite soft aren't ya'," I ribbed as I elbowed him gently.

"Fuck! Don't let everyone know, baby. I'll get mugged," he joked but smiled softly at me.

Rolling my eyes at him I took a pull on my bottle as Aaron bounced to the side of me. I smiled up at him. "Hey, gorgeous" I teased. It was a regular joke between us as we were both the spit of each other. It was kind of like complimenting ourselves. I always wondered how we were identical but he had at least a foot on me. Jealous!

"Spanner!" I turned to find the man behind the voice. Romeo lifted a bottle to me "We got a gig at Brandell's tonight. You coming?"

"Sure. Could do with getting a little wrecked," I winked.

His eyebrows pulled together. "Thought you were immune, Spanner?"

"Just Tequila."

He pulled a mischievous grin. "Then prepared to be destroyed. There's gotta be some way to pull you."

Laughing I walked over to Bulk who was manning the barbeque. "Hey," he grinned, hugging me into his side and holding out a fork that speared a sausage. Smiling appreciatively I slid it off the fork and took a bite.

"Can I ask you something, Bulk?" he nodded. I leant in closer, "Who's the girl on Jax's wall?"

His posture altered slightly before he rectified himself and scanned the area close to us. His eyes found mine and I frowned as I saw the sadness in them.

"His little sister." It was no more than a whisper and I knew immediately that he had disclosed some private information that Jax wouldn't be enthusiastic about being revealed.

I nodded. "I take it something happened to her?"

Flipping the burgers before he continued, he eventually turned to me. "You know E, you're the first girl he's ever let into his bed."

I was stunned at his words and tilting my head in puzzlement I regarded him softly. He sucked in a deep breath, as if preparing a nice way to say his next line. "He's a good guy, E. Doesn't deserve to be hurt. Dealt with a lot of shit but he deals a lot of shit too." I frowned. "You know what I'm saying, E?"

Thinking it over for a while I smiled softly, "Yeah, I understand ya' Bulk."

Squeezing me tighter he leaned in again, "She died."

CHAPTER 9

We all piled into Brandell's that night and the guy's immediately set about setting up their gear whilst Cam and Aaron went to get the drinks as me and the girls settled into a booth on the back wall. Melissa had joined us after we'd gone round to her dorm, insisting that she join us and to be honest, I really liked her, she was fun, kind and really sweet.

"SPANNER!" Romeo shouted across the room. He waved me over when I acknowledged him but as I got closer I noticed Jax sat on the edge of the stage talking to a blonde girl who was giggling as he whispered something to her. I bit my bottom lip severely when he took her earlobe between his teeth and tugged lightly before pulling her in for a kiss.

Romeo looked in the direction of my gaze and frowned before turning back to me. "Jax wants to know if you wanna duet again?" What the hell?

I shook my head. "You sure? You rocked it last time."

I scoffed slightly. "If Jax wanted to know then Jax should've asked," I said without removing my eyes from Jax's exploitation of Blondie's tongue.

Romeo cocked his head and smiled wickedly, leaning a little closer, "Then you wanna solo?" I frowned at him, not sure whether I could do that. He nodded encouragingly. "Sure you can," he answered without waiting for the question. "Come on E, the crowd will big it up! They love us here; they'll enjoy the fresh arrangement."

Biting my lip and racking my brain for a song, I smiled playfully and leaned in to inform Romeo of my choice. He smirked and nodded, "C?" I nodded in confirmation when he asked about the starting note.

"Good Girl."

The band played their usual composition and after the last song Romeo took the mic and placed a hand on Jax's arm to halt him from continuing.

"Hey guy's. You rockin' it?" he shouted to the mass.

"*FUCK YEAH!!*" they shouted back.

Romeo nodded and grinned as he glanced at me. I nodded my confirmation as I made my way over to him. Jax wore a puzzled expression as his eyes shifted between Romeo and me. I jumped onto the stage and Romeo held out his hand for me.

"I want a huge Brandell's welcome for E!"

The crowd went wild, wolf whistling and stomping their feet on the floor as Boss drum rolled. I quickly realised most of them were Room 103's most loyal fans who followed them around the city and they recognised me from last night.

"Well I have a fucking hell of a special treat for you tonight."

The crowd whipped up a chant of "E, E, E, E…" I smiled and blew them a kiss initiating a roar of appreciation. "SIT ON MY DICK, E!" someone shouted from the crowd.

"Sorry, I only practice safe sex and you don't look very safe to me!" I retorted loudly. The room went wild and I heard Jax's deep chuckle from beside me.

Romeo laughed, "Well Hell... that told you dude."

Rhythmic clapping hands appeared in the air as the chant of my name persisted and Romeo had trouble calming them down before he continued. "We gonna let her rock the room folk's?"

"*FUCK YEAH!!*"

"Wanna hear her TALK FUCKING DIRTY?" I closed my eyes against the thunderous cheers for the *Poison* song I had chosen.

"Fuck yeah, babe." Jax whispered beside me before he jumped into the throng of fans.

Bulk brought me in and I just let myself enjoy my moment of fame as the crowd sang with me.

"You know I never
I never seen you look so good
You never act the way you should
But I like it
And I know you like it too
The way that I want you
I gotta have you
Oh yes, I do."

As soon as I got to the chorus Jax suddenly appeared beside me and leaned in to share my mic as he joined in.

"Cause baby we'll be
At the drive-in

In the old man's Ford
Behind the bushes
Until I'm screamin' for more
Down the basement
Lock the cellar door
And baby
Talk dirty to me."

I gave him a laugh and a shoulder nudge as he growled the words in my ear. He returned my laugh when I changed a line and pointed to Romeo.

"Romeo
Pick up that guitar
And talk to me."

Romeo saluted and came to front of the stage. The girls went wild as he thrashed out a solo riff whilst he stood beside me, leaning close and giving it to me.

We fucking rocked and I loved every second of it. I could certainly get used to this.

The room exploded when I finished. I squealed when Jax hoisted me up onto his shoulders, carried me down the stairs and perched me on the bar. "Get this girl a drink!" he demanded to the bloke behind the bar.

He handed me a bottle and I held it in the air to the crowd. "ROOM 103!" I toasted at full volume.

"ROOM 103!" they all saluted.

Jax winked at me before Cam came to save me. "Christ E... brilliant." I smiled as I jumped down and my friends hugged me.

"Always said your voice ate shit, E." Luce winked.

I didn't need to buy a drink all night as my new fans kept them coming fast and frequently. I left with a pocket full of phone numbers, very drunken friends, someone's boxer shorts in my bag, twelve condoms stuffed down my bra and no idea who the hell I was!

***

Some stupid person had turned the light up to maximum and my eyes screamed in protest. Satan himself had burnt my mouth to a cinder. A drummer had crawled through my ear and took up residence in my head. And the Bermuda triangle had invaded my stomach.

"Ooh, Goddd," I moaned to myself, not daring to move.

"Okay, babe?"

My eyes shot open with the rest of my senses as I swiftly sat up and stared at Jax lying beside me in his bed, with nothing but a huge smile and a mighty fine chest on display. Shit!

Lifting the duvet, daring a peek at my body I was horrified to be greeted with only my see-through white bra and knickers.

"M&S, babe?"

I nearly died... Primark!

"Please tell me we didn't?" I asked ultra-quietly. I wasn't sure he heard me.

His laugh was deep. "Babe, you didn't even know your name never mind whether you wanted to fuck." I nodded slowly as relief flooded me. "What *is* your name?"

I frowned at him. What a stupid question, "Eve."

"Then you know if you wanna fuck, babe?" he winked before he placed his arm over his eyes.

Shaking my head in exasperation I contemplated how to get the hell out of bed without Jax getting an eyeful of my lady parts.

"Already seen ya' E."

How the hell did he do that? Did my thoughts flow out of my ears before I had a chance to speak them?

"Nice tat by the way."

I swat him on the arm when he referred to the tattoo I had on my pubic area, '*Desire*'. "Christ, Jax."

He laughed as he rolled over and pulled me back down with an arm around my waist, "Go back to sleep, it's too early to fuck."

I must admit it felt good to be snuggled in a pair of strong arms. The erection pressing into my bum, I wasn't so sure of.

CHAPTER 10

I woke with my face pressed against his solid chest; my thigh straddled over his and my arm around his waist as his arm was wrapped around me, holding me close.

I mentally inspected myself and was pleased to feel a little better than I had earlier.

Rotating my head around my neck I opened my eyes to brave the light. Jax was staring at me intently. "Hey babe," he said softly.

I gave him a soft smile, "Mornin'."

We lay just looking, gazing at one another in silence until a thought occurred to me and I cocked my head slightly, "What's your proper name?"

His shoulders lifted a little with his soft chuckle, "Jaxon Cooper."

"I like that," I whispered as he ran his finger down my nose. "How old are you?"

"Twenty three, babe" he whispered back.

I was on a roll. "Favourite group?"

"Probably Sabbath but Nirvana's up there too." His finger trailed across my jaw. "Yours?"

"G N' R, Journey and Poison but I like Sabbath too," I grinned. "Favourite food?"

He laughed at this question, "Everything. You?"

"Undoubtedly coffee."

He frowned at my answer. "Coffee's not a food, babe."

"Oh but god, it is." I smirked then decided to slip in the one I really started the conversation for, "Siblings?"

I felt him stiffen instantly. I pretended not to notice when his breathing sped up a bit, and I looked up at him expectantly.

His silence was heavy, went on for too long and my heart was breaking at his distress. "She's very pretty," I whispered eventually, biting the bullet and praying I didn't push him too far.

His eyes snapped to mine. The raw pain held in them hurt so much. "She was babe... a stunner." He smiled and nodded as he remembered.

"What was her name?" I encouraged gently.

He swallowed heavily, "Mary Ann."

"Suits her."

He smiled down at me. "She was so lively, so full of life, E." I smiled sincerely and he ran his thumb across my lower lip. "You would have liked her, babe." He paused and took a shaky breath "She was just 13 when... when..."

"Shush," I whispered as I stretched up to him, my mouth hunting for his. My need to soothe his pain was immense as I reached out for him. He reached out for me too as he brought his mouth closer and gently took my lower lip in his teeth, luring it between his lips.

I groaned faintly.

He growled loudly.

Then he kissed me, dear god did he kiss me. He owned me as he worked me, his mouth taking mine prisoner, hostage under his own. The passion he radiated as he controlled me was the exact same I kissed him back with.

This man knew how to kiss, in fact this wasn't kissing... this was something else entirely. He had invented his own brand of kissing and I wanted to purchase every single share on the market.

I pulled him closer as he continued to dominate me. He rolled onto his back and took me with him so I was straddled over him, my chest pressing into his. My hands slipped into his soft mane as his own fingers twisted around my long waves.

He moaned again, a deep rumble in the back of his throat that shot straight to my womb before his hands ventured down my back to cup my bottom. He caught my gasp in his mouth as his fingers caressed my soft flesh. I left his mouth and grazed my teeth across his jaw, my tongue soothing the bite as I made my way down his neck.

"You need to stop E," he breathed.

I barely registered what he said. I carried on, suckling my way down his throat as my tongue traced around his adam's apple. "Fuck, babe" he growled as his hands came round to cup my breasts. I moaned and pushed them further into his touch, my lips now working their way across his defined collarbone as my hips started to grind against the straining erection in his shorts. I was silently thanking his decision to remove his jeans last night.

His cock was huge and the knowledge wiped out my inhibitions. "I need to taste you," I whispered against his nipple piercing, my teeth now tugging gently at the silver ring.

I moaned loudly when he growled and pinched my rigid nipple. "We need to stop E, before I can't."

I pushed myself up, his words hitting me like a bucket of cold water. "Why?"

He shook his head gently as his palm cupped my cheek, "Babe, you're… not me."

What the hell was he on about?

"I'm fucked up babe, proper mind fucked."

Pushing myself further up I scrambled off him, hurt by his rejection, embarrassed by my wanton behaviour and angry at my reaction to his words.

"Babe!" Ignoring him, I pulled on my clothes that were folded in his chair again. Sitting up he growled at me, "E!"

I shook my head frantically but refused to look at him, "It's okay Jax, I understand."

"No! Babe, you don't." His hand shot out and his fingers wrapped around my wrist as I attempted to get to the door as quickly as possible.

"It's okay, Jax. Hell, even I know I'm not…" I pulled at my wrist, desperately trying to get him to release me so I could get my humiliated ass out of there.

"Not what, E?"

I pursed my lips. "Not your usual…" I shrugged, couldn't make my lips sound the words.

"No. You're not my usual. You deserve more, Babe. Fuck, you are more! That's why I don't wanna hurt you. Cos' I will. I'll fucking drain you dry… cripple you until you can't fucking breathe. You hearin' me, E?"

I frowned at the most words that had ever left his mouth in one stretch, not sure what he was saying but I managed to wrangle my wrist free.

"I've gotta go anyway... essays to do so..."

I flung myself through the door and out of the house as fast as I could move before he saw my tears.

***

I didn't see Jax again all week. In fact I didn't see much of anyone all week, my classes, lectures and work kept me relentlessly busy. The band had been in the bar each night, minus Jax, but I had been too busy to take any time with them.

Boss had kept his word though and walked me back from Z Bar each night but I hadn't seen anything of Austin since the incident.

Thursday night as he and I were walking through the village back to my dorm he gently placed his hand on my arm and stopped me. "E."

I frowned at his expression, realising something he was about to ask or say was difficult. I raised my eyebrows and smiled gently to urge him on. He bit his lip before looking at me, "What happened Sunday between you and Jax?"

He sensed my composure shift and his brows deepened. "Nothing!"

He sighed and tilted his head at me. "E, come on. Jax has been like a bear with a sore fucking arse all week, you've kept your distance from everybody and if Cam gives Jax anymore dead eye I'm gonna have to put a stop to a serious fight... and I don't really wanna do that, hot stuff. They're both my friends."

Bewildered, I shot him a glance. What the hell had gone off between Jax and Cam? "I can't help you with the Jax and Cam argument but me and Jax... well like I said nothing happened!"

He continued to stare at me, not believing a word I said, so I sighed and resumed, with a lot of blushing, "Not for want of trying." Confusion covered his face and I gave him a shameful smile. "I came on to him, he didn't..." I gave him a shrug instead of finishing the sentence.

His eyebrows hit his hairline, "He didn't...?"

I shrugged again but shook my head faintly "No. Told me to stop."

"Fool," was all he said but he continued to wear a confused frown all the way back to my dorm.

Being the protective gentleman he was, Boss always made sure I got into my room safely before he left me, just in case Austin the Aggressive, as Boss had labelled him, was hanging about.

"Not sure what to say E," he offered as he opened my door to leave. He was staring at Luce's painting of me on the beach, determined not to meet my eye.

"It's okay Boss. I just misread the signals that's all."

"Nah hot stuff, you didn't."

He closed the door quietly behind him and I flopped onto my bed with exhaustion. I didn't think I had either.

***

Friday night gave me a rare free night so Cam, Aaron, Luce, Kaylee, Melissa and Josh dragged me into Huddersfield town centre on a pub crawl.

By 3am we were all hanging onto each other for support and singing our way home. Cam's house was closest and because Melissa was busting for the toilet, we decided to carry on the party at his.

We all fell through his front door in one fluid movement, ending up in a heap of bodies in the hallway.

"Shit guy's, I really need to pee. Get off me!" Melissa wailed from near the bottom of the pile.

"I can't get up," I laughed from the top of the body mountain.

"Oh Goddd!" Melissa cried. Oh dear!

"Don't you dare piss on me, Mel." Cam snorted from underneath Melissa, "I'm not into that kind of thing."

We all laughed and Melissa groaned loudly. "Can you shuffle out?" I asked her as I rested my head on Josh's back who was directly underneath me.

Everybody tried to wrestle about and I smiled at Josh as he managed a 180° turn and was now face to face with me. He grinned at me, planted his hand behind my head and pulled my mouth to his. Just like that!

He slanted his mouth and deepened the kiss but when he swept my bottom lip with his tongue I pulled back.

"Sorry," he whispered. "Couldn't resist."

"That's okay." I shrugged as hands came around my waist and lifted me up, planting me upright on the floor.

"Spanner!" Romeo greeted with a huge beam on his face.

"Romeo, Oh Romeo." I swayed drunkenly before I jumped up and swung my arms and legs around him. "Take me to the kitchen slave boy!" I demanded.

He grinned playfully and made his way towards the room. "Might wanna shut your eyes for this bit Spanner," he warned with a small chuckle but I frowned and stupidly ignored him.

He opened the lounge door and took a step in. I really wish I had heeded his advice!

My eyes zeroed in on Jax's bare arse pumping furiously at a moaning Fran, who was underneath him on the sofa.

My heart clenched, my throat closed in and my lip split under the bite of my teeth as the little bubble of forbidden pressure built in my blood. Shit no!

Romeo didn't sense my discomfort as he continued to carry me through to the kitchen, plonking me onto the table in the middle of a card game the other band members were playing.

Boss frowned at me and glanced at the door we'd just appeared from before he narrowed his eyes on Romeo. "Shit man! Did you bring her through the room?"

I diverted my gaze as I continued to chew rapidly on my lower lip. A tingle in my tongue made me pull in a breath.

Romeo gave him a confused look and Boss swore under his breath before he grabbed my hand, his worried eyes fixed on me, "You okay, hot stuff?"

A shiver racked my body and I fought against it. I plastered a fake smile on my face and nodded before jumping off the table and made my way to the fridge, pulling out a beer, popping the cap on the edge of the worktop. I swallowed back the electric shock that jolted my brain.

Boss was glaring at Romeo; Bulk was throwing a bewildered look between the three of us and I just took myself outside, needing the fresh air to bite down the familiar urge that was starting to build. Christ E, not now!

I took a long pull on the beer as my other hand gripped the railing, crushing it under the force of my hold. Trying desperately to control my breathing I struggled to stop the itch that started to vibrate my veins. Crap!

Pulling my phone out I hit the internet button and fired up Google.

Just once. Just once wouldn't hurt E, then you can pull it back again.

You just need it once, E! Then you'll feel good, not this sad crap!

My heart beat rapidly, excitement coursed through my soul as Google became my new best friend and an address displayed the nearest club. Then I booked a taxi.

Then I smiled to myself, closing my eyes as the tension twisted through my muscles.

Nearly there E... an hour! Just an hour and everything will be fine! Release E... sweet fucking release!

My hands were shaking as the air from my lungs started dispelling itself in short little gusts and as the roaring in my ears became too loud, I made my way round the side of the house on trembling legs and waited for the taxi on the roadside as I gave anxious glances towards the house.

Please don't come out, please don't come out, please don't come out!

The tightening in my chest was becoming unbearable and I dug my nails into my palms to fight the pain whilst my teeth ravaged my bottom lip.

I nearly orgasmed with the exhilaration as the taxi pulled up, knowing I was so close, so close to euphoria. My body energized powerfully, the hum pulsing at my nerve endings as I climbed in and recited the address.

I heard Cam shout as we pulled away but I didn't turn around.

I heard the tune of my phone ring but I didn't answer. But most of all I heard the soft voice in my head say 'Nearly there E. Sweet, sweet surrender is yours' and I did answer this as I walked into the club.

CHAPTER 11

I was grinning like a lunatic as I pushed open my room door, the exquisite high now flowing through my body made me giggle as I fell through it.

"You stupid, stupid fucking fool!" Cam raged at me as I stumbled to a stop in front of him. He was sat on my bed beside Luce, both of them held a rage so strong I could hold it in my hand.

"Sshhh," I told them as I placed a finger on my lips and giggled again.

I could see the heave of Cam's chest as he struggled to hold back the fury. Luce just looked at me sadly. "Don't be sad Luce, I'm good now. So good hun," I beamed as a stray tear slid down her cheek.

"Take it off!" Cam demanded. I just scowled at him and shook my head melodramatically. "I said, take it off!"

"It's not supposed to be my brother who says those words. It should be…"

"TAKE IT OFF!!"

I jolted at his rage, closing my eyes as realisation of what I had just done started to penetrate my mind. Oh God. What had I done?

"Now!" he growled slowly.

I sucked on my lips as I turned around, grasped the hem of my top and lifted it over my head wincing in pain as I did so.

"*Holy Christ!*" A sob tore from Luce's throat and I heard Cam suck in a huge breath.

"I'm sorry," I whispered.

"You got a bath here?" Cam asked.

"No, just showers," Luce replied.

"*Fuck!*" he seethed, "You need to soak, E." I nodded but remained silent. "You got your cream and bath oil?" I nodded again.

"Fuck, E!" He was so angry and I winced at the tone in his voice as I replaced my shirt with a loose blouse. "You'll have to come back to mine."

I shook my head at him, "No it's good." There was no way I was going to witness a lovey-dovey Jax and Fran this morning.

"YOU'VE GOT NO FUCKING CHOICE!" I think he was angry with me.

Rubbing his temples he closed his eyes in frustration. "Sorry," I repeated on a choked whisper.

He shook his head in disappointment and gave me a tortured look before he wrapped his arms around me gently and tenderly hugged me. "It's okay, E. It's gonna be okay," he whispered as I started to shake now the high was coming down.

"Come on." He held out his hand to me and I squinted at it.

"Please Cam. I don't really..." He shook his head at me and I sighed before extracting the things I needed from the back of a drawer, things I hadn't needed for eleven long weeks.

***

Cam opened his front door and I was relieved to find the house quiet. He placed a finger against his lips before leading Luce and me up the stairs and into the bathroom.

"I'll be downstairs if you need me," he whispered. I nodded and closed the door behind him before Luce started to run the bath, expertly measuring the correct amount of oil before pouring it under the stream of water.

She didn't speak to me. I knew at the moment it was safer not to talk to her either, her disappointment in me strained the atmosphere in the small room.

I climbed in the warm water, routinely crossed my arms over my chest and sank down slowly. The sting took my breath and brought the tears.

"Oh E," Luce whispered sadly as I began to sob, heart wrenching disgusting sobs that tore through both our souls.

"I'm so sorry Luce, I... I..."

"Ssshhh, darlin', it's gonna be fine, E. Everything will work itself out. I promise." She cried with me as she stroked my hair until we were both snotty and spent.

Luce helped me out of the bath and gently patted me down before turning my back to her so she could apply the cream onto my back.

"Fuck E, it's really bad this time." She winced as she struggled to bring herself to apply the cream, not wanting to cause me any pain.

I nodded and swallowed heavily, "Yeah... needed it... raw."

She hissed through her teeth and I could feel her hand shake. "You need to lay down, E?"

Luce knew I usually zoned out at this stage and I could sense her anguish if I passed out on her while stood up. "I'm good, I'll hold onto the shower frame."

She pulled in a large breath as I gripped each side of the cubicle and grit my teeth. The first swipe of the cotton ball took my breath; the second made my knees buckle and the third brought a snarl.

"Shit E, I can't do this."

"Just do it, Luce!" I hissed through clenched teeth.

She was trembling as I struggled to hold myself upright but she determinedly persevered and I loved her all the more for it.

I could feel myself sliding down the frame. "Fuck E, stay with me," Luce shouted.

"I'm trying.... Lu..."

"CAM!"

The blackness took me to oblivion.

***

I woke laid out on my stomach, the cool air soothing my sore back and my mouth squashed against the pillow, "Urghhh."

"Ssshhh, babe."

Fuck!!! I daren't move. What the hell was I doing in Jax's bed?

Shit! Shit! Shit!

His hand settled in my hair as he gently stroked down the length of it, soothing me. *CRAP!*

Pushing myself up without giving him a glance, I clambered to my feet. Closing my eyes and biting down the shame of being naked in front of him.

"Lay down."

Shaking my head I scurried around for my clothes, finding them in their usual spot on the chair.

"Why, Babe?"

"I need to go," I whispered, still refusing to look at him or answer his question as I slipped into my blouse, wincing as it brushed against my welts.

"E!"

"WILL YOU STOP!" I screamed at him, humiliation and pain bringing fresh tears, ones that I refused to let him see.

His hands gripped my upper arms as he lifted me up and slung me back on the bed, his powerful frame caging me underneath him as his raging eyes pierced through me.

Turning my head to the side, I refused to look at him but his large hand gripped my jaw and forced me to look. His eyes were dark and angry, his chest heaving vigorously as a warning snarl left his throat.

"Let me go," I grated through clenched teeth.

His head shook slowly, "Talk!"

I gave him my best glare. His eyebrows rose in a silent dare and I closed my eyes, denying him the attention. He settled above me, straddling my thighs. As I opened my eyes he was sat, arms crossed with a 'whatever, I have all day' expression.

"Fuck you!" I spat.

He leant down, his face an inch from mine, still declining my need to look away. "Why?"

"Screw you."

"Why?"

"Go to hell!"

"Why?"

"Piss off!"

"WHY?"

"WHY?"

"BECAUSE I FUCKING NEED IT!" I eventually screamed.

"WHY?"

"GO FUCK YOURSELF!"

"WHY, E?"

"BECAUSE I FUCKING DESERVE IT! OKAY, I DESERVE IT... every fucking piece of it. Every thrash, every sear, every fucking slice of pain... I deserve it...I deserve it..."

The keening noise came from somewhere in the room and I tilted my head to identify it. A sob tore through me as I realised it was coming from me, the long pitch echoing through my body.

He swept me up, pulled me in tight as his large arms framed me and gripped me so firmly I was sure he was breaking a rib.

"Ssshhh, babe" he whispered as I cried against his chest, his strong powerful chest. A chest that made me safe, protected me and also broke my heart.

He let me cry for a long while, his fingers stroking through my hair as he whispered words of comfort in my ear, his relentless persistence to soothe me pulled me further into him and I knew I had to break free.

I drew back and lifted my face to his, "Sorry."

He shook his head slightly as he slipped his hand over my ear and held my head, "Don't be." I looked away, didn't want to see what was behind his eyes as I tried to pull free from him but he held me firm before his finger tilted my chin back.

His eyes blazed as he bit his bottom lip, his obvious struggle to hold back was consuming him and he wasn't winning.

His mouth brushed mine so delicately I wondered if I had imagined it until it became firmer and I knew it wasn't my imagination... this was real, very real.

His tongue demanded entry and as I opened to him he released a small groan and wrapped his fingers in my hair, twisting it almost painfully in his grip. I returned his moan with one of my own and joined in the dance, sucking desperately on his tongue, telling him just how much I needed him before his teeth started to graze my neck, his stubble scratching deliciously against the heat of my skin.

"Fuck E, I need to be inside you so bad."

I groaned at his words and pulled his head further into me, giving permission to his words. Hell, I would give permission for anything if he made me feel like this.

His fingers found the buttons of my blouse and slowly, torturously began to undo them whilst I silently urged him to hurry the hell up.

"So fucking beautiful," he whispered as he opened my blouse to reveal my bare breasts. The flat of his tongue slowly brushed over my pert nipple and I rewarded him by wrapping my legs around his hips and pulling him in. "Fuck, babe."

"Hurry, Jax," I whispered. "I need to feel you."

A growl erupted from his throat as he unbuttoned my jeans and swiftly pulled them down my legs, along with my knickers, and as promised he kissed each of the stars that decorated the outside of my right leg all the way up until he discovered the tiny diamond dermal piercing and ink at the end of the trail.

"Holy shit." His nose rested against my mound, "Fucking sexy, babe."

I lifted my hips, encouraging him to get on with it. I needed to feel him, feel his tongue on me. Christ! I was gonna combust!

A long drawn out groan erupted from my chest as his tongue swiped the full length of my sex, "Oh Goddd."

"So good," he whispered before he began his torture, expertly working me into a fever as he sucked my clit then released it and fucked me with his tongue. Always so close but he wouldn't let me go, refused to let me fly.

"Christ, Jax!" I breathed. He chuckled! The bastard chuckled!

He relented and began frantically flicking his tongue over my clit until I jumped; dived over the edge with an almighty explosion... I think I shook the bloody room.

"Fuck yeah babe, feel it," he growled as my hips lifted off the bed so high I wondered if I'd snap my spine.

"Oh Jesus," I wheezed as he reached into his side drawer and extracted a condom before stripping down and rolling it on.

He palmed my face tenderly as he nudged in slowly, "You ready to take me, babe?" He pushed a little deeper, "You ready to be fucked into extinction, E?" A little further, "Cos' I'm gonna make you fuckin' scream, babe."

I groaned and rolled my hips at his unhurried pace. My back arched and we both groaned in satisfaction as he pushed all the way in and filled me completely. "*Christ,*" he rasped.

We lay unmoving, our eyes connecting and saying so much in the silence before he pulled back out slowly and slid back in, so easy, so deliberately and so god damn good.

"So tight babe, I can't..." His teeth sank into his bottom lip as he closed his eyes and rested his forehead against mine. "E," was all he said before he took control and worked me into a wild panting mess, whimpering with each powerful thrust as he drove me up the bed and into oblivion with his relentless rhythm.

"Fuck yes," I screamed as I felt my body tighten.

"Give it up babe, give it me," he growled. I exploded around him, detonating his own violent climax as we both clawed and clung to each other, fighting to breathe.

"*Fuck,*" he snarled out. His head flung back in ecstasy as I pulled him in, lifting my hips and grasping him tightly with my thighs, draining every bit of pleasure from him that I could.

His face dropped to my shoulder as he fought for equilibrium whilst I panted my way back to consciousness.

"Christ, babe." He pulled out then rolled onto his back as he dragged me with him, pushing my head onto his chest before he took my hand in his and held it tight, threading his fingers through mine as his thumb stroked soothingly across my own.

His other hand came to rest on my back, just a natural stance but I hissed and tensed. "Shit babe, sorry."

Shaking my head I squeezed his hand to reassure him.

Silence engulfed us and when it bore down a little too heavily I knew he wanted to talk so I did what I always did. Diverted!

"I have stuff to do." The lie left my mouth easily and I hated myself for it.

"The hell, babe!" He lifted my chin to look at him, his eyes were narrow and fierce as he shook his head slowly, "Don't do this, E!"

Swallowing back the retort I flung myself out of bed, "I said I have stuff to do, Jax."

He scoffed and then hissed, "Babe. It's really doesn't look good from where I am."

I spun around so fast I nearly toppled over, "Then don't fucking look!"

The growl was fierce and I bit my lip in anguish. "Babe..."

Turning away from his warning, I squeezed my eyes shut, desperately trying to fight the urge to just give in, to just for one moment let it all flow out but I knew I couldn't. I had this secret that needed to be taken to the grave with me. I owed him that much.

"Who the fuck did it?" he asked. There it was; the question I had seen in his eyes earlier.

"Don't worry Jax, they enjoyed it too. They both screamed in fucking ecstasy as much as I did," I spat nastily, his relentless push tipping me over the edge. I regretted it immediately.

His face tightened as his jaw twitched, his eyes darkened so much they appeared to be solid black. His fists clenched as he slowly climbed out of bed and stalked towards me, gradually backing me up against the wall.

Swallowing heavily I closed my eyes against his rage. "Open them," he growled.

"No." A whisper was all I could manage as my heart beat wildly against my chest.

"FUCKING-OPEN-THEM!!" I opened them!

His fury was edible, the thickness it coated me with made me shiver and I gasped as he traced my cheek bone with his finger. "Don't ever talk like that again!" His intensity held the breath back in my lungs. "You hear me, babe?"

"Yeah, I hear ya'," I whispered back.

He nodded once. "We need to talk babe, but when you've calmed the fuck down."

"I can't, Jax." I winced when his eyes flinted.

"You can, and you will." He pushed off the wall, pulled on his jeans and left. Just fucked right off!

Nice!

CHAPTER 12

"We ready to ROCK THE ROOM?" Jax led the rowdy crowd into Room 103's signature track and I risked a glance at him from my spot behind the bar. His masculine beauty captured my breath and I pushed back the urge to touch him, just touch him.

The craving for him hadn't subsided since he had taken me this morning and I was angry at myself for the reactions I was feeling towards him.

Jax didn't do relationships, Hell, a girl was lucky if he invited her back for seconds and I wasn't stupid enough to think I was any different.

I watched him as he worked the crowd, feeding them as he consumed them.

"Help me feed it, feed it, serve it, the growl to open the tomb
Yeah, yeah, yeahhhhhh
Make me feel it, feel it, touch it, while we Rock the Room."

"E." My eyes shifted to the guy sat on a stool watching me warily.

"Austin." He must have seen the stiffening of my shoulders and the flint of fear behind my eyes but he didn't respond to it, "What can I get you?"

"Jack and coke."

I nodded and fixed his drink and as I placed it on the bar in front of him his fingers wrapped around mine. I heard Jax's voice stutter and I shot him an 'I'm okay' look. He nodded once but continued to watch us. I turned back to Austin as he started to say something.

"I... God, I'm no good at this... I just wanna apologise, you know for..."

I pursed my lips and frowned, "You need to apologise to Melissa, not me Austin."

He shook his head marginally. I noticed he still held my hand under his so I slid it back, gently releasing myself from his grip. "I'm not supposed to go near her. That's why I'm here; I need you to tell her something..."

I shook my head firmly, "I don't think that's a good idea, Austin."

His teeth sank into his bottom lip and I noticed the glint filter through his eyes. Christ, this guy really needed to invest in some anger management!

"Please E, you have class with her."

I shook my head at him, "I'm sorry Austin."

"God damn it, E!" he snarled nastily.

I flinched inwardly at his tone but remained outwardly impassive, not wanting to alert Jax to my concern but his hand clenched around my arm and he practically pulled me over the bar, my small legs kicking the air behind me as my body slid across the beer slops on the old wooden counter. "Just fucking do it," he growled as a loud screech sounded from the stage speaker and guitar amp.

Austin was dragged across the room by his hair, Jax's fingers gripping so tightly I could make out his white knuckles. Boss, Bulk and Romeo followed behind, their wrath physically touchable in the air as every single eye in the room watched the commotion.

"Shit," Rachel said from behind me, making me jolt in surprise.

"Yeah... Shit!" I repeated.

Twenty minutes later the band walked back in, walked over to the stage and resumed their act. Nothing happened here Officer!

*** ***

"Okay, babe?" Jax's voice came from over the bar while I was crouched down under it refilling the shelves.

Z Bar was closed but the boys were still packing their kit away whilst I cleaned and restocked, and to be honest I was grateful of their company.

I looked up to be met by his face peering over the edge of the counter at me, a wide smile on his glorious face. I grinned back up at him and nodded. "...12...13...14...15...16..." I held a finger up and counted loudly to indicate I would be just a second.

"19...18...17...16...15..." he smirked.

I closed my eyes and counted in my head, trying desperately to shut him out. "...14...13...12... Arghhhh, you..."

His deep laugh brought a smile to my face and I stood up and swat his arm. He grabbed my wrist and pulled me over the bar... Jeez, again!

His mouth crashed over mine, his lips working me into a hot wanton mess as his dominant work-over made my knees tremble.

"Carry on, I don't mind watching," Boss shouted from across the room but Jax didn't pull back, in fact he seemed to do the opposite. His hands settled on my upper arms as he dragged me fully over the bar and perched me on the edge.

I wrapped my legs around him as his hand slid into my hair and wrenched me harder against him. My intense arousal brought a groan forward and Jax replied with a growl as his arms spanned my waist. He lifted me off the bar and walked us towards the stockroom, his lips never leaving mine. I wondered how the hell he could see where he was going?

Kicking the door shut behind him, he pushed me against the wall while he resumed his passionate kiss. "Legs down babe," he whispered against my lips. I did as he asked, dropping my feet to the floor.

His fingers popped the button on my jeans before they were swept down my legs with my knickers as I hastily yanked at his jeans, releasing his stiff cock into my hand.

I smirked at him as I slowly worked him up and down. "Fuck yeah," he growled. He grabbed one of my legs, pulling it around his hip as I tried to balance on my tiptoes when he positioned himself at my entrance. He nipped my bottom lip between his teeth just as he impaled me viciously. "Fuck! You're too short. Put your legs around me, E."

I jumped up, clamping my legs around his hips. He thrust back in so forcibly my head whipped back and banged the wall. "Shit, you okay, babe?"

I nodded. "Yeah, just fuck me, Jax."

He didn't need to be told twice. His thrusts were hard and fast, our bodies slapping loudly against each other as my back pounded a rhythm on the wall in tune with our erotic moans. My teeth sunk into his neck, making him hiss and pound me brutally.

Before we knew it we were both coming hard. "*Eve*," he growled out as his spunk hit my womb and my orgasm milked him dry whilst I screamed my release.

"Oh Jesus," I breathed as a loud palm drum roll sounded on the door.

"Fucking epic. That rhythm was awesome guy's," Boss shouted.

I groaned as Jax smirked, "Fuck. Off."

I blinked and gulped. "Jax." His head tilted as he frowned at me.

"Babe?"

"Condom, Jax."

I grimaced but he shook his head adamantly, "Not you, babe!" What the hell?

"What the hell?"

He shook his head again, "I said, not with you." I blinked again. "Need to feel you!"

I didn't quite know how to take that really. "But Jax..."

His eyes narrowed on me and his finger ran down my nose "You on birth control, babe?"

"Well yes but..."

"Then no buts, babe. Need to feel you," he repeated. "Fucking ace."

I just nodded. What could I say? Then my brain registered other problems with this scenario but my mind wondered how to broach the subject, "But..."

"Spit it out, E." He glanced up at me as he crouched before me, wiped my lady parts with some paper tissue he had whipped off a clean roll, then held my knickers open for me to step into. How totally sweet!

"Well, what about... you know..."

"Clue me in, babe." He frowned while now pulling my knickers up my legs and over my hips.

"You know Jax... are you clean?" I finally managed, hoping I didn't insult him.

"Yeah babe, you?" Bit late to ask me now!

"Of course, I've never gone with anyone saddleless but I just needed to check. You know?"

He planted a small kiss on my nose. "Sure babe. I hear you," he said then dipped back down to help me back into my jeans but I noticed his face darken when I propped my hand on his shoulder to steady myself.

Grabbing my wrist he studied the purple bruise left on my arm by Austin's hold. He was furiously biting his bottom lip as his eyes blazed wildly, "Fucker!"

I palmed his face, trying to placate him. "Hey, I'm okay."

Remaining silent, he tapped my foot to remind me to pull my leg through before he stood up and regarded me intently. "Bastard shouldn't touch you."

Nodding, I reached up and planted a kiss on his cheek. "Thank you for being my knight in shining armour," I whispered with a happy smile, his response was to take me in another toe-curling kiss.

"Turn around babe," he whispered when he pulled away. I frowned and shrugged but did as he asked but as soon as I realised what he was doing I tried to turn back. "No," he warned.

Closing my eyes in shame as he rolled my shirt up my back to check on my lacerations, I braced myself for the reappearance of his temper but he surprised me when his lips gently kissed each and every lash on my back.

A tear slid down my cheek at his tenderness, not really believing I deserved it. "Does it hurt?" he asked softly before he gently kissed another.

"Not at the time... not until after," I divulged quietly.

I felt his small nod as he continued to caress my broken skin, "Why the whip, babe?"

I paused before I spoke. "Please don't do this in a fucking cupboard, Jax" I pleaded.

His chin rested on my shoulder as his breath tickled my cheek. "It needs saying babe, don't care a fuck where it's said."

"Jax," I took a deep breath before I said the next words. "Look, no offence but we hardly know each other. We've fucked twice..."

His growl was deep and I swiftly shut the hell up. "Babe... coulda' fucked once, coulda' fucked a trillion times... don't really give a shit how many times we've fucked…" He spun me around so I was facing him. "But what I do give a shit about is the fact that someone's fucking with my girl." He leaned in a little closer, "and I don't like my girl to be fucked with. You hear me, babe?"

I nodded slowly. "I hear ya' Jax." Did he actually just call me his girl? Holy Hell! Little dude dance inside my belly!

He nodded then took my hand. "Tomorrow! Me, you and words. Okay?" he informed me sternly.

I swallowed heavily, "Okay, Jax."

CHAPTER 13

I spent Sunday morning catching up with assignments, essays and cleaning the dorm.

Austin hadn't turned up and I was a little anxious about what the guy's had done with him so I made a mental note to ask Jax when he picked me up later.

We had arranged, or rather I had been told, Jax would pick me up early in the afternoon and my stomach was currently revolting against the fact that he wanted to talk. What the hell did I tell him? My life wasn't one of the simplest. In fact it was damn complicated and I knew he wouldn't approve of any of it but I suppose he needed to know some of it. There was no way I could disclose all of it, some secrets were just that... secrets!

✳✳✳

"Ah, ah, ah, it was the Germanic settlers from the Netherlands that brought it over," Josh argued as I chewed the end of my pen so thoroughly it was now in dire need of plastic surgery.

"Yeah, but it was originally the Anglo-Saxon's that developed it." Josh rolled his eyes at me but I persisted, "and *'Beowulf'* is practically the earliest English we translated from."

"Folklore, E."

I smirked at him when he grinned. "You go with yours and I'll go with mine." I winked as I rose from the table and went to brew a coffee.

Josh nodded when I held up a cup, silently asking if he wanted one, but then he came and stood beside me, fidgeting with his fingers nervously. I frowned at him. "Listen E, about Friday night..."

"It's fine Josh, just a drunken kiss..."

"Babe?" *Fuck!* Always happens doesn't it!

Planting a smile on my face I turned to find Jax leaning against the doorframe regarding Josh and me intently with his brows high. I knew I would be getting a grilling about the kiss Josh and I shared. "Hey." I grinned when my eyes flicked down to the Starbucks take-away cup in his hand.

Rolling his eyes he winked and passed it me. "Cinnamon latte, extra shot," he declared.

I cocked my head. "How did you know?" This man never ceased to amaze me.

"I listen to people, E."

My smile slipped and my breath hitched when his eyes blazed at me before he swooped down and governed me in a possessive kiss which I knew was for Josh's benefit. His fingers twisted through my hair and his teeth clamped gently on my bottom lip as he owned me.

"Wow" I breathed when he pulled away. His wicked smile brought forward my own. "Behave," I whispered.

His grin widened. "Ready, babe?"

"You're a little earlier than I expected. Have I got time to change?"

"Sure."

Turning back to a gloomy Josh, I smiled. "We okay to break off?" He shrugged but nodded in confirmation before swiping up his books and trudging from the room. Jax raised his eyebrows at me but I just shook my head at him before I led him into my room while I changed.

He plonked down on my bed and gazed at the beach scene whilst I changed into jeans and my faded *Mötley Crüe* T-shirt, before sitting at my dresser to sort out my wild hair.

My heart stuttered as I looked at the reflection of Jax on my bed, laid flat with his arms behind his head appearing utterly relaxed as though he belonged there. He glanced at me when I swallowed heavily and I quickly diverted my gaze, pulling my hair up high on my head.

"Okay, babe?"

Shifting my eyes to his in the mirror I nodded and smiled. "Sure, baby." His grin at my endearment was breath-taking and I instantly promised myself that I would do anything to earn more from him.

"Fucking gorgeous," he whispered in my ear after removing his magnificent body off my bed. Our eyes locked in the mirror for a second before he gently clamped his teeth over my earlobe "We need to go before I bend you over the bed and fuck you raw."

The whimper that escaped my mouth made his eyes darken and flash. "Or we can just stay here so you can bend me over the bed and fuck me raw," I offered with a frantic nod of my head. I beamed happily at him when he sucked in his lips to stifle his laugh.

"Later, babe." He grabbed my hand and led me out to his car, his beautiful car.

***

"Where you taking me, handsome?" I asked as I browsed through his iPod for some tunes as we cruised round some country lanes.

"Handsome?" he smirked at me with a lift of a brow.

I turned to face him and let my eyes wander over his body slowly. God this man made me throb. "Sorry... Where you taking me, *Hot and fucking* handsome?" I rectified as I switched the music to some AC/DC.

He laughed deeply and shook his head in amusement, "Swimming, babe."

I reared back with a frown, "I haven't brought my costume." His answering mischievous grin had me a little worried. "Don't answer that!" I informed him.

We both thrashed out *AC/DC's 'Highway to Hell'* before he veered off onto a dirt track. I gave him a worried glance. "Now you're gonna tell me you're some sort of perverted axe murderer aren't you?"

He chuckled and shook his head, "Nah babe, just a pervert."

"Ace," I retorted happily. "My own pervert, whenever, wherever, however," I declared excitedly.

"Fuck yeah." He winked as he carefully steered through a clearing between some trees.

Where the hell was he taking me? I was getting a little worried about his car when the tree branches started to batter the side of it as he drove deeper into the wooded area. "Jax?"

"Chill, babe."

My eyes widened when the trees opened up onto a small clearing and a little vista welcomed us. A towering rock waterfall flowed into a small but adequate pool, which was surrounded by masses of multi-coloured flora and fauna. A large grassy area was scattered with an expanse of bluebells and miniature weeping willows.

"Oh my God," I breathed as I practically stumbled from the car and took in the scene before me. My breathing was heavy as I stood immobile for a long time just exploring the beautiful landscape with my eyes.

It wasn't for at least ten minutes that I realised Jax hadn't joined me. Turning to look for him, I gasped when I saw him leaning on the bonnet of his car, his face white and his breathing laboured as his fists clenched tightly. "Jax?"

I very slowly walked over to him until I was stood in front of him. His eyes were trained in the distance towards the mass of bluebells and the pain radiating from him was raw and real. "Baby?" I whispered as I cupped his desolate face, "Hey."

He looked at me and smiled sadly, there was so much pain in his eyes that it took my breath. "Mary Ann and me, we... used to come here. She loved it, said it made her feel like a fairy." I smiled softly and nodded, encouraging him to open up. He laughed lightly. "She used to hide in the bells thinking I couldn't see her." He shrugged and smiled at me, "She always wore a bright yellow dress."

I chuckled with him. "Yeah, that'd work."

He took a heavy breath and I took his hand. "First time I've been back, E."

My heart broke as his voice stuttered. "She still here with you?" I asked softly.

His eyes swung to me, the expression in them when he realised I understood him, honoured me. He nodded slowly, "Yeah, babe."

I gave his hand a tug. "Then let's go say hello," I whispered.

His eyes brimmed but he nodded firmly as I led him over to the field of blue and sat in a tiny clearing, patting the ground beside me. He gently dropped beside me and stretched out his long legs in front of him. "Tell me about her."

Swallowing heavily he grabbed my hand and I squeezed against the tremor that ran through it. "She was just so bright babe, intellectually and personally." I smiled as I pictured her running through the bells, Jax laughing as he chased her. "Always wanted to be with me, you know?" I didn't answer, he didn't expect me to.

"Her voice was..." He sucked on his lips and turned to me, his head tilted with a small smile, "Like you babe, husky and low but god, so fucking beautiful."

A tear slid down my cheek and he brushed it away with his thumb as his face saddened. "She was close to my Dad, they were like twins, same sense of humour, same likes and dislikes, just together. You hear me, babe?"

I nodded, "I hear ya', baby."

"He was so... so dark, E." His hand tightened in mine and I grew a little anxious at his change of mood, his smiling face had now disappeared as a sombre black one took its place.

"Hated me, babe." What did I say to that? Nothing, so I remained silent. "Always said my music was a waste of space, would never amount to much just a low life busker, a junkie he used to call me." He laughed bitterly then. "Never touched drugs in my life E, but him, he couldn't fucking get through a day without 'em."

"Yeah," I scoffed softly.

He turned to me, "Ya' know, babe?"

I nodded, "Yeah, I know Jax."

His hand squeezed mine as we shared a connection, a childhood experience we had both lived through. "Your Dad?"

"Yeah." I pulled in a heavy breath, "And my Mom."

He nodded solemnly. "Yeah babe, I hear you."

We were silent for a while until he found the courage to continue. "He loved my Mom though. God, too much." His vision was glazed as his memories took him back to some horrific moment. I knew this because his hand started trembling and sweat beaded on his brow.

"Wasn't right the way he loved her. Too intense, too black and manipulative! You hear me, babe?"

I squeezed his hand again. "I hear ya'," I whispered, understanding every tragic fucking word.

He sighed profoundly before he carried on. "Got too much for her after a bit. She left." I closed my eyes at the distress in his voice. "Left us all."

Looking up at him I could see the utter devastation he felt at being abandoned. "Just upped and fucked off." I clambered onto his lap, straddling his thighs as I rested my forehead against his and took both of his hands in mine.

"He couldn't cope when she went." I tracked the single tear that rolled down his cheek. His bleak eyes found mine.

"Shot Mary Ann then shot himself."
Oh Jesus Christ!

A sob tore from both of us as I pulled him in as tight as I could, trying to get him close enough to absorb his pain, swallow it whole from him as his heart wrenching cries tore at my soul and ripped straight through my heart.

"Just... fucking... took her, babe. Right from under me."

I kissed away his tears; bore the weight of each one of them as I desperately tried to shoulder his pain. I let him cry, listened to his distraught howls and felt each horrifying rack of his body as he finally grieved for his sister.

CHAPTER 14

"More?" I shook my head at Jax's offer of more food. He'd packed enough to feed the 3000. His back was leant against a tree as I perched between his open legs, my back to his chest as he fed me from the picnic he'd lovingly packed himself.

I peeked over my shoulder at him, "Can I ask you something, Jax?"

His eyebrows rose but he said, "Sure, babe."

"How come on stage you're like... a talk show host on speed but in normal conversation you're like... very UN-conversational?"

He chuckled quietly, "My Mom used to say 'Jax, you have the conversational skills of a three year old with fuckin' Tourette's'."

I smirked and looked back at him as his finger nudged my rib. "Wow, I think I would've like your mother a hell of a lot, baby. Wise woman."

He laughed loudly but nodded. "Not sure babe, just who I am." I nodded at his statement. "Just me and always will be me."

I skated round to face him, "Well I like just you, Jax."

He smirked as his eyes dropped to my mouth. "And I like just you, E."

His hands slid round the side of my face as he gave me a hot and demanding kiss, his hunger and need evident in each sweep of his tongue but he pulled back and ran his finger down my nose. "Need to hear those words now, babe."

Grimacing, I turned back around and remained silent for a while but he didn't push until a little later, giving me the courage boost I needed to build. "You know, these words that you lock up, they might be the reason you hold so much pain."

He planted a small kiss on the top of my head. "Free 'em babe, get 'em out of there. Just fucking throw 'em out there. Launch 'em so far out there that you finally get to fuckin' face 'em." I thought his Tourette's was getting worse!

I fidgeted with my fingers that were settled on my lap as a tear broke free with his words. The most words I had ever witnessed from him in a single sentence were the very words I needed to hear, probably the only words that would liberate my own.

"I really don't know if *you'll* wanna face them Jax, not me," I whispered honestly as I chewed my bottom lip frantically.

I felt him nod behind me as his fingers took hold of mine; halting my nervous play, "They're just words, babe."

Swallowing heavily I drew my knees up in front of me and hugged them, needed that tiny bit of distance before I put a wrecking ball through the pedestal he had put me on.

"I loved my Dad so much and he loved me," I sighed, feeling the sadness start to envelope me. "He wasn't my real dad, my Mom had an affair but he... he just took us on, nurtured me and Aaron as his own, but me, well I was his princess, his Rockin' Princess he used to call me." I hadn't realised I was trembling until Jax's finger slid down my spine in a comforting act.

"He was a roadie with Guns N' Roses as we were born and every opportunity he got he'd drag us along with him."

"The Gibson, babe?"

I nodded, "Yeah, practically grew up with the lot of them. They were like my family. God, fuckin' great times." I laughed at some memories. "But my Mom, she wouldn't come, never wanted my Dad never mind the tours or the weeks on a bus and the draining schedule, but my Dad and me, Hell it was what we lived for."

"I hear ya', babe."

I nodded at Jax's understanding. "Would you do it again?" he asked as his finger ran along the tattoo on my neck.

"God, yes. Without a fucking thought, baby." I could sense his smile as he pulled me back and snuggled me back into him.

I hesitated and sighed before continuing my story but Jax sat patiently, never pushing, never rushing me. "I was about 13 when we came back from a five month tour and we noticed something odd with my mother. Aaron had stayed home for this latest tour and he'd become withdrawn and edgy but it was my Mom who frightened me."

I swallowed back the nausea and the slight tingle in my veins but it was beginning to win, I could feel its raw power igniting my craving, my need to rid the pain. As though he'd noticed my struggle, Jax's arms surrounded me and pulled me tighter. "You're good, babe. Let 'em free. I promise E, I promise it'll ride the hunger."

So taking a deep breath I told him the rest. "It was about six weeks later when my Dad had to go back on the road but my Mom refused to let me go, said I'd missed too much school and she needed me with her. Cos' it was a short tour, Dad agreed."

Diverting my gaze to the lake I closed my eyes. "She'd always dabbled in drugs but it soon became apparent that she'd got into the real heavy stuff." I heard him suck in air through his teeth as his thumb started a rhythm across my palm, helping me fight the sweats and shakes.

"The bills started piling up, then my Dad returned and I thought everything would be okay." I let a bitter laugh expel from me as I shook my head. "He became addicted right along with her."

"Fuck!" Jax hissed and I nodded.

My brain was jerking with every single shot of electricity that pierced it. My shakes were becoming unbearable as my leg started twitching rapidly. "Ride it, E." His stern voice filtered through and I inhaled harshly a few times, desperate to settle the itch.

"They built up a drug debt with the wrong people," I told him outright. I felt him stiffen behind me. "Couldn't pay off what they owed so... so..." I stood up swiftly, my leg tapping rapidly on the floor as I yanked at my hair. "Fuck!"

"Fight it, babe."

My fingernails had become imbedded so far in my palms the blood was dripping from my hand. I concentrated on the drip, drip, drip. "I can't," I wheezed.

"Listen to me, babe. I won't let it win so you might as well fucking fight it cos' there is no fuckin' way you ever getting that shit again."

My teeth sank into my bottom lip so much that I think they crunched my jaw as my stomach clenched in anger and my eyes blazed as I turned back to him. "Try fuckin' stopping me Jax," I growled.

His answer was to slam me against a tree trunk, pin my arms above me and thrust his groin against me. "Oh I will, babe. No way… no fucking more. You hear me?"

"Go fuck yourself," I spat nastily.

"I'd rather fuck you babe," he growled back and I turned away.

"Just let me go, Jax."

Shaking his head slowly he leant in a bit closer, "Can't do that till you calm the fuck down."

"Get the fuck off me, Jax. You've got no right to do this!"

He shrugged but refused to let me go. "Tell me."

I squeezed my eyes shut and shook my head. "No!"

"Tell me."

"NO."

"TELL… ME… WHAT… HAPPENED…"

A sob broke free, a gut wrenching cry before I pinned him with my gaze. "The bitch pimped us out!" I whispered.

He dropped his arms immediately and stared at me, "*Christ!*"

I looked away, couldn't look at the disgust on his face as I battled my demons. "She pimped us to pay for her drug debts," I repeated. "Just let them fuck us, Jax... But my Dad; he couldn't go through with it and tried to stop them but... they... they...."

I sank to the floor, my stomach revolting at my words as I upended all of Jax's wonderful lunch. The pain was horrendous, as though my heart was being torn straight through my chest as my mind tried in vain to shut down my body against the memories.

"They killed him because he changed his mind and wouldn't let them touch me... they fucking stabbed him like a piece of fucking meat... left him to bleed all over my god damn bedroom floor like... like he wasn't worth a fuck!"

And that's when I just started screaming, loudly and violently, my lungs forcing air through my mouth so forcibly it burnt the sides of my throat.

I felt myself being lifted and carried over to the pond before I was unceremoniously dragged in with him, right into the centre. It was so cold it stunted my breath and stopped my screams instantly, letting free the tears and heartache.

He held me tight, refusing to let me go as he shouldered my pain like I had taken his. "Good Girl."

My legs wrapped around his waist as I claimed his mouth with my own. The need to forget demanded his attention and I let him know just how much I needed him. I needed to feel him, feel something other than the racking agony that cursed my body.

He replied by kissing me right back, his passion, his hunger and his own need for me was reflected in his control of my lips but then he pulled back and softened the kiss, slowed it right down until it was nothing but tender and sweet. "Need it slow, babe. No fucking, just loving, E."

A choking sound left my throat but he swallowed it whole as he carried me out of the water and over to the mass of bluebells before lowering me down and rearing back to gaze at me, "You hear me, babe?"

"I hear ya', baby."

His lips devoured me before he slowly undid my jeans and leisurely peeled them down my legs, his eyes never leaving mine as he travelled down my body. His mouth kissed each toe, then each of the soles of my feet, then each star that decorated my skin, until he reached my knickers and when he discovered their obstruction he ripped them, just ripped them clean off. Good God!

His answering smirk to my gasp heated my blood so much it felt like I was on fire. "Jax, I need you so much," I whispered.

"I'm here babe, right fucking here. Right fucking beside you, and I aint going anywhere until I'm right inside you, loving you hard."

I nodded wildly as I sucked in my lips and as he sensed my pain his tongue swiped the full length of my sex. My head tipped back as I released a long moan. "Watch me devour you, babe. Watch me taste your delicious pussy."

My eyes opened and I propped myself up on my elbows to do as he asked. "So fucking good. Your cunt should be illegal cos' it's a fucking drug, E." Oh Christ! I was going to explode.

His tongue swirled around my clit as his finger entered me, its calloused tip brushing roughly against my inner wall. "*Oh Fuck,*" I hissed as he hit the sensitive sweet spot inside.

"Oh yeah, you like that don't ya', babe."

"God yes... oh shit... JAX!" I was gone, floating somewhere beyond pleasure and pain, the clash of both took my breath and my senses, but more importantly, it took my craving.

Before I had even reached the ground Jax was very slowly entering me. So slowly and so totally smoothly it brought tears to my eyes. "Eve," he whispered as his mouth rested beside my ear. His cheek pressed against mine as he made love to me so beautifully I never wanted to let go.

He tugged at my T-shirt and lifted it over my head before unclasping my bra and then devoured my breasts, worshipping every inch of skin and idolising my heavy nipples. "You have beautiful tits, babe." He growled as he started to speed up, his need to claim me had my hips lifting in time to each thrust.

"God, take me, Jax."

He growled as his teeth sank into the soft flesh under my ear but he refused to up the beat any more, his thrusts still at a regular rhythm as his hips drummed a soft rock tune, refusing to make it heavy. "I'll take you E, cos' you're mine, all fucking mine."

That was it, I exploded wildly, forcefully and so utterly intensely I think I broke a toe. I felt him swell and harden inside me to an incredible thickness as my orgasm triggered his and he erupted so powerfully he actually stopped breathing. I grew a little worried, but he eventually pulled in a long ragged breath and I sagged in relief.

"Thought you'd left me there, baby" I grinned.

He opened his eyes and smiled a heart-clenching, breath-taking, utterly devastating smile that captured each and every piece of my broken soul. "I thought so too, babe."

CHAPTER 15

"Come on little girl." Jax laughed as he dipped into the water and emerged under my legs, lifting me high on his shoulders before catapulting me across the lake and deep into its depths.

"You Bastard!" I choked out as I emerged to his raucous laughter.

"It's not cold, babe."

My chattering teeth were arguing with him. "Jax, it's bloody freezing." I swan back over to him and wrapped myself around him, gaining any bit of heat he was producing as his lips warmed my blue ones.

"Christ E, you're freezing. You should have said."

I narrowed my eyes on him before he winked mischievously. His bright eyes lowered to watch my pebbled nipples bob on the surface of the water. "Fuck. Now I wanna take you all over again," he said before he mouthed one.

Groaning I pushed my hips against him, letting him know I was right there with him. His teeth delicately grazed my sensitive flesh and I rewarded him by slipping down on his rigid length. "Yeah, babe," he growled out. "Fuck me!"

I didn't argue with him as I rode him hard and fast, both of us loudly acknowledging another orgasm as we clung together in the depths of the cold water. I just couldn't get enough of him and he seemed to experiencing the very same obsession.

We were sat on a rock, still naked but shrouded in the plaid blanket he'd brought for the picnic, both of us waiting to dry off before we re-dressed.

"I need to fetch something," he told me as he stood up and walked over to the car. My eyes tracked every part of his delicious naked backside as he moved smoothly across the distance; each buttock rippling magnificently with each stride.

"Wow," I whispered to myself on a sigh.

"Heard that, babe."

I was still chuckling when he returned with what looked like a piece of paper in his hand. He grinned at me before reseating himself beside me, and wrapped the blanket back around us.

I frowned as he passed me the paper. "Need your thoughts?" he said quietly. I could hear the stutter of nerves in his voice.

It took me a while to read what he'd wrote but I knew by the tingling on my neck and the flutter in my stomach that this song was going to be epic, in fact *fucking* epic was a better description.

I looked at him. "Did you write this, baby?" He nodded once. "About me, Jax?" He nodded again. "It's... Wow... yeah; I dunno what to say really Jax, but wow."

He nodded and pursed his lips. "Wrote it for us, babe."

His eyes found my wide ones as he silently asked what I thought he was asking. "You wanna duet with me?" He nodded again. "This song will be... ours?" I whispered.

A small smile lit his face and he cupped my cheek, "Just ours, E."

"I dunno what to say, Jax." I was stumped. He'd written a song just for us, with us in mind.

"Nothing to say but yes, want you there right beside me when it rocks out the fans." His eyes were searching mine for an answer but he really didn't need to look too deep.

"Yes," I said softly.

"Yeah, babe?" It was my turn to nod now. I was greeted to his beautiful grin, "Gonna rock it hard, babe."

I smiled wide. "Try and fucking stop me, baby!" He launched himself at me, rolling us around as I laughed loudly. "I take it your glad I said yes, Jax!"

He turned onto his back and had me straddled on his lap within seconds. "Babe..." he whispered as his eyes grew dark.

I nodded as I whispered back, "Yeah, I hear ya', baby."

He gulped and scrunched up his nose, "Need to say it, babe."

His eyes softened as his hand cupped my cheek. "Okay," I wheezed.

"Never said it before, E. Never felt it either, but you, you've dragged it out there, cracked me open and dug deep, fucking deep, babe."

I swallowed heavily, my heart pounding so strong I think we both saw its pace through my chest bone. As if he felt it, he lifted a finger to the piercing on my chest and gently traced around the edge of the tiny pink diamond. His eyes lifted to mine, their intensity took my breath away as each frantic beat of my heart stuttered wildly.

"I'm falling in love with you, Eve Hudson."

Taking two small breaths then one large one, I cupped his face with both my hands, "And I have already fallen, Jaxon Cooper."

He growled, sat up and engulfed me in the most passionate kiss yet. The power and desire in it brought me to my knees as they literally buckled underneath me and my arse plonked onto his lap. His strong arms wrapped around me, supporting me while he devoured me. Every single piece of his heart was expressed while we connected so deeply we became a single entity, each of us refusing to end the kiss as it lasted for an eternity.

"Fuck babe," he whispered as he finally pulled away and rested his forehead against mine, his eyes locked on mine. "Say it again, E. Need to hear it again."

"I love you Jax," I stated firmly. "All of you, baby. Your beautiful heart, your tortured soul, your pain, your pleasure, your mind, hell even your bloody Tourette's!"

He grinned at me and planted a soft kiss on my nose. "There aint one inch of you that aint perfect. I see through your pain E, and all I see is your beauty, your bright spirit and the largest heart I've ever known, and the most amazing pair of tits on the planet," he finished with a wink.

I laughed. "Yeah baby, your arse is pretty magnificent too," I winked back.

Jax sulked tremendously when I asked him to drop me back at my dorm early that evening. He wanted me to spend the night at his place but after the emotional turmoil we had both endured that day, we both needed the silence of our own thoughts.

His pain as he told me about his sister would never leave me. I thought my life was hell, but to lose his sister so cruelly, well, I was surprised he wasn't fucked up more than I was.

We both knew how it felt to drag yourself through life. How to pick the shattered pieces of your soul up off the floor, tuck them in your pocket and carry on, yet we did it and to be honest, I thought we did it damn well, even if I did have a penchant for whips.

Luce beamed widely at me as I entered the kitchen and flicked on the kettle. "You okay, hun?" I asked her with narrow eyes. She was up to something and that always worried me.

"Uh-huh."

My eyes narrowed further as I spooned coffee granules into my cup, holding up the coffee canister to Luce, asking if she wanted one. She nodded and sighed happily. "If that smile has been put there by my brother then I really don't wanna hear it, hun."

She barked out a laugh as her eyes twinkled but my eyes widened when she exaggeratedly rubbed her left hand over her cheek. A huge diamond twinkled from her fourth finger. "Oh My God! Oh My God!"

She grinned and squealed. "You're gonna be my sister, E!"

My mouth dropped open. I couldn't form any words never mind any thoughts, "Shit, Luce!"

She stood in front of me when a nervous expression flitted across her beautiful face. "Are you okay with this E, I mean really? And don't lie."

I shook my head in astonishment, "Are you bloody serious?" Her face dropped and I realised she had took the context of my words completely the wrong way. "Hey, hun. I'm so excited I think I just pee'd my pants."

She rewarded my words with an almighty squeal as she flung herself in my arms and we hugged like the best friends we were. "Oh Luce, I'm so happy for you."

She pulled back and I wiped away the tear that was hanging off her long eyelashes. "He's so much more... content E, now that he's here," she disclosed honestly as she leant against the worktop.

I nodded as I poured kettle water into our cups, "I know, and if I've got anything to do with it, he won't be going back."

"And you, E?" I just gave her a small nod but her narrow eyes found the truth behind my tight ones. "Shit, E."

I bit my lip. "Luce, she's still my Mom, whatever she's done, you know."

"Actually, no I don't know, E. How the hell can you..." She bit back the rest of her words when she saw my face and held up her hands in submission, "I'm not doing this now Eve Hudson. I'm too happy to let you spoil it!"

I scoffed back a retort and forced out a smile when I decided to give her my own news. "I have something to tell you," I said quietly as I walked over to the table and dropped into a chair. She smiled expectantly and I took a deep breath. "Jax and I are... together."

Her reaction was not what I expected when she gulped and bit her bottom lip as her eyes took on a pained expression. "What the..." she spat.

"Okay, I'll try that again... Me and Jax are together." I lifted my eyebrows at her expectantly but she just looked sad, or angry, I couldn't tell which. Maybe a little of each.

"Right..."

Standing, I walked over to the door and turned. "Thanks for being pleased for me, Luce." Her pained face hurt me; she obviously had something to say on the matter but daren't say it. I thought she would have been pleased. For me to open up to the male species was somewhat rare, but hey!

Just as I went to open the kitchen door she spoke. "He told you about Fran, E?" My hand froze on the door handle but I refused to turn round. If she had anything to say, she could say it to my back.

"What's the problem, Luce? You want all the limelight on your pretty face instead of mine?" I snapped; her lack of support hurt like hell.

"Fuck you, E! I suppose he hasn't told you she's fucking pregnant!"

What the hell?

My knees jarred slightly. I held on to the door, frantically trying to hold myself upright as my lungs emptied in one fell swoop.

"Shit E, I'm sorry. I shouldn't have told you like that." She appeared beside me but I held up a hand and shook my head at her. I didn't want to hear it now. I felt sick and my head was spinning. I needed to get the hell out of there.

She was still shouting me as I slammed the dorm front door behind me and took myself off at speed to... anywhere, fucking anywhere; all the time fighting the familiar urge to give into my pain.

CHAPTER 16

"Goddd, I lurve this songggg," I slurred to the random sat beside me as I saluted the track with my glass of… whatever it was, its funny pink colour spilling over the sugared edge of the glass and onto my favourite *Mötley Crüe* T-shirt.

"It's fucking skill, Friend." We both nodded reverently as we dedicated a melancholy moment to appreciate the skill of *Scorpion.*

"....Babe, it wasn't easy to leave you alone
It's getting harder each time that I go
If I had the choice, I would stay
There's no one like you
I can't wait for the nights with you
I imagine the things we'll do
I just wanna be loved by you…"

The tears came as I sang the last line, "I just wanna be loved by him Friend, you know?"

Random nodded grimly, "Yeah, Friend. He's a fucking fool, especially with a hot voice like yours."

I nodded in agreement as I signalled the bar tender for another of… whatever it was. "I mean he's fuckin'… God he's so fuckin'…" I groaned as his magnificent hard body appeared in my head and I sighed.

"That good?" Random sighed along with me.

I nodded firmly. "Oh yes friend, he's fucking hot. He has the most amazing arse I've ever seen... Oh Jesus now I'm horny!"

"...I imagine the things we'll do
I just wanna be loved by you
No one like you"

I finished the song and Random tapped my glass with his in a toast, "To two-timing bastards!"

I barked out a laugh and returned his toast as my phone rang for the twentieth time. "Yo. This is a hologram. E can't talk to you right now cos' she's getting wasted," I answered this time, not sure why, just thought I'd better let my friends know I wasn't dead.

"Where the fuck are you?" Cam growled through the earpiece.

My brow knitted and I nearly toppled off the stool as I reared back from his voice. "Cam, do you know how much I love you?"

His huge sigh was loud and drawn out but his voice softened, "Please tell me you're just drunk, E."

"I'm just drunk Cam... very, very drunk, Cam." I giggled. Random spat out his drink in laughter and leaned in to my phone.

"Hey Dude, she's *very, very, very* drunk!"

I nodded and laughed. "Too right my friend."

"E, who the fuck are you with?"

"I have no fucking idea but he's my friend," I retorted. Random grinned at me.

"You're my friend too." I returned his grin.

"Christ sake, E! Where are you?"

"I have no… fucking… idea." I chuckled, and then turned to the bar tender, "Where are we?"

His eyebrows rose at me as if I was stupid. "The Hell Pit," he informed me.

"Cool name," I nodded with respect and he laughed.

"Thanks, sugar." I gave him a grin before he shook his head in amusement.

"Apparently I'm in a cool place called 'The Hell Pit' and it's fucking awesome. I have made an awesome friend, Cam. He likes me."

Random nodded seriously, "I like you very much my friend."

We grinned happily at each other like escapees from the local asylum. Cam chuckled through the phone. "Stay there E, I'll be there soon."

I nodded even though he couldn't see me and ended the call. "My Bro is coming to join us," I told Random, who nodded earnestly.

"That's cool, Friend. I would love to meet your brother." His face lit up as he waggled his eyebrows, "You wanna do karaoke, Friend?"

"Hell yes!"

We both wobbled over to the stage, supporting each other and as we picked up the mic's the whole room cheered, all four people… and the dog.

"What you wanna sing, Friend?" He asked me as we both squinted at the list of options.

"I dunno Friend, I can't fucking focus on the titles," I tittered.

He nodded solemnly, "I'll just pick one and we'll hope for the best, Friend."

I nodded in agreement and took stance at the front of the stage and waited for the song to open. I laughed loudly when it started:

"Why do birds suddenly appear
Every time you are near?
Just like me, they long to be
Close to you."

Random took over and I grimaced at him as his tones made my ears bleed but I swayed happily alongside him before it was my turn again.

"On the day that you were born the angels got together
And decided to create a dream come true
So they sprinkled moon dust in your hair
Of golden starlight in your eyes of blue"

Random again:
"That is why all the girls in town"
Me:
"Girls in town"
Random:
"Follow you"
Me:
"Follow you"
Random:
"All around"
Me:

"All around"
Together:
"Just like me, they long to be
Close to you
Close to you"

We finished the song as Cam, Luce and Boss walked through the door. "My family!" I declared as I introduced Random to them.

Boss grinned at me. "I fucking love you Boss," I shouted as I launched myself off the stage and leaped straight into his arms. "You wanna fuck, Boss?" I smacked my lips over his and gave him a snog of the century. He returned it obviously.

"Hey, Hot Stuff," he said softly. I grinned at him as he walked me back over to the bar stool and settled me onto it.

He palmed my cheek with a sad expression. "Why so sad, Boss?" I pouted to him.

"Cos' I love you back, hot stuff and right now you're hurting sweetheart."

His words pierced my heart and under my drunken stupor I understood what he was saying. "I hear ya', Boss."

He nudged me with his elbow, "Great rendition of the Carpenters, hot stuff."

I giggled and looked at him seriously. "Do you know Jax has that song on his iPod?" I winked cheekily as Boss stared at me in astonishment.

My sombre mood returned swiftly at the thought of Jax and my face fell at my heartache. "Oh God, E." Boss wrapped his arms around me as the tears fell;

his strong embrace held me tight, so safe and secure in my friend's arms. "He's a fucking dick for doing this to you!"

"I told him Boss, I told him every – fucking - thing..." I sobbed as I fiddled with his pony tail, twisting it around my fingers as I concentrated on it.

"You told him what, sweetheart?" Boss's soft voice lulled me into calm.

I looked at him sadly, "...Everything..."

"E?" Cam asked from behind me, "You told him?"

I nodded marginally. "I trusted him. He told me everything and I told him everything."

I knew I wasn't making any sense to them in my half trance and I think I was rationalising everything to myself instead of them, but maybe that's what I needed to make sense of it all.

"Let's get you home, hot stuff," Boss said as he turned round and patted his backside, telling me to hop on for a piggy back.

I jumped aboard and looked for Random, finding him perched on a bar stool with his head in his arms, resting on the bar top. "Friend, you need a lift?" His head lifted and his bloodshot eyes met mine as he frowned at me in confusion. "Lift home? Wherever home may be, Friend," I reiterated.

He grinned widely, "Sure, Friend. Blythes Hall Student Village if it's not out of your way?"

"No Shit! Me too." I grinned broadly and he nodded in admiration.

"Fucking awesome, Friend."

"Come on." I swooped my arm at him, gesturing for him to follow as I rested my chin on Boss's shoulder. "Take me home, baby."

Boss carried me out to the car park and over to a clapped out white van. "Holy Shit!" I breathed, "Is this gonna get us home?"

"Hey hot stuff, don't diss the tour bus." I laughed hysterically, so much so I had to clamp my legs harder around Boss so I didn't pee my pants. *Tour Bus!*

He opened the rear doors, turned round and plonked me down on the edge of the floor. Random and Luce climbed in, I rolled over and crawled up the floor, clambering precariously over their stage kit until I reached them.

"I'm sorry, E" Luce whispered in my ear as we held on tight against Boss's erratic driving. He seemed to be taking corners at 160Mph and all three of us clamped hold of each other for dear life.

I banged on the partition wall between us and the front cabin. "Fuck Boss, if you don't want my face imprinted in one of your drums, slow the hell down!" He slowed down.

"It's okay, hun, it wasn't your fault. Both of us said some things."

She shrugged and remained silent for a while. "So what are you gonna do?"

What was I going to do? Face him? Kick the shit out of him? Create a voodoo doll of him and stick extra-long pins in his testicles? All of the above?

"Nothing!"

She nodded solemnly. We both raised our eyebrows when Random started moaning and talking in his intoxicated sleep... "Brad, oh God, Brad! Sooo good baby...."

She smirked, I giggled, she laughed, I fell over.

CHAPTER 17

"Oh, Christ!"

Rolling over and laying my arm across my eyes to shut out the horrendous light, I groaned again as my phone sang from somewhere in my room.

"Please go away." I sounded like a hoarse Kermit the Frog high on marijuana as I forced a swallow. I was begging now. The damn thing had been chirping happily for the last hour and I was seriously considering teaching it how to fly.

It rang off.

It rang again!

"God damn it!"

Fumbling around on the floor under the bed, my hand seized the damn thing and I threw it unceremoniously through my en-suite door. I cringed when I heard an unwelcome splash. "Shit!"

Shrugging, I rolled over and succumbed to the wonders of sleep.

Ooh that felt sooo good, so good that it made me moan in appreciation.

I loved these types of dreams. Erotic dreams were always that so much better when they were lucid dreams and I thanked the wonders of alcohol for delivering this one to me.

"Mmm." My hips rolled as I felt the brush of fingers over the outside of shorts. Now come on dream! You could have at least removed the shorts!

The pressure built as my dream answered my demand and the finger now slid inside the crotch and straight into the very core of me, "Yes." Thank you!

The finger worked me well, rapidly pumping until another finger joined it and a thumb brushed over my sensitive clit, making my hands lift to my own needy breasts, caressing the flesh until my orgasm approached and blew my head clean off. "Fuckkkkk" I growled.

I relaxed and sighed. Thank you very much, Mr Sandman.

I smiled to myself then my eyes flew open when I felt someone crawl up the bed, their body caging me underneath as their nose inhaled deeply.

"What the hell, Jax?" I scrambled up the bed, trying to etch the outline of my body into the old wooden headboard.

His eyes narrowed on me as he watched my reaction, "The fuck, babe?"

I stared at him, my mouth hanging open as my eyes blazed. "What the hell are you doing?" I asked, holding on to my temper by a thread, a very fine bloody thread.

He reared back and sat back on his heels, "Now, looks like I'm trying to love my girl, babe."

I scoffed loudly.

He glared sternly.

"And which girl would that be Jax? Me? Fran? Or the one currently residing in her fucking womb?" I snarled.

The thread had split; in fact it had bloody severed. His eyes widened slightly. He reined it in quickly, but I had noticed it and he knew I had noticed it.

My eyebrows rose in question, "Well?"

He inhaled deeply and turned to sit on the edge of the bed. "Fuck, babe."

I shook my head in disgust as I watched him rake his fingers through his soft black spikes. "It's definitely *'Fuck babe'* or we could try *'Fuck off babe."*

He spun round so quickly the bed creaked its disapproval loudly and I pressed further into the headboard. His large hands slammed beside each of my trembling thighs as his eyes transferred every ounce of the rage he was bearing, "You wanna repeat that, babe?"

My own eyes widened now. How dare he! How fucking dare he!!

"Yeah...*babe*... 'Fuck off'," I growled feeling pretty pleased with myself at my show of bravery. Good Girl, E!

The growl that ripped from his throat brought forward a whimper. I swallowed heavily, wondering if I sucked hard enough I could vacuum the words right back into my voice box.

"If I had thought you needed to know then I would have fucking told you, babe." His anger was palpable and I urged down the need to run.

I nodded slowly. "So it's not important that your long term fuck buddy is pregnant? Which I find pretty amazing seems as though you told me you only went bare-back with me but," I shrugged mockingly. "Hey, I obviously don't understand simple things like that because you didn't feel the need to tell me *before* you fucked me."

His narrow eyes were blazing. "You need to calm the fuck down, babe."

Oh... My... God!

"I NEED TO CALM THE FUCK DOWN?" I was furious. Jesus Christ, had this man no shame?

He pressed his body further into me and nodded slowly, "Don't do this, babe." His warning was not lost on me but I stepped right over it.

"I will fucking do it *babe*, cos' it needs fucking doing!" I snarled at him. "I trusted you Jax. I shared fucking... *things* with you because I thought you were important enough to share with. Now get the fuck out of my room until you think *I'm* important enough to share important things with me."

He hissed through his teeth and continued to glower at me but I glowered the hell right back at him. "Christ E, I just.... fuck!"

"Go," I whispered because by now my hurt was starting to ride the anger and I was desperate he wouldn't see my tears. I wouldn't give him that.

A lone tear tracked my face.

Okay, maybe I would give him a little.

"Babe..." he whispered as his fingers reached for the tear but I turned away and closed my eyes; turned away from the heartache in his eyes and closed my eyes to the despair on his face. I didn't breathe until the door shut behind him.

Then I went and fucked myself right up!

✳✳✳

The darkness was oblivion.
The light? Not so much.
Oh God, it hurt. It hurt way too much this time. I couldn't hold back the vomit as it erupted forcibly from me as my cheek squashed against the filth of the dorm carpet.
The darkness was oblivion.

The light was back.
A mumbled scream from somewhere made me groan. It still smarted, the agony tore through me everywhere; it was too soon E, way too soon!
The darkness was oblivion.

"E."
"E."
The light returned. "Cam?"
I didn't want to move. I couldn't move. But I felt myself lifted before a scream tore through me. So sore, so damn sore.
"Sshhh, sweetheart."
"Boss?"
The darkness was oblivion.

Christ almighty. I wanted to scream. The pain was torturous and I cringed as every nerve ending in my body loathed me. I swallowed back the bile as I opened my eyes and squinted against the brightness of the room.

I was laid on my stomach with my face turned sideways on a crisp linen pillow, my back was open to the air of the room but it didn't ease the agony.

Where the hell was I?

I closed my eyes again and groaned... and groaned again.

"E?"

"Mmm," I mumbled to Cam but refused to open my eyes to the brightness. I felt him beside me even if I didn't see him. I felt his hot breath as he closed in and kissed my cheek. That was surprising. I was expecting his wrath.

"How you feeling?" he asked softly as his hand palmed my cheek gently.

"Not so good," I wheezed.

I could feel his anguish in the air. Its potency made it physical and my heart broke at the distress I'd caused him. "I'm so sorry Cam," I choked out. "I... I... I don't think I'm doing so well," I admitted.

There! It was said! It was out there, wide open and willing to be dissected. The weight that lifted from my shoulders with those few words was immense.

"No, I don't think you are either, E."

I nodded; I couldn't do much else. "I love him, Cam."

They came then, with the words, the racking sobs that tore through each and every part of my soul along with the devastation that ripped straight through the tenderness of my already frayed heart.

I loved him. Simple. No, not so simple.

I had to bury my face in the cold hospital pillow and cry because I'd made such a mess of my back that Cam couldn't hold me. He couldn't comfort me and it tore him to shreds.

"Christ, E," Was all he said but he sat, sat and listened, sat and devoured all my pain, just sat and waited and took every damn piece of my misery.

CHAPTER 18

Two days later I rubbed my eyes in exhaustion as I listened to the nurse rattle on about the need to attend each of my psychiatrist appointments and the horrors of misdosing my medication, but I nodded in the right places and smiled when I wasn't sure what reaction was needed.

"An appointment has been made with Mr Trayson for next Monday, Eve. A confirmation letter will be sent to your address."

I nodded dutifully.

"You must ring this number immediately should you feel the need to harm yourself before Mr Trayson's appointment."

I smiled politely.

"If you have any other queries regarding your bandages or medications Eve, then don't hesitate to contact us."

I mumbled a 'Yes'.

Boss rolled his eyes behind her.

I stifled a laugh.

Cam elbowed Boss.

Boss shoulder barged Cam.

Cam glared.

I rolled my eyes.

I stood staring with concern at Boss's van, wondering how the hell I was going to climb in without splitting my back open again.

Boss's hands gently circled my waist before he smoothly lifted me and placed me in the seat. Could I love this man anymore?

"Thank you," I whispered with a small smile, a hint of shame sending a blush up my neck and onto my face.

"No sweat, hot stuff." He winked and closed the door. Cam rested a reassuring hand on my thigh whilst Boss stashed my bags in the back of the van.

I turned my gaze through the window as I plucked up the courage to tell him. When Boss climbed in beside us, I inhaled deeply and kept my face turned out to the roadside. "I'm not going back to the halls," I told them both whilst bracing myself internally.

"What? Where do you want dropping then, hot stuff?"

I swallowed heavily. "The train station."

Silence.

"What? Why?" Cam stuttered. I bit into my lower lip a little too harshly but swallowed it back and kept going.

"I'm going home."

Silence.

More Silence.

Very painful Silence.

"Stop the van!" Cam said so quietly that I wondered if I'd heard him correctly. Obviously Boss didn't hear him because he continued driving at his regular 160Mph.

"STOP THE FUCKING VAN!" Okay, here we go!

Boss slammed on the brakes so hard I had to put my hand out to stop my head bouncing off the windscreen. They both turned to look at me; both glaring but only one knew the reason why my decision was such a horrific choice.

But I needed to go. I couldn't be near Jax. I couldn't sit back and watch him love somebody other than me. Couldn't watch them be... together.

"You go back and we're done, E." The wrath Cam emitted made my bones ache.

"I have to Cam, I can't... I need to get better and I can't do that... here."

He laughed; a bitter manic laugh. "And you're gonna get better around... *them*?"

Sucking on my lips, I turned to look at him. The distress he wore crushed my lungs but I grit my teeth and nodded. "I have to Cam," I answered softly, desperately trying to communicate with my eyes.

"Fuck! Fuck! *FUCK!* I'm gonna kill that bastard." He banged the dashboard so hard I was sure I heard it crack.

His anguish brought a tear free. I grabbed his hand but he shook me off, clambered over the top of me and flung himself out of the van, giving me one last pained look before he shook his head sadly, wiped a tear from his cheek and walked away.

Boss's hand slipped into mine so softly it broke my heart. "You wanna tell me why he doesn't want you to go home?" His voice was so soothing and calm that I found myself opening up to him.

"My mother... my Mom..." I used the heel of my hand to wipe away my tears but Boss remained silent and patient, just waiting for me to proceed. "My mom has an extreme drug addiction."

He nodded gently and I raised my blurry eyes to his. I trusted him unreservedly. I knew he was my friend and I knew he loved me like I loved him.

"She gets me to... to pleasure her dealer for her drugs."

He nodded slowly but I noticed his adam's apple bob about wildly as his teeth clenched together so severely I heard them crack under the pressure.

He swallowed before he spoke. "And why... why do you need to go... back?"

The struggle in his voice made my heart bleed and I squeezed his hand. "I'll be okay" I told him softly.

He scrunched up his face and shook his head. "You see, hot stuff... I don't think you will be."

Chewing my bottom lip to within an inch of its life I nodded despondently. "I have to be, Boss. I have nowhere else to go," I whispered sadly. I really didn't have anywhere else to go. How shit was that realisation!

His pained eyes found mine as his hand cupped my cheek. "You don't go back there, E. I know why you can't stay here but you can't go back there, sweetheart."

I smiled softly but shook my head faintly.

"I have a cottage in Cornwall, well my grandfolk's do. You can go stay there for as long as you need to." He offered.

"What? I can't do that Boss," I argued shaking my head wildly.

He took both of my hands in his, his eyes pierced mine. "You can and you will, E. You need to mend sweetheart and I know you won't do that here or at home. But if anything E, I'm gonna make it my fucking mission to fix you cos' you're one hell of a girl and I need that girl back, sweetheart. I need that girl rockin' her pretty little ass right beside me." Oh Christ!

I nodded firmly through my tears. "Okay," I managed to choke out.

"Right, we have a small diversion to my folk's house and then we'll get your stuff and get you on that train hot stuff."

He started the engine again and pulled away from the curb.

***

"Did he show you the song?" Boss asked me quietly as we sat on the platform bench waiting for way train to arrive.

I nodded, "Yeah."

His eyes found mine as his finger tapped his thigh with his nerves. "I know right now you hate every single hair on that thick bastard head of his, but promise me while you're away you'll think about still doing it."

I sighed heavily, "I dunno, Boss."

He took my hand and squeezed. "E, when you got up on that stage last week, something... something came alive in you, something deep down in you roared to life and fuck, it was fucking mesmerizing to watch it unfold. You're ace out there sweetheart... it's you E, and by God you rocked every fucking soul in that room."

I smiled, blushing at his compliment and took another breath, "All I can promise is that I'll think about it."

His smile lit my heart. "That's all I ask, sweetheart."

"The 09.38 Huddersfield to St Ives is now arriving on platform 3."

"That's me."

Boss nodded firmly and pulled me in tightly. "God E. You need to beat this, hot stuff. Promise me..."

I nodded tightly, refusing to let my tears flow. "I promise," I whispered hoarsely as I leant in to kiss his cheek.

His hand gripped mine and he squeezed tightly before he nodded once, turned and walked away. I watched him walk away before I picked up my case, took a deep breath and boarded the train.

CHAPTER 19

"For Christ's sake, Kellan," I grumbled as I powered down my kindle. "What the hell is wrong with these bloody Rock God's?"

Still shaking my head to myself I walked across the patio and entered the rustic little kitchen.

It was absolute heaven here. A small but adequate thatched cottage right on the heart of the Cornish coastline, which I had instantly fell in love with as soon as I had turned the key three weeks ago.

After managing to postpone my out-patient appointment and procure a sickness declaration from the hospital, I had arranged with university to take a four week medical absence. I was deeply indebted to Boss or rather Boss's grandparents for letting me stay here.

I was due to go back the following Monday, just three days away, but for now I was still making the most of the peaceful resort.

I had become good friends with a guy who was renting the holiday cottage next to mine. Evan and I had discovered we had a lot in common from our love of rock music to the wonders of beer and coffee, and we'd had some pretty heated discussions over a few bottles of beer and a barbeque.

Our friendship was purely platonic and we were so comfortable in each other's company we found ourselves chilled out in pyjamas most of the time, movie on the TV and a pizza delivery to devour.

I had splashed out on a new tattoo.

'We accept the love we think we deserve' now embellished the inside of my left thigh. I adored it and I thought the words described my life to a 'T'.

Evan had accompanied me and I had managed to talk him into receiving his own. I'd been honoured when he'd had a replica of my neck tattoo inked onto the nape of his. Our friendship was sealed.

My phone rang from atop the kitchen table and I grit my teeth as I peeked at the display.

Jax had been bombarding me with texts and calls, all asking where the hell I was.

I had been grateful to Boss and Cam for keeping that nugget of information to themselves, knowing that once he knew where I was, he would be storming through the door saying 'The fuck babe?' in that low growl of his.

I had managed to reach quite a few decisions in my convalescence and I hoped I would be strong enough to see them through. I needed to be strong enough.

I'd had some small yearnings for the whip but Evan had dragged me up and hauled my ass to the nearest pub or along the nastiest hiking trail he could find, whenever he saw my fists and teeth clench.

I was slowly but surely picking myself up, and to be honest I was damn proud of myself.

I had opened up to Evan one drunken night. Told him about my compulsion with pain and then I had told him about Jax.

He had sat, listened and then comforted me but then he had told me in no uncertain terms that I was here to relax and recuperate and would talk no more of these things while I was here. They were the wisest words I had heard for a long time.

"Hot Stuff!" Boss greeted me when I answered my phone.

A grin erupted on my face at the sound of his voice. He was slowly becoming one of my best friends and I loved him immensely for all the support he had given me over the previous three weeks. He had never missed a daily call and I found myself looking forward to hearing his voice every day.

"Hey, baby."

"I have news, E."

I crossed my fingers and closed my eyes as I waited for his words. Room 103 had been approached the previous week from an industry scout about their involvement in a huge outdoor festival in a few months. They were currently waiting on confirmation that they would be listed as an act in the upcoming band listing announcement. If they made it, it would mean big things for the group that had captured my heart and I found myself sick with waiting for news.

"We're in!"

My silence brought forward his laughter and a single tear from my eye. "Oh – My – God - Boss!"

"I know, E. We - Are – Fucking – In, Baby."

I laughed, cried and screamed simultaneously just as Evan walked through the door.

He lifted his eyebrows and I nodded. His own grin was bright and wide, he didn't even know the people who had become my family, only what I had told him about them.

"GRATZ," he shouted through my phone.

Boss returned his thanks. "Jesus, Boss. Room 103 are gonna be so fucking hot. You'll have groupies hanging from your balls, baby."

He laughed hard, "It's my dick they need to hang from hot stuff, not my balls." I returned his laughter. "Listen, sweetheart…"

I pursed my lips at the start of his question but hung on to his words. "You thought about what I asked you?"

I knew he would ask and I'd really expected it sooner than this to be truthful. "I have" I answered. His silence was my encouragement to continue. "I will."

I heard him suck in a breath. "Then you're all the way with us, baby."

My eyes widened when I realised what he was saying. "Oh shit, Boss. I don't think I can…"

"Yes you fucking can and you fucking are. You will rock that field, E and you'll blow the fucking roof off the place." Well, what could I say to that! Apart from fields don't have roofs.

"Okay," I squeaked.

***

"So, E. You thought about what's gonna happen when you get back?" Evan glanced at me as we dug our toes into the sand, both of us building little caves over each toe.

"Some," I answered evasively. He nodded but left it alone.

He sighed wearily and suddenly grabbed my hand. I ignored the pained expression on his face because it matched my own. "I'm gonna miss you," he whispered as he twisted my thumb ring around.

I nodded, blinking back tears.

Evan was returning home to London in a few hours and I was both relishing the thought of having my final days alone and hating the thought of him gone.

"You know, you can always come and visit, E. Anytime. Anytime you're feeling..." he shrugged, a slight blush creeping up his neck.

I smiled and squeezed his hand, "And you know I expect you at that festival."

He smiled widely. "You are so gonna rock that place to the ground."

He sensed my hesitance as I looked to the horizon with my top teeth deeply embedded in my bottom lip. "It's just... gonna be so hard. You know," I admitted, hating myself for submitting to my worries.

Could I really do this with Jax? Stand by his side and let the passion in the song take me away, knowing that each word we sang together, side by side, was written for me.

"Right, come on misery. Let's go watch some porn, have mad sex and roll about on that God damn ancient rug before I go."

I glanced sideways at him and chuckled. "Such a romantic," I mocked.

He nodded sternly, "Always, darlin'."

I let him pull me up and as he did he pulled me tight against him, his arms wrapped around me as though he was frightened I would fall. "I'm gonna go now. Hate goodbye's and all that shit E, makes me look like a pussy." His whispered breath in my ear made me shiver. I didn't want to let go. I wanted to hold him forever and never face the world again.

I swallowed heavily and nodded. He smiled softly, planted a gentle kiss on my lips and walked away.

A tear left my eye as I watched his back retreat.

As he rounded the corner, he turned back, nodded once and then disappeared.

Then I realised he still owed me for the pizza last night.

Damn!

***

Stepping off the train Monday morning, I sighed heavily. I could already feel the weight bearing at my heart.

Damn it E... Get the hell on with it.

"HOT STUFF!"

I grinned widely and looked around immediately for the voice I had grown to love so much. I saw him, barrelling at speed towards me and I knew he wasn't going to stop. *Shit!*

He charged at me and jumped right aboard. His arms flung around my shoulders and his legs wrapped around my waist.

Now, bear in mind, I'm 5ft 2" and Boss is like 6ft... you can see where I'm going can't you?

I clung to his large body as we both slowly toppled backwards and my arse hit the floor with so much oomph I'm positive I felt my coccyx bone hit my tonsils. Boss ended up straddled over me and I'm sure to all the commuters in the station it looked like a position from the *Kama Sutra*.

"Christ, Boss. You need to shape up boy."

He landed his lips on mine and kissed me hard. "I fucking missed you, baby."

I nudged him with my elbow, "Kinda missed you too."

He picked up my case and we made our way to the car park. There was something he was holding back on, I could see it in the way he held himself and I was almost too frightened to ask.

He plonked my case in the rear of the van and then opened my door for me before he climbed in beside me.

"You gonna talk to me?" I asked as soon as he sat down.

He stole a quick glance at me and I could see the worry behind his eyes. He sighed and turned towards me, "Your Mom... she, well we're not sure what's wrong but she's been in hospital, E."

"Oh. Okay." Not quite sure what to make of that.

Boss nibbled on his bottom lip. His frown was both assessing and anxious.

I smiled and squeezed his hand. "I'm not gonna go get whipped if that's what you're worrying about, Boss."

He sighed and scrunched his nose up, "That's not all, E."

He was hesitant and my blood rushed at his distress. "Is... is she okay?" Please God!

He nodded and smiled reassuringly. "God, sorry, yes she's okay now. They sent her home the day after, did some tests and all that but..."

"Will you bloody spit it out!" I urged.

He held his hands up. "Okay. I'm just gonna say it."

About time!

"She turned up at yours while you were in Cornwall."

Oh God!

He looked at me with a cringe and it all became clear. I could feel the anger bubbling away inside. "Did she take it?" I practically growled.

Boss shook his head, "No. But not for want of trying."

My fist slammed on his dashboard.

"Christ. What is it with my dash?" He huffed.

"It takes it, Boss. Your tour bus is solid stuff. It's like a man cave on wheels," I winked then mouthed sorry.

He side huddled me and kissed my cheek. "Go for it, hot stuff. Better than my face." I thoroughly agreed with him.

I barked out a laugh then sagged and rubbed my face with my hands.

"So how come she didn't get the Gibson?"

"You have good friends, E."

I turned to look at him with wide eyes. "Did you...?"

He nodded. "Luce rang Cam in a panic, said your Mom was there trying to take it. Well it's a good job Jax has a fast car!"

I groaned and closed my eyes. Could my life embarrass me any further with that man? "Oh God!" A huge blush covered my face. I was mortified they had all seen my mother in one of her 'moods'.

Boss grabbed my hand, "Enough, E. We're your friends. Your shit became our shit when you drank my tequila and stripped down to your bra."

I shook my head in amusement but grinned at him.

"I love ya', hot stuff. Even if you did refuse to blow me," he said so earnestly I thought he was serious. Then he grinned and elbowed me.

I just adored this man. "Think you might deserve one now."

His eyes widened and sparkled as he made for his zip. My own eyes widened before he belted out a laugh and tilted his cheek in my direction. "A kiss will do, hot stuff."

I reached over, palmed his face and turned him to me before planting a huge smacker on his lips. "Thank you," I whispered sincerely.

He winked and started the engine.

And then started the engine again.

And then started it again.

I looked at him cynically as I pursed my lips.

Boss stuck his nose in the air, ignoring my high eyebrows and gave me a blasé glance. "Give her a moment. PMT week."

I stifled a laugh and looked out of the window. "Sure. I have chocolate in my bag if she needs it."

The engine started and it kept ticking over this time. *Woohoo!*

"She gonna make it, Boss?"

He glared at me, his eyes narrow but I could see the humour behind them. "She's a woman, hot stuff. Even on her back she can do the job."

My jaw dropped and I slapped his arm. "We are good for other things you know."

He nodded wildly, "Of course baby... we men have to eat as well."

CHAPTER 20

I walked into Z Bar that afternoon to a raucous welcome back. Everybody wanted to know where I had been so I just told them I had been caring for a sick relative and no more was asked.

I hadn't seen Jax yet but Boss had informed me we were to rehearse the song that night in his garage. Apparently that was where they did all their rehearsals and I was slowly building myself up for the grilling that I knew would come.

"You wanna give me a hand for an hour, E?" Rachel asked when she was snowed under in orders.

"Sure." I hopped onto the bar and swung my legs over, stashed my bag and turned to my first customer.

"FRIEND!"

Friend's beaming face was bang in front of mine. "Christ, Friend." I beamed back, leant over the bar and planted a wet kiss on his cheek.

"I've been looking all over the halls for you, Friend." He stated as he kissed me back.

I nodded at him. "Been away for a few weeks but I'm back now. Anyway drink?" His brows huddled together in puzzlement. "Drink? You know. Beer, spirit, cocktail, pop?"

"Oh god yes, sorry. I'll take a Stella and your proper name."

I laughed. "E. Short for Eve."

His head tipped and his brow furrowed again, "You're never the E that everybody's been talking about?" Ooh dear! Did I want to hear this?

"Not sure. What has everybody been saying?"

He grinned and waggled his eyebrows and I narrowed mine on him. He held up his hands and laughed, "Nothing bad, just about how the band and their fans missed you for the past few weeks. My mate dragged me here last weekend to hear you but you weren't here."

I nodded as I popped the cap on his bottle and passed it him. "Yeah, I'm back now. Performing Saturday if you can make it."

He pulled a long swill on his beer and nodded. "If it's anything like our rendition of Close to you, then I wouldn't miss it for the world."

I laughed loudly as I turned to the next customer and took their order. "You gonna hop on that stage with me on Saturday and give it another blast?"

He shook his head in horror as he finished his beer then pulled out his phone, "Gimme your number, Friend."

We exchanged numbers before he left to return to class. I found out his name was Trent but I still entered him under 'Friend' as he did me.

I worked until the lunchtime rush had died down then hopped over the bar and treated myself to a sandwich and beer whilst I was filled in on the gossip by Rachel.

"SPANNER!"

I smiled as I swallowed the last of my sandwich and turned to the voice. I desperately tried to keep the smile on my face for Romeo but it was hard when I saw Jax stood beside him.

Here goes. I wasn't sure if he was pissed off or aroused. Maybe both. Hopefully the latter.

His dark eyes found mine and I gulped at their intensity. My body screamed to life at the sight of him and I silently cursed myself as I felt the rumble between my thighs.

Every time I saw him, he seemed to get hotter. If that was possible.

He was stood staring at me in hot tight faded black jeans, the ones that hugged his strong thighs and magnificent arse so nicely and a worn Guns N' Roses t-shirt that clung to each muscle on his glorious chest. His customary black boots were on his feet. His eyes just wore me.

Romeo planted his backside in the stool next to me and side hugged me. "Where have you been, Spanner?"

I removed my gaze from Jax as he slowly stalked across the room, each impressive leg taking a torturous route nearer and nearer.

"I... I well, I..."

I could feel him behind me, his breath warm on the nape of my neck. I bit my lower lip harshly at the force he emitted.

"Clue us in, babe?" he growled and I shivered at the huskiness of it.

Romeo's eyes were switching between us wildly and as if he sensed the coming storm, he battened down his hatches and buggered off. Traitor!

Jax slid onto Romeo's vacated stool and tilted his head at me in query, his eyebrows high as he sucked on his bottom lip. "The fuck, babe?"

There it was! To be honest I had missed it!

I lowered my face, refusing to see the question written all over his. His finger and thumb gripped my chin and he turned me to look at him. "Please don't," I urged quietly.

I couldn't handle this now. I was doing so well and he just came tearing back in and ripped all the pain back into the open.

His eyes flicked from my eyes to my mouth, to my hair and then back to my mouth. "What the fuck happened, E?"

Why did he have to keep bloody digging? He had a family on the way, why didn't he go eye-fuck his girlfriend instead of me? Even though he eye-fucked really, really well! God, so well.

"What the fuck do you want from me, Jax?" I managed to stutter out, proud of myself for forming a sentence.

He leaned in close. I swallowed back the need to run my fingers through his soft spikes, the urge to just touch him was overpowering and I clenched my hand into a fist to control myself.

He rested his mouth beside my ear. "What I want is you, underneath me and beggin'. I want my mouth on your perfect pink nipples, worshipping them with my tongue. I want to bury myself so fucking far in you that I tattoo myself on your womb. I want my name ripped from your lips when I make you come hard; hard enough to make you clamp me so fucking tight that every ridge of my cock etches onto the walls on your delicious pussy, babe."

Okay, yes, that's sounded really nice. Thank you.

I just gulped and stared. Was that actually a paragraph? Christ, it was a fucking poem!

"You hear me, babe?" he rumbled as his thumb traced along my bottom lip.

"I hear ya' Jax but I don't think you're hearing me," I whispered.

His eyes continued to watch the route his thumb was taking as it now trailed straight down the middle of my throat. It's touch singeing each of my tiny hairs on the way down.

"We need to talk, E."

I nodded, "Yeah."

He nodded with me. "And you need to listen, babe."

"You gonna do the same, Jax?"

His eyebrows lifted but he smiled, "Yeah." I gave him a small smile in return.

He suddenly jumped off the stool but held my eyes. "After rehearsal tonight, babe" he ordered and I nodded.

"Yeah."

Before I could move, his lips were on mine, moving so slowly and tenderly I didn't have the courage or the inclination to refuse.

God, he felt good. I had missed him so much. My hands finally relented and slipped through his shock of black softness, curling round the thickness tightly.

He groaned and stole my mouth with his tongue, drawing mine into his mouth and sucking on it relentlessly. One of his huge hands cupped the side of my head while the other curved around my neck. I knew he was claiming me back, demanding my attention and control.

His knee nudged itself between my closed thighs and I opened them immediately and let him in, dropping my hands around his neck and pulling him in closer.

Both of his hands now dropped to my bottom and bumped me across the stool until I wrapped both legs around his waist. He picked me up and held me tight as he continued to fuck my mouth with his expert tongue. I moaned and drew him closer to me, my rock hard nipples pressing against the firmness of his chest.

"Fuck, babe. Need you. Need to fuck you so damn hard." Who said romance was dead?

"Put me down Jax," I whispered in his ear.

He growled softly but removed his hands from my backside. My feet dropped to the floor. He rested his mouth on my forehead. "7 O'clock," was all he said before he turned and left.

7 O'clock then E!

CHAPTER 21

"I think we got it covered, Bulk." Jax growled after hours of relentless practice.

I agreed with Jax. We sounded awesome, even after only a few hours.

The song had gripped everyone. It had just flowed effortlessly between us all. Each member of Room 103 and me, syncing with the other as we all worked our parts to perfection.

Even though we had another four rehearsals before Saturday, I knew we would nail it.

"Yeah. It's cool guys. That'll do until tomorrow."

As soon as the words left Bulk's lips, Jax stalked over to me, lifted me over his shoulder and carried me straight up to his room. Man cave and club came to mind.

He dumped me unceremoniously in the middle of his huge bed, and then stood at the bottom of it just staring at me.

He stayed there so long I wondered if he'd actually slipped into a vertical coma. Suddenly he grinned; a huge dirty smile lifted the corners of each of his pink lips as his eyelids dropped to half-mast. He palmed the bed and proceeded to leisurely crawl towards me, his hands and knees penning me underneath his huge frame as he climbed higher up the bed.

"Ah, ah, ah. No nookie until after you apologise, buy me a field of flowers, finger feed me masses and masses of chocolate and kiss my feet," I chastised playfully.

He paused on his adventure, his eyebrows rose but I caught the slight twitch of his lips.

"Babe. Who needs flowers and chocolates when I got a fucking hard dick right here for you?" Okay. That worked as well!

I bit my bottom lip as I tried to stifle the grin that was threatening to erupt. "You are so romantic, Jax."

He smiled and carried on towards me until his forehead was resting against mine. "Just need to breathe you, E."

Oh Christ. Why did he have to say things like that when I was trying to be angry with him?

He softly planted a kiss on my forehead then ran his nose down mine until his lips were gently resting against mine. His eyes held mine for what seemed like forever, the darkness of them swallowing mine. I could see straight into his soul, into his damaged and broken soul. The twin to mine.

He eventually rolled over and lay flat on the bed beside me. I turned onto my side, propping my head on my hand to look at him.

"We're not together, me and Fran."

He opened his eyes and turned to face me so we were both side by side, our faces inches apart. Our warm breath mingled as he gazed at me, begging me to see the honesty behind his words.

I nodded. "But...is that your choice or Fran's?"

He puffed out a breath and scrunched up his nose. "Mine."

"Is she happy with that?"

He pursed his lips and shook his head slowly, "Nah, not really."

I sighed and nodded. Lifting my hand, I palmed his face. "Then we have a problem, Jax."

His eyes closed for a moment and when he opened them I flinched at the fire he held in them, "Nah, no problem, babe." God damn this man!

"Jax. I will not be slung into the middle of a volatile relationship. It's just not me, baby."

His teeth pulled at his lip as he growled faintly. "Babe, you're not hearin' me."

One of his fingers traced the contours of my cheek bone and followed round to outline my ear as he inched just a little bit closer. His mouth was now a mere centimetre from mine. I couldn't keep my eyes away from it, the curve and softness of his lips were demanding my attention. My body was screaming at me to just take him, to lay my lips over his and make him beg for mercy. To drag his bottom lip between my teeth and bite he until he gave me what I need.

"I am hearing you, Jax but you're not hearing me. I won't be the bitch that took someone's man," I stated.

His hand now slid past my ear and he gently took a handful of my hair. "Was never hers, babe." His lips came to hover over mine. "Always yours E, always…"

I released a long groan as he finally joined us in one of his magnificent kisses and he began his unyielding torture, turning me into a quivering, begging beast.

My body surged to life as my womb pulsed viciously, demanding that I sort out the throb that was making it clench tight.

Wrapping my arms around his shoulders and flinging my leg over his, I rolled us until I was straddled over him, taking him under me whilst he continued to devour me. He was eating me alive and I wanted to smear myself in his favourite food stuff so he would never stop, never remove his mouth from me, just forever consume me... all of me.

His hands snaked around my back as he pulled me further onto him. I could feel his ready erection straining under his jeans.

One of his hands burrowed under my t-shirt to unhook my bra and then ventured round to cup my breast, his large calloused hand caressing me so rigorously that I begged for the same attention to my other breast. I moaned and arched myself into his huge palm, begging for some sort of stimulant, any as long as it made me feel good.

He understood instantly and rolled my stiff nipples between his thumb and finger, sending a jolt of energy straight down to my clit.

"Please... oh God, that's so good... please..." I whispered against his lips.

"You want this, babe?" What a stupid time to ask that! I wasn't going to say no, was I!

"God, Yes. I want everything you're gonna give me," I breathed against his mouth triggering a growl from him as he gently flanked my bottom lip with his teeth.

I gripped the hem of his t-shirt and bunched it up. He lifted slightly so I could pull it over his head, then I sat upright and feasted my eyes on his glorious naked torso... and what a god damn exceptional torso it was.

Hot and hard and so bloody firm... yum! His wide strong shoulders curved superiorly from his neck line, the curve of them made me want to nibble furiously along the very edge of them. Each commanding Celtic inked bicep and forearm brought a hunger for them to be wrapped around me, holding me and protecting me.

His powerful muscular pecs made my mouth water, the contrast of his small tight brown pierced nipple against his bronzed skin made my blood heat. His six-pack rippled fabulously and each contour of those incredible abdominal muscles made me want to run my tongue along each groove.

And then down to those magnificent wing tattooed hip bones either side of his delicious 'V'. The very aspect of each wing made me want to trace each feather with my tongue.

I palmed his chest and devoured him with my eyes, then explored each contour and form with my fingertip, delicately adoring each of his mouth-watering regions before I continued my idolisation with my tongue.

"Fuck, babe. Your tongue's wicked."

He groaned loud when I kissed down his man trail and popped the button on his jeans before I nudged them and his shorts over his hips and down his long legs.

Looking up at him through my eyelashes, I grinned lasciviously before I unhurriedly kissed and licked my way back up his leg. I stroked his scrotum with the tip of my tongue before I mouthed his testicles and sucked on each one gently. I smiled to myself as I planted tiny kisses all the way up his velvety shaft until I reached the very tip.

His strong fingers twisted in my hair as he emitted a loud moan. "Shit, babe. Fucking suck me!"

Then I slaughtered him. Wrapping my lips behind my teeth and curling my fingers around the base of his mighty cock, I slid my mouth down as far as I could, relaxing my throat and swallowing as he hit my tonsils.

"Oooh Fuckkkk," he growled as his fingers tightened in my hair with each plunge.

Gripping my head firmly he took control as each movement of my mouth drove him nearer to euphoria. "Gonna come right down your throat, E."

I groaned with his words sending a vibration through his cock and forced his climax from him. His hips lifted high and he roared his release as his hot, creamy cum hit the back of my throat so forcefully I couldn't take it all, it dribbled out of the edge of my mouth.

God, I was so turned on I came right there with him, just from the pleasure of his own reaction to his orgasm.

Kissing my way back up to him, he palmed each of my cheeks as soon as I reached his face and kissed me feverishly before he gripped my t-shirt and pulled it over my head, pulling my bra along with it.

He rolled us so I was underneath his huge form and he frantically pulled off my jeans, stripping them down my legs with a swiftness that made me giggle.

He grinned up at me from my toes before he softly clamped his teeth over my little toe and bit down before swirling his tongue around the tender flesh. I was utterly surprised to find this action extremely erotic and a soft growl erupted from me.

His eyes darkened as he made his way up my leg, his tongue tasting and teasing all the way up until he came to the new tattoo on my inner thigh.

"Fuck, babe. Love it!" he snarled before he dipped right into my sex and swiped his tongue from my anus to the tiny piercing on my shaved mound.

"Christ. You fucking rip me apart, E."

I lifted my hips to encourage him to ravish me, begging with my actions for him to bring me to explosion point.

He slid a finger inside me, swirling it round and round, preparing me for his intrusion. Groaning I clasped his hair and pulled him further onto me "Jax, please..."

"You wanna come hard, babe?"

"Fuck yes... please... god, yes. So hard," I pleaded feverishly.

He inserted another finger as his tongue flicked over my clit rapidly, urging a choked whimper from my throat.

"God, you taste epic."

That was it. I detonated right over his face, erupting in an almighty orgasm as he growled and lapped at me religiously.

"Fuckkkk," I screamed loudly as my hips lifted us both off the bed.

Before I caught my breath he was pressing his solid cock straight into me. We both groaned in appreciation as he tipped my womb and I rolled my hips, grinding myself further onto him.

"So good, babe."

I was panting manically as he pulled out slowly and then slid back in at his leisure, never speeding up until I was frantic with need. "Christ, Jax. Harder. Fuck me, damn it."

His mouth sucked on a nipple, elongating it with his teeth and driving me wild. "Damn it," I snarled and punched him in the arm. "Will you fuck me hard. I need it... please."

I grunted as he pulled out and then thrust back in powerfully, yielding to my desire. "Harder," I urged again. I needed to feel him rough and ready; needed to feel his ultimate power when he took me.

He pulled back, snarled, and then drove into me with so much vigour he knocked me up the bed. "Yes," I hissed at him, "More!"

"Take it all, babe" he rasped as he drove right to the tip of me and I yelped when he bounced off my cervix.

He pushed up onto his hands and continued to work me crazy and feral, each forceful drive brought me nearer to rapture while his eyes held mine, and never let them free from his intense stare.

We were both moaning and panting wildly as we fucked like animals... raw, primal and unrestrained as we took what each of us gave; fed from it, devoured it whole and then gave some more.

"Need your orgasm, babe." He grunted and I could see his teeth clench as he held himself back for me. His whole body was strung so tightly I could decipher where each of his muscles ended and another started.

I was building so rapidly that each of my muscles was screaming at me for release, my teeth chattered and my nerve endings hummed violently.

I don't quite know what happened then but I kind of went a little savage. I flung my head back so far I heard my neck crunch; I bit my bottom lip so severely I brought blood, my fingernails scoured all the way down Jax's back; drawing blood as they raked through his skin and I screamed so loudly I tore my throat as my cum poured from me and drenched him and the bed.

"*Fucking Christ,*" Jax roared as he bared his teeth and came as powerfully as I did, his head dipped into my shoulder as his teeth clamped onto the soft flesh at the base of my neck and he muttered a string of curses as he pumped into me uncontrollably.

"Oh. My. God" I panted as he remained immobile against me.

I couldn't catch my breath as my body trembled wildly, each of my nerves, muscles and organs chaotically attempting to find their correct status in my jumbled body.

I was starting to think Jax had died when he still didn't move his body and I lay staring at the ceiling until he suddenly shifted.

"What the fuck, babe?" Jax gasped as he rolled over and pulled me into his side.

"Sorry," I whispered as shame and embarrassment surged through me.

He reared back and scowled at me, "What the hell for?"

I grimaced and lowered my face, burying my heated cheeks in his chest. His fingers tilted my head so I was facing him again and he raised his eyebrows in a silent question, "For?" he repeated.

"Well... I went a bit... a bit... wild."

I could have died. I had never acted like that during sex and I was utterly mortified by my untamed behaviour.

"Are you shittin' me?"

I just shrugged and silently wished he would shut the hell up before I died of humiliation. He shuffled round so he was looking straight at me and took my hand in his, bringing it up to rest on his chest between us. "Babe, been fuckin' for near ten years now and I have never been fucked like that before." Well... okay... help me someone!

I frowned in confusion. A slow delicious grin erupted on his cheeky face and the sight warmed my insides. "Was – Fucking – Utterly – Awesome, babe... Mind-fucking-blowing!" he stated slowly. Oh okay... that was a nice thing to say.

"Yeah?" I asked quietly.

He belted out a bark of laughter, "Christ. Fuckin' exploded, babe. Passed out at one point."

"I think you gave me one of those female ejaculation thingy's."

Jax's eyebrows rose with a hint of humour, "Female ejaculation thingy's?"

I grinned widely when he started laughing and pulled me in, hugging me closely. "Christ, E. Go to sleep now. Class tomorrow, babe" he ordered with a soft chuckle as he planted a soft gentle kiss on my forehead. Well that was a sudden change of direction!

I nodded and snuggled down with him, now utterly exhausted and sated.

But I lay listening to his steady breathing for a long time, treasuring our close time together.

The sensation of just been held by him had a bout of energy coursing through my veins and I stayed awake for a long time that night... just being intimate and fused to the man I had fallen so deeply and entirely with.

CHAPTER 22

We practised our song religiously all week and with all my study, work and love making with Jax in between, by the time Saturday night came I was completely shattered.

I was working the bar but Trish had popped in to cover for me whilst I performed, she was as excited as everyone else to hear the duet and I must admit I was slightly terrified. The guy's had been really supportive and Boss had even offered me oral relief to calm my nerves... Jax's face was epic.

Friend AKA Trent had come in with his group of mates and introduced me to all of them. I was stoked when they asked me to autograph their chests; one had asked for a buttock signing... again Jax's face was classic.

I had dressed for the gig in a tight leather black dress, fishnet stockings and knee high 5 inch boots; my make-up was sexy and smoky and my hair was messed up wildly; I had even died the tips of it red to match my fringe and it looked awesome.

Each member of Room 103 had just stared immobile and wide-eyed when they came to pick me, Luce, Kaylee, Aaron and Josh up from my dorm; apart from Jax who dragged me back into my room and pummelled me against my door whilst the guy's waited in the van for us.

Needless to say we got a cheer and Jax received some back slaps as we returned. Mortifying!

Room 103 worked through their regular set and as it came nearer the time for me to join them I was a dithering wreck. My heart was pumping wildly, my blood was so hot it scorched each of my veins and my legs trembled so violently I worried I was going to have to crawl onto the stage.

"Z Bar!" Jax held a finger in the air and held his hand against his ear feeding the crowd with attention.

The room screamed and cheered.

"You know what's coming don't ya'."

Screams, whoops and whistles erupted before the chants began. "E, E, E, E, E..." sung out as feet stomped on the floor rhythmically.

"Then let's get her up here. Come on, babe."

I wobbled slowly up to the stage. Boss jumped down and gripped my waist to hoist me up as it was impossible to climb up lady like in my short dress.

The throng erupted so loudly I had to cover my ears.

"Come and blow me, E!"

"Gotta' hard dick here for ya', E!"

"Love you, E!"

The sentiments kept coming until Jax glared at the crowd. "She's mine," he growled out and I suppressed a smile at his possessiveness.

"Let's do this!" Boss shouted, "Give it up for the new band member of Room 103... E as she duets with Jax with '*Shocking Heaven*'."

I took my position on set which was on the right hand side of the stage whilst Jax stood on the left as Romeo came in with a slow melodic introduction, causing the room to start swaying already with the beat of the music.

Jax stepped forward and came in with the first verse which was slow and mellow.

"You're there, seen from the stars
Peaceful dignity with so much quiet misery
Trying to hold on, to breathe
Just stay and don't ever leave
I'm beggin' ya', ya' need to believe."

I stepped a little closer to him as he looked over at me as the chorus shifted into a faster rock composition, upbeat and at a heavier pace. I noticed the crowd eating up every word as they swayed, then rocked, then pumped the air in time with our music. The passion and excitement surged through my veins, lighting up every single nerve ending in my body as my heart injected each vein with electricity.

We came in together for the chorus, walking slowly nearer each other whilst singing as one. The emotion and passion that Jax expressed through the words had me believing he'd written every word for me, which he had.

"But if you're going through hell, keep going
Cos' you're just shocking heaven
Shocking heaven
And shaming angels
Cos' you're just screaming in silence
Bringing me to my knees
With each of your silent pleas."

Then it was my turn for my solo, at a melancholy and sorrowful tempo again as Jax took another step towards me.

"You're near, touching my mind
Forever seeing with so much abandon
Trying to take back, to live
I've not much more to give
But I'm beggin', make me believe."

We rocked out the chorus again, triggering whistles and dancing bodies from the mass of fans before Jax came in with another verse.

"You're here, inside my soul
Brutal caress with so much tender slaughter
Trying to break free, to run
Don't leave me when you're done
I'm beggin' ya, don't fire the damn gun."

After Romeo gave a solo riff, we both came in with the middle 8 section as we came together in the middle of the stage. Jax grabbed my hand, squeezing it tightly as the crowd whistled and cheered their approval.

"But we're trying to carry on and love
Gently fighting against each other for the passion
Linking together as one, no more lonely souls
And now we're shocking heaven, just shocking
heaven"

And after another chorus Jax sang the outro.

"If you're going through hell, keep going
Keep going, keep going
Don't ever stop, never stop
Keep going, keep going"

We finished, Jax growled, lifted me up and kissed me passionately as the room erupted in screams and a deafening applause that seemed to go on forever. Their explosive levels of noise shook the walls.

"I think they liked it, babe."

"That's because you did a damn fine job of writing it, Jax."

He grinned and cupped my cheek, "You did a damn fine job of singing it, E."

I returned his passionate kiss with one of my own, forging my lips violently on his, telling him just how much his words meant.

Boss came over and pulled me from Jax before swirling me round and planting a huge sloppy kiss on my cheek. "Fucking awesome, hot stuff!" he cheered in my ear as I got a thumbs up and a 'SPANNER!'

from Romeo. Bulk grinned at me then picked up all the boxer shorts, condoms and roses thrown on the stage and handed them to me.

The feeling was phenomenal. I felt euphoric, incredible and fucking electrifying. The vitality that flowed through me made me feel like I was high as the crowd still chanted mine and Jax's names.

I was on a high and at that moment in my life I was seriously debating whether it might be a good idea to make a career using my voice. Hell, why the heck not?

***

We were all sat round Room 103's regular table after hours. The door was bolted and the centre of our table had been filled with Tequila and Jagermeister shots as we celebrated my official initiation into the band.

Boss and Romeo had picked up a couple of girl's but Boss's was already asleep under the table and he was currently been ribbed to death by the rest of the band.

"Looks like a hand job tonight, Boss." I winked as someone rattled on the pub doors.

"Yeah, *your* hand, E?"

Poking my tongue out at him as Jax growled at him, I slid the bolt across and pulled open the door to a fist, right it in my cheek bone.

"What the fuck!" I stuttered as I stumbled backwards.

Fran was stood in the doorway glaring at me. "You fucking Bitch!" she screamed as she swung again. Luckily I was ready this time and shifted pretty quickly.

"I swear to God, Fran. You might be pregnant but hit me again and you'll be on you back." No change there then!

"Whoa!" Jax shouted before he pulled me behind him. "The fuck, Fran?" he growled at her.

She stood there, just gawping between me and Jax. Her face contorted in rage as she glanced at Jax's hand in mine. "So that's it, is it? Now you've got a new whore?"

My mouth dropped open and I pulled my hand out of Jax's, much to his displeasure. "You see what I was trying to tell you?" I snarled at him. "I won't be *that* bitch, Jax."

I turned my back on them both but Jax's hand shot around my arm, "No, babe. Wait."

He turned back to Fran, his eyes frantically shifting up and down her face. His hand tightened in mine so much so it was beginning to hurt. "What you on, Fran?"

Her eyes flicked but her face remained impassive. I frowned as I looked between them both. She wouldn't take drugs whilst pregnant. Would she?

She pursed her lips and glowered at Jax. "So what now?" she asked with a shrug. "You just gonna dump me for that... skank!" Okay, now I was getting a little irritable!

Jax sighed heavily beside me. "Fran. I can't fucking dump you cos' we were never together."

Her eyes went wide and her face slackened. I had a small twitch of sympathy for her. Just a tad.

She seemed to consider his words for a moment, her face showing each of the emotions her mind went through. "But... We're having a baby, Jax" she choked on a whisper.

"And?..."

Okay Jax. Maybe a little harsh there!

She shrugged again. "And... I... I... I love you, Jax," this time it was a whisper.

I shuffled my feet uncomfortably. "Okay you guys. I'm just gonna let you both..." I murmured as I tried to pull away.

"Stay the fuck there babe," Jax said softly.

I shook my head at him and squeezed his hand as I leaned in to whisper in his ear, "Jax. You need to sort this out with Fran. She doesn't know what is gonna happen. She's pregnant with your baby..."

The growl that rumbled through his throat stilted my words. "Stay – the – fuck - there, babe." What the Hell!

"If you don't want me to embarrass you in front of your ex, then I suggest you get your hand off my arm and let me fucking go," I hissed.

His head turned to me so slowly it reminded me of the girl on 'The Exorcist'... he seemed to have inherited her eyes as well, I was hoping it didn't stretch to the green vomit.

"Not gonna say it again E," he growled.

"Okay fine!" I uttered through my teeth. I was so going to kill him when Fran had gone!

He turned back to Fran, his eyes narrow and blazing and I saw her swallow heavily. "E and me are together... fucking like animals, Fran. All – the – fucking - time. You got that?" Wow. That must have hurt.

I squeezed his thigh and he glanced at me. "Need to say it, babe."

I screwed my face up at him. "Not like that though, eh?"

I risked a quick look at Fran and cringed. She was white, her fists were tight and sweaty and I could see the tremble in her legs. "You... you wanna sit down, Fran?" I asked quietly.

She flicked me a glimpse, her eyes full of tears but she shook her head before she turned and left, closing the pub door quietly behind her.

Jax shrugged and turned back to the table but I stood immobile, stunned at what had just occurred.

He turned back to me, a confused frown on his face as he tilted his head in query. "Clue me in, babe."

I gave him an incredulous look before I shook my head at him. "You gonna treat me like that when you're done with me, Jax?"

His eyebrows hit his hairline and his eyes widened before his lip curved up into a wicked smile. He took two steps to reach me, the darkness in his eyes made my stomach heat and my other bits squeeze tight. He deliberately shook his head twice and leant into my ear. "Never gonna stop needin' you,

E... never. You're always gonna be there for me, with me; whenever, however and wherever cos' you're in here, babe." He grasped my hand and held it over his heart, "As well as here." Then he put my hand elsewhere... use your imagination!

I gulped and nodded wildly.

"You hear me, babe?"

Fighting past the lump in my throat I took a breath, "Yeah, I hear ya', Jax."

He gave me his dirty grin before he took me in a mouth-watering kiss that blew my socks off... well my stockings.

CHAPTER 23

It was late Sunday morning and Jax and I were snuggled in his bed, relaxing under his huge fluffy duvet whilst he fork fed me fresh fruit and coffee... the coffee wasn't via a fork though!

We had made a declaration that neither of us was leaving his bed for the day. We had a pile of DVD's and CD's piled up beside the bed, a mass of chocolate which Jax had ran to the shop to get for me... sweet, I know, and the numerous remotes for each of his gadgets lined up on the bed.

"You gonna clue me in then, babe?" he asked after he popped another slice of peach into my mouth.

"What would you like clueing in on, baby?" I asked him as I slid a blueberry in between his very kissable lips.

The way he pursed those lips made me think I wasn't going to like his topic of conversation. "Where and why you went?"

My top teeth sank into my bottom lip as I diverted his attention with a piece of apple. He lifted his eyebrows, telling me he knew it was a diversion but I refused to look at him.

"You know I need to go and see my mother soon. I might be gone for a few days," I told him out of the blue, using it as a distraction.

"The Fuck, babe!" How did I guess that's what he'd say?

"She's ill, Jax. She might need me," I argued.

"Yeah, she needs you, but not for care..." he growled.

"Jax... don't..." I hid my shame as I turned my head and studied the TV remote, my finger outlining each of the buttons to shift my concentration.

"Babe..." He lifted my face towards him with his fingertips but I shook my head.

"Jax please, just... just don't."

He huffed loudly but nodded. "Then I come with you, E."

"I don't think that's a good idea, Jax" I warned and he scoffed. Yeah right E! Not a hope in hell.

"So babe... where?" God this man was relentless. Push, push, push.

I sighed heavily. "I went to Cornwall for a few weeks," I divulged as he scowled.

"Cornwall?"

I nodded. "You ever think about finding your Mom, Jax?" I asked quietly as my fingers tugged on a loose thread on his duvet. Please just change the damn subject!

He rolled me over so I was pinned underneath his magnificent frame. His hands took my wrists and held my arms above my head as his solid body held me prisoner underneath him.

He glared at me as my heart and breath stuttered simultaneously. "Why, babe?"

I looked away, "It doesn't matter, Jax."

His nose twitched before he ran the tip of it down the length of mine "Think it does, babe. Need to know."

"Why do you need to know, Jax? It doesn't concern you."

I ignored the deep rumble in his chest, it was just wind! "Tell me."

"No."

"Tell me."

"Nope."

His tongue trailed a delicate route across my bottom lip and my body hummed in delight as my vagina argued with me about divulging information. 'Just bloody tell him so he fucks the living daylights out of you' it was saying! Damn hormones!

"Babe... Tell - Me."

"Jax, please" I whined as his tongue now trickled down the centre of my throat, my breathing speeding to a pant.

"Need to know, E."

"Why?"

He had now reached the edge of the 'V' neckline of my shirt. He tortured the swell of my breasts ruthlessly, planting lots of open mouthed kisses along the edge of the hem.

"Oh God..." I breathed as I slid my hands around him and cupped his glorious backside through his shorts. Christ, his arse was pure sin. I raked my nails over the taut muscle, triggering a groan from deep within him.

"Tell me babe," he reiterated tenaciously.

"You'll be cross," I whispered.

He elevated slightly, his face expressing confusion. "Never, babe."

I nodded solemnly at him before his finger stroked along the edge of my face, his eyes tracking his movements. "Promise," he whispered gently as he cupped my cheek tenderly.

He held my eyes with his own as he vowed by his pledge, urging me to trust him. "I... I had a...relapse. A bad one," I whispered. He had to turn his ear towards me to hear my words.

The fire lit his eyes and his teeth sunk into his bottom lip so forcefully I thought it was going to pop under the pressure.

In for a penny...

"I made a bit of a... mess."

His breath stunted as he knelt up and narrowed his eyes on me. He didn't say anything, he didn't have to really; his eyes told me his exact thoughts.

"You promised..." I reminded him cautiously.

He ground his teeth but nodded and grasped my hand, his beautiful green eyes held mine as he fought against his own temper. "Turn over," he ordered gently.

Shaking my head at him, I tried to nudge backwards up the bed but he gripped my hips and flipped me right over, no effort needed. Damn his strength!

I desperately tried to escape from his hold but the back of my shirt was already around the nape of my neck.

Shit!

He sucked in a large breath as he studied my scars. I could feel the full body flush that ascended from my toes to the crown of my head.

The humiliation of my actions was now coming back to haunt me in front of the man I loved, the man I was so desperate to please. His pride and faith in me meant everything and the shame of disappointing him was aching my heart.

"I'm sorry," I threw out, more sternly than I meant to.

His fingertip traced along each welt whilst he remained silent, his harsh heavy breaths sounding loud against the silence of the room.

"I'm sorry, baby" I repeated distraughtly, trying to hold back the feeling of failure.

"Babe…" he choked out eventually.

I burrowed my face in the pillow as I echoed my apology on a sob. His body dropped beside me with a loud thunk on the mattress before I was huddled tightly into his protective embrace. "Need to see someone about this now, babe."

I nodded, "Yeah. The hospital has made arrangements for me to see a councillor," I shrugged.

His fingers softly swept the outer edge of my arm, up and down, up and down, its hypnotising rhythm was extremely comforting and I felt myself relax into him. "You… Hospital?" He stuttered out and I nodded against him.

"Yeah… I told you, I made a… it was too soon after the last session and it kinda', well it… tore me up a bit and I passed out…" I trailed off as I felt him stiffen, his whole body clenching rigidly beside me.

His fingers now moved down to my hip, continuing their soothing strokes along the edge of my knicker line. "Why?"

I was dreading this question and I was frantically trying to come up with a lie to cover the embarrassment of the truth but the thoughts filtered through my ears again as Jax said "Truth, babe." Crap!

"I dunno really... just things that had built up," I said, a little economical with the truth.

Jax nodded lightly then tucked his thumb in the edge of my knickers. My pussy moistened in anticipation as my womb yelled at him to rip them right off.

"You fucked off right after our argument about Fran," he divulged. No flies on this man!

Swallowing heavily I relented and nodded. "Yeah," I whispered against his ribcage.

He was silent for the longest time. I was internally trying to gauge his emotions but Jax was always closed off and good at hiding every damn thought he had.

"I hurt you."

I wasn't sure if I had heard him correctly. "What?" I said softly.

He growled and gently pushed me off him before he abruptly clambered off the bed, picked his jeans off the floor and pulled them on with his t-shirt before slamming his bedroom door behind him.

Well that went well then.

I sat immobile and stunned in the middle of his bed, not quite sure what to do. Hell. I really hadn't expected that reaction from him. I thought he might have been a bit irate but I hadn't anticipated this.

He seemed angry with himself instead of me and my frazzled brain couldn't work out how to respond to it. I hated the fact that I had upset him and I sat still, not knowing what to do.

Did I stay? Did I go home? I just sat there tracing the buttons on the bloody remote.

Eventually I climbed off his bed and pulled on my own jeans, and ventured down for coffee.

Boss was sat at the kitchen table with a skinny blonde girl, both of them silent and staring through the window in an awkward silence.

Boss's head turned towards me and relief flashed over his face as if my presence would shift the uncomfortable atmosphere.

"Hey, hot stuff." He grinned a little too happily. I smiled at him and his eyebrows drew in. "You okay, baby?" he asked softly.

Blondie huffed and stood. "I'll get off then shall I?"

Boss and I glanced at her, not appreciating the attitude rolling off her. "Sure, see ya'." Boss shrugged. She huffed again and left via the kitchen door.

Boss shook his head as if to clear his thoughts then stood and lifted the kettle, waggling it at me. I nodded and slumped into a chair, tracing along the edge of the scuffed table with a finger.

"What's up?" he asked without turning around.

"He asked why I'd gone," I divulged.

"Uh huh."

"I told him, he realised it was because of the argument we'd had about Fran, which of course didn't help." I sighed and frowned, still baffled by Jax's behaviour. "Then he said he'd hurt me and took off," I finished with a shrug.

Boss sighed and sat in the chair next to me, gently placing my coffee in front of me on the table. "The thing with Jax is... he kinda' grew up without any attention what so ever. Nothing from both parents and the only interaction he got was with Mary Ann," he started to explain.

I nodded but my heart was breaking for the huge strong man that wanted to protect me before himself, always before himself.

"His emotions, mental state and social skills have always been... stunted because of it. Hell, even his speech skills never developed past the childhood stage because he'd only ever had a child to communicate with."

Boss traced the rim of his cup with his finger as he divulged private information about his friend, the awkwardness of it was making him guilt ridden but he was telling me for my benefit, now his friend as well as Jax. "He was never sent to school you know."

He shook his head sadly, "That's why he started singing. It was really the only thing he could teach himself. That and guitar."

I took a huge gulp of my coffee, just to force down the lump that was forming.

"When his mum took off, then his dad and Mary Ann... Well, he kind of forced himself into education.

Think he thought he needed to prove something to himself. That he wasn't a deadbeat like his dad used to call him. It was his way of coping with the grief I suppose."

I nodded silently again, my teeth frantically chewing on my bottom lip to encourage the tears to stay in their ducts.

"Mary Ann was his life, he'd hate himself every time he hurt her because it was the only time he never had anybody. She'd lock herself in her room and refuse to talk to him and it... it killed him. They never talked things through, she would just come back out, hug him and that would be that. He just doesn't know how to deal with emotions, feelings and it kinda' sends him crazy when he has these feelings he doesn't know how to deal with."

The tears had been flowing for a while now and I swiped my hands over my face.

My strong Rock God; so tough and confident on the outside and yet so destroyed and lost on the inside. So emotionally alone and abandoned that he didn't realise just how clever and compassionate he really was and that people loved him for who he was, for exactly *how* he was.

Boss grasped my hand tightly. "Be patient with him, E. Everybody left him. To him, even the sister that loved him immeasurably disappeared. I know she didn't do it intentionally but in his head, she still left him alone just like his parents did."

He frowned at his own words. "It's hurt him because he knows he hurt you. He's just trying to deal with that. Maybe he thinks you'll leave him as well if he hurts you. I dunno what goes off in that head of his."

I nodded, "Yeah."

"He loves you E," Boss declared on a whisper.

"I know. I love him more than life Boss, more than my soul can consume, but I don't know how to...how to find him. Not where he's gone now, but just *him*. Ya' know?"

He nodded sombrely and squeezed my hand tight. "He's gotta find himself, E."

I nodded in agreement. I had to step back and let Jax establish who he was for himself. Not for me, not for his group, not for his friends but for himself. I just hoped I could cling on while he made that discovery.

"You ever loved someone so much, it actually hurts your heart, Boss?"

I noticed him stiffen and he nodded once but didn't divulge any more apart from a heavy sigh and a sad painful expression covered his face. The look broke my heart when I realised Boss had his own demons and experience of heartache, but I didn't dig, it was his story to tell not my place to probe.

CHAPTER 24

I decided to stay and took myself back upstairs, stripped naked and pulled out Jax's old G N' R t-shirt, tugging it on as his male huskiness enveloped me, and curled up on the bed to watch some movies.

Jax's DVD compilation genre consisted of action, action or action (Oh, and a few porn), so I settled on an action movie after much deliberation.

I was near the end of my second film when his bedroom door suddenly opened and he stood there, all hardness and hot, simmering sex.

Good God!

His narrow eyes found mine and he crooked a finger in the air. "Get up." My eyes widened. He repeated his command, "Up, babe."

Clambering off the bed, I kept my eyes trained on him, trying to gauge his mood but his eyes were like black pits, pools of darkness. The intensity in them burned straight through his t-shirt and singed every hair on my little body.

"Shirt off," he growled at me as his tongue swept across his bottom lip. I wanted to follow its route with my own but I answered his demand and lifted the shirt over my head, revealing my naked form to him.

A low rumble rattled his chest as his eyes scrutinised every part of me. I swallowed harshly, trying to draw in what air remained in the room.

"Come here!"

I liked this next command. It brought me nearer to him, close to the raw sex he was radiating. I stumbled on the first step but managed to drag my trembling legs across the room until I was stood before him, my chest heaving with every hard intake of air.

Suddenly he lifted his own shirt over his head, then removed the remainder of his clothes, sweeping his jeans and shorts down his legs whilst he silently commanded I never left his gaze.

His stern stare wouldn't allow me to look at his glorious body as he held me firm in his eyes. He took a step closer and I whimpered involuntary, desperately trying to stay upright as my whole body shook in pure unadulterated need.

Every puff of his warm breath lit another synapse in my body, stimulating each of my neurons until my very essence was screaming at him to touch me.

He prowled around me until he was stood directly behind me. I jolted as I felt his lips brush the side of my neck. "You mine, babe?"

I nodded as I struggled to breathe never mind answer him.

"I asked if you are mine?" His rough sound penetrated my core.

"Yes," I whispered harshly.

"How much?"

My chest rose and fell vastly, goose bumps erupted over every part of me as I closed my eyes to attempt some sort of control.

"A... All of me. Everything I am, Jax."

He sucked air savagely through his teeth before his fingertip brushed from the nape of my neck, straight down my spine to my bottom.

"Even this, babe?" he asked quietly as he cupped one of my buttocks in his large hand. Oh God! Oh God!

I sucked on my lips as my breath stuttered wildly, right along with my heartbeat. "Well..."

He mouthed the soft flesh under my earlobe, his tongue dipping out to taste me as he ran his finger along the groove of my backside. "I need all of you, E. I need to take every - single - piece - of - you." A tiny groan reverberated from my lungs as they deflated in a single gush. "I need to own Every – Single – Inch – Of - You, Eve Hudson."

Could I really give him this part of me? A part that had never been touched before; a forbidden zone of me. I mean it was my... my... Oh just say it E... arse!

"But... it might hurt..." I choked out, feeling utterly stupid. Here was a God of sex that had probably had more women, in more ways than I'd ever dreamed about. And here was little old me, a quivering wreck because he wanted to... take me there!

"Won't hurt you babe, I promise," he breathed against my ear.

I took a deep breath before I nodded.

"Need to hear you, babe."

I swallowed again and pulled myself together.... well tried to. "Yes," I puffed out.

I heard his breath hitch before he swept both hands up my back and circled the back of my neck with them, both of his thumbs rubbing along my tat.

"I'm gonna make you feel so good, E… so damn fucking good," he growled.

I nodded again as my mouth dried and my insides vibrated.

"Bend over and hold on to the chair," he ordered softly.

I closed my eyes and took a calming breath before I did as he asked and bent forward, placing my palms flat on the seat of his song writing chair. I felt him kneel behind me and I cringed as he viewed me openly, every part of my sex on display for him.

"*Fuck!*" he hissed, "So fucking beautiful."

My eyes shot open as I felt his face bury against me, his whole face in my lady parts. "Oh God," I whimpered.

He inhaled then moved back a little before he circled my inflamed clit with his tongue, then travelled it upwards and dipped it into my pussy, lapping at my already formed juices. I whimpered again before he carried on his voyage over my perineum and then he reamed my anus. I sucked in a huge shuddering breath as he inserted a finger into my slick vagina.

"Oh my God," I panted.

"Yeah, you like that," he stated. "You're gripping my finger tight, babe." His tongue continued its exploration of my ass before he suddenly stood and disappeared. "Stay there," he ordered. I couldn't move if I tried.

He returned with a tube of lube and slid behind me again before I felt his cold slippery finger teasing my tight hole as his tongue idolised my clit.

He sucked on my nub as he inserted his finger into my backside. I gasped at the intrusion but he ventured on gradually, painstakingly slow. His talented tongue brought my attention back to my clit as he rolled his finger inside me, preparing my anus for his penetration. He pulled out and then I felt a tightening as he joined it with another finger, increasing the pressure as well as the access.

"Oh shit, Jax... I... God..." I was a spluttering fool. The pleasure hadn't been expected but it was very much welcomed.

"Ready, babe?" I nodded. God yes, was I ever?

He came to stand behind me. I felt the tip of him press against me and I whimpered. This was going to hurt!

"Relax, babe" he whispered as he leant over my back and nudged in gently.

"Oh, Oh, Jax... Shit..."

"Easy. Bear down and push against me," he instructed softly in my ear.

Gulping, I did as he asked until he was fully inside me. He remained motionless, completely still as my body acclimatised to the intrusion. The pain lessened and when his finger found my clit, I gave out a deep guttural growl. Shit. Had I just made that sound?

Jax growled in reply before he slowly pulled out. "You okay, babe?" His voice was a low rasp and I nodded.

He pushed back in so slowly it was near torturous. "Baby... Jax, for god's sake... move!"

The groan that left his lips was animalistic and inhumane; a huge turn on and I pushed back onto him as he pushed into me. "Fuck me damn it!" I ordered.

His right foot landed on the seat of the chair beside my hand then he went for it! Christ! Did he go for it?

We were sweaty, loud and brutal as he took my virgin arse. His power and lust worked me into a panting, groaning mess. "Jax... Fuck! Fuck! Christ... I... Oh God. Oooh Goddd..." I'm sure he laughed at me... Bastard!

I exploded ferociously, screaming wildly as my whole body bucked and shivered violently.

Jax growled, grunted, and then roared as he spilled his load into my backside, pumping for what seemed like forever. "Fuck E," he wheezed as he collapsed on top of me, squashing my cheek into the seat cushion.

"I...Wow... I..."

He chuckled as he pulled out gently, then scooped me up in his arms and curled us both up on the bed. "You okay, babe?"

I nodded into him as I struggled for composure. My body hummed delightfully and I had never felt so relaxed in all my life.

***

"Babe." His warm breath whispered against my cheek and I grumbled at him.

"Bugger off."

His deep throaty chuckle brought a smile to my lips. "Babe. You need to eat," he tried again, forcing my eyes to squeal as I opened them and was greeted to his gorgeous smiling face.

"Mmm," I mumbled as I palmed his cheek. "Hey, beautiful," I whispered. The grin that lit his face fluttered my heart. "What time is it?" I jolted upright, dragging myself out of my slumber.

"Relax. It's only 4 O'clock."

I nodded to him as he perched on the edge of the bed and handed me a mug of coffee. "Gotta go out babe," he informed me as I blew lightly over the rim of the cup before I took a sip.

I frowned and pouted. He tilted his head and shrugged an apology, "Sorry."

"Will you run me back? I've got to get ready for work."

He kissed my forehead and took a huge sniff of my scent before he stood up. "No time, babe. Boss will run you back."

I smiled and nodded to him. "Okay."

He turned to leave but halted in the doorway. I watched him intently when he didn't turn. "You okay, baby?" I asked hesitantly.

He seemed to be struggling with something but then he turned to me, his pain was written all over his face.

I clambered up and knelt on the bed, my heart in my mouth, "Jax?"

He scrunched up his nose then sighed heavily, "Fran..."

I closed my eyes to the torture in his voice. "Oh God. Go, Jax," I urged.

He turned towards the door again but then flashed back over to me, surrounding my whole body with his as he kissed me so passionately I thought he was trying to consume me.

He stroked my face as he pulled away. "I... I'm still yours, babe" he choked out.

I nodded and took his hand. "I know, Jax. And I'm still yours, every single molecule of me. Lock, stock and barrel, baby." I reassured him.

He puffed out a breath and rested his nose on mine. "I love you, Eve Hudson," he whispered and before I could replicate his sentiment, he had gone.

CHAPTER 25

My shift at Z Bar had never gone so slow before. I had been constantly watching the door for Jax but by midnight, my stint was over and he was still nowhere to be seen.

I had texted Boss to see if he had returned home yet but no joy there either.

"You go Rach, I'll lock up tonight. I owe you for covering for my few weeks off anyway," I said to Rachel as she plonked some dirty glasses on the bar top.

"You sure, hun?" she asked seriously, but I could see the excitement in her eyes. She had just got together with the hottest member of the university football team and her eagerness at leaving early had made me chuckle.

"Go hump your man, Girl." I winked.

She squealed joyfully, grabbed her bag from behind the bar and shot out before I changed my mind.

I piled the glasses into the dishwasher, wiped down the tables and made sure the shelves were restocked before I poured myself a glass of vodka and settled on a stool at the bar.

I checked my phone again but nothing. Surely he had news by now. I wasn't even sure what had actually happened but I presumed she had lost the baby.

Hating to be that pushy woman but needing to know, I braced myself and decided to send him a quick text.

Me:
Hey baby. Any news? x

I left it at that. Didn't really need any more but I was tempted to tell him all sorts. The simplicity of expressing yourself via a text was so much easier than actually saying the words in front of them.

I wanted to tell him how much I loved him. How proud I was of his utter strength to carry on after losing everyone he held close. To tell him I would die for him, walk through hell for eternity to see his brilliant smile. Tell him I would drag him back from the darkness when he was swallowed by it, but then I wanted to tell him how frightened I was of our relationship, how totally consuming it was. How it ate at my soul and I was terrified I would somehow lose him, not be able to keep my hold of him.

After another half hour of phone silence, I seized my bag, locked up behind me and trekked across the student village back to my dorm.

As I passed through the passageway between the shop and the tennis court I heard a stutter of a footstep behind me. I turned to look but shrugged and carried on when there appeared to be nothing there. There was always students hanging about at all hours and I put it down to an amorous couple in the bush.

The more my feet moved the more I was sure there was someone behind me. My heart was starting to surface through my throat, so I pulled out my phone from my bag and dialled Jax. I knew with every instinct in my body that there was someone following me and my legs were starting to tremble.

Jax didn't answer and I cursed under my breath as I tried again. I sped up, desperate to get out of the walkway and into the open area behind my halls. "Fuck, Jax" I scolded when he still didn't answer.

I dialled Boss. As soon as I heard his voice answer, I felt a hand around my mouth. My phone skidded across the pathway and I was dragged into the bushes from behind.

"Hello E," Austin hissed, as he shoved me down on to the ground.

My eyes went wide as I took in his crazy features. His face was red and angry, his teeth were bared, his eyes were wide and frenzied, and his sweaty hands were shaking against my face with his adrenaline.

I struggled against him but his firm grip held me secure underneath him. I shook my head desperately trying to tell him to stop before he did anything he'd regret.

"Thought I'd left?" he snarled. I managed to swallow the bile that was surging up my throat. One of his clammy hands stroked down my face and over my neck, triggering a whimper from my squashed mouth.

"Always thought you were better than me didn't you, E?"

I shook my head wildly. What the hell was he on about?

"All I asked was that you passed a message onto Melissa but you had to get your henchmen to... to beat the shit out of me. All for asking for a favour E," he spat, his spittle splattered my face and I closed my eyes against it.

"No," I mumbled under his hand but I doubt he could understand me. I don't think he was really listening to me anyway; he seemed phased out, somewhere in his own gaga land.

"I think that deserves a bit of retribution, E." *Oh Shit!*

"Austin. No," I muffled under his hand as his other hand slid further down and over my breastbone, his eyes tracking their undertaking before he came to my breast and fondled it harshly.

A sob tore up through my throat as I bucked and thrashed under him. The punch of his tight fist on my cheekbone smarted and a tear slid free.

"Keep – Fucking - Still. Or this will be fucking painful," he jeered.

His hand reached the button on my jeans. I shook my head rapidly, my eyes wide and wild as I started crying properly. I closed my eyes and prayed as he gripped the waistband of my jeans and nudged them down over my hips with my knickers. I screamed under his hand, however, as it slipped down a little, I managed to get my teeth into the flesh at the base of his thumb and I bit down savagely. His blood filled my mouth and I gagged at its taste.

He squealed and when he removed his hand to punch me again I screamed at the top of my voice. I was so proud of my lungs… singing must have helped because the pitch of my scream perforated my own eardrums as well as Austin's.

"You fucking bitch," he shouted as his fist connected with the side of my head and everything went black.

***

My head throbbed, the pain was a thumping pressure and I moaned before I had even opened my eyes.

"E?" Luce whispered from the side of me.

"Mmm," I moaned but still refused to open my eyes.

"You okay?"

"Mmm."

I finally peeled them open to find Luce sat beside me on a chair with her hand in mine. I was desperately searching my brain to try and remember why I was laid in hospital. As she sensed my confusion she squeezed my hand, "You're in hospital, E."

"Yeah." I moaned, then my eyes widened when it occurred to me exactly why I was there.

I scrambled backwards up the bed; my eyes were wide as the terror set in and I gripped Lucy's hand tightly. "Luce... Austin."

She nodded and smiled gently, "Yeah hun, I know."

"Did he... Did he...?" I asked as I squeezed myself to ascertain if there was any soreness.

"No," Boss declared from a dark corner of the room. I jolted in surprise at his voice.

"Boss?" I squinted in the direction of his voice. I saw him approach slowly, his smile was soft even though his eyes showed so much pain.

"Hey, hot stuff." He bent to plant a tender kiss on my forehead.

"What happened after... he punched me in the head. I can't remember... I don't know what he did... I don't know..." I was starting to panic, unsure of what Austin had done when I had been knocked unconscious.

"Hey. Sshhh," Boss soothed. "It's okay, E. Bulk, Romeo, Cam and me got there before he...before he..." He swallowed heavily. I puffed out a large breath and nodded wildly.

"Okay," I choked out and glanced around the room, "Jax?"

Boss shrugged his shoulders. "We can't get hold of him. I have no god damn clue where the prick is!" he snarled.

"What time is it?" I asked, now growing concerned with Jax's disappearance.

"Just gone 5," Luce informed me. I frowned then winced as my cheek bone throbbed.

"*Shit!*" Where the hell was he?

I looked between Luce and Boss, "Did you report it?"

Boss nodded. "Yeah," was all he said before he looked away.

I grabbed his hand. "Boss?"

He rolled his eyes at me. "Well. I realised you were in trouble when I heard you on the phone and we came looking for you. The others kinda' kicked the shit out of the bastard while I picked you up. Police dragged them in."

My eyes widened and I kind of hiccupped... don't ask me why I hiccupped because I have absolutely no idea!

"What the hell? They were just protecting me!" I declared. Boss nodded and shrugged but settled his hand on mine.

"E. Don't blame yourself for this. It's not your fault."

I couldn't help it. I did blame myself. "But... Shit! You shouldn't have reported it, Boss."

He glared at me so hard I quaked under his stare. "That's bullshit, E and you know it. The guy's will be fine and Austin deserves fucking locking away... fuckin' animal!" he snarled as he turned away from me.

"They got any previous, Boss?"

I noticed he cringed but he didn't respond as his phone rang in his pocket. He pulled it out and released an almighty huff when he answered. "Where the fuck are you?" he roared. I could hear the silence on the other end of the line.

Boss was livid, I gathered it was Jax that had called him, probably to find out why the house was empty at 5 O'clock in the morning. "E's in hospital and you had better get your fucking arse down here now. She fucking needs you, you arsehole!"

"Boss, it's okay… it's fine. He had stuff…"

He gave me that killer glare again. "The fuck it's okay, hot stuff… You rang him… You fucking rang him!" he hissed at me.

I heard Jax scream down the phone at him, asking him what the hell had happened.

"Austin tried to… Fuck Jax; he tried to rape her…"

He planted the phone back in his pocket. I presumed Jax had disconnected on the other end. He spun around and punched the wall before he disappeared through the door.

Luce and I stared at each other. "I think he's pissed cos' he didn't get to kick the shit out of Austin," she divulged with a tiny laugh. I nodded. "He cares a lot about you, E. We all do…" Tears flooded in her eyes and she blinked rapidly as she tried to fight them.

"Hey. I'm fine," I whispered as I pulled her hand to my mouth and gave it a small kiss, followed by a smile.

She nodded her head rapidly but sucked in her teeth. "When Romeo called me… I… I really thought he had…"

I clutched her hand tightly and shook my head. "But he didn't. I'm okay," I whispered.

She nodded sternly and wiped her tears away with the back of her hand before she rolled her eyes. "The police wanna talk to you."

I nodded. "Of course," I sighed heavily as the nurse entered the room.

"Hello, Eve. You decided to join us?" she smiled kindly.

I returned her smile. "Didn't wanna be too lazy." I winked then winced as a sharp pain shot through my pupil.

"No winking, love. You've got a right proper black eye there." She chuckled. I knew she wasn't being offensive, just trying to put me at ease.

She took my obs and checked me over before she shoved some pain killers in my hand and passed me a cup of water, "These will help with the pain."

I nodded and swallowed them down as the door opened and a policewoman appeared. "Hi, Eve." She ducked her head slightly as she smiled gently and I groaned internally.

I hated false sympathy. To her I was just another attempted rape victim. One of many, just another number in the sexual assault statistics and to be honest... it fucking stank!

"Are you up to answering some questions?" she asked as she ventured across the room and dragged the spare chair to the other side of the bed.

Didn't look like I had much choice then really.

"Before I answer any questions I want to know what's happening with my friends," I told her sternly.

Her eyebrows elevated slightly. "Your friends?"

"Yes. They got into trouble for coming to help me and apparently now they are all down at the police station."

She nodded and stood before she left the room and went into the corridor.

Luce scowled at me and I narrowed my eyes on her. "I need to know they're okay, Luce. They beat him up for me and now they're in trouble."

"I know, E, but I'm sure they'll be fine." I shrugged. Who could tell?

The policewoman re-entered the room and smiled at me. "They've just been given a warning and they have all been released."

I sighed heavily and beamed at her. "Thank you so much."

She retook her place in the chair and scrunched her nose. "It's no problem, love. I can understand why you are concerned and to be honest I wish I had friends like that." She winked at me and I decided I liked her.

"Yeah, they're..." I sucked on my lips as I suddenly felt emotional. "They're..."

She patted my hand and flipped out her notebook for a diversion. "Okay, Eve. I'm WPC Gemma Broadley, and I'm here to take a statement from you about the incident which occurred in the early hours of this morning in the vicinity of Blythes Hall Student village. Are you okay to answer some questions?"

And so it began...

CHAPTER 26

Jax came barrelling into my room just as Gemma finished my statement and had taken photographs, scraped my fingernails and bagged my clothes for evidence.

She had been lovely, never rushing me. Her questions had been tactful and discreet as she had taken me through it all step by step.

"Babe," was all he said. I saw his Adam's apple bob up and down as he scrutinised my face.

"Your fella?" Gemma whispered in my ear. I nodded. Her eyes twinkled. "Wow," she mouthed. I chuckled slightly but nodded and waggled my eyebrows.

"I'll be in touch Eve," she reassured me as she left.

Luce stood up. "I'll leave you two alone." She nodded comfortingly before she smiled at Jax, then left.

Jax stood chewing frantically on his bottom lip for a while before he crossed the room in three long strides. His fingers stroked across each bruise on my face as his face darkened and his breathing deepened.

"I'm okay," I whispered as I looked up at him.

A low growl reverberated from his chest but he sat on the bed beside me, scooped me up and pulled me onto his lap. His hand threaded through my hair before he pushed my head onto his chest and he settled us back down on the bed.

We lay like that for ages. Just curled up with each other, me taking comfort from him as he took solace from me.

"Babe," he whispered against the top of my head. "I... Fuck!"

"Hey. I'm good. The guy's got there in time," I pacified but he sighed heavily.

"You rang me. Fuck, babe. You fuckin' rang me."

I buried my face in his chest when I couldn't hold back the tears any longer. His breath stunted as I sobbed but he didn't say anything or even move, just let me let it out as he tenderly stroked my back and arm and I gave it him all. Each tear, each piece of my pain, each part of my terror and each chunk of relief for what could have been so much worse.

"So fuckin' sorry babe," he breathed out eventually. "I should have..."

I peeked up at him and shook my head. "Hey, no. You had to deal with Fran. How is she?" I asked as I turned and knelt beside him so I could see him properly.

He puffed out a large heavy breath. "She took an overdose. Lost the baby." Oh God!

"Oh, Jax. I'm so sorry, baby."

I straddled his legs, my thin thighs encompassing his thick ones as I cupped his face and rested my forehead against his.

He clicked his tongue as his face threw out many of his emotions. Something I had rarely witnessed from him but this time he was hurting and he needed me to know that.

I placed a gentle kiss on his nose. "Before you say it Jax... it wasn't your fault. She was already high when she came to the pub." I knew exactly what was going through his head and it was crucial that I helped ease his pain.

"But you said it, E. In the pub."

I frowned and took hold of his hand as I gently traced around each of his fingers, anything to just touch him and try to absorb all his horrible thoughts. "I said what, baby?"

"You said that I was... cruel." His face screwed up as though he was experiencing real physical pain. I bit my lip and wished I could rewind time, just take us back to that night in Z Bar when she came knocking. But who knew if anything would be different?

I swallowed back my guilt and cupped his face. "Baby, yes, there are ways to say things but you are you, and however or whichever way you say things... you're just you. Fran knows you didn't mean to be cruel. Hell, she stormed in fists flying. If a person's gonna behave like that, then they should expect some sort of reaction to it."

He nodded slowly. "Well she got revenge didn't she!" he hissed. I cocked my head, shrugging with incomprehension. "She took me away from you when you needed me." His voice broke as he said the words and my heart ached for him.

"Jax, baby I'm okay. A little shook up yes, a little sore, but I'm okay."

He closed his eyes tightly. "You still mine, babe?" he asked on a whisper as though he was nervous of my answer.

"Lock, stock and barrel, baby" I whispered back as I leaned into him and brushed my lips over his.

A whimper left his throat before his arms surrounded me and he drew me into him. "I love you, Eve Hudson," he hummed against my lips.

"And I love you, Jaxon Cooper."

So fucking much!

✳✳✳

Friday afternoon came around way too quickly. Jax and I were singing loudly to a Kings of Leon song as we made our way down the motorway, back to my Moms.

I had decided to just go for one night with Jax chaperoning me. The last thing I needed was to push my luck that my mother would behave for more than that length of time. I had told her we were coming, so I was hoping she had no orgies planned, especially with Jax being with me... I would have died, and I was optimistic that she would be clean. Well not optimistic... hopeful really!

"You ever think about finding your Mom, Jax?" I asked carefully after our forth song duet.

He sucked air through his teeth and seemed to consider my question but he didn't seem to be offended by it. "Dunno, babe. Tried once when Mary Ann and my Dad died but..." He trailed off, checking his mirrors and I knew it was a diversion. Hell, I was expert at diversions.

I glanced over at him and flipped through his iPod, trying to appear nonchalant. "So what... you couldn't find her or she just...?" I didn't want to finish that sentence.

His lips made many movements, both of them being sucked in and out, pursed, nibbled and licked as he fought with himself about opening up to me.

Eventually he cast me a narrow glance and sighed. "She just didn't wanna... come."

I desperately tried to forbid my eyebrows from hitting my hairline. What sort of mother didn't want to attend her own child's funeral? Bloody Hell!

I was suddenly so angry with that woman. I wanted to hunt her down and hurt her... bad; punish her like she had punished her children for just being there, for just breathing. I wanted to drag her home by her hair and tell her, instil into her how wonderful and caring her son was. How much pain and self-suffering he carried around with him because of her actions, because she was so bloody selfish. Out of all the things I had discovered about her this was just... just beyond belief.

I pulled in a breath and just nodded. I had to be strong for him, not flip out every time he trusted me enough to share a piece of his suffering with me.

"Say it babe," he said quietly. At first I didn't understand what he was saying. "Fucking - Say - It!" He growled this time. I now understood every word and every emotion that was strewing from him.

"I don't think that's a good idea, Jax," I whispered.

He reached over and took my hand, giving me a quick look. "SAY IT!"

I closed my eyes, internally fighting every damn thing I wanted to say... no scream!

"You can say it, babe cos' I fucking think it... all the fuckin' time."

I nodded and swallowed but suddenly I couldn't say them, couldn't get them out because I was crying so hard; crying for this beautiful, loving shell of a man. A man that would have had so much potential in life if it wasn't for the injustice of having fucked up parents! Hell, I knew all about that.

I sobbed in the silence of the car, *beside* him as I wept *for* him, all the time holding onto his hand, never wanting to let him go.

***

We pulled up on the driveway of my old home. The prickle of pressure ran through my spine as I sensed its foreboding welcoming.

"Okay, babe?" Jax whispered beside me and I jolted.

I nodded, took a deep breath and climbed from his car. He pulled our overnight bag from the boot and came to stand beside me.

I felt the body shiver pass through me and I grit my teeth against it. I would not let this win, would not allow its return.

I had seen my head doctor this week for a couple of sessions and so far I hadn't benefitted from anything that had been discussed but I supposed I had to give it time.

"Fight it E," he said sternly as he took my hand.

I exhaled heavily and smiled at him, "Yeah. I'm okay."

His lips hovered over mine as he leaned towards me, "I'm here, babe. You need it, you give me the word."

I swallowed heavily then reached into him and took him under my mouth, reciting each of my emotions as I controlled the kiss and thanked him physically for his assurance.

The front door to the house opened and my mother stood there, a huge grin on her face. I quickly scanned her to see which of her moods manipulated her today. She looked okay but then who could tell with my mother... she was the queen of mercurial.

"Eve," she squealed as she walked down the many steps in front of our affluent, immaculate house; the charade of a happy home.

I walked over to her as Jax flanked me, his presence relaxing me as my mother swept me into her arms. I noticed her frail frame as I embraced her and I furrowed my brow by it.

My mother had always been beautiful, stunning even and now at 37 (Yes, she had been a teenage mum), the drugs had ravaged her body, giving her a drawn face and a skinny frame but she was still striking.

I pulled away and ventured into the house. My whole body tensed as I took a step through the doorway. Jax must have noticed because I felt his comforting hand settled at the base of my spine as his thumb stroked lightly.

Turning to my mother I cringed when I saw her checking Jax out. Her eyes scanned his body slowly, up and down before her lips lifted into a sexual grin. "Well, hello you," she breathed. Christ Mother! Once a groupie, always a groupie.

I coughed slightly and she turned to me, her eyes narrow and steely.

I saw Jax lift an eyebrow at me, bewildered by my mother's outright flirting. "Mom, this is *my* boyfriend, Jax Cooper. Jax, this is my mother Lisa Hudson," I introduced.

"Pleased to meet you, Honey," she whispered huskily as she approached him and reached up to kiss his cheek. Jax smiled tightly and nodded but didn't return her greeting.

Had she just sneaked a look at Jax's crotch? Christ, she had. She had been checking to see if he'd had a reaction to her kiss.

Oh my god!

He hadn't thank god. I sneaked a peek just because I thought you'd want to know, not because I really thought he would have, but I needed the information to reassure you!

"Eve, why don't you take your bag up to your room whilst Jax and I have a little chat," she smirked.

Hell, I was going to prison for murdering my own parent before the weekend was over!

"Jax doesn't chat, Mom."

Her eyebrows lifted in his direction but Jax just shrugged.

"You gonna put the kettle on Mom, we're gasping," I near growled at her. She seemed to shake off some thought before she smiled at me and we walked into the kitchen.

I had always hated this room, its cold steel appliances and fittings always made me feel like it was a hospital lab and I forever expected her to have some young male tied to the metal island that spanned the middle of the huge room; his over large penis stood upright as she experimented with it.

I sat on a stool at the breakfast bar and Jax settled beside me. He cringed at me when my Mom turned her back on us to make coffee and I gave him an apologetic look. "You wanted to come," I mouthed. He returned my look with a resigned expression. I stifled a smile at my huge hulk of a man's embarrassment.

My mom perched on another stool when she had handed us our drinks and I studied her.

Her bleach blonde hair was styled professionally on top of her head, her make-up applied expertly on her face and her clothes screamed money but there was something different about her and I couldn't quite put my finger on it.

Her gaze landed on Jax again and her eyes narrowed marginally. "I seem to recognise you from somewhere, Honey," she purred and I rolled my eyes.

Jax ground his teeth and his own eyes narrowed. "We've met," he growled out in that rough timbre of his.

My mother seemed delighted by his low sexy voice and I grimaced when she squirmed on her stool. "We have?" she gushed.

"Yeah, when you tried to steal E's Gibson," he smirked.

The smile on my mother's face drooped a little and a flash of something ran across her face but she managed to pull it together quickly. "Yes... I apologise for that. I must admit, it wasn't one of my best moments."

I couldn't hold the scoff back. She turned to me but before she could say anything I jumped in. "You gonna tell me what happened?" I asked her.

She pursed her lips and she shrugged, "Just went a bit far, Eve."

I shook my head slowly. "Mom, you've always gone too far before but you've never ended up in hospital," I persisted.

She flapped her hand at me. "I'm fine, Eve. Stop going on!"

I narrowed my eyes on her as I saw the lie in her eyes but decided to drop it whilst she was being defensive.

"So how long are you here for, Honey?" she asked, her whole demeanour morphed into her caring mother personality.

"Just until tomorrow. I have work and Jax has a gig."

She nodded but I saw the disappointment on her face and I felt the usual guilt surge up. She turned back to Jax. "You're in a band, Honey?"

He just nodded at her, she nodded back faintly. I loved that she wasn't getting the attention she wanted from him.

I placed my empty mug on the counter. "I'll take Jax up. He probably needs to freshen up after the run down." I gave her the excuse but I had really just wanted Jax on his own for a few minutes without her eyes on him.

Jax shot off the stool, as if relieved that I was dragging him away. He picked up our bag as I led him up to my room.

I sighed heavily as I shut the door behind us. "Christ, babe." He blew out on a puff and I winced.

"Yeah, sorry. I should have warned you what she was like."

I left Jax to nosey around my teenage bedroom whilst I entered the en-suite.

As I closed the door I gripped the sink tightly and sucked in a huge breath. The urge was overwhelming and I struggled to control it, so I ran the cold water tap until it was bitter cold and held my wrists under it as I counted to thirty.

My hands were blue by the time I removed them but the itch was still in my veins and every hair follicle on my body tingled.

"*Fuck!*"

I started again with the cold water and the counting but this time I tapped my foot with every number I counted.

I reached 24 as Jax came in and I cringed at the fact I had been caught. "Babe, you struggling?"

I nodded but carried on until I reached forty.

Jax had started to run the bath and poured in a vast amount of crème. He took my hands in his and brought them up to his mouth, placing a kiss in each palm. "You need a distraction?" he whispered with a grin.

I grinned back and returned his affectionate kisses with my own. "You still mine, baby?" I asked, needing to hear the reassurance from him.

"Lock, stock and fuckin' barrel, babe."

His hands gripped the hem on my shirt and he lifted it over my head. His eyes roamed over my chest, he brought his lips to my piercing and sited a kiss over it before he ran his tongue over the edge of my bra.

"So fuckin' sexy, E." He breathed as his fingers reached around my back to unhook it.

As he pulled it down my arms, his mouth had already taken advantage of my bare skin as he sucked in a nipple, releasing a groan from me when his teeth gently nibbled on it.

"That's nice," I whispered as I threaded my fingers into his hair and pulled his head further into me.

He moved onto my other breast as he undid my jeans and began his worship again as he pushed my jeans and knickers over my hips.

Suddenly he pulled away and paid attention to the running bath, turning off the taps and swirling the water.

"In," he tipped his chin towards it and I removed the rest of my clothes and climbed in.

I watched Jax hungrily as he peeled off his clothes, revealing a new delicious part of him with every item he removed. "You are so beautiful," I told him and was rewarded to his handsome grin.

He climbed in behind me and pulled me against his chest as he started his labour on me with the sponge, soaping it to an extreme before he proceeded to wash me. His religious dedication to each inch of my skin relaxed me and I soon found myself sighing as I leaned more against him.

His mouth settled on top of my head, "She always like this, babe?"

I knew he was talking about my mother and I tensed up again. If Jax felt my change of posture he didn't mention it but I nodded, "Yeah. She's always been... highly... you know..."

He was quiet for a moment. "Sexed?" he finished for me.

I nodded again and I felt him nod slightly.

He dropped the sponge but continued to bathe me with his hands, both of his huge palms caressed my breasts as his feet hooked around my ankles and pulled my legs wider apart.

"Ace tits, babe." Romantic, was Jax, all the way through!

I smiled to myself. "Ace cock, baby," I replied when I felt his cock rising to attention behind me.

He chuckled with me but I stuttered to a stop when his fingers walked over my ribcage, across my stomach and down until he reached the piercing on my pubic mound. He traced the edge of it and I lifted my hips, begging him to take his fingers lower.

"I need you, Jax" I rasped, then moaned when a single finger stroked downwards and began circling around my pulsing clit.

"How much, babe?"

I groaned again and tried shifting my bottom to get him in the position where I needed him, "God, so much, Jax."

His mouth found my neck and he started sucking in my soft flesh as his fingers dipped inside me.

"Yes, thank you… Ooh that's so… Oh God Jax." Why did this man always turn me into a dithering wreck every time he laid a finger on me?

I was panting, moaning and practically begging for him to bring me off. I reached behind me and took his mighty erection in my fist. He groaned deep into my ear and we fired each other up, working each other towards the oblivion we both craved.

"Make me come, Jax. Please… I need to…" I begged as I drove him in my hand, fast and hard.

He knew what to do. His finger curled into my vagina wall, stroking my G-spot as his thumb flicked relentlessly on my clit.

I shattered into pieces all over him. He growled, bit my neck and pumped his own climax right onto my back. "Christ... Yes..." he choked out as I arched my back and lifted my hips off the bottom of the bath with the force of my climax.

I laid my head on his shoulder. He kissed my nose when I turned my face towards him. "Love you, Eve Hudson."

I smiled widely, never tiring of hearing those words tumble from his lips.

"You hear me, babe?"

I sighed happily. "I hear ya', baby."

I reached both hands around me and hooked them behind his neck "Love you, Jax Cooper."

"I hear ya' babe," he whispered in reply.

CHAPTER 27

We descended back downstairs an hour later as my mother was preparing dinner in the kitchen.

She smirked at me as though she knew exactly what we had been doing but I chose to ignore her, hell, she did it more than I did.

"You need any help?" I asked but she shook her head.

"No it's all good. Sit it's about ready," she replied as I climbed onto a stool beside Jax.

I could hear a phone ringing from somewhere and I glanced questioningly at Jax but he shook his head. Then I spotted a mobile on the edge of the counter and reached for it, checking the name on the display.

"Mom, Frankie," I shook the phone at my mother when she turned as I called her name.

She paled and shook her head whilst she swallowed heavily, "Just leave it." She turned back to dishing out the food but I could feel her tension physically in the room.

"You okay?" I asked her.

She didn't turn but nodded, "Sure, Honey." The smile on her face was forced and excessive when she placed the food on the counter. "Enjoy" she said and walked to the door.

I spun around, "You aren't joining us?"

She shook her head, "No. no I have to... go out. I have to go out."

"Mom?" I urged but she smiled falsely again and left.

Something was really wrong. I worried that she was up to her tricks again and had gotten involved with the wrong people all over again.

"Babe?" I looked at Jax and he was frowning at me. "Okay, babe?" he repeated.

I smiled and nodded. "Yeah, baby, I'm good."

But really I wasn't and the feeling intensified when I heard the front door slam.

***

Jax and I were laid in my bed after making love... mind-blowingly, I might add.

He then asked a question that would change my life forever, or rather, the events that followed that question being asked would alter the course of my life. I just didn't know it yet.

"Babe?"

"Mmm," I mumbled back to him but I could sense his hesitance.

"Is this the room where your Dad died?"

I tensed immediately but he didn't apologise or try to alter his question, just sat patiently waiting for me to answer. "No," I revealed. "We moved here after his death. Mom couldn't wait to spend his insurance money," I added bitterly.

We were both silent for a while. Jax's fingers were rhythmically stroking up and down my back as he rested his mouth in my hair. "Did they ever find them?"

I shook my head but I was fighting with myself whether to open up and tell him everything, my final secret, to tell him my father's last request and the sheer terror that had followed me around for the previous five years because of what he told me.

"Jax," I said quietly.

"Babe?"

"You... you with me baby?"

He paused and at first I thought he didn't realise the context of my words but he answered slowly and confidently. "Babe. If I was any further with you, I'd be your fuckin' soul."

I nodded and took a deep breath. "I need to get something."

I clambered off the bed and entered my bathroom before retrieving the small flick-knife I had in my cabinet and prised the front side off the bath. I felt across the ridges of the floorboards until I felt the slight groove that ran across the edge of one of them and dug the knife into it, popping the small joint of wood up. Reaching through the tiny space I extended my fingers into the gap and pulled out the tiny item.

I flicked it around a few times in my fingers before I stood back up and turned to enter the bedroom. Jax was leaning on the doorframe, silently watching me. "Shit, Jax." I jumped a mile.

His eyes were narrow and he cocked his head slightly. "Clue me in, babe."

I nodded. "That's what I'm doing, Jax" I whispered.

He frowned. "Why are you whispering?"

I took a deep breath as well as his hand and led him back over to my bed, snatching my laptop off my desk on the way. "Sit down."

He studied me but perched himself in the middle of the bed and I crawled up beside him, sitting on my knees I looked at him seriously.

"What I'm gonna show and tell goes out to no-one, Jax." His eyes narrowed on me but he nodded. "I need to hear ya', baby." I needed the confidence behind the spoken words before I disclosed any further.

"I hear you babe," he said as he took my hand and squeezed it.

He could sense my nerves and he stroked his thumb across my knuckles soothingly.

After a long moment I opened up to the man I loved.

"When I was twelve I was madly into all things criminal, spies and CSI and all that kind of crap." Jax smiled softly and I nudged him humorously. "Hey, I was twelve," I defended.

"Well, for Christmas that year my Dad bought me all kinds of spyware. You know invisible pens, booby traps and stuff but one present was a video camera and it was disguised as a book."

I climbed off the bed and walked into my walk-in wardrobe and grabbed the item off the shelf then took it back to Jax. I regained my position next to him but held the book in my lap, smiling at it and also hating the thing with my very core. Jax noticed the pain on my face and rested his hand on my thigh.

I smiled at him and continued. "When I became thirteen I became addicted with movies like any normal teenager. Many nights I'd hole myself up in my room and watch DVD after DVD and I built up a supply of sweets and chocolate to divulge in whenever I watched."

Jax's brows rose and I grinned mischievously. "My mom would have killed me if she knew I had that much stash so I hid it."

I puffed out a nervous breath. Jax patiently waited for me to carry on, his thumb now spinning patterns gently into my bare thigh. "I noticed after a few nights that my hoard was depleting quite rapidly. I knew either Cam or Aaron was stealing it so..."

I paused and Jax clicked his tongue. "You set up the camera and recorded your room." he answered for me.

I nodded slowly and sucked on my teeth. Jax's eyes closed painfully and he hissed through his teeth. "You taped them didn't you," he said quietly and slowly, more of a statement than a question.

I nodded again. "Y...Yeah..." I near choked out.

I reached over for my laptop and plugged in the USB and fired up the video, my heart beating way too rapidly when it started.

A sob tore from me as it showed my dim bedroom the night of my father's death. Jax grabbed my hand tightly and shuffled nearer so his thigh was resting against mine as he watched a thirteen year old me asleep.

Voices were heard through the tiny speakers of my laptop as it displayed my bedroom door open and my father and a man enter.

Teenage me scrambled backwards on the bed as the man sat beside me and stroked my cheek.

Jax stiffened beside me whilst he watched but I couldn't keep my eyes off the fuzzy image of my wonderful Dad, the man who had loved me unconditionally, besides my many flaws as a child.

The footage continued to show the man fondle my under-developed breast whilst discussing something with my father, then my Dad left the room.

Jax growled when it displayed the young me shoot off the bed and flatten myself against the wall as the man shouted at me. He near roared when it revealed the man grab my hair and yank me back on the bed when I made a run for it.

"*Shit, babe.*" Jax snarled and squinted at me, as though the image of what was happening on the laptop screen burnt his eyes.

"Keep watching," I grated out.

He closed his eyes for a moment then returned his agonised gaze to the screen. It was now showing the man trying to force my small nightdress over my chest. Jax began to shake, "I can't watch this, E... shit... it's..."

I palmed his cheek and nodded in encouragement, "It's okay, it stops in a moment. Just after the point where I scream..."

And it did. It stopped showing me being molested as it now showed my Dad rush back into the room, another man close on his heels as if to stop my Dad entering back in the room.

I was now struggling to breathe as I watched in horror as my father yanked the man off me and a fight ensued. I watched in tortured silence as my Dad struggled with the two huge men.

I made a funny gurgling sound when my father suddenly dropped to the floor and the two men stood over him, one with a knife in his hand and one with a gun pointed at my head.

"Ooh Christ..." Jax choked on his own sob.

I was becoming a little hysterical. It had been near five years since I had watched it and it brought back so many... just so many...

It then exposed one of the men yank my hair and hiss at me that if ever I told they would hunt me down and torture me painfully and slowly.

Jax was struggling with his composure beside me. I climbed onto his lap to offer comfort to both of us.

The men left my room and it then revealed me kneeling beside my Dad, my ear to his face while he choked out his last words.

"What did he say?" Jax asked on a whisper.

I swallowed down the lump in my throat and touched my father's face on the paused screen. "He told me he loved me so much and then he said... he said... 'be careful, Eve. Use it as insurance only because they will hurt you princess, they'll hurt you real bad if they know you have it'."

The tears streamed down my face as I heard my Dad's final words loud and clear in my head as I watched him die on a fucking computer screen... over and over again!

Jax placed the laptop on the floor before he scuttled me in tightly. "He must have known I was recording it, it used to show a red light as it taped so I presume he noticed it," I divulged between heart-broken retches.

"Shush, babe," he whispered in my ear whilst he let all my emotion flow as I finally freed my final secret, to the first person ever, but to a man I trusted impeccably. The secret that had tortured me for years, the secret that, if ever revealed would no doubt cost me my life.

Jax rocked me and whispered loving things to me. We remained like that, just rocking and loving until we both fell asleep emotionally and physically exhausted.

CHAPTER 28

My mumbled brain registered a noise but I couldn't fathom out if it was in my dream or outside of it. Opening my eyes, I soon found out the reason.

I couldn't move; my body and brain both froze as I watched my mother sat on the floor beside my bed with my laptop on her knee whilst she watched my home movie.

I choked out an incoherent noise as my brain finally kick-started. I shot off the bed, completely and utterly naked and snatched it away from her horror-struck face.

Glancing at the screen I was horrified to find she had watched the whole film. Her eyes lifted to mine and they widened in shock. "E... E... Eve..."

"Shit, Mom," I shouted. "What the fuck are you doing in here?"

Jax shook himself behind me then groaned when he realised what was happening. "Fuck!" he hissed.

I spun on him. "You shouldn't have fuckin' left it there. You shouldn't have let us fall asleep with it... there." I pointed harshly at the floor as I screamed at him.

He grimaced and nodded his head painfully, "E..."

I shook my head wildly and turned back to my mother. "Well? What the fuck are you doing in here?" I barked at her.

She seemed to be in shock as she remained immobile and silent. I approached her and placed my hands on her shoulders as I shook her hard like a rag doll.

"Fuck!" I screamed as I pulled on my jeans and t-shirt, foregoing any underwear. Then something occurred to me and I narrowed my eyes on her. "Did you sneak in to catch a glimpse of Jax?" I asked coldly and calmly.

Her eyes flashed and I knew I had her sussed. "Fuck, Mom!" I spat in disgust. She finally scrambled to her feet and floored me in one punch.

"Don't you ever fucking talk to me like that again, you ungrateful little whore." Spit flew in all directions and I realised she was high as I scurried back towards the bed, knowing exactly how violent she became when she'd scored.

Jax was off the bed in one large movement before he grabbed my mother by the back of her shirt and carried her out of the room, leaving me sat on the floor stunned by both their actions.

What the hell was I going to do? I knew she would use this to her advantage so before she returned I quickly hid the USB back where it had rested silently for five years.

Jax came back in and it wasn't until that point I realised he was in all his glory. "Christ, Jax. That's exactly what she came in for and you have just given it to her on a fucking platter." I shouted at him as I pulled out our bag and stuffed everything we had brought into it.

His brows raised and he sighed. "I take it we're going back early, babe."

"Aren't you a clever boy?" I snarled at him, absolutely furious with him even though I knew he wasn't at fault but he was just there...

I was pinned under him on the bed within a fraction of a second. "Calm the fuck down, babe" he said gently but I shook my head at him and punched his arm when the familiar itch vibrated my veins.

"Do you even realise what she will do with this?"

He reared back and frowned at me, "What? What can she do with it?"

I scoffed incredulously as I stared at him, "Fucking leverage, Jax. Fucking great big drug sharks and she now has info on them. Info that could get me killed! What do you think she'll fuckin' do with it?"

Realisation crossed his face and he knelt back, releasing me from his hold. "*Shit,*" he hissed as he ran his fingers through his hair in frustration. I nodded slowly at him.

"You put it back, babe?"

I nodded again and sighed as I saw the guilt cross his face. "I'm sorry, Jax. It's not your fault and I shouldn't have... shouted at you."

He shrugged but nodded, "I hear ya', babe." He pulled on his clothes then turned to me with a serious expression, "She hit you a lot, E?"

I pulled in a breath. "When she's high, yeah. Or when she's withdrawing, or when she's craving, or when I won't open my legs for her dealers, or when she's in a mood…"

He clicked his tongue and swore under his breath as he stroked the new bruise on my cheek.

"You ever wish you could go with them, Jax?" I asked quietly.

He frowned and drew breath, understanding what I was saying, "Sometimes." He palmed my cheek; the emotion on his face broke my heart. "I miss her more and more every day but… she's gone, babe, just like your Dad, and there aint anything we can do to get them back."

I sighed as a tear slid free and he tilted my head back. "But following them doesn't mean you'll join them, babe." I gazed at him as his words penetrated my brain and I nodded. "You hear me, babe?" he asked softly as his mouth rested against my forehead.

"I hear ya', Jax."

"You still mine, babe?"

"Lock, stock and barrel, baby," I whispered as his lips found mine. His kiss was everything I needed at that moment, soft, tender and so full of love it forced the tears to drip free.

"Love you, Eve Hudson," he breathed against my mouth as his hand settled on the nape of my neck. "So fuckin' much, babe. You're inside me E, you own me, possess me and fuckin' rule me… every god damn fibre of me, every beat of my heart and every fuckin' breath I take. They're yours, babe because I'm yours."

I gripped his hair and pulled him back to me. The emotion in his kiss and the words he had just spoken drown out all the vibrations in my blood, all the electric surges that had been building in my brain and all the cravings for the release in the pain.

"And I'll always be yours, baby. Wherever I am or whatever I'm doing. I'm yours. All of me, every inch of my body, every fragment of my soul and every piece of my heart because I love you right back, Jaxon Cooper."

CHAPTER 29

3 MONTHS LATER

"Oh My God. I can't do this Bri," I choked out to Brian, Room 103's new Tech guy.

They had hired him part time to tune all their instruments, now more and more bookings were coming in for gigs.

Room 103 had been so popular lately, even the local TV and radio had dragged them in for interviews and performances and the guys were lapping it up.

Luckily I still only sang 'Shocking Heaven' with them and I was so grateful for that as I stood stage side, waiting to join them in mine and Jax's song whilst they sang their first four songs at the festival.

The place was heaving, the noise levels were astronomical as was the atmosphere and I smiled as I watched Jax lap it up. He was in his element and had interacted and rocked the crowd with ease.

There were at least 70,000 people out there, and Room 103 had enraptured each and every one of them and I was so proud of them.

"You'll rock their fuckin' socks off, sugar," Bri inspired as he stepped aside whilst a festival sound man checked my mic and earpiece. I nodded to him when it tuned into the action on stage.

Aaron squeezed my arm and I gave him a wobbly smile to which he chuckled and then he stuck his thumb up as Jax reeled in the crowd ready for me.

The stage set guy motioned me up the stairs so I was nearer to the stage. He grinned and winked when I let out a whimper. "It will all disappear when you get out there. Don't worry, love."

I nodded and checked myself over. I had chosen tight low rise black jeans and a cool white leather Basque and everybody had lifted their jaws off the floor when I stepped out of the changing rooms in one of the porta-cabins.

I had left my hair loose but Luce had mashed it up before applying my make-up for me when my hands had shaken so much I couldn't apply any of it without resembling a clown.

The stage team were frantically trying to set up our props below the stage as Jax started to introduce the next song. A woman with a stern glare ushered me over and I sat on the small wrought iron table that was part of our set.

I was to be sat outside a cardboard café on a little table, drinking coffee alone while Jax would be perched on a motorbike on the other side of the stage, surrounded by girls.

It had cost a fortune to hire the dancers and choreographers, but it had been worth every penny when we'd hired a professional to film our music video, and at the last count it had received 817, 592 hits on YouTube.

I raised my hand and made an okay sign to the sound guy when he asked if I was ready through the little earpiece stuck in my ear. He started counting down to me with his fingers and as he put each one down my pulse went up. And then the middle section of the stage started to rise and so did my stomach.

"Give it your all for the fuckin' amazing, Eve Hudson... my beautiful fuckin' woman, and let's start shocking those fucking angels!"

I rolled my eyes at Jax's introduction but the crowd roared when I appeared from below. Jax strode across the room and straddled the bike whilst the stage filled with gorgeous women in skimpy outfits as they surrounded Jax around the bike. I bet they were frozen... it was bloody February!

I glanced over at Jax as Romeo started the song with a small slow riff, he gave me a small wink. I picked up my false coffee cup and pretended to drink whilst Jax sang his first verse as I looked the other way and he watched me whilst he sang. When Boss hit a rock rhythm on the drums to bring Jax in to the first chorus I could feel myself calm as my section approached.

Jax diverted his attention to the girls at the same time as I looked over at him and sang my verse. I could feel myself flow and open up as my blood surged through my veins when the crowd roared their appreciation to my part, and I recognised our loyal fans start a trend when the crowd started the regular chant of 'E, E, E, E...'

Jax and I looked at each other across the stage as we both delved into the chorus together, his smile was awesome as he sang and I couldn't help but smile back.

I diverted my gaze again when Jax sang another solo verse and then after another chorus, Romeo came in with his solo riff and I stood and took a step towards Jax. He mirrored my movement after climbing off the bike and we slowly made our way over to each other just in time to come in with the middle 8 section.

The mass of people all swayed as we sang and then when Jax finished with the outro, the crowd roared and whistled and cheered. Jax grabbed me and kissed the damn life out of me. He was primed and pumped, "Gonna fuck you so hard, babe. Fuckin' epic."

He always had such a way with words.

I laughed loudly as the crowd continued to cheer. Boss, Romeo and Bulk came forward to take the applause now their set was over.

We all walked off the stage to Cam, Luce, Aaron and Brian as they popped the cork on a bottle of champagne and we toasted Room 103 success.

A tall man approached Jax and held out his hand, "Jaxon Cooper?"

Jax nodded to the bloke he smiled, "Hi. Harry Galloway, RMG."

Every single eye in our group widened as we stared at the man from the hottest British Recording label. "Oh… Hey…" Jax stuttered.

Harry smiled at Jax's stunned expression, "I'm wondering if we could go somewhere for a discussion about signing you up with us."

Jax's jaw dropped and Boss kind of whimpered whilst I just stood immobile.

Harry turned to me. "This involves you too, Miss Hudson. We want to promote your duet, Shocking Heaven."

I sort of coughed as my legs trembled. "You want me?" I choked out.

He laughed and nodded happily, "Yep, Miss Hudson. We want you too."

My eyes widened and all I could think of was if I'd get my teeth whitened. Maybe? I mean they would look better for it, even though they were quite decent, a little whitening never hurt.

Six weeks later our song shot to number 1 in the British charts and it stayed there for nine weeks.

***

Over the next six months, Room 103 had three number one hits, made an album that shot straight in at number two and we were currently on tour of the British Isles, performing at all the major cities from north to south… in an upgraded tour bus though.

We had made music videos, had interviews with top talk show host's and had many photo shoots and even been asked to perform at a charity concert.

I had dropped university and had become either a backing singer for Jax or a joint lead vocal on a few songs. I had a small solo part in our new song 'Bring it home' but what had mostly amazed me over the previous months was the attention I received from our fans. They seemed to adore me. For some strange reason.

I received gift after gift as well as huge appreciation from them when I sang at our concerts. I had even been approached by a top cosmetic company asking if I would be the face for one of their products.

It had all been overwhelming and a little surreal but we were doing great and we coped with everything like professionals.

The only thing I hated was the lack of privacy and the god damn groupies who hung onto Jax like withdrawing leeches at every bloody moment, even though we were notorious as a couple.

Mine and Jax's relationship had gone from strength to strength and our love had grown to a level that neither of us wanted to break from. It consumed us as well as fed us. I loved him with my very soul and he loved me with all his heart.

Boss had been hinting that Jax was going to be asking me the biggie. I had slapped him for letting it slip, but I was secretly excited, every time he took me out or we had a romantic moment I was on tenterhooks waiting for him to ask.

***

We were in London, just after performing the last concert of our summer tour when we received a phone call that would change everything.

Jax and I had just climbed into bed, exhausted from a gruelling few months of back to back concerts, but desperate for a quickie when I heard a yell from the living area on the tour bus.

Boss and Bulk were screaming wildly like children on E numbers and fizzy pop. Jax groaned as he elevated himself from my breasts. I quickly pulled his head back down, "Ignore them, Bulk will have scored on Fifa."

Jax chuckled as he pulled a nipple back into his mouth and I moaned in appreciation. His tongue circled as his teeth nibbled and I was soon squirming my hand under his boxers and yanking them down his legs.

We were both always horny after a concert. I knew why the other band members hooked up with the many groupies. The adrenaline from a show always quickly turned into arousal once we came down from the high and Jax was like an animal... I was never quite sure where he got all his sexual energy from. Not that I complained... of course!

Rolling us both over I straddled him and slid down on him immediately, causing us both to groan in satisfaction.

I rode him hard as he grabbed my hips and rocked upwards, spearing me brutally. "Fuck yeah," he growled as I spun round so my back was to him and continued to pump myself wildly on him.

He sat up behind me and brought his hands around to cup my breasts, teasing my nipples with his fingers as my orgasm built briskly.

"Fuck Jax," I whimpered when I suddenly found myself on all fours and Jax now thrusting into me deep and hard.

"You – Like – It - Hard." He roared between each thrust as he grabbed my hair and yanked me upright. "Ride me, babe" he ordered. I didn't argue as I drove us wild and just as my climax hit, the bedroom door flew open. Typical.

"Arghh" I screamed as Jax's hands covered both of my breasts from Boss as I scrambled for the sheet to cover myself with.

"What the fuck, Boss?" Jax glowered but Boss was on a high and didn't notice. Or didn't care.

He just grinned widely. "America want us," he declared bluntly.

My head tilted as though I hadn't heard him correctly, "What?"

He couldn't keep the grin off his face. "Red Music just contacted Gary. They want us; they want Room 103 to storm fucking America!"

My breath stuttered and I stared at him, "You shittin' us, Boss?"

He shook his head slowly, "Uh-uh, hot stuff. We made it big, baby."

"Oh. My. God." I breathed and fell back onto Jax, who just placed a gentle kiss on my neck.

"You want this, E?" he asked and I frowned at him.

"Don't you?" He smiled and nodded but it looked a little strained. "You sure Jax cos' if it's not what you want then we don't do it, baby?"

"I just want you to be happy, babe." Was all he said. I cupped his face as I turned to him but he smiled widely and I wondered if I had read him wrong.

"I am happy, Jax" I assured him.

He nodded and smiled, "Then we do it, babe."

Boss squealed and left our room as he went in search of the others. Jax snuggled us back down under the sheet. I rested my cheek on his hard chest but he let out a sigh, "You still mine, babe?"

"Lock, stock and barrel baby," I whispered back to him.

Jax always needed to hear this whenever he was feeling insecure or unhappy, so I knew something was on his mind but after numerous nudges that night he never disclosed what was troubling him, so I just put it down to nerves.

It was a huge life change, moving to America, even if it was temporary. I knew I would miss my family and Luce with my very core but it was also something the band needed to undertake to find themselves.

It was a massive opportunity and although Jax realised that, I still had the suspicion that he didn't want it as much as the others. But Jax being Jax, he would grit his teeth just to see everyone else happy.

The contract was signed in the next few days and within four weeks we would officially be American rock stars.

All the arrangements had been made. Where we would live, our schedule and start out tour had been planned to within each daily minute and the studio had been reserved. We had been booked onto an American talk show and numerous music channel attendances.

All our personal staff had been hired, from bodyguards to personal assistants and it was all extremely exciting.

CHAPTER 30

The week before we were due to leave I received a phone call from the hospital to say my mother had collapsed. Aaron and I waited in the waiting room for the doctor to discuss her condition.

"You ready now then, E?" Aaron asked, as a diversion to all the waiting.

I nodded and smiled. "Yeah. I've just one or two things to see to. I wish you'd come with us, Aaron."

He squeezed my hand, "No, E. I need to finish my Bachelors and I'm not leaving Luce."

I nodded in understanding. "Yeah I know, I'm just gonna miss you, bro."

I glanced around the dismal room, the torn sofa and the peeling wallpaper gave me a sense of foreboding. I couldn't shake the ominous feeling that had engulfed me. "I see Cam came then," I said snottily.

Aaron scoffed. "Yeah, okay E. Like you expected him?" he answered as the doctor entered the room and both of us shot upright.

"Are you both Lisa Hudson's family?" he asked as he settled on the sofa and gestured that we did the same.

My stomach dropped through my arse. There was only one reason a doctor would ask you to sit, and that was so you didn't fall the fuck down when the news hit you.

He took a deep breath and I grabbed Aaron's hand. "I'm afraid your mother's had a gastrointestinal bleed caused by her cancer."

I frowned and then giggled, "I'm really sorry Dr...?"

"Waters," he divulged.

"Dr Waters, but I think you have the wrong family. My mother doesn't have cancer." I felt quite awful for him because he could get in trouble for a blunder like this.

"Miss Eve Hudson?" he asked and I nodded.

"Yes. My mother is Lisa Hudson."

He nodded slowly and took my hand but I snatched it back and shook my head. "I am afraid your mother was diagnosed with gastric cancer about three months ago, but has refused any treatment so far."

His words kind of became physical, because it felt like they had just formed into a solid being and slapped me around the face.

"No, I'm sorry doc but you really ought to get your facts right before you come in here and frighten people," I scolded just as Jax came in.

He took one look at my ashen face and was instantly beside me, his arm wrapped around my waist. I turned to him and laughed. "This stupid doctor's got the wrong patient," I giggled to Jax.

His face was painful. "Don't look like that, it's fine. He's just got it wrong that's all," I informed him. Jax turned to Dr Waters.

"Doc?" Jax asked. Even in front of professional's he never conversed properly.

"You are?" Dr Waters asked.

"Husband, Doc", Jax informed him. I quickly covered my left hand fingers.

The doctor nodded but he wasn't stupid, although he let it slide. "Mrs Hudson was diagnosed with stomach cancer three months ago. She has refused to have any surgery and until she agrees there is nothing we can do. She suffered a gastric bleed yesterday. We've drained the blood so she's comfortable at the moment."

"No. Look, I want to speak to your superior. I am not sitting here and listening to your bullshit," I spat out.

Jax swallowed and Aaron remained silent.

"Babe." Jax turned my face to look at him but I jumped backwards.

"NO! No, Jax… No… no… n…" Jax huddled me up as a strangled scream erupted from my throat, "Noooo."

"I'm here, babe" Jax whispered in my ear as I broke down and wept against him.

"I'll let you have a moment. Come and find me when you're up to discussing the options for your mother." I heard the doctor tell Aaron.

"Yeah," he said quietly.

"No Jax, she can't. Why does she have to be so damn selfish all the fucking time?" I cried.

"Shush, babe." He led me over to the sofa and I scrambled onto his lap, desperately trying to climb inside him so he could absorb all my pain, take it all away and stop the torment I felt at that moment.

Yes, she was a bitch and had never been a great mother, but there had been times when I was little where she would play dollies and we would sit in the garden and have a teddy bears picnic. Or she would roll up her trousers and splash in the puddles with me on a rainy day, or the time we had both decorated the shed for my dad by just splattering paint all over the walls; we'd had so much fun that day.

She was still my mother and had been a good one until she'd found the joy of heroin.

"She can't, Jax. No, I won't allow it!"

"E. Talk to her." He urged but I shook my head.

"Why should I? She hasn't given me a second thought," I barked.

He nodded solemnly but deep down I knew he was right.

Aaron was still silent and I cast him a glance. He was sat on the sofa with his head in his hands, the sight of him so defeated, broke me. He was my twin brother and I was here to help protect him. There was no way I could protect him from the horrors of cancer.

I closed my eyes for a second then picked up my bag and went in search of my mother.

***

She was asleep when I walked into her dimmed room alone. I looked at her ravaged figure. I hadn't seen her since the night Jax and I stayed over, the sight of her was a shock and it brought an involuntary gasp forward. She had lost a vast amount of weight, her eyes appeared sunken in her head and her face was long and drawn.

She opened her eyes and squinted against the darkness. "Eve?"

I swallowed and approached her slowly as my jellied legs wouldn't let me go any faster. "Hey," I said simply.

She reached her hand out to me and I softly clasped it, noticing how bony and rough it was. "Why didn't you tell me?" I asked quietly.

She looked away as if ashamed by her actions but when she turned back I saw her own pain and desolation. "Because you weren't there, Eve. You went and didn't..." She swallowed her words. I was suddenly so angry with her.

"And why wasn't I there, mother? Why? Because you tried to get your eyes on *my* boyfriend's body *before* you punched me and called me a whore," I spat at her.

"You know mom, I've put up with so much of your shit over the years and I have always stood by you, always took whatever you dished, always received every fucking punch you ever gave me, always swallowed whatever abuse you said to me."

And then I leaned in close so she wouldn't miss my next words. "And I always *paid* your drug debts! What kind of mother does that to her only daughter?"

She flinched bodily but I saw her shut down and lock me out. "God damn it, mother! Don't bolt out on me again. We need to talk about this," I shouted at her.

"I'm dying, Eve... I'M FUCKING DYING!! ISN'T THAT ENOUGH?" she screamed.

I stood in silence, listening to her ragged breathing, sucking on my damn lips like a sulking four year old who wanted her mummy.

"But I need you," I whispered.

She scoffed loudly. "You never needed me, Eve. Your father made sure of that!"

I took a step back at the bitterness in her voice. "Don't you dare drag him into this."

"Why not, Eve? He wasn't the fucking saint you thought he was!" she spat out and I clenched my fist.

"No! That man died for you. Died because he tried to stop your fucking pimp collecting on a debt!"

The laugh that erupted from her froze my bones. "You believe that Eve because I've let you believe that."

I took another step back. "Don't do this," I choked out.

"Why, Eve? You've blamed me for the last five years. Don't you really wanna know what happened that night?"

I shook my head rapidly. "No. It was your fault. You took too much mother, always took too fucking much. Take, take, fuckin' take, never ever fucking gave anything back," I bellowed at her.

Her face contorted in rage. "Your precious father made me fuck three men that night, Eve. Just because he wanted to fucking score! And it was him that owed those bastards who wanted you... not me, Eve. Not me!" she screamed at me.

I fell backwards, my legs finally giving way. "You're lying!"

She shook her head sadly. "Why do you think I never came to help you? I couldn't get to you after they... after they killed him!"

I shuffled backwards, desperate to get away from her lies. My Dad was a good man, he wouldn't... he wouldn't do that... "No..." I whispered. Her face scrunched up in pain at my pain. "But you, you let them all at me after he died..." I argued.

She sighed heavily. "Yes Eve, I did. It was too late for me by then. I know I was a shit mother, hell, I *am* a shit mother. I had followed your father for so many years, because he didn't give me a choice. Always had to do what Robert said!" she said resentfully. "Do this Lisa, do that Lisa. Make these men happy, Lisa. I need to score, Lisa. Open your legs, Lisa..."

"STOP IT!" I screamed, covering my ears with my hands.

"NO EVE! It's about time you knew. Your real father... he..."

I shook my head rapidly, covered my ears and started to sing loudly. "Please stop..." I whimpered.

The tears flowed down both of our cheeks as she finally released her biggest kept secret ever, her biggest pain, and her biggest heartache. "He loved me

Eve, so damn much. He adored the ground I walked on. Made me feel like a princess."

She had a glaze over her eyes now as she reminisced. "I was going to leave Robert for him. I was so in love with him. He was my one, you know? Just like you and Jax, Eve... so fucking in love. He was my soul, my life." A huge dirty, snotty sob tore from her lips. "Robert he... he hunted him down Eve, hunted him like an animal and... and... I never saw him again. He took him from me..."

I was going to vomit and I frantically searched the room for anything to be sick into but it was too late, it exploded everywhere along with my mind.

I saw my mother drop out of bed and start crawling towards me, her hands and knees shuffling on the cold tiled floor whilst the drip stand trundled behind her as she tried to reach me.

I remained immobile, just staring at her as she came closer. Her face white with her obvious agony, but it was her emotional pain that ripped through me as she finally got hold of me, finally and at long last, held the daughter that just wanted her love.

She finally loved me. And she told me, over and over and over again.

Her heartache was written all over her face and I knew then that she hadn't received the treatment because she just didn't want to be here any longer. She had taken enough and she was desperate to finally let it all go. She wanted to be free.

CHAPTER 31

I slowly walked back to the man I loved… to break his heart, my heavy legs not wanting to make the journey that would end my life.

He knew as soon as I opened the waiting room door that I was going to hurt him because he shook his head, wildly at first then more slowly, then with a sob as I took his hands in mine.

"I… she needs me here, Jax." I whispered as he cried into my chest, his hands frantically pulling at my clothing when we'd dropped to the floor in the waiting room.

"Babe, no, no, no… I won't go either, E." He said but I shook my head and cupped his face.

"Baby, you can't back out now. The contract has been signed. They won't let you out of it without a hefty court war, everything is set up in America and most of all, and you can't do that to the guy's. They've worked as hard as us for this."

I sobbed right along with him but I knew I couldn't go to America. My mother would need me now. She had relented and finally agreed to have her stomach removed and start a bout of chemotherapy, and there was no way I could let her go through that alone.

My heart tore right in two on that hospital floor that day, right along with my lover's.

My soul shattered into a million pieces in that hospital waiting room that day, right along with my lover's.

And my life ended that day, whilst I sat on my lover's knee and witnessed his own life end, right alongside me.

***

It was the night before the band left. Jax had taken me out for a romantic meal and we were sat, cross legged in the middle of his bed, just touching each other.

Our fingers explored each other, committing every damn groove, every ridge, every bump and blemish to memory. He reached behind him, opened his bedside drawer and pulled out a small blue box. He turned back to me and took my hand, his face fighting with each of his emotions.

"You mine, babe?"

"Lock, stock and barrel, baby" I whispered in return.

He nodded and opened the box. My breath caught. Inside was the most exquisite platinum eternity ring I had ever seen. It was utterly breathtaking.

He sucked on his teeth. "Wanted it to be a wedding band babe, but... well... we'll save that for when I return."

He took it out and slipped it over my finger. He'd done his homework because it was a perfect fit. "It's beautiful," I breathed.

"Nearly as beautiful as the woman wearing it," he whispered as he cupped my face and drew my mouth under his.

I burnt his kiss to my mind, making sure I would remember exactly how perfect he felt as he joined our mouths.

He pressed us backwards onto the bed as he consumed me in his kiss, as though he wanted to soak up every part of my soul. My hands found his hair as I held on for dear life, holding him to me, wishing I could keep him there forever.

He moaned into my mouth as I drew his t-shirt over his head, desperate to touch his skin, feel every inch of him and that's exactly what I did. I rolled him over and idolised every single part of him, torturously slow because I didn't want to ever stop.

I knelt between his legs as he knelt before me and unbuttoned my shirt, slowly peeling it off my shoulders before his fingers studied me; tracing the edge of my bra, my breastbone piercing and along my collar bones. His thumbs leisurely ran up my throat, across my jaw, over my lips and along my cheekbones before his mouth repeated their trek.

He removed my bra and as he cupped my breasts in his large hands. He just sat and gazed at me, his hands caressing me tenderly.

I arched my back and pushed into him on a sigh. "So beautiful," he whispered before his mouth sited wet kisses over the swell of my breasts and then down to my nipples as he adored them softly.

He slid the zip on my skirt and pushed it over my hips as I wriggled out of it, along with my knickers.

He trailed a finger down the centre of my chest and stomach until he reached my Christina piercing, twirling it around his finger as his eyes held mine. "This will always be mine."

I covered his hand with my own, "Always, baby. Always yours."

He nodded at my reassurance and slid his finger further down and into my vagina. "Mine."

"Yours," I moaned as my eyes closed.

"Need to see ya', babe. Need to see your soul." I opened my eyes and gazed at him as he gave me a soft smile.

He gripped the tops of my arms and pulled me flat on top of him as he lay backwards on the bed and kissed me forever. I slid onto him and made love to him tenderly, torturously slowly and so lovingly that neither of us wanted it to end.

He rolled us over until he was above me and continued our gentle loving, all the time holding my eyes with his.

His fingers slid onto the side of my head. "I love you so much, Eve Hudson. I'll never stop. Wherever I am, I'll always love you."

A tear slid free as Jax came forcefully when my own climax erupted. At that moment I hated that orgasm with everything I was because I knew it would be the last one Jax would ever give me.

✳✳✳

"Gonna miss you, hot stuff," Boss choked against my ear as he hugged me tight in the private departure lounge at Heathrow airport the next morning.

I had already said my goodbyes to Romeo and Bulk and now I was saying farewell to one of my best friends.

"I'm gonna miss you too, Boss."

He leaned back and studied me. "Take care of him for me, Boss" I whispered as I kissed his cheek. He squeezed my hand and headed through the gate.

And then there was my man, stood before me, his beautiful face white with pain and sorrow as we both silently gazed at each other. He stepped into me and I felt my throat close in.

God, I couldn't do this. It was too fucking hard.

He kissed me so heart-wrenchingly we were both drinking my tears as they slid down my face, over my lips and into our mouths, their saltiness penetrating our taste buds.

"I love you, Eve Hudson. I'll always love you, babe. You're in my heart so deep a piece of you injects my veins with every beat. You're in my head so intensely, every time I close my eyes I see your beautiful face and you're in my soul so entirely, I feel you inside me."

Christ!! This was so unfair... so fucking unfair.

I wanted to claw at him, scrape him under my fingernails just to keep a part of him. I wanted to learn the art of osmosis so I could absorb him.

"You hear me, babe?" he choked out, his own rough and sexy voice breaking before me.

"I hear ya', Jax. I'll always hear you, wherever you are, baby. I love you so damn fucking much, Jaxon Cooper and don't you ever forget it!"

I couldn't see him through the ocean of tears I was spilling and I frantically wiped them away. I needed to see his beautiful face, burn it memory and take as much of it as I could while he was this close.

My heart was now shattered and my soul died as he stepped back, his hand still tight in mine as I desperately clung onto him.

He stepped back into me and pressed his lips to my forehead. "Christ..." he sobbed.

"Go..." I whispered. "Please..." I couldn't let him see me fall to pieces, I wouldn't let him witness my breakdown and I didn't want him to hear my screams.

"You mine, babe?"

"Lock, stock and barrel, baby."

He nodded once, walked to the gate, turned, pierced my soul with his...

...then left me.

I sank to the floor, my heart in shattered fragments around me as Cam scooped me up and held me as I screamed and screamed and cried and cried and yelled for him, hollered for him to come back.

I refused to move for three hours in case he changed his mind and came home, came back to me.

He didn't.

He couldn't.

He never would.

***

Jax phoned every day for the first four weeks.

He phoned once the next month.

He phoned once in the next six weeks.

And then he never rang again.

And he never came home.

My Mom died six months after Jax left.

Cam left to chase a career in Australia.

Aaron and Luce moved in together.

I fell back into my old routine of submitting to the whip and hating myself, along with hating Jax.

The day I buried my mother, I laid a pink rose on her coffin and swore to myself I wouldn't turn out like she did; desperate for something, anything in her life; so I pulled out my phone and dialled a special someone.

"Saul... I need your help....."

PART 2

CHAPTER 32

2 YEARS LATER

"Christ, Leah." I flapped her away as she touched up my make-up. "It's a bloody radio interview. No one is gonna see me."

"Pete fuckin' Burrows is gonna see ya'," she nodded wildly as she smeared lip gloss over my already primed lips.

"You ready, Eve?" A studio technician asked and then led me through to the studio.

Pete waved as he spoke through the microphone then someone ushered me into the seat opposite him and donned a pair of headphones on my head. So much for Leah's hair style!

"You okay, Eve?" Pete asked while he waited for a track to finish. "Just gonna be routine questions Eve, boring stuff really." He smiled and I relaxed a little.

This kind of thing wasn't my thing.I always hated doing interviews, so Radio 1 was ecstatic when my manager, Brent Howard, had agreed to it, much to my displeasure but I knew it was needed.

I fidgeted with the headphones as Pete introduced me and the interview went started:

P: We have a special exclusive now that I know you've all been waiting weeks for, so let's not hang on any longer. A huge welcome to Eve Hudson from Hell's Eden.

E: Hey guys.

P: How you doing, Eve?

E: I'm good thanks, apart from these damn headphones, they really hurt your ears ya' know.

P: (laughs) Well us here at radio 1 have been excited since we knew you were gonna give us this exclusive. What a whirlwind of a year you've had. Five number ones, one of those 'Let me Breathe' is currently at number 1 this week, and the fastest selling album in the last ten years. How's it been for you?

E: God, absolute manic. It's been brilliant though and I just wanna shout out to my fans... what can I say? But god, thank you, each and every one of you. I love you all.

P: What everyone wants to know is how it feels to duet with the one and only Sed Tyler from Platform 2?

E: He's great. I was scared to death at first but he's a real sweetheart, he made me relax instantly and that voice... God, that voice does things to a girl you know.

P: (laughs) I bet it does. Your duet comes out tomorrow and we've got an exclusive coming at the end of this interview folks but I can reveal it's a little bit raunchy. Now, I've seen the video, Eve and I must say I really like your outfit.

E: Thought you might, Pete.

P: You're singing your debut performance with Sed tonight at the Bafta's; please tell me you're wearing that outfit, Eve.

E: God no, I think I'd get arrested for indecent exposure, but something close enough.

P: (laughs) I've heard that Room 103 are over from America and will also be performing tonight. Nobody forgets the epic number 1 hit, Shocking Heaven, you had with them. We know you value your privacy Eve, but I heard you were all quite close before they hit the big time.

Oh God. Oh Shit. He'd be there... tonight! I hadn't seen him in two years, apart from on the TV.

E: Well. It's true I sang a few songs with them way before they made it big in America and yeah, I owe those guys a lot. They were the ones that encouraged me to get up on stage and well, I wouldn't be here without them really.

Pete nods.

P: What's it gonna feel like to see them again after, what is it 2 years?

E: Yeah about two years, and it'll be great to see the guy's again.

P: Can you tell us why you never went to America with them?

E: It was because of some personal issues that I was going through at that time.

P: You got quite close to a certain member of room 103.

Shit! Divert!

E: Boss and I became good friends. He tries to make out he's a bit of a tough guy, but I'll tell you Pete... he's all soft and gooey. But don't tell anybody I told you, he'll tie me up and beat me.

P: (laughs) So what's happening in your life at the moment, Eve?

E: Well. I have just finished my tour, so for a few weeks I'm gonna kick back and relax at home, concentrate on the new song and snog the hell out of Bruce.

P: Bruce?

E: My cocker spaniel. I miss him so much when I'm away. He's my monster.

P: Right gotta hit you with the usual rapid fire questions the listener's sent in and I must say, some of the questions have me cringing so be prepared. By the way you can't pass.

Groan.

P: Ready?
E: Hit me.
P: Bikini or snowsuit?
E: Bikini.
P: Classic rock or hard rock?
E: Both, all rock.
P: Love or sex?
E: Definitely sex.
P: I finish at 4.
E: I can't wait that long.

P: I'll get some cover.

E: (Laugh)

P: Who would you rather bed, Sed Tyler or Jax Cooper?

Cringe. Already done them both!

E: God! One of them, the other can watch.

P: Ahh, but which one?

E: Either way round.

P: Chocolate or fruit?

E: I'm a girl... chocolate.

P: Chest or arse?

E: I'm definitely an arse girl.

P: Against the wall or in bed?

E: Christ. Who sent these in? Both.

P: What's the weirdest thing a fan has ever sent you?

E: Oh God, I don't think I can tell you that live on air.

P: Go for it, it's my job on the line.

E: Well, one guy sent me his... his foreskin.

P: (laugh) you are joking?

E: Uh-uh, he'd just had a circumcision and thought I might like... his most prized possession.

P: Okayyyyy.

P: Final one, you ready for this...you have a piercing *and* tattoo on your lady parts... yes or no?

E: OMG! You can't ask me that.

P: Apparently we can. (Laugh)

E: Well... Oh God... okay... yes.

P: Oh Christ... I'll let you all know what it says tomorrow folks.

E: (Laugh)

P: Well a huge thank you to the one and only Eve Hudson. It's been an absolute pleasure. Good luck on your new single and here's our exclusive performance of Eve Hudson and Sed Tyler singing, Please me baby.

"That's it Eve. Thank you so much." Pete held out his hand, I gripped it and smiled at him.

Leah propelled me through the building when I exited the studio. "God, Leah! I'm not on wheels."

"We've gotta get round to the Bafta venue and get sound checked before rehearsals," she barked severely. God, I was knackered.

She practically pushed me into the waiting car where the guys from my band were already clamped in. "E. How'd it go?" Angel, the lead guitarist asked, his pure white hair stuck up in different directions. Each time I looked at it, it made me smile. It was the reason he got his nickname 'Angel'.

"Yeah, was okay." I yawned, whilst Leah shoved some correspondence on my lap to sort through.

Sponsor for a clothing range... No.

Sponsor for a cosmetic range... No.

Duet with Ted Candy... Definitely no.

Attend a TV interview with somebody I had never heard of... No.

Perform at a cancer charity event... Yes.

Respond to mail from H.A.S.H T.A.G.... Yes.

H. A. S. H. T.A.G. was a self-harm charity I was president of. It stood for **H**elp. **A**gainst. **S**elf. **H**arm. **T**herapy. **A**nd. **G**uidance.

When I had been determined to take control of my life two years ago, they had been an enormous help and comfort, and I now put my name to their company. So far I had managed to raise over £2 million for them.

I handed the papers back to Leah and spotted Hunter, the keyboard player for Hell's Eden, staring at me, the numerous piercings in his eyebrows lifted high on his forehead.

I lifted an eyebrow in query and he smirked at me. "Gonna clue me in, Hunt?"

He grinned mischievously. "Room 103. Tonight."

I shrugged at him and peered out of the window. "Actually I think I have the penthouse suite, not room 103," I smirked.

Mad (Real name Gavin, but you can guess why we call him Mad. Even though he was soft as a brush with me), my drummer, put his hand in mine. "You gonna be okay, E?"

I smiled widely at him and nodded. "Yeah, all's good," I lied.

Was it?

Christ, I didn't think so.

CHAPTER 33

I had locked myself away in my dressing room since I had arrived at the Southbank Centre just in case I bumped into... people I didn't want to.

A knock came on the door. Jack, one of my security guys, answered the door and spoke quietly to someone. "They're about ready for you, E," he informed me as he turned to me.

I nodded and smiled and entered the corridor where Sed was waiting for me. He smirked when he saw my outfit. "You like?" I asked with my tongue in my cheek, before I pulled on my leather jacket and zipped it up.

My costume team had kitted me out in tight black leather hot pants, a black leather bustier and a floaty, cream sheer top with knee high four inch boots. Sex on a stick, Mad had said.

"I like what's underneath it, E" Sed whispered in my ear.

"I know you do, you dirty boy." I winked as we approached the stage and took our positions. The set was a pub scene. A long bar ran across the back and a few tables were scattered around. The dancer's had already taken position at their tables and I was to sit on a bar stool.

Sed blew me a kiss as he walked across to his spot. I perched on my stool, touched the ring that was hidden in my bra, and whispered to myself 'Lock, stock and barrel, baby'; my ritual before any performance.

"And here with an exclusive performance of their new single, 'Please me, baby', Give it up for Sed Tyler and Eve Hudson," Tom Holder introduced. The crowd applauded as the light strobes hit us and Sed's guitarist brought Sed in.

I swivelled around on my stool, my legs provocatively crossed as I tried to pull off a sexy pose, and Sed started his verse.

"You shock it baby
Make me wanna rock it baby
Demanding me on my knees
Beggin' you for the release
The pleasure's so damn fine
I'm gonna put ya' on a hell of a shrine."

I hopped off the stool while the guitarist played a harmony and slowly unzipped my jacket, whilst keeping my eyes on Sed, then slung it aside before I started on the chorus.

"So breathe me baby
Just feel me baby
Yeah, yeah, yeah
Just god damn feel me baby
Yeah, yeah, yeah
Let me ease it baby
And just please you baby
Oh yeah."

I wowed the crowd, and myself, when I took to the huge pole in the middle of the stage and threaded myself around it, as I began to dance round it while Sed sang the next verse.

"You ace it baby
Make me wanna taste you baby
Always such a cold hard tease
Gives me the need to please
The thrill is so god damn great
You always make me take the bait."

I started the chorus again as I slid down the pole to a waiting Sed at the bottom. At the end of the chorus, Sed took hold of my top and ripped it straight down the middle, leaving me in just the black bustier.

The sultry smile on his face lit my insides.

The crowd roared as I came in with my own verse.

"I'll give it ya' baby
Make ya' wanna feel me baby
Give in to my temptation
Concede to my flirtation
My touch'll make you such a bad guy
But I'll make you feel so damn high."

Sed and I sang the chorus together this time, our hands roaming over one another as we hip grinded, then Sed sang his last verse as I pole danced for him whilst he knelt before me, as if worshipping me.

"You work me baby
Make me wanna jerk it baby
Surrender to the deep desire
Needing to put out this fire
The need's so god damn hard
I know I'll always be badly scarred."

The crowd went ballistic as we both finished together.

"Just please me baby
Please me baby
God damn ease it baby
Just please me baby
Please me baby
Feed my release and please me baby."

The audience were up on their feet as Sed and I took to the front of the stage and took the applause.

Tom Holder walked over to us and waited for the clapping to die down before he spoke.

"Wow guys," was all he said. The crowd roared again. "I've got a feeling that's gonna knock you off the top spot, Eve" Tom joked. "How you doing?" He asked as he thrust his microphone in front of me.

"I'm really good thanks, but these boots are bloody killing me! Would anybody mind if I took them off?"

Tom and the audience laughed as Sed shook his head in humour. "Go for it," Tom said.

I grinned as I unzipped them and then pulled them off, "Oh God, yes."

The crowd cheered and as I turned to smile at them, I spotted a beaming Boss stood in front of the stage. He saluted me. "Hot Stuff," he mouthed with a wink.

A small bubble popped in my chest and I swallowed back the lump. Before I could think about it, I was running across the stage, leaping off the edge and launching myself into his arms, wrapping my legs tightly around his waist as he spun us both round.

"God, I missed you, hot stuff!" he shouted in my ear as the crowd erupted in whistles, cheers and appreciation.

Tears were streaming but I didn't care a shit what I looked like. I had missed this man with my entire soul. "Boss!" I whispered. He squeezed me tightly.

"That was fuckin' epic, E. How ya' doing, baby?"

I leaned back a little and nodded as he wiped my tears away with his hand, both of our gazes said everything we felt.

I could see Jack, my bodyguard beside us and I glowered at him. "It's fine, Jack" I assured him.

"Need to get you back up, E," he said as my brain kicked into gear and I took a glance around at all the people watching us.

Boss dropped my feet to the floor and I palmed his cheek and smiled softly. "We'll catch up later, hot stuff" he said as Jack helped me back up on stage.

"Make sure you find me at the after-party."

He nodded.

Tom grinned at me as I smiled guiltily and walked back over to him, "Sorry about that."

Tom shook his head, "No problem, Eve. I take it you know Room 103's drummer?"

Smirking, I nodded. "Yeah. Something like that." I said softly.

Tom turned to Sed. "So Sed. What's it been like to duet with the Hell's Eden goddess, Eve Hudson?"

Goddess? Seriously? Creep!

Sed lifted his eyebrows and smirked, "Fun!"

I blobbed my tongue out at him but gave him a smile and a wink. We'd had some fun alright!

"Fun," Tom repeated and smirked at Sed, as if he understood the innuendo in Sed's words.

I shook my head at the pair of them before Tom turned back to me. "And you'll be back in a short while to perform a new charity song you have written, Eve?"

"I will. I'll tell you all about it later," I smiled in confirmation.

"Okay. Show your appreciation for Sed Tyler and Eve Hudson," Tom said to the stars in the audience and they clapped loudly as we left the stage.

Leah was flapping about as usual when I had descended the stage steps.

"Quickly. You need to get changed for your next song," she flustered.

"My God, Leah. I've got forty five minutes yet. All I've gotta do is get out of these clothes and put others on."

She stared at me as though I'd just told her the Prime Minister was a transvestite and I rolled my eyes, "Your hair. Your make-up," she scoffed as she gestured to each section on me with a wave of her hand.

"Of course, Leah. I'm so sorry."

Sed nudged me and I held back as Leah scurried ahead.

"You wanna catch up later?" he asked quietly and I smirked at him.

"Catch up? What would you like to chat about, Sed?" I teased as I strode in front of him and swayed my hips seductively.

I heard his low growl behind me and giggled as I rounded the corridor and slammed into Romeo.

"Spanner!" he cried. I laughed and smiled.

"Christ. Romeo!"

He lifted me up and hugged me tight. "Fuck, E. It's been forever," he sighed as he refused to let me go.

I could sense Sed patiently waiting behind me but I continued to embrace this huge hulk of a man. "It has," I breathed. "How have you been?" I asked as he put me down.

He nodded determinedly. "Good, E. I've been following you. You've done really well. Jax..." He stopped himself and seemed to curse under his breath.

I felt his discomfort so I diverted quickly. "Romeo, this is Sed Tyler. Sed, this is Romeo, lead guitarist of Room 103," I introduced.

Sed cocked his head. "We've met," he said with contempt. I frowned at his behaviour.

Romeo lifted his eyebrows at him but didn't say anything.

"Problem, Sed?" I asked with a hint of a warning.

I wouldn't have him offending my friends; they would always come before Sed.

Sed glanced at me and shook his head slightly, "Not with him, no. His vocalist? Oh, yeah."

"Why?" I asked hesitantly.

Romeo looked really uncomfortable and I suddenly didn't know if I wanted to find out the reason for Sed's disdain.

"Let's just say, the prick can't keep his hands off other people's women," he hissed.

My brows rose and Romeo glanced at me uneasily. "Don't worry about it, Romeo. I didn't expect him to wait... I certainly didn't," I divulged. "Hell, I'd be dead before then," I added resentfully.

Romeo gave me a pained look, as Sed glimpsed between the two of us, and grabbed my hand. "I... I... Shit, E..."

I scrunched up my nose and shook my head in sadness. "I know, Romeo. Don't worry about it. I'm all good."

"E." Leah shouted from a doorway down the corridor and I smiled up at Romeo, "Gotta go. Catch you at the party later?"

He smiled and nodded. "Of course, E. Free booze," he winked.

He stroked his thumb over my cheek as though an apology for leaving me, his eyes held mine and silently asked for forgiveness.

I nodded and smiled softly before I walked away.

CHAPTER 34

The costume people had grumbled at me when I returned to my dressing room, whining about the time limit I had to change.

Christ. These people really pissed me off at times.

I wasn't a diva, far from it, that's why I couldn't understand all the commotion about not having at least an hour to climb out of some shorts and a bra and slip a dress over my head.

They had put me in a dark blue silk Chinese style dress. I admit it was exquisite and I had loved it as soon as it had arrived. It was knee length with a split up to my hip on the right hand side, showcasing the tattooed sprinkle of stars all the way up.

It was high-necked but there was a teardrop shaped section cut out at the chest, which showed off my dermal piercing and the swell of my breasts. The back was completely missing and I had specified this as a requirement when I had ordered the dress for a specific reason. Along the hem and up around the side split it was embellished with a beautiful cherry tree design.

I adored it and I wore it with pale pink heels. The hair people had pulled my hair back into a severe bun, until every single strand was screaming in pain.

I looked elegant. First time for everything. Shame my gob wasn't.

Mad was bouncing on his heels beside me as we got the all clear to take the stage. "Mad, cool it. You're making me nervous," I disciplined softly.

He sighed heavily, "Sorry. Just really nervous for you, E."

I nodded. "Yeah. My stomach's like the Bermuda fucking triangle. Am I doing the right thing, Mad?"

I was totally nervous at what I was about to do. People would either love me or hate me and I knew the statement I was about to make would cause uproar. But I had to do it... for me and for some of the other people I had met recently.

The set technician rolled his arm around and we all established our places.

I turned and smiled at the violinists and they nodded in welcome. I then looked to Hunter who gave me a thumbs' up on the piano, Angel and Mad nodded from their places.

Tom started to introduce us, "Now we have another performance from Eve Hudson with her band, Hell's Eden. But this song is a little bit special and I'll let Eve tell you all about it."

Tom turned to look at me and nodded.

I took a step up to the mic as I touched my ring, this time in the palm of my hand because I needed the strength I always drew from it. 'Lock, stock and barrel, baby' I whispered before I took a huge breath.

The lights in the crowd dimmed and a spotlight appeared on me.

I smiled and swallowed the nerves. "Hi all" I started.

Everyone shouted 'Hi' and I nodded in thanks.

"About seven years ago, I started to self-harm," I confessed bluntly.

Gasps and shocked murmurs extended through the room and I gave everyone time to come to term with my words.

My legs and voice wobbled but I grit my teeth and carried on. "The appeal of self-harming is different from victim to victim. I say victim because that's what we are. We are victims of whichever reason we each harm for."

The room lights rose a little so I could make out each person in the room.

"The appeal for me? Well, it's kind of hard to explain but I'll try my best."

Each eye in the room was trained on me. I felt like I was being swallowed whole, each of the individuals wanting a piece of me but I needed to speak out to raise awareness of something that was considered taboo, unmentionable and baffling to most.

"Each victim that self-harms does so in many different ways. Some cut, some burn themselves, some people even stay in violent relationships for it. My personal method of self-harm was to be whipped... severely."

My voice broke and I clenched my fists to control myself but I turned around and showed everyone the scars on my back. The spotlight illuminated my back and the image was mirrored on a huge screen behind me.

Gasps rang out again. Out of the corner of my eye, I saw someone walk across the stage towards me. I turned to see Boss striding over to me with a soft smile on his face.

When he reached me he slipped his hand in mine and squeezed before nodding for me to continue. At that moment I couldn't love that man more. Even after two years he continued to support and love me.

The damn lump in my throat that had appeared the same time Boss had, was proving difficult to remove. I blew out a long breath as I turned back round. "Why we do it? I can't speak for each individual but as recent statistics tells us, for most us it helps us cope with some sort of emotional or physical pain."

I paused and looked around the room. "Since an incident that happened to me in my childhood, I held a lot of pain and anger inside. To me, the internal pain actually felt like a physical pain. Sometimes it grew to such an extent that my body physically seemed to boil. My veins would scream at me that they were burning with the agony. My brain would send electric synapses into my nerve endings that actually, to me, felt like genuine electric shocks and my bones would literally vibrate as a pressure inside me built to a roaring degree."

I took another scan of the room, each and every person was giving me their whole attention. I noticed some people, mostly women, were crying and my heart surged at their understanding.

"Someone once asked me why the whip. Well for me, the external physical pain seemed to, if only for a few hours, engulf the internal pain. But it wasn't just that. I'm going to get descriptive now but I need to, to help you understand."

I paused to see if anybody wanted to leave the room but the whole place remained still and silent.

Boss leaned into me whilst I paused. "Proud of you, hot stuff."

I turned to him and it was those very words that brought my tears. I took another breath and he nodded firmly, encouraging me to do this, so I did.

"Each time the whip brought my blood flowing, it released all the build-up of pressure and pain. Every drop of blood that fell rid a small fragment of torture. Every time that whip slashed through my back, it made me feel I was repenting for some guilt I carried about inside me."

I faced Boss for my next words. "Quite a while ago, I hit a really bad spot and if it wasn't for my friend here, I wouldn't have survived the episode I subjected myself to."

Boss stroked his thumb over my chin and smiled tenderly as I squeezed him. "Every self-harmer needs a friend. Each and every one of us."

I closed my eyes and sucked in my lips before I carried on because I knew my next words would hurt some people in this very room. "Two years ago, I fell really hard after a very heart-breaking time. The harm I did to myself was so bad, it was a turning point in my life. I was going through some really terrible personal issues. As well as losing my mother to stomach cancer, I found out some sickening secrets that had been held for many years. Secrets that changed my outlook on my childhood and at that very same time, I lost... some very close... people in my life. "

I squeezed Boss's hand because I knew he would be torturing himself over it, he squeezed back.

"At this point the pain was too unstable, too severe. It felt like my whole body would explode if I didn't find the release and I did a stupid thing... I told the person whipping me not to stop. They were stupid enough to listen and I nearly bled to death," I finished bluntly.

Boss was staring at me, his eyes rimmed with tears but I shook my head at him before I turned back to the room.

There were many people crying now. I glanced around the room, my heart stuttered wildly and my stomach dropped, when I saw the back of Jax retreating through a door at the back of the room. It had been two very long years since I'd seen that back but I'd recognise it anywhere, all the old feelings overwhelmed me as my legs wobbled. Boss caught my reaction to Jax and swung his arm around my waist to support me.

"Thank you," I whispered to him. He shook his head and I realised he couldn't talk because he was extremely emotional at my words.

I cupped his face, "Hey. I'm good. I'm here and I'm better."

He nodded and bit his lower lip before I resumed my statement. "I know you probably think I'm getting too personal but I am telling you for a reason. Many self-harmers suffer in silence, frightened to tell people because the topic is extremely taboo. Many people are appalled by the very idea of it, but if my honesty, my openness about my illness, helps even one of those people then I have achieved something with my life."

I looked around the room again and smiled. "After spending a while in hospital I was very alone. I felt so isolated and desolate, that I would have done anything to escape that room and do it all over again. The pain inside me was so bad that I just wanted to... well, you get the gist."

I turned to the edge of the stage where a woman walked towards me and I smiled widely at her. She stroked Boss's shoulder as she passed him, silently thanking him for being there for me, and stood beside me as she took my other hand, once I'd flicked my ring onto my finger.

"I'd like to introduce Isla Gregory, the lady who saved my life."

A thunderous round of applause broke out in the room. Isla blushed ferociously as her eyes filled with tears. I joined in the cheers as well as the tears.

I waited for the noise to die down before I continued. "Isla is a volunteer for the wonderful charity H.A.S.H. T.A.G. which stands for 'Help Against Self Harm, Therapy And Guidance'."

Another round of applause erupted and we both smiled happily at the attention the charity was receiving.

"Isla was the woman who turned my life around. She talked to me, listened to me, guided me and became my friend. Something every self-harmer needs... a friend. Plain and simple. We need someone to talk to, someone who listens without judging and Hell, even someone to swear and throw plates at."

Isla nodded and pointed to me as the room laughed and I rolled my eyes.

"Hash Tag is a non-profitable charitable foundation and they need all the help they can get."

Isla nodded again. "They treat each harmer as a person, an individual and not like a leper. They give guidance, support, and arrange therapy but most of all they listen. And believe me, I can rattle."

Both Boss and Isla nodded this time and I nudged them both.

"The song 'Endure', which I'm going to sing for you now, is one I wrote a couple of months after my one year free of harm marker."

The crowd stood up and congratulated me with a standing ovation as a sound tech guy ran on with a stand for my mic and Isla kissed my cheek before she strode off the stage.

Boss pulled away but I held him firm, to which he frowned but I shook my head.

I turned to the band and the violinists and they all thumbed up.

Standing at the mic I looked around at each section of the room. "All proceeds, and I mean all, including all recording and individual expenses from this song goes to Hash Tag and it's available for download and retail purchase from tomorrow. A huge thank you to RMG Music for foregoing their fee."

The room applauded. "But this performance is dedicated to my amazing friend Boss, the drummer for Room 103, who once picked me up off my university dorm floor, broken and bleeding and took me to hospital while he held my hand, and then he kicked my butt and sent me to recuperate in his own personal holiday home."

I heard some cheering from the back of the room and spotted Romeo and Bulk hailing Boss whilst grinning wildly.

I turned to a weeping Boss. "This time it's my turn to dedicate to you," I told him as a stage tech brought him a stool.

Once he had perched on it beside me, I lifted my finger to Hunter, who came in with a slow melody on the piano as I touched my ring and closed my eyes, 'Lock, stock and barrel, baby'.

The song was an immensely slow and melancholy track and I closed my eyes for the first verse.

"I've watched you camouflage the agony
Striving to shield the affliction
The very essence of your soul

Destroyed by their corruption
Your heart massacred by their poison
The guilt you hold so close
The pain you fight to endure"

Angel played a solo riff whilst Mad drummed out a muted beat and then I came in with the chorus.

"Endure the torture
Endure the torment
Cos' I'll take your pain
Take it, break it, and destroy it
I'll break you free
Help you to rejuvenate
Bring you back to life, to life
Bring you back to me, to me"

All the band and violinist's played together in a sad section as I sang the second verse.

"I've witnessed the darkness take you
The craving your conscience dictates
The sheer force of your spirit
Crippled by their depravity
Your trust shattered to the bone
The blame you think is yours
The burn you fight to endure"

Angel and Hunter joined me vocally in the next chorus and then when I came to sing the last section, it was pitched up and the entire band joined in together as I belted out the final verse.

"But now I'm bringing you the light
The release your body does demand
The very core of your heart
Caressed by my devotion
The bliss, it's yours
The love, it's yours
The love, it's yours to endure
Yours to endure
Cos' I just set you free
You're free to brave your dreams."

The violinists played the song out and the whole room roared, the walls and floor shook and as I looked into the crowd, he was there... watching me.

He wouldn't release my eyes, just held me to him without touching me.

My breath caught as I gazed at him.

My whole body and soul roared to life, and my heart stopped beating for a fraction of a second, even though my blood pumped frantically around my veins.

Every single hair on my body reared to attention and goose bumps exploded all over me as my soul reached out for its mate.

But I turned, and I walked away as a tear slipped free.

CHAPTER 35

"Give it half an hour after I leave, then come round," I breathed into Sed's ear as we danced at the after party.

He groaned as his hands slipped down to my hips and he pulled me in to him further, giving me a stroke of his hard erection. "Can't we make it ten minutes? I'm so damn hard I could strip you naked and take you right here."

"You're always so damn hard, Sed." I chastised playfully.

"Only for you, babe."

I flinched. "Sed, I've told you, don't call me that!"

He sighed heavily and held his hands up as my mood was broke and I ended the dance.

"E... Shit..." he moaned as he followed me to the bar.

I smiled to the tender as I leaned over and gave him my order as Sed stood beside me, apologising over and over.

"Okay, I get it! Christ," I barked at him.

He reared back and shook his head. "Come get me when the moods fucked off, E." he snapped and strolled off, probably to some other faceless fuck!

I huffed and downed my drink, closing my eyes in desperation to get out of the room currently full of big-headed celebrities and wannabe's.

Jack appeared at the side of me and side hugged me. "You okay, girl?"

I scrunched my nose. "Nah. You okay if I get gone. I've had enough of these egotistical fucks!" I whined.

He barked out a laugh but nodded. "Give me two minutes to get the car round."

I held up a finger to the barman and gestured one more.

Just while I waited for Jack!

My body sensed him before I felt him. I closed my eyes in distress as I held back the whimper that wanted to vocalise.

His finger swiped up my spine and my whole body tingled at his touch, the touch I had craved for over two years. He leaned into my ear, his warm breath triggering an unwanted desire to flood my system.

"Babe."

I didn't know whether to laugh, scream or cry when I heard it... that god damn 'babe' was all my dreams had consisted of for the last two years.

"Jax," I returned unemotionally, without turning to him.

He appeared beside me, his huge masculine frame leaning on the bar as he gazed at me, his eyes drinking me in as they skimmed over every inch of me.

I kept my face forward and refused to look at him.

My eyes were demanding that I turn so they could get their fill. They had been withdrawing for too long.

I was not going to look. I was not going to look!!!

I fucking looked.

God damn it!

"Fuckin' epic song, babe," he growled out in his unique husky tone.

My whole body turned to a liquid mess. *FUCK!* I had promised myself I would not do this.

"Did you want something, Jax?"

His eyebrows rose and he tipped his head but Jack disturbed his next words.

"There's been some trouble at the Grande E, security alert. Gotta give it another half hour," he stated.

Why does it always happen? Every time you're desperate to escape!

I nodded and sighed, "No problem, Jack. Come and find me when it's sorted."

He nodded and disappeared, leaving me alone with a simmering Jax.

I signalled for another drink and the barman nodded in acknowledgement.

"Babe?" Jax asked.

I turned to him, my eyes blazing as my breathing increased. "What Jax? *What?*"

He closed his eyes and swallowed before he traced my ring finger with his. I knew what he was asking.

I scoffed bitterly. "Fucking eternity rings don't actually wait an eternity, Jax." I slammed as I pushed off the bar and scurried across the room to find anybody…anybody but the man crushing my heart at that very moment.

***

Kicking off my shoes and peeling off my dress I walked across my hotel suite naked, apart from a black lace thong, and stood in front of the huge landscape window, in the dark gazing out at the London nightlife with my cinnamon latte, with extra shot, in hand.

Closing my eyes, I concentrated on my meditating technique to drown the hum in my veins.

Picking up the sound system remote, I flicked on some music and started swaying to it as I blew out some deep breaths and just lost myself in the beat.

I could beat this. Eighteen months Eve. Don't fucking lose it now. I wouldn't let it win.

Breathe in, breathe out, sway left, sway right, tap left thigh, tap right thigh, breathe in, breathe out.

If anybody from below could see me through the window I must have looked a right duck!

I sipped my coffee as I continued to sway to OneRepublic's 'Everybody loves me'.

Sway and breathe E!

"Very nice. Dance, baby" Sed said from behind me and I spun round, spilling coffee all over my arm.

"God damn you, don't you ever knock?" I bristled. "Who let you in?"

"Jack," he shrugged. "He's used to me by now, baby" he grinned lewdly as he swayed across the room to me, matching each of my sways eagerly.

God, he was sexy!

His soft blonde hair was highlighted with light brown streaks. His lean chest wasn't overly pumped but he still had a fantastic body and every time my eyes set on it, my core heated intensely.

I couldn't hold back the smile at his movements. His hips swinging from left to right as he pulled his t-shirt over his head, waggling his eyebrows when I giggled at him.

I raised my arms and swayed towards him, both of us rocking our hips in sync and rhythm as his hands shimmied beside his hips to the beat of the music.

When we joined, he pulled me in tight against him and rocked into me, whilst he sang the words in my ear.

I spun around so my back was to his chest and worked my backside down his body, rotating my hips until I was crouched in front of him, turned and then worked my way back up. He palmed my breasts, his thumbs skimming over my pert nipples whilst his lips found mine and he controlled me in a smouldering kiss, driving me wild with need.

"Fuck! You are one sexy fucking bitch," he growled as his hands cupped my bottom as I pushed it out and into his embrace.

Rolling my hips against his impressive hard crotch, I gripped his thick blond hair and yanked his head back sternly before I ran my tongue up his throat. "Fuck me against the window," I breathed.

"*Jesus!*" he moaned as I nibbled along his jaw.

He danced us backwards until my back hit the clear glass and I gasped at the cold sensation. He smirked at me as he twisted the edges of my thong and ripped it off.

I took his nipple between my teeth and tortured it as I popped the buttons on his jeans and slid them over his hips.

"You want me, E? You want my hard dick inside you?" he hissed as I fisted his erection.

"You know I do," I whispered as I kissed down his chest and over his stomach until his rigid cock was at my lips.

I gazed up at him lasciviously as I ran my tongue over the tip of him, lapping up the small amount of pre-cum that had pooled just for me. He sucked air through his teeth and gripped my hair as I sank my mouth over him, my knees wide either side of his knees.

"Fuck yes. Blow me, E" he snarled.

I worked him hard, up and down, my hands teasing his balls; tasting him, teasing him and enjoying his addictive flavour until he groaned loudly and pulled me up before spinning me around and pushing me flat onto the window.

His mouth rested beside my ear. "How hard do you want fucking, E?"

"Hard!" I groaned as his finger swept down the groove between my buttocks and then into my vagina.

"Your sweet pussy's panting for me, E." So was I, Damn it!

"Please..." I whimpered.

"How hard, E?" he repeated as he rolled on a condom.

Hadn't I already told him? I was sure I had? "Fuck me hard. Brutal, fuck me till I scream!"

He impaled me in one forceful thrust and we both groaned loudly, as my palms splayed on the window.

"Fuck yes!" he snarled as he powered into me, each of his ferocious thrusts slapped my cheek on the cool glass.

His hands gripped my hair as he held on tight, each of his fierce hammers driving me deeper into ecstasy as I struggled to hold the glass with my sweaty palms.

"Fuck yes; yes that's it, harder *Jax*!"

We both stilled immediately and I closed my eyes, cringing vehemently.

Oh dear!

He pulled out and I daren't turn to look at him. I just remained naked and squashed against the damn window.

I swallowed loudly and risked it. "I... I... well... I meant to say... Sed..." I kind of trailed off towards the end and whined his name out.

He stood staring in shock at me, his eyes wide and bright.

"Sorry," I whispered. I really didn't know what else to say.

He took a step back and looked at me as though I'd just bit his dick off. "Did you just call me Jax?" he spluttered.

"Well..." I pulled my top lip behind my bottom lip.

"Well?" he barked out so intensely I jolted.

"I didn't mean to Sed. It's just... well, it's just cos' I've seen him tonight and... well and..." I pursed my lips and flinched when he picked up my coffee cup and threw it across the room.

It bounced off the huge, hopefully not Picasso, painting that donned the back wall and splattered all over the three thousand pounds a roll wallpaper.

Shit! That was my deposit gone. Stupid man!

"Sed, look..."

"Don't fuckin' bother, E. Just don't okay..." He pulled his clothes back on and left, slamming the door so hard it bounced off the wall and snapped a hinge.

Well, that went real well E!

As I started to pick up the broken crockery my phone rang from somewhere and I scanned the room to hunt for it.

Where the hell was it?

Luckily it kept on ringing until I found it and seeing Aaron's name on the screen I took a huge breath before I answered.

"Go!"

"A girl!"

I squealed loudly and jumped up and down. "Oh my fuckin' God!!" I beamed happily. "How are they?"

Aaron laughed loudly and I couldn't hold back the huge grin on my face. Someone was looking down on me tonight because this was exactly what I needed.

"Both are great. She is so beautiful, E... a little stunner, looks like Luce."

A sob choked from my throat. "How big?"

"She weighs 7lb 6oz. Her hair weighs 6lbs of that," he laughed and I giggled.

"Oh Aaron..."

"I know, E. We want to call her Evie Kara."

I made a funny strangled noise and plopped my arse on the plush hotel carpet... sod my nakedness, they could afford carpet cleaners.

"You want to name her after me and... Oh, Aaron."

He paused. "Roger phoned me after your Bafta performance, E." Roger was one of Hell's Eden's tech guys and one of Aaron's good friends.

I was silent. Didn't know what to say really.

"I'm so proud of you, sis. So is Luce. What you have achieved in the last two years, especially after everything you lost. Well, if my daughter holds a fraction of your spirit, then she will be a fucking joy," he said softly.

"You know I'm proud of you too Aaron?"

"I know."

I paused then sighed. "He's here, Aaron," I whispered and peeked around the room as though I was a bloody spy for the MI5.

He was silent for a good few moments. "He speak to you?" he hissed out.

Since Jax had never come back to me, Aaron had hated him for what he did to me. He was the one that held me night after night when I sobbed with the heart wrenching pain of missing my lover.

"Yeah, but I didn't let him say much. Just left him stood there and came back to the hotel."

"Please don't give in to him, E." he urged and I scoffed.

"Aaron, our lives are completely different now. He won't feel the same way about me anymore. If he did he would have answered my calls and come home to me, wouldn't he?"

"Mmm," he murmured quietly.

"Listen. Give both my girls a kiss and I'll be up tomorrow," I told him.

"You're coming up tomorrow?" he asked. I could hear the grin in his voice.

"Yeah, I've just got a couple things to do but I can see to those in the morning and then I'll come up in the afternoon. I have to talk to you about something anyway. I'll be bringing Bruce though cos' I've missed the shit out of him."

"Okay. Text me when you are about here. Love you, E."

"Love you too, Aaron. Tell Luce and Evie I love them. Bye."

I sighed and brought my knees up for a hug, suddenly I felt so lonely.

I was close enough to my band mates but I missed Aaron and Luce so much. Cam and I Skyped every Sunday but apart from that I had no one. You never knew who to trust in the music industry and you had to be wary of anyone who wanted to befriend you. Most of them just wanted a story to sell to the papers about you, and that would be my worst nightmare.

My phone pinged a text through and a teary smile erupted on my face when Aaron had sent me a photo of Evie.

She was beautiful and I replied telling him exactly that. Then I forwarded the photo to each of my boy's (That's what I called my band members), walked to bedroom and pulled on a robe before I went to run a bath.

Just as the bath reached halfway, they all charged into my room, each of them picking me up and swirling me round before popping the cork on a bottle of champagne.

They were good to me. They looked after me and dragged me through the muddy darkness when I needed it, especially Mad, who had grown quite close to me. I had started to get a feeling it might be more than platonic on his side. I hoped not because I didn't see him like that, and I didn't want to spoil our friendship by exploring those feelings.

We ordered sloppy pizza, played cards and drank lots of champagne until we all passed out drunk and exhausted.

Yep. I loved these boy's.

CHAPTER 36

Oh Wow. I felt as rough as I looked. I reluctantly peeled myself out of bed, frowning when I realised each of the boy's had joined me in it.

Well, why not? It was certainly big enough and I sighed in relief when I realised I was wearing shorts and a vest. Then again, it wouldn't be the first time I had woken with these boys, when they were naked after a night on the juice.

I stumbled into the kitchen area and ordered room service, including three cinnamon lattes with an extra shot in each.

"Christ, babe. You look like shit!" Jax growled from my sofa.

I squealed loudly as I turned to find him on the couch, one ankle propped over his other knee as he drank coffee and read a morning newspaper, leisurely leaning back into the huge plump cushions.

"What... the hell, Jax?" I stuttered.

He tipped his head. "You always sleep with your band member's, E?"

"What the hell, Jax?"

Yes, I had said that once.

He stood slowly and prowled towards me causing my knees to buckle at the sheer raw sex emanating off him. His strong pecs rippled with power as his tight t-shirt clung to each contour of his deliciousness. My mouth watered as I watched him approach.

His tattooed solid arms lifted to hold the tops of my arms when he reached me. He pulled me against his chest as his nose rested in my hair. "Need to breathe you, babe."

I was too weak to move, too in love with him to say no and too desperate to feel him, to not inhale him. I closed my eyes and just took, seized everything he was giving me right at that very moment. My whole body hummed in delight as my soul coupled with its mate.

"You mine, babe?"

Whoa!

What the hell?

That ruined the moment!

I reared back and stared at him incredulously. "I was!" I spat.

He sucked air through his teeth and nodded, "Shit happened, babe."

Was that it? Was that all the excuse I was going to get?

I laughed bitterly. "Oh yeah, Jax. Shit definitely happened. Get out!"

He narrowed his eyes on me and I glared at him. "Need an answer, E."

I shook my head in confusion "An answer to what?"

"Band. You sleep with 'em, babe?"

Oh My God!!!

"Yeah, Jax. Fucked 'em all. Hard, wild and all at the same time! Fucking ace, *babe*!" I sneered.

A growl rumbled from deep inside him. He took one huge stride into me, locking me down with his eyes. "Calm the fuck down, babe."

My face made many expressions with the many astounded thoughts that skimmed my brain. "What?" I asked so quietly I wasn't sure he heard it.

He studied me intensely, then his hand lifted and he ran a finger across my jaw and down my throat. "There been anyone lately?"

Christ almighty!!! Did he have any limits?

"Jax. You need to leave now before I get seriously pissed at you and knee you in the fucking balls." I warned.

His brows lifted as his face held a smirk before he spotted the champagne bottles lined up behind the couch. "Celebrating?"

Was he just ignoring my request for him to leave or was he just ignorant?

"Yes," I sighed. "Aaron and Luce had a little girl last night."

His grin made my heart flutter, "Shit, babe."

I grinned back and nodded. "They've called her Evie. I'm gonna go up and squidge her later. I can't wait."

Wait a minute, E! What the hell were you telling him all this for?

His face seemed to contort with pain for a moment before he cleared it and we just stood staring at each other. Our eyes saying everything our mouths couldn't.

His hand cupped my face tenderly. We both sighed heavily at the contact as I nuzzled into it.

"I hurt you bad babe," he whispered and I couldn't hold back the sob that erupted.

"Yes," I agreed.

"You took the whip for me."

"It was for lots of reason, Jax. Don't worry about it," I whispered.

"You never left me, Eve Hudson. You never escaped from in here." He lifted my hand and placed it against his heart. "It was just too damn hard, babe. The gap, the longing, the sheer need for you. Too fuckin' painful, my body ached. I... I... couldn't stand it when I saw..."

I held up a hand to quieten him and pulled away before turning to look through the window. "Go, Jax. I don't wanna hear it. It's two years too late..."

He was quiet for a second. "You'll always be mine, babe" he stated softly before he left.

"Lock, stock and barrel, baby" I whispered as the door closed behind him.

***

"You made the papers," Leah informed me as soon as I answered my phone. I growled at Hunter, who was currently trying to steal my coffee.

"Good! That was the idea." I smiled but my nerves were antsy about what was to come.

"Well it must have been a good idea E, because Hash Tag has been inundated with donations. Since last night they have received over another £250,000 in contributions."

I could feel her grin through my phone but it didn't match mine, it couldn't... mine was a whole mile wider. "You are shittin' me, Leah?"

She scoffed loudly. "Nope. And that's before the income from the single."

"That is fantastic." I beamed as Mad smiled at me, obviously clueing into my conversation.

"Listen Leah, while I've got you on. I need you to handle all my shit for a few days." I cringed as she laughed falsely.

"You are joking, E?" she chuckled again.

"Nope."

Silence... deadly silence.

I waited for it to click into place.

"You're not joking are you," she stated slowly and I clapped her silently.

"Nope," I repeated.

"What the hell, E? I can't just press a pause button and suspend the next three days itinerary!"

"I don't care what you have to do Leah, but I am going north to spend a few day's with my new niece. I need you to sort it. I know how fabulous you are, so you will sort it." I cringed as I disconnected.

All three boys were staring at me, shocked expressions on their faces and I shrugged. "I'm sorry boys but I need these few days," I pouted and fluttered my eyelashes. "You don't mind do you?"

Each of the six eyebrows facing me lifted at my attempt to butter them up but they smiled.

"Go for it, I think we could all do with a break," Angel said.

"Where are you going?" Mad asked nonchalantly.

I noticed something in his eyes but I couldn't ascertain what it was. "Huddersfield. It's where Aaron and Luce live... oh and Evie. I have a house up there for when I visit them," I added with a grin.

He nodded and smiled tightly as Tom, my other personal security man came into the suite. "E, group of guys wanting to see you," he informed me and I frowned.

"I know I'm a goddess but I don't usually get a *group* of blokes after me," I joked.

He smirked as Hunter barked out a sarcastic laugh producing a glare from me in his direction.

"Band members of Room 103," Tom informed me and I grinned widely.

"Well send 'em up," I urged giddily.

He nodded and spoke into his phone and ten minutes later, they all dived in and scooped me up, Bulk first as I hadn't seen him yesterday.

"Good God, E. Look at you, all grown up." He winked and I slapped his arm.

"Look at you Bulk, still exactly the same!" I winked back.

Jax stepped forward and passed me a take-out cup from Starbucks. "Cinnamon latte, extra shot,

babe." He smirked and I couldn't hold back the smile
that he had remembered which beverage I preferred.

"You gonna introduce us, E?" Mad asked with a
hint of a glint in his eyes as he scanned Jax from top
to bottom. I narrowed my eyes on him in warning but
made introductions.

Jax took a step closer to me, bringing him within
touching distance as he checked out Mad.

It was like pistols at dawn and I stifled a smile
when I caught Boss's humorous expression whilst he
watched the pair of opponents square up to each
other.

Boss grinned at me and winked playfully. "Guess
what, hot stuff?"

I shook my head in blankness before he slipped
his eyes to Jax and then back to me. "We're coming up
The Hud with you."

I narrowed my eyes on him and cocked my head,
"What?"

"Huddersfield babe," Jax enlightened

I swung round to him slowly, my brows high.
"Sorry, what?" I repeated, a little stunned.

I heard Boss scoff and Romeo had an amused
expression on his lips as they all watched Jax and me.

"Coming home, babe."

Unreal!

I nodded slowly as I pursed my lips. "Only took
you two fucking years, Jax!" I spat.

He sucked air through his teeth loudly and flinched but took a step into me as he bent towards my ear. "Calm down, babe" he whispered.

I laughed bitterly and looked at him in astonishment. "Calm – Down - Jax? You don't bother to get in touch for two fucking years; you don't ring, you don't answer my calls, you don't... you don't give a holy fuck for two long fucking years! And then you turn up out of the blue as if we'd... as if... as if... Shit!"

My hands shook in anger and I held them over my mouth in anguish as he stared at me. I didn't care that everybody was watching me. I was too damn angry!

Boss walked over to me with a pained expression and took my hand, then led me through the suite and into my bedroom, shutting the door quietly behind us.

He sighed heavily and turned to me with a sad look. "It's been hard for him, E" he said softly and I scoffed.

"Yeah?" I said bitterly.

"E... he didn't cope well with the distance. It hit him hard and he just... he gave up E, god damn it! He just gave up when you...!"

"He gave up?" I interrupted his words as anger surged through me. "You know what, Boss? You wanna know how *HARD* it was for me... you wanna know?" I shouted loudly, all the pain of the last two years finally coming to a head.

"He fucking promised me Boss, he promised me he would come home and do you know what? I fuckin' waited for him. I waited for him for eighteen fucking months like a sad, desperate twat because I couldn't let him go." I sobbed and held my hands up to him when he approached.

"I sat on that airport floor for three fucking hours, begging him to come back Boss... three fucking long and torturous hours, because my heart and soul went with him that day, and I couldn't breathe, I *haven't* fucking breathed since he walked through that fucking door in that fucking airport!"

He looked at the floor to shield himself from my anger and my pain.

"I lost my mother, my brother, my friends, my lover, my faith in my father and my... within six months and all I wanted to do was die... *was fucking die*! And you're here telling me he didn't cope well. Well you know what, Boss? I was just on the end of a phone... just a simple press of thirteen buttons and I would have been there for him. Or even one just to answer my damn calls."

He sucked on his lips and nodded in despair, "He didn't want to talk after..."

"Boss!" Jax barked in warning from behind us and I jolted.

"How long have you been there?" I asked stiffly as his eyes found mine.

"Long enough," he said quietly. I looked away in awkwardness.

"Boss. Give us a minute," he asked. Boss nodded and left.

"Sit down," he ordered. I stared wide eyed at him but refused to move. He grit his teeth and glared at me, "Sit the fuck down, babe."

I stood immobile just looking at him in amazement, my jaw dropped and my eyes round.

He poked his tongue between his teeth and bit down, as if to control his anger. "Babe..." he growled softly.

"Just who the fuck do you actually think you are, Jax? You are nothing to me anymore, so don't tell me what the fuck to do."

He closed his eyes and I saw his fists clench as his nostrils flared slightly. "You're not hearin' me, babe."

"Well... no, I don't think I've fuckin' heard you for two years Jax, so there's nothing new there, is there?" I smirked, now past the point of caring whether I wound him up or not because I was just about ready to blow.

The growl that rumbled from deep within him, made my toes curl as he set his black eyes on me. "Gonna ask you once more, E. Sit the fuck down!"

I laughed. I couldn't help it. I laughed... loudly, humorously and uncontrollably.

Within seconds I found myself flat on my back on the bed, pinned under his body... his strong, delicious and fucking fabulous body.

I whimpered! Whether it was in fright or desire, I wasn't sure.

Both our chests heaved as he caged me with his body. His eyes were the darkest I'd ever seen them;

his anger, his pain and his obscene desire blazed in them desperately.

And then I broke!

I screamed and pummelled him. Two years' worth of hatred came to the forefront and I savagely beat the crap out of him, pounding my fists into him as I shouted and screamed at him, "You bastard! I hate you, I hate you, I fucking hate you!!" I yelled.

He remained there, immobile and staring at me as he took each of my hits, took each piece of hatred and all he gave me back was patience, tenderness and love.

Yes, love was right at the front of his face and it was this that made me do it!

I grabbed his hair with both hands and tugged his mouth onto mine.

He groaned loudly and kissed me with such passion I thought I was going to pass out. His fingers twisted almost painfully in my hair as his tongue invaded my mouth and wrestled frantically with my own.

I took everything he gave me, his whole soul and spirit crashed into me as we brutally clashed our mouths together, bruising and biting and demanding, both of us whimpering and moaning over each other as we reconnected after so long.

He pressed up, his eyes were so intense, they were liquid. His hands fisted my vest and he shredded it in one forceful tear. I gasped and fumbled with the belt on his jeans, desperate for him; eager to feel him, to take him and claim him back.

"Fuck me, Jax. Hard and fucking wild. I need you inside me," I snarled as I ripped down his jeans and shorts.

Pulling at my shorts until they were off, he loomed over me and then he entered me.

We both groaned loudly and arched together in satisfaction. A deep intense sensation of coming home surged through me as our souls danced and our broken bodies fused.

His eyes were on mine, holding me hostage as he took me back, devouring me with his gaze as we became a whole entity once again.

"You..." He thrust hard. "Are..." *Thrust.* "Fucking..." *Thrust.* "Mine..." *Thrust.* "Eve..." *Thrust.* "Hudson..." *Thrust.* "MINE!"

He roared out the last word as we both climaxed painfully and violently. My whole core lit up to extreme levels, my body shook forcefully under his, as my hips lifted him clean off the bed. My eyes rolled to the back of my head as he bucked and jerked wildly, his teeth sinking into his bottom lip as he cried out my name and filled me with a part of him once again.

And then I cried!

CHAPTER 37

He pulled out and embraced me but I jerked away. "Don't, Jax."

He cocked his head and frowned. "E?" I sighed and sat on the edge of the bed, my back to him.

"Don't..."

He settled behind me, his long legs flanking mine as his arms snaked around my waist and his hands took mine.

"Please don't do this, Jax." I pleaded and he sighed.

"Clue me in, babe" he whispered in my ear as he swept my hair over my shoulder.

"This..." I gestured between us with my hand. "It was just sex, Jax. Don't make out it was anything more."

He was silent for a while then the tone in his voice made me flinch. "Fuck sex, babe. Always different, always more with you and you know it!"

I clicked my tongue and sighed, "You leave for America soon, Jax and I can't do all that shit again. We both have different lives now."

He kissed the soft flesh under my ear. "You feel so good, babe. You smell good. Christ babe, you even sound good; those little whimpers and moans that you give me, they light my fuckin' core. I can't just... just not..."

I stood up and rummaged through the dresser for some clean underwear just as the door flew open and

Mad came barrelling in. "What the hell, Mad?" I scoffed as Jax came to stand in front of my naked figure, with his own naked figure.

Mad was silent as he took in the scene of a nude Jax and me. His eyes were furious but I chose to ignore him and pulled on some jeans and a shirt.

"Did you want something, Mad?" I asked, encouraging him to get on with it.

"Just checking up on you, E. You've been in here a while but it's pretty obvious why now." He said with a hint of disgust.

I heard a low growl in Jax's chest as he tipped his head. "Well now you know… leave."

"Jax…" I warned and Mad glared at him.

"Well I was also wondering if…" He looked a little nervous and I frowned at him. "…well if you minded if I came up to Huddersfield with you to see Aaron and Luce…"

I smiled gently at him, "Sure. They'd like that," I said softly to calm his nerves. "Are you travelling with me?"

He grinned then nodded. "Yeah, I suppose it saves taking my car." He smirked at Jax, but Jax was having none of that.

"He can travel with the guy's and I'll share with you, babe" Jax ordered and I turned to him with high eyebrows.

"Well that's okay, Jax but I have to pick Bruce up first and you might not get on with him."

His eyes narrowed on me, "Bruce?"

I smirked mischievously "Mmm, Bruce…"

Pulling out my case I started to pack up my belongings when I caught Mad's wicked grin. "Yeah. Bit of a big guy and he's kinda funny with people he doesn't know," he divulged but Jax just shrugged and followed me back into the living area where everybody was sat around getting on brilliantly.

"I'll risk it, babe."

I rolled my eyes and shrugged. "Whatever," I conceded much to Mad's furious face.

"You got anywhere to stop up there?" I asked Boss who grinned at me when he caught the huge love bite on my neck which Jax had decorated me with.

"Gonna book into a hotel, hot stuff."

Rummaging through my bag, I pulled a key off my bunch and passed it to him with an address. "This is my house up there. There's plenty of room for you all but I'll be later than you cos' I have some stuff to do first. Just don't wreck the place before I get there!" I cautioned playfully.

He shot up off the couch and hugged me. "Gonna have some serious fun baby," he grinned playfully.

"Why am I worried, Boss?" I laughed as he rounded up the others.

"Mad's coming with you, Boss" Jax said and Mad sighed heavily.

"Let me just get some stuff and I'll meet you in the lobby," he said to Boss who nodded his agreement.

"Sure. Not a problem." Boss shrugged.

Angel and Hunter pulled me into a hug. "You back for the MTV thing Thursday?" Hunter asked and I nodded.

"Yeah. I'll be back Thursday morning," I assured.

They both nodded and left with the rest of Room 103 and Mad, leaving just Jax and me.

"Don't you need to pack a bag, Jax?"

"Good idea. I'll be back in half an hour." He came towards me, a sexy little smirk on his face.

"No rush. I'll nip home and pick up some stuff then meet you here," I offered but he shook his head as his finger ran across my bottom lip.

"Think I got competition," he muttered. I stared in confusion. "Mad."

"Mad's just a friend... and so are you," I reiterated my words from earlier.

He scoffed and walked away.

Somehow I don't think he had taken me seriously.

***

I pulled up outside my neighbour's house and killed the engine before I turned to Jax. "I'll just be two minutes if you wanna go into mine and wait."

He frowned at me, "Why?"

"Because I have to fetch something first," I explained slowly. Christ. It was living with your parents... What, why, who?

"I'll come with you," he ordered. I didn't have the energy to argue.

"Whatever!" I sighed and climbed out of the car then made my way up the path as Jax followed dutifully behind. I just knew his eyes were on my arse. A girl knows these things!

Pete opened his front door and grinned at me. "Eve, baby" he declared as he huddled me up into a powerful hug.

"Good to see you. How's he been?" I asked. Pete's eyes shifted to Jax then widened when he realised who he was.

"Oh my God! Jaxon Cooper," he declared gleefully.

I leant in to him and winked. "Thought you'd appreciate my small addition," I chuckled.

"Fuck small! He's all fucking man... every single glorious inch of him," he drooled and I nudged him before I turned to Jax.

"Jax meet Pete. Pete meet Jax," I introduced before I pushed past Pete and made my way inside.

"Mommy's home!" I shouted.

That was all it took.

Bruce came barrelling around a corner and I knew he wasn't going to stop. He collided with my legs at 100Mph and then jumped straight into my arms, kissing me hungrily with a huge doggy grin on his face.

"My boy," I giggled as I kissed him back with as much relish.

"Where's my song?" I asked him. He slipped into a howl, his canine lips forming a perfect 'O'. "There it is" I grinned then wobbled into Pete's kitchen to retrieve a treat from his box.

"Bruce?" Jax inquired from behind me.

As I turned I held a huge grin and looked at Bruce. "Bruce, this is my friend, Jax. Now you need to like him cos' he's staying with us for a few days," I told him seriously.

Jax's eyebrows hit his hairline as though I was completely mad for having a conversation with a five year old dog. Bruce glared at Jax,I knew he felt threatened by this huge hulk of a man who wanted all of his mummy's attention.

"Don't worry, you're still my favourite boy," I whispered in his ear.

He blew off into another song and I joined him, both of us singing to Fun, *'Some Nights.'*

Kissing Pete, I left his house, walked a little way down the path and entered mine. Jax followed me in and I made my way to the kitchen.

"You want a drink before we go?" I asked but he shook his head as he took a look around.

"Ace place, babe."

I smiled my appreciation. "Thanks. I'm just gonna nip up for some stuff. Make yourself at home."

He nodded as he eyed a wary Bruce. I presumed they'd be okay for a few minutes while I packed some things for the trip and left them to it.

I presumed wrong!

I came down ten minutes later to a white-faced Jax cornered into a kitchen chair and an angry Bruce, staring at him with a slight curl to his lip, guarding his biscuits.

I had to close my eyes for a second to stop the laugh that was threatening to rumble at the sight of Jax's face.

"Good boy," I said as I desperately tried to control my laughter.

Bruce took a glance at me, and then backed off away from Jax. "You tell him to hate me, babe?" he asked with narrow eyes and I laughed.

"He thinks you're a threat to his mummy," I explained and Jax smirked.

"Wise dog," was all he said. I chose to ignore him as I scooped Bruce's stuff into his travel bag.

"Let's go see Uncle Aaron," I told Bruce who barked in agreement and went to retrieve his car harness from his low peg near the door.

I had found Bruce, a black and tan cocker spaniel, at the back of an alley a year ago after a concert, he had smothered me in love and gratitude ever since. I couldn't understand how someone could just dump such a clever dog. Everything I had taught him, he had picked up in a couple of days and each time he mastered another trick it amazed me.

Even though he only had one eye and half his right ear was missing... he was butt ugly, but to me he was adorable. He had surprised me time after time and I showered him in love and comfort just for being him.

He was brill!

He trotted behind me and pee'd up the small tree on the front, before he clambered into the back seat and gave me his harness; his large tongue having sex with my ear as I clamped him down.

Jax watched from beside me. I could see the respect in his expression but he didn't say anything.

"Ready?" I asked as I belted myself in next to Jax.

Bruce barked just as Jax was about to confirm, and I stifled a laugh when every time Jax opened his mouth, Bruce woofed over him.

My dog was telling Jax who was boss! Good boy!

What a wonderful journey we had up the M1. Bruce barked every time Jax tried to talk or touch me. Jax actually started to growl back to Bruce, it got so bad they were snarling at each other before we reached Sheffield.

Bruce sang to the radio for half of the journey, much to Jax's annoyance and I tried to stop peeing myself all the damn way.

My boys' hated each other... Epic!

CHAPTER 38

"Romeo texted me. They've gone straight to Z Bar. They'll meet us at yours later," Jax informed me as we entered Huddersfield.

I nodded as my stomach gurgled in excitement at being close to home.

Jax's phone had been ringing constantly all the way up and every single one was declined by him, raising my suspicions that it was obviously someone he didn't want to talk to in front of me and it made me start to wonder why.

"When do you go back home?" I asked nonchalantly, but actually bracing myself for his answer.

"Home?"

"Yeah. America. Home, Jax." I echoed.

He looked confused for a moment as he glanced at me, "Huds always been home, babe."

Seriously? Could have fooled me!

I just nodded and left it at that before I said something I would regret as I turned into a country lane. Jax looked at me then looked on the horizon at my house. "Fuck, babe!" he stammered as he took in the sight of my large house.

Bruce barked loudly and started panting when he smelt home and I smiled to him through the mirror.

"Home, Bruce." I declared. He answered me with a long drawn howl.

Turning into the double gates, and entering the pin code on the security panel, I drove up the gravel drive and sucked in a comforting breath through my window.

Home!

"Welcome home, boy." I grinned to Bruce as I let him escape. He immediately bounded towards the meadow and I knew where he was going. "You come back dirty and you're running your own bath," I shouted after him. He barked and kind of wiggled his bum before he disappeared over the small hill to the little brook; his eagerness to torment the ducks that resided there carried his small legs as fast as they could.

Jax was stood in astounded silence, just staring at my beautiful home. I was suddenly quite nervous of his opinion. Did he hate it?

"What do you think?" I asked quietly.

I had fallen in love with it as soon as I had viewed it. I had bought it for a steal because it had been so run down, but now as I looked at the stunning white structure, its many latticed windows and ivy covered brickwork, it enveloped me in calm and comfort.

Jax turned to me, his jaw low and his eyes soft. "You renovated it didn't you," he stated and I stared at him in shock.

"How did you know?"

He smiled and cupped my cheek. "Because it's just as beautiful as you, babe. It *feels* like you." Fuck me! Why did he always say stuff that made me want to cry?

I smiled sadly and nodded. "Yeah. My Mom and I found her before she died. We both knew... it was where I needed to be."

His eyes were sad as he stood before me. He continued to cup my cheek but his thumb ran across my lower lip. "You said to Boss that you'd lost faith in your father?"

I nodded and looked towards the hill where Bruce had vanished over as I stood in silence debating how much to tell him. I had always been able to tell Jax anything, and he always listened.

"Yeah. She... Mom told me some stuff that... well that kinda changed everything," I disclosed painfully. "Stuff I haven't had chance to deal with yet but hopefully this week, well..."

His hand slipped into my hair and he reached closer to me as he held my eyes. "I'm here babe," he whispered and then he kissed me. God, did he kiss me! Slowly. Tenderly. Lovingly, and it broke my heart all over again but I reflected it all back as I gripped his hair and held on to him for dear life.

A choked sob erupted up my throat at his soft and gentle worship of my mouth. He moaned as his tongue sought out mine and I played just as affectionately as he did. "Babe..." he whispered against my lips before he wrapped me in his arms and pulled me closer. I settled my head on his chest as we stared out to the meadow.

He reared back a little and stared intently at me. "Bluebells," he said simply.

His breath hitched when I nodded. "They're what drew me here," I said and then I took his hand. "I want to show you something," I said as I inhaled deeply.

I had to do this.

I led him towards the meadow and we made our way through the mass of bluebells towards a huge tree that spanned the back section.

It was a large and dominant Major Oak and it was absolutely perfect for the memorial monument I needed it to be.

I walked him over to it and showed him. "It's for everyone special to me," I whispered as his fingers outlined the name 'Mary Ann' that I had carved lovingly into the trunk.

He stood silent as he read his sister's name aside my parents and then he looked lower down the trunk. I could see the confusion on his face before realisation hit him.

He palmed the tree for support when he saw it, but then fell to his knees. "Oh dear god…" he choked out as he read the name.

'Kara Ann Cooper'

"I didn't find out until after you had gone." I whispered sadly, "I lost her at 24 weeks and she was so utterly beautiful."

His head was drooped but I carried on as Bruce came bounding up, but he always showed his respect at the tree and he sat immediately.

"I didn't tell you because I wanted to surprise you when you came home but... you never did... and... and she died."

"You should've rung me when she... when you lost her, babe."

I scoffed loudly. "What? I tried Jax but they wouldn't put me through to you, your damn PA kept declining my calls to you." I explained and I saw him stiffen.

He released a sob, just a simple exhale of a choked cry. I dropped to my knees beside him and grieved with him for the daughter he never met.

"The whip?" he breathed as he took my hand and gazed at me.

I nodded and smiled sadly, "Yeah. It all got a bit too... too much and after Kara died... well I wanted to... go with her."

My hands shook as did my body, but he held on tight. "I can't have any more. They had to do a hysterectomy when they got her out. Everything inside was just too ravaged to save, and now... now I'll never... hold my own..."

He bundled me up and held me as tight as he had ever held me. "Babe... I... you were never out of my heart or head. You were always with me, E."

He lifted his shirt over his head and I stared at his chest, my mouth wide open.

A tattoo now inked his left pectoral muscle, just over his heart. '*Lock, stock and barrel, baby*'

My finger traced the words. He took hold of my hand and followed it with me.

"You mine, babe?" he whispered.

"Lock stock and barrel, baby" I whispered back as I slipped off my shoe and lifted my foot so he could see the sole of my foot.

Inked up the centre were the words 'Lock, stock and barrel baby'. "It's written on my soul," I disclosed, giving him the reason it was under my foot.

His forehead came to rest on mine. We stayed there for an age, our eyes just holding each other's until eventually Bruce muzzled in and we laughed.

***

We made our way back to the house, hand in hand and silent, but as I opened the front door my breath gushed out.

"Shit," I hissed as I took in the state of my home.

Bruce growled and went off in front, protecting me as usual.

"Fuck..." Jax spat as he grabbed my arm and pulled me behind him. "Stay here," he ordered as he went to check the house.

Everything was thrown everywhere. The furniture had been slashed, the contents of every single drawer in the house was scattered everywhere. The fridge and cupboards had been cleared but luckily they hadn't contained much food due to me being away. The carpets had been ripped up and all the pictures from the walls were thrown about the room.

"They were looking for something," I said slowly to Jax as my eyes spanned the room.

He spun around as he hadn't heard me enter behind him. "Fuck, babe."

I stood silent and calm as I narrowed my eyes. "She told them."

"Shit!" Jax hissed and came over to me. "She tell you she'd told them?"

I shook my head and nibbled my bottom lip furiously. "No... if she wasn't dead, I'd fucking kill her right now!" I growled.

I was so damn angry with her!

"How could she do this to me? After everything we sorted out before she died." I walked over to the fireplace and picked up the smashed photograph of Aaron, me and Luce, taken on Luce's twentieth birthday.

"God Damn it!" I screamed as I threw it across the room.

Bruce started barking wildly and Jax held a hand up to me as he went to investigate.

Sinking into my ruined sofa I gazed around my home. Everything I had worked for, every piece of love and devotion I had put into it had gone... ruined.

I knew they hadn't found what they were looking for but I also knew that they wouldn't stop the hunt until they recovered the prey... Me!

"Shit, Hot stuff" Boss gasped when he walked into the room.

I looked up at him and shrugged, "Just stuff right."

He gave me a pained look and came and sat beside me. "Disadvantage of being famous, E." he said and I scoffed.

"Disadvantage of having a mother like mine," I rectified.

He gave me a confused expression but I shook my head as the others came in. "I have to clean up," I said unemotionally. Jax grabbed my hand.

"I'll get someone in," he offered but I shook my head.

"No, Jax. It's my stuff," I said and then I saw it and my lungs gave up.

Jax caught me and followed my gaze to the small framed picture that had been ripped in two.

I screamed, loudly and uncontrollably as he went to retrieve the two small pieces of paper with the footprints of our baby. His fingers gently swept across the pink paint, dried long ago, as he bit his bottom lip and his chest heaved.

He approached me, passed them to me, and then disappeared.

Just walked out.

Just... left.

CHAPTER 39

The guy's had been brilliant and within a few hours, my house was liveable again. Mad had scoured the internet and ordered a replica suite but nothing would replace my baby's footprints and it was the fact that some bastard was cruel enough to do a thing like that that hurt me.

It just went to warn me who I was dealing with. Merciless bastards!

Jax had returned an hour later, his eyes bloodshot and his shoulders stiff but he had swallowed it back and pitched in to help everybody else after Boss had dragged him into a private room to let loose.

Mad had started to worry me. He was frequently plying for my attention in front of the others, touching me, wanting to be near me continually and I knew it was because of Jax's presence. He had even grabbed the bedroom next to mine before the others could claim one; causing Jax to glare at him but Mad had just smirked back.

Boss and Bruce had bonded like best buddies. No surprise there then!

Jax wisely kept out of Bruce's way as he worked his way around my home. I stalled at my bedroom door as I watched Jax quietly staring at the framed photo of him and me when we had attended a charity dinner dance, back when Room 103 had made it big in Britain; him in all his gorgeousness as he wore a tux and I had sprayed on a tight red cocktail dress.

"You were so beautiful that day," he said softly without turning around, sensing my presence behind him. "Still are, babe."

"As were you. As are you." I replied. He turned to me, a small smile lifted his lips as his eyes twinkled.

"Jax?" I said softly.

"Babe?"

"I… I'm really struggling right now," I confessed awkwardly. His eyes lifted to mine and the pain in them was indescribable.

"You need it, babe?"

I nodded and clenched my fists. "It's been over a year but this… and Kara's picture… it's… it's eating me Jax, choking me." I stifled a sob but I knew it was coming, threatening to rip me apart.

He strolled towards me and took each hand in his. "How do you feel, babe?"

I frowned in confusion but he nodded slightly, encouraging me to tell him but it wouldn't help, just saying the things I felt out loud. It never did.

"Angry. Scared. Consumed. Empty." With each of my words he planted a small kiss against my jaw, his tongue flicking out to taste my skin and every one generated a huff of air from my lips.

"Unloved. Guilty. Disgusting. Sad" I just wanted to keep going to earn another sweet but hot kiss.

My body was firing on all cylinders as his mouth crept nearer to mine; each individual erotic graze launched another hiss of air from my lungs.

I could feel the itch in my blood turn into a heat. The pressure that was pulsing through my body transformed into arousal, each of my words and every one of his kisses dampened down the craving of release and built the hunger for him.

"Hot. Aroused. Desperate. Needy. Stimulated."

He groaned before his lips crashed onto mine. I whimpered at the contact but clung to him, feeding from him as he devoured me hungrily and dominantly.

"Jax," I breathed as his mouth trailed down my throat, his hot lips wetting a route down to my collar bone. I held onto his strong biceps to hold myself up.

"Babe…" he murmured as he found the swell of my breasts above the V in my t-shirt and ran his tongue across the edge. "…you smell fuckin good. I need you, E. All the damn time. I need to breathe you, I need to feel you. I need to consume you and take you. Take you under me until you lose your damn mind and I find mine."

Holy Fuck! I was on fire. "I need you too, baby" I whispered.

His chest rumbled loudly as he came back up and took my mouth, making love to me with just his tongue.

I couldn't get enough of him as I fought back with my own, both of us duelling passionately as our hands roamed over each other, ravenously exploring one another's bodies, taking our fill after such a long withdrawal.

My back hit the wall and I hopped up and embraced his waist with my legs, pulling him further into me.

It was like I could breathe, finally after two long years, I could take a breath; a huge inhalation, a ginormous gulp of air that slammed into my lungs and flooded life throughout my whole body. Synapses lit my brain and brought my dried ravaged nerve endings to life, feeding each of them voraciously as my heart finally took a beat, like a lightning bolt had unfrozen it and restarted it.

He turned and walked us over to the bed, laying us slowly down as he continued his own brand of kissing. The brand I thought had gone bust and sold out so long ago.

My shirt was lifted over my head as he lay next to me, his eyes roaming every inch of my bare torso with a blaze that ignited my own fire.

He cupped my breasts with both hands, softly caressing them as his mouth found my ribcage and his tongue moistly travelled down to the waist of my jeans where it continued to idolise me around the edge of the band.

My hands found his hair and I moaned as he undid the button and lowered them down my hips with my knickers, immediately slipping a finger into me, prompting a loud groan from me.

He took them off completely, then crawled back up to me and slung each of my legs over his shoulders and growled... deep and gruffly.

Christ! Why did he do that? I was practically begging.

I moaned long and loud as his tongue swept the length of me. "Missed your honey, babe," he breathed as he began his tongue fucking. I arched into him, my pussy controlling my hips as I lifted them further onto his mouth.

He worked me in a wild, panting mess as his tongue flicked rapidly at my clit whilst his fingers stroked my internal walls, forcing my orgasm to build hastily.

"You ready to scream, babe?" He smirked up at me sexily, before he slipped his finger into my anus and wrapped his lips around my nub and sucked.

And I did just as he'd predicted... I screamed, loudly, breathlessly and wildly as my body fought between the pleasure and the pain.

"*Jesus,*" I whispered as he suddenly straddled my body, his huge cock in his hand as he pumped it urgently until he shot his spunk all over my chest. The warm creamy liquid covered the whole of my breasts and I climaxed again just at the sight of him.

"Eve," he roared out as his head flung backwards fiercely and his hips flexed until he'd emptied everything he held.

He stayed spanned over me as he placed the flat of his hand into his own cum and started to spread it around my upper body, smearing it over my breasts and up my throat. It was utterly dominant and brazen and I loved it.

I took his hand and licked it with the whole of my tongue, from bottom to top, devouring every single drop of *him*.

His eyes darkened as his cock bounced to life again and before I took a breath he was inside me, his hips rocking into mine urgently and frantically as our carnal appetite ruled us both and we rode each other hard; him over me, me over him, back to chest, hands and knees and then chest to chest as I straddled his hips while he knelt before me.

His hands and mouth were everywhere, tasting and touching every single inch of me as he moaned out erotic words and shameful requests in my ear and my body loved every single fucking second of it.

My climax built so fast it shocked me when it surged through me and I did something stupid as I was overtaken in the moment...

I told him I loved him! Loudly, angrily and passionately. Just shouted it out there *at* him, not to him. In fact I think I screamed it at him. As soon as it left my mouth he exploded into me, a loud cry burst from him as he hit the tip of me, rebounded off it and then filled every single bit of me with his sperm.

I had stiffened as soon as I had said it. Jax eyed me curiously after he had come back down to earth, "Babe?"

I smiled tightly and shook my head, "I'm good."

He sighed and rolled over but then turned on his side and looked at me deeply, his eyes boring into mine and seeking out my soul.

"Need to hear it again, E."

I cringed and shook my head. "Was just habit, Jax." I lied.

His breathing deepened and I watched his chest rise and fall heavily as he bit into his lower lip like his life depended on it, "The fuck, babe?"

"God damn it, Jax. What the hell do you want from me?" I leapt off the bed and pulled everything back on as he lay and just watched me.

"You, E. Just you."

I stared at him incredulously. "You gonna give up America for me then, Jax? Stay here and break the guys' hearts?"

His face said it all.

No!

"No. Didn't think so." I turned away from him so he couldn't see the pain on my face.

I was so stupid. Such a bloody fool for letting him back in once more. I knew he would break me all over again. I shouldn't have risked it, should have bit back the urge but he was like a damn drug, my need for him was too intense and I couldn't fight the hunger and the ache.

I had swapped one addiction for another and this one would be harder to overcome. This one could kill me.

"I have to get to the hospital. It's near visiting time," I said bluntly before I left the room, left him immobile and quiet on my bed, as he realised the truth in my words.

We were both stuck in a vicious circle. Our careers destroyed our hearts.

CHAPTER 40

Evie was snuggled against her Mummy as me and all the guy's entered the hospital room, weighed down with balloons, teddies and chocolates.

It had only been because they were famous rock stars that the Duty Sister had let us all in, and I had rolled my eyes at each of their flirtatious banter to suck up to her.

I stood and took a steady breath before I approached her. My heart was both soaring and breaking at the same time.

Luce gave me a sad but encouraging smile as I emotionally settled my hand on my niece's mass of brown hair. "She's beautiful," I whispered.

She stood up and handed her to me, resting her into my arms so I could cradle her.

"Hey Evie," I breathed as Jax came to stand beside me, his huge frame supporting me both physically and emotionally.

This should have been me with my daughter, but now, it never would be, and Jax knew exactly how I was feeling as he leaned into me. "You're the cool aunt," he murmured. I smiled and nodded.

He was right. I would be the cool aunt; the aunt who Evie could go to when she needed to talk about sex and boyfriends, when she couldn't tell her mother. The aunt that would take her to the park and the zoo, and shower her in the gifts that had been refused by her parents.

I would be *that* aunt. And I would love every single day with her.

"Evie Kara Hudson," I told Jax whose eyes widened and a gentle smile lifted his lips.

"Evie Kara Hudson," he repeated softly as he palmed her tiny head.

"Jax," Aaron muttered from the corner of the room. I groaned to myself as Jax turned and Aaron tilted his chin towards the outside corridor demanding Jax outside the room.

Jax nodded simply and followed him outside. Luce laid her hand on my arm as the other guy's came for a look at Evie.

I passed her to Romeo as Luce pulled me to the corner of the room, her eyes bright with anger. "What the hell are you doing, E?"

I turned away from her wrath and shook my head. "Nothing is going on, Luce."

"Bullshit. I can even fucking smell him on you."

I scoffed. "What are you, a fucking vampire?" I barked out bitterly but cringed when she heaved in a heavy breath.

"Don't, E. Just don't take the fucking piss with me. Don't you dare make fun of me! Who the hell was it picked you up when he left and never came back? Who rocked you to sleep night after night whilst you screamed for him? Who sat and took your resentment, took your heartache and took your rage?"

I nodded and sucked on my lips. "Sorry," I whispered. She grabbed my hand.

"I just don't wanna see you go through all that again E, when he leaves. Because he will. He will turn and leave again and you will be the one left behind. You will be the one fighting the god damn whip. Not me!"

I knew she was right but her words cut into me, the truth in them hit me hard but I understood her resentment.

It *had* been her that had tried to drag me out of the darkness, each of her attempts failing and making her feel like a failure time and time again. And that is what had hurt her, her inability to help her best friend.

I nodded and side hugged her. "I know. We both know… we just…"

She placed her finger over my lips to silence me as her eyes showed me her pain. "End it, E. End it now before it's too damn painful," she urged. I sighed but nodded.

***

We all piled into Z Bar to celebrate Evie's birth and it felt like visiting your granny; familiar, homely and comforting.

A huge round of applause erupted and chants of 'Room 103' and 'E. E. E. E…' hit the rafters and shook the place.

Drinks were bought for us and lined up on the bar and as the night progressed we all slipped into a happy and relaxed mood. Nobody treat us like huge celebrities. We were just the old Room 103 and that's what we loved about the place.

After about an hour Rod, the manager, asked Room 103 if they'd do a couple of songs for old times' sake.

I grinned when they agreed. Rod dragged their old instruments out of the store room and the place erupted when they saw it been set up.

I settled on a bar stool next to Mad as the guy's clambered on the stage and took their places.

"Z Bar!" Jax shouted, "God. It's so good to be back folk's."

The crowd cheered and Jax looked around the room, a slight nostalgic expression on his face and then he took a hefty sigh. "I've missed you all, you know that right?"

Everyone cheered in acknowledgement.

"Gonna start with one of the old ones guys, one that means a lot to me because I once dedicated it to a girl. A girl, who took me as I am, took all my shit and my pain and made me hers. And now, once more I'm gonna dedicate this one to, E. She oozes it boy's, she makes me hard... she *IS* fuckin' *Allure.*" He winked at me with a cheeky grin.

I ignored Mad's huff from beside me.

The band started to play as the mass of people screamed in approval at the song choice as Jax came in, his eyes on mine the whole way through and once again he finished it with the altered line.

> *"But me, I always say*
> *Break it down boy, the Allure's fucking E,*
> *Just fucking E."*

Everyone was up on their feet as Room 103 played a few more songs; a couple of their new big hits and a couple of old ones, rocking the room into orbit and I loved every minute, watching and rocking with the crowd.

As they finished their last song, Jax grinned at me and took the mic in hand.

"Who thinks we should get Eve fuckin' Hudson up here?"

The room exploded into uproar as every head in the place turned to me and I suddenly found my small body being passed from person to person until I reached the stage.

I glowered playfully at him but smiled when he side huddled me and turned back to the crowd, "Any requests?" Jax smirked.

"Shocking Heaven" was yelled from every single mouth in the building.

Shit!

I shook my head at them and Jax frowned at me, "Babe?"

I just shook my head again and took the mic from Jax. "Sorry guys. Not tonight. Pick another," I told them.

After a round of 'boo's, they all shouted "Let me breathe", this being my current single in the charts, it was fresh on their minds.

"Can't. Room 103 don't know the..."

The band surprised me when they began to play my song perfectly and I turned to them open mouthed. Shrugging, I turned back to the room. "Guess they do," I grinned.

A huge cheer echoed through the room and I caught Jax's face. He was angry, no he was furious and I knew it was because I had declined to sing *that* song with him.

He'd get over it!

Boss started me in with a beat on the drums as the first verse was sung with just a throb on the drum and for the whole song I held Jax's gaze.

Because, unbeknown to him, I had written this song for him.

> *"I'm stood here in the dark*
> *Waiting for your call*
> *Waiting for the pain to end*
> *But you never even dare*
> *Never even tried*
> *Just left me in the dark*
> *Alone and broken."*

The rest of the band came in now with the chorus and I could see the realisation sink into Jax as he read my eyes.

"So just leave and let me breathe
Just leave and let me breathe
Cos' I aint giving it no more
Aint openin' you the door
It's locked and dead
To the very core
Right to my empty core."

His expression was painful as I hit the second verse and I caught the question in his eyes.

"I'm feeling all the pain
Hating the void you left
Longing for the fire you took
But you ripped it all away
Stole it away
Just gave me all the hate
Lonely and severed."

He definitely knew now, and when I entered the chorus again, I could see his adam's apple bobbing about manically as his chest heaved with his large gulps.

The last verse was once again just sang accompanied with the drum beat and I belted it out to him, burnt him with it, made him feel every inch of my pain.

"*But now I've burnt the hurt*
Brought my soul back to life
Closed my heart to your world
Cos' that's what you did
When you flew
Just flew and let me die
Empty and barren."

Jax slammed the bar door as he left, stormed out as the room hit the roof in appreciation.

Boss eyed me suspiciously and Mad smirked happily.

But me? I broke all over again.

CHAPTER 41

The ringing in my ears was sending painful jolts through my poor addled brain.

It was still dark out and I was snuggled too comfortably to be ripped so annoyingly from my sleep. It had been singing to me for about an hour on and off and I had been cursing the damn thing in my poor hung-over state.

Eventually relenting, my hand shot out in the dark to grab the offending item before I was tempted to smash it with my fist, and answered without even opening my eyes.

Skill!

"E. Where the fuck are you?" Sed growled down the earpiece.

My eyebrows rose but my eyes remained as they were... glued shut, "Home." It was all my rubber mouth could manage to spit out.

"Where the fuck is that?"

"Okay, Sed. Has something pissed you off cos' you really sound like it has?" I asked and was presented with a loud huff. I rolled my eyes, beneath my eyelids. More skill.

"You kidding me, E?" he barked. He really was in a mood, "After what you did?"

"Look, Sed. I said I was sorry and really... I am. I shouldn't have called... said what I did but I don't know what you want me to say?"

He sighed loudly and paused before he continued. "I just thought... well, stupidly I thought we had a good thing going," he said slowly and I cringed.

"We have, Sed. It is good but I think you're thinking there's more to it than what there is." Did that make sense? Because it didn't to me.

His silence was loud and I grimaced again, "You still there?" I asked quietly.

"Yeah, E. I'm always fucking here," he answered sarcastically.

"Christ, Sed. I told you this when we jumped in. It was always just gonna be sex between us. You said that's what you wanted, so... so we...dived. If I had known it was gonna be a problem for you, well I wouldn't have..."

He was silent again and then the phone went dead.

Brilliant, just brilliant!

"You fuckin' Sed Tyler?" Jax's voice growled across the dark room and my eyes finally opened. Pretty damn quickly!

"What the hell are you doing, Jax?" I spluttered as my eyes adjusted to the darkness. I spotted him, sat in the corner of my bedroom, in the rocking chair I had bought when I had found out I was pregnant.

"Need to hear it, babe?" he reiterated quietly.

I sighed heavily, really not wanting to do this now but I clenched my teeth and went for it. "Yes."

I heard him suck air through his teeth. "You fucked him while you fucked me, E?"

I couldn't decipher his mood through his words. He was very calm and I paused before I answered.

"No, Jax."

His eyes finally met mine as he flicked on the lamp beside him but I still couldn't read him. He rose from the chair and made his way across the room. His strides were heavy and slow and I bit my lip as he drew closer, his gaze fixed to me, sucking the breath right out of me with his intensity.

He stood beside me, peering down at me with a glint in his eye and his head cocked. "No more, babe. Stay the hell away from him," he demanded bluntly and my brows flew high.

"Excuse me?"

"Mine, babe. You - Are - All - Fuckin' - Mine! Every, single, beautiful inch of you. He's just... no, babe." he rumbled quietly as he shook his head firmly.

My arousal surged at his dominance but my anger rose with it and I glared at him. "You fucked anybody else, Jax?"

His eyes narrowed on me and he palmed the mattress, each one of his hands beside my head. "Yeah. I fucked babe, but now I'm yours and we love, not fuck. So, now? No, I don't fuck!"

"That's not what I asked Jax and you know it," I stormed at him but of course he ignored me.

His knees now settled beside each of mine and he leant into me, his mouth resting on my neck. "You give me all you got E, and I'll take it all. Devour every fuckin' drop of you, every fragment and piece of you and then I'll surrender everything I am. You hear me, babe?"

His light kisses on my skin were driving me wild for him and he knew damn well what he was doing. And he knew it would work.

"I hear ya'" I whispered as I slid my head to the side to give him better access to me.

He moaned low and sucked my flesh into his mouth, his teeth biting down as he claimed me, marked me dominantly as his hands rewarded my answer and worshipped my breasts.

"Jax..." I breathed heavily, but he rolled onto his side and regarded me with narrow eyes.

I knew what was coming so I scrambled out of bed before he asked. His hand clamped around my forearm before I made it to a safe point. Damn his reactions!

"Words, babe. Need to hear 'em," he stated as he pulled me back onto the bed. Yeah! You need to bloody learn some!

"What about, Jax?"

He snorted and glared at me, "The song, E."

I just shrugged and tried to escape again but he was adamant I was going nowhere. "Babe!" he practically growled.

I settled beside him and sighed "It's just too..."

He laid still expectantly, his silence notifying me to continue as I tried to find the words to explain.

Rubbing my hands over my face I sighed again and looked at him hesitantly. "It just became... too hard to listen to... you know? When you went, it seemed to be playing everywhere I bloody went. The pub, the car, the TV even the god damn doctors played the chuffing thing and it... it hurt, Jax. Every time I heard it. In the end my whole body related that song with pain and I can't bear to..."

He nodded slowly as if my words had physically hurt him. "And every time I heard it, it made me happy, E. Cos' it was ours, just ours. Something of the two of us." he said as he diverted his gaze to the dark window.

We were silent for a moment but then he turned to face me, "It hurt, babe."

I frowned at him, unsure of what he was referring to. "Which part?" I asked hesitantly.

"When... when you forgot me."

What the hell? How fucking dare he!!

"What the hell are you on about, Jax? I never forgot you... never! All the bloody time, you were there, but never *here*. Just... there. Fucking haunting me cos' I couldn't get the damn smell or feel of you out of me. Couldn't get your face out of my head or the memory of how you used to feel inside me, loving me, kissing me..."

I bounced up, absolutely furious at him. After two years of pausing life, just waiting for him to walk back through that door and he had the damn cheek to say I forgot him.

"It didn't take you long to move on, did it babe?" he scoffed, his eyes full of anger and accusation.

I shook my head in bewilderment. "Jax, just tell what you are on about cos' I think we're both reading a different book here."

He clambered off the bed and went to pick his phone up from the side table. After scrolling through it, obviously looking for something, he thrust it in my face.

I stared at the photo of me in David's arms, and then looked back at Jax with a shrug. "Yeah. David. And?"

He glared at me wide eyed and his jaw dropped. "Seven weeks after I left, babe. I mean, Fuck, E."

Then it sank in. "Is David the reason you never came back?" I asked quietly.

He turned his attention to the window before he answered, "Yeah, babe. Hurt like fuck!"

I couldn't speak.

Fucking unbelievable!

"You stupid fucking man!" I roared at him.

He spun round and before my next breath I was pinned to the wall, his hard body pressed into me.

My anger swelled and my palm swiped his cheek with so much force, his head shot sideways. I ignored his growl because I couldn't hear it for the pounding in my ears.

"He was my mother's Macmillan nurse, Jax!" I bellowed at him. "He was fucking comforting me when I found out that she wouldn't survive surgery. That photo some dick sent you, was the day I knew my mother was going to die. You think I fucked him?"

I pushed my hands against his chest forcefully when he didn't answer, needing to get him away from me. This was just too implausible and I was shocked to my bones as my whole mind couldn't conceive what he had just divulged.

Holy bloody Hell!

"Two years of bloody heartache because you were too fucking stubborn to pick up a bloody phone and ask! JUST BLOODY ASK!!"

He stood silent and pale, just fucking staring at me.

"I don't know what hurts the most, Jax? The fact that you believed some... some jealous person on a photo that doesn't even suggest anything apart from a hug or the fact that you didn't trust me."

"Babe..." he choked out. His shock was just as immense as mine but I shook my head in disgust.

"Just go, Jax. I can't even bear to look at you," I whispered.

The pain and remorse on his face was just a slight indication of how he felt, but at that moment I couldn't give him the forgiveness he needed. "Get out," I repeated as I turned away from him.

The whole pain of the last two years just doubled; in fact it tripled because it could have been so easily avoided.

He hadn't even tried to sort it out. That's what hurt the most. A ten minute conversation on the phone could have saved our relationship but he had chosen to believe whoever, probably Fran, over the woman he was supposed to have loved.

"I asked you to leave," I said without turning.

"Babe, Fuck..." I could hear the desperation in his voice but I refused to cow down to it.

As soon as the door closed behind him, I let the tears flow.

CHAPTER 42

Aaron and I walked up the gravel driveway to our old home, hand in hand. The need to support each other was incredible and we both sucked in a huge breath before Aaron slipped the key into the hole.

When Mom had died, I walked out and never came back, just left everything as was. The same went for Aaron, but he had refused to enter even before her death.

"Ready, E?" he said on a hefty sigh and I nodded.
"Yeah. We need to do this."
I knew it had been ransacked. I knew it before he opened the door.
After my home had been done over, I knew their next step would be here, but Aaron didn't, and it was a huge shock for him as his knees buckled in the doorway when he took in the sight before him.
"Oh God" he breathed. I slipped my hand in his for encouragement.
"It's okay, come on," I said gently.
He narrowed his eyes on me but didn't question my composure as we led each other into the house.

The place had been destroyed worse than mine and I could tell they had been here first.

Aaron walked through to the kitchen, carefully stepping over the broken picture frames on the floor and I ventured into the lounge.

My breath caught when I spotted an envelope with my name on, pinned on the wall above the fireplace.

I managed to stash it in my pocket before Aaron came in. "Fuck, E!"

"Yeah," I breathed as I glanced around the room.

"Do you think we ought to phone the police?"

"Nah, it'll be too late. This was done years ago. You can tell by the dust that covers everything," I lied.

Luckily he bought it and bent to pick a crumpled photo off the floor. He frowned and passed it to me, his face silently asking if I knew who the man in the photo was.

Ironing it out with my fingers I smiled faintly. I had never seen this photo before but I knew exactly who it was. I glanced at Aaron with a soft smile, "It's our father."

His eyes widened significantly as he stared at me. "But I thought he was a... just a one-time screw of hers."

I shook my head, he deserved to know this much. "No, she told me before she died. They had a full blown affair and she loved him as much as he loved her."

Many emotions crossed his face and I gave him a moment as I passed him the photo and went upstairs. It had come as a shock to me when my mother had told me, so I knew how Aaron would be feeling and he needed to come to terms with it himself.

There was nothing I could do or say that would help him comprehend that, after years of thinking your dad had been some dead beat pervert, he was actually a loving and caring man, who had loved my mother entirely.

It was kind of a nice feeling, once you came to terms with the fact that your life had been based on a lie.

I made my way into my old bedroom and into the en-suite and chuckled to myself when I saw the front of the bath ripped off.

Smart girl, E!

I had moved it to a security deposit box when I had released my first single. I knew the status of being a public figure would bring some attention I wouldn't appreciate, but I hadn't anticipated it would be these people I would be hiding it from.

Hearing Aaron downstairs banging about in the kitchen, I locked my bathroom door and pulled out the letter from my pocket.

I sat and stared at it apprehensively for a few minutes before I plucked up the courage to open it.

Eve Hudson
We know you have it.
Ring now 09978345123
Don't even think about ignoring us.
Really isn't worth a leg or even your life.

My eyes closed involuntary as though the words scorched them and I sucked in a huge breath.
SHIT!

God damn my mother. After all we sorted out between us, I thought we had said goodbye with a clear conscience each. Why didn't she just tell me she had told them? Then I could have been prepared.

Aaron banged on the door and I jumped in alarm and banged my hip on the corner of the vanity.

"Coming," I said quickly, as I gave my hip a rub and flushed the toilet as a cover-up.

"It's a waste of time trying to do anything here," Aaron declared as I opened the door to him.

Nodding, I sighed. "What do ya' wanna do?"

He shrugged and glanced around my bedroom. "There anything you wanna keep?"

"Nope," I answered sadly.

Aaron nodded in return "Yeah. Me neither."

How sad was that?

"You don't want to look for any photos of Dad?" he asked and I shook my head.

"Nope," I replied too easily. He narrowed his eyes but didn't speak.

We left as we came. Hand in hand.

And never looked back.

***

"You dirty boy," I scolded Bruce with a chuckle as he exited the brook and splattered me with mud and water. "Mummy's mad." I glowered playfully at him. He sat before me and whimpered but he knew the game, his frantic wagging tail gave him away.

He barked in reply before I grinned and threw his stick again. He watched it launch straight across the banking and land bang in the middle of the stream.

I am sure he grinned mischievously at me before he launched off his hind legs and leapt into the water.

"Oh Christ, Bruce" I sighed.

"Hey, E." Mad spoke from behind me. I smiled and turned to him before I went to stand up but he shook his head and settled on the ground beside me.

"I take it Bruce is on one of his missions," he smirked when he regarded my muddy clothes.

I nodded to him but frowned slightly. His voice was a little off and I knew the reason why but said nothing to him.

He grinned at me wickedly and pointed his chin to the brook. "Fancy skinny dipping?"

I stared at him incredulously but he stood up and pulled his shirt over his head. "Come on, E. I dare you," he bounced on his feet and I swallowed back what I wanted to say to him.

Next went his jeans and I started to panic. "Mad! What the hell are you doing?"

"Come on, E" he said excitedly, too excitedly, taking hold of my hand and pulling me up.

I shook my head at him, staring at him like an idiot but then he got a little scary. His eyes glinted as he took a step towards me and I took a step backwards.

"Mad?"

He kept coming as he scrunched his nose. "Come on E... strip."

"Whoa!" I held my hands up at him and continued on my rearward journey.

He just kept coming, his eyes were wild and his chest was heaving outrageously. As I took another step back, my foot caught on a root in the grass and I stumbled backwards, landing on my ass with a heavy thud.

He was on me within a second. His hands grabbing at the hem of my shirt as he tried to pull it off. "Mad! Christ! Stop it" I exclaimed but he was too strong.

"Come on, E. That fucking hot body of yours should be on fucking display."

I smacked at his hands and scrambled backwards, shuffling my bum across the mud. "What the hell is wrong with you?" I yelled at him.

He had managed to get my shirt up over my breasts and I kicked out at him. "Fuck yeah, E. See... fuckin' stunning." Oh Shit!

"Mad, please. You're scaring me now. Just stop!"

His eyes blazed and I knew he had taken too much this time, he was way over the clouds. I frenziedly looked around to see if there was any means of escape.

He was clambering on top of me know, his fingers at my jeans. "Oh come on, E. You know how I feel about you. We'd be fuckin' awesome together," he whined before he tried to kiss me but I turned my head away.

He gripped my chin harshly and twisted my face back around and tried again but I refused to kiss him back. "Fucking kiss me, E. God damn it! You'll fuck everybody but me." How fucking rude!

"Mad, please" I whimpered as one of his hands grabbed my breast harshly and the other started to pull down my jeans.

Bruce came from nowhere and had Mad's foot in his mouth before Mad could get any further.

He was growling and dragging him off me. I breathed a sigh of relief, but it was short lived as Mad's other foot thudded into Bruce's head with force.

He yelped and lay still and silent on the ground.

"Nooo!" I screamed as I scurried across the ground to Bruce's lifeless body.

Mad stumbled upright and watched in horror as I scooped Bruce up and pulled his ear away from his face. Placing my ear against his mouth, I whimpered as I felt his shallow breath.

Lifting him up with me, I ran towards the house as fast as I could. My god damn jeans were falling down my arse and my t-shirt was still bunched above my boobs but I didn't give a shit.

"BOSS!" I screamed as I ran into the house. "Boss!" I yelled again.

He came hurdling out of the kitchen and stopped dead when he saw me cradling a limp Bruce. "Fuck!" he declared as he went to retrieve his boots.

We both hurried out to my car. I threw the keys to Boss as I huddled in the back with Bruce.

"Come on big man. You stay with me you fucking brute. Mommy needs you," I sobbed as Boss squealed out of the driveway.

"What the fuck happened?" he asked as he screeched around the junction and onto the main road.

"Fucking Mad happened!"

Boss frowned at me through the mirror and then his eyes widened when he saw my disgusted expression. "E...?"

I chewed rapidly on my lower lip and just looked back at him.

"Just tell me if Bruce was protecting you?"

I scrunched up my face and nodded wildly.

"Fucker! I knew there was something weird about him."

My hand was desperately stroking Bruce, as I smoothed each section of his fur down. "You gotta look beautiful for the vet big boy. So handsome. Get all the lady doggies hot, don't you? They all chase after my boy. We gonna sing a song Bruce? What would you like?"

He didn't answer.

He couldn't.

But I sang in his ear softly, all the way to the vets.

CHAPTER 43

Boss quietly shut the door behind us then went straight into the kitchen and pulled out the whisky.

He didn't ask if I wanted one, he didn't need to. He passed me a glass and he raised his own to me. We both saluted and downed it. He refilled me and I downed that one too.

Then I cried. Loudly and heart wrenchingly, as I sunk to the floor and prayed for my boy. Boss sank down beside me, pulled me onto his lap and huddled me tightly, rocking me to and fro as I sobbed and sobbed.

"He's gonna be okay, E. I promise," Boss whispered into my hair and I nodded.

"I don't know what to do, Boss?"

"What do you think you should do, hot stuff?" he asked gently, his hand now stroking my tears off my face.

I shrugged heavily. "It's just... the band, hell what do I tell them? 'Hey guys, Mad tried to rape me then nearly killed my dog' Fuck! It's such a mess!"

"Where the hell did he go anyway?" Boss asked, taking a glance around the kitchen as if he expected Mad to jump out from behind the fridge, brandishing a samurai sword and waving it around wildly.

I shrugged, not actually caring, and then stood and wandered around the kitchen, not really knowing what to do with myself.

It was too quiet, too still and too empty.

I smiled sadly as I looked at his peg, his car harness and lead sat waiting for him.

I felt Boss's hand on my arm before he quietly left the room and I still stood immobile, staring at Bruce's things.

Picking up his biscuits, I poured some into his bowl. "Hurry home my darling before the duck's steal your biscuits," I whispered as I blew him a kiss and retreated to my bedroom.

The night was going to the longest ever as I waited for news and I silently sang to him, singing for him to come home alive.

***

I woke in the darkness with two hulky arms wrapped around me. I pulled him closer needing his closeness and comfort.

"Babe," he whispered against the back of my hair.

"Hey," I whispered back.

"Okay, E?"

"Not really, Jax." I shrugged and he held me tighter.

"He hurt you, babe?" I could hear the chill in his tone and sighed heavily.

"No. But Bruce... Bruce..."

"Sshhh." He tenderly stroked my hair and we lay in silence for a while.

"The band, babe?" Jax asked cautiously and I shrugged.

"I have no idea," I said honestly.

"They know yet?"

"No, not yet, but I've gotta let them know. We have a charity concert Saturday. How the hell am I gonna perform with him...?"

"You don't go near him again, babe. Find a new drummer." He ordered.

Oh so easy! I scoffed loudly, "Before Saturday?"

"Boss, babe. We don't go back till Monday. He's yours."

I tensed at his words. "You go back Monday?" I asked, desperately trying to keep my voice calm.

"Yeah," he answered quietly.

I nodded but didn't say anything, although my heart was screaming at me. What could I say? Apart from 'here we go again'.

My phone rang and I shot my hand out to pick it up, swiping the screen before it was even at my ear. "Bill?"

"He's doing good, Eve." Bill said quietly and a relieved sob erupted up my throat.

Jax scurried behind me and flanked me from behind in a comforting pose but I nodded and smiled to him.

"He's not out of the woods yet though, Eve. We've managed to drain the bleed but there is still some swelling around his brain." Bill divulged and I chuckled slightly.

"Hell Bill, you found one?"

Bill barked out a laugh, "Yup. Definitely one in there so I think he's been playing you all this time, Eve."

I smiled and nodded even though I knew he couldn't see me. "I'll ring for an update in the morning. Thank you so much, Bill. You're Bruce's guardian angel and I'll make sure he gives you one of his unique kisses."

"Don't bother," Bill gasped before he ended the call.

"Oh my God!" I breathed out and Jax nuzzled my neck.

"Okay, babe?" He asked in my ear.

I sighed and nodded. "Just gotta wait now but Bill seems optimistic."

"That's good. I think you need to relax," he whispered and a shiver racked my whole body as he planted wet kisses along my skin.

God, this man could take me from zero to a million in seconds and I moaned against him and palmed his head.

"You mine, babe?" he whispered as he nibbled his teeth along my jaw.

"Lock, stock and barrel, baby. Ooh that's nice. Yeah, just there, Jax." I whimpered.

I felt his smile against my neck as his teeth nipped the length of my throat. "You want more, babe?"

Was he stupid? Of course I wanted more. I wanted everything.

"The whole damn hearts and flowers, Jax" I whispered back.

He stiffened immediately and I suddenly realised he didn't mean what I had thought he meant.

Fuck! Shit!

I closed my eyes and sat up quickly, desperate to hide my humiliation. "Babe" he choked out and I shook my head.

"Dunno where that came from, Jax." I laughed nervously as I scurried around the room, picking up my clothes.

"Babe," he growled as he made a grab for me but I diverted and hurried into the en-suite.

Standing in front of the basin, I turned on the cold tap and held my wrists under it, counting loudly as I battled against the pressure and pain. And yes, heartache was at the very top.

How could I have been so bloody foolish?

There was nowhere to go with our relationship. There was long distance, and then there was fucking stupid long distance. Our distance was *incredibly* fucking stupid extra-long distance!

"Babe?" Jax asked as he jiggled on the doorknob but I ignored him. "E. Fucks sake, babe!"

"Sixteen, seventeen, eighteen...."

He just got angrier and louder. "The door's coming down, E" he growled at me and I snorted.

"Good luck with that, baby." I smirked.

After seven attempts he stopped and I chuckled. This was quite fun actually.

Little did Jax know that the door he was currently bashing his body against was a security door I'd had fitted when I bought the place, just in case I got attacked. Kind of like a panic room but mine was a panic bathroom... very handy when you pee'd your pants as your attacker attempted to murder you.

"Giving up so soon, baby?" I tittered when I caught his snarl behind the door.

"The fuck, babe?"

Well I'll say one thing for him; he wasn't a quitter, as I discovered when he continued to bang the door with his giant frame.

"Jax. You really need to stop now." I laughed loudly.

"Babe. Get out here now!" he demanded and I giggled to myself.

"You lonely out there, baby?"

"Who the fuck made this door? Ironman?" he barked and I rolled in laughter.

He was silent for a moment, and then he spoke. "Babe... My dick is so fucking hard right now!"

Okay. I stopped laughing instantly and listened. But you knew I would.

"Really?" I said loudly. The door muffled each of his words and I was hanging on to each one he said.

"Yeah, babe. So... Damn... Hard. My hand is slowly stroking up and down its stiff length. There's a little bit of cum on the end, babe and it's all yours."

I licked my lips involuntary as I imagined that tasty little treat sat on the tip of his cock.

"Swipe the end with your thumb Jax and scoop it up for me," I told him, quite breathless. I heard his groan through the door and my pussy clenched as I pictured him masturbating for me. "Stroke harder, Jax. Imagine it's my hand, sliding up and down your cock. Squeezing at the crown and then sliding back down. So, so slowly, baby."

"Fuck, babe" he snarled and I slipped my hand between my legs, gasping at my own wetness.

"Is that good, Jax?"

He groaned again and my whole body shuddered at the sound. Sliding a finger inside me and resting my forehead against the door I moaned with him.

"Oh God, Jax" I murmured.

"You fingering that sweet pussy, babe?"

"Yes." I whispered as my hand moved faster, bringing me closer but never quite touching it. It was too far away, too out of reach and I frantically pumped harder.

"Babe...?"

Fuck this!

I flung the door open and vaulted myself onto him. "Fuck me, Jax. Hard and fucking furious," I demanded.

He wasted no time and I was suddenly bent over the bed, his hands wrapped around my hips as he viciously thrust into me.

"Fuckkkk," he hissed as he hit the top of me and banged me hard.

"Christ yes," I shouted at him. "Harder. Fucking take me, Jax!"

His drives got harder and fiercer as he pounded into me powerfully. A hand yanked my hair as he pulled me upright, and then his arms circled my waist and he carried me to the wall.

"Hands behind your back," he ordered harshly. My arousal flew wildly and I groaned with lust as I did as he asked. He rapidly tied my wrists with something and then I was pushed flat against the wall, his hard body pressing into me as his mouth came to my ear. "Don't. Ever. Fucking. Run. Again!" he growled.

Christ! I was on fire. One more word and I would orgasm without the need for his touch.

"You hear me, babe?"

I nodded frantically. "I hear ya'," I whispered.

He palmed my butt cheeks and spread them wide. "Open your legs, babe."

My legs parted impulsively; no motivation needed, and I groaned loudly as his finger swept along the length of my sex, teasing my entrance as it passed then arrived at my clit. I wiggled my hips, trying to get his finger where I needed it.

"Ah, ah, ah. You don't deserve it. You've been bad!" he smirked from behind me. I moaned, still straining to get his touch to where I wanted it.

"God, Jax..." I whined as his finger circled around my clit without actually touching it.

"How much you want it, babe?" he said slowly as his teeth bit down gently on my buttock.

"God. With everything I have, Jax. I need it. Please," I begged.

His mouth climbed higher up my back, his soft lips idolising my tat before he travelled all the way up my spine and rested them on my shoulder. "And how much you want *me* babe?" he added and I frowned.

"I'm not sure what you're getting at Jax?" I asked as his finger plunged inside me.

We both moaned loudly at his intrusion and I pushed against him, desperate for the stimulation.

"So damn wet, babe" he breathed heavily, his mouth now at my ear. "Do you want me? All of me. Lock, stock and barrel, babe?"

He circled his finger inside me, igniting a roar through my body. "Fuck Jax. You know I do. All of you, every single god damn fucking piece of you. Lock, stock and barrel, baby!"

A low growl rumbled through his chest before he brutally drove into me again; his rock hard cock filling every single groove inside me.

"Yes!" I hissed.

About bloody time!

My head bounced off the wall as he began to pound into me, his anger and passion driving him wild. "Come back with me," he cried out as he continued to fuck me ruthlessly.

I was too far gone to acknowledge his request so I just pushed back against him, meeting each of his forceful drives.

"You're mine Eve Hudson!" he roared as he erupted into me. His spunk hit the very tip of me and triggered my own climax. I bucked wildly against him as his arms circled my waist and he pulled me further onto his throbbing cock, making me take every single drop of him as we both squeezed each other tight.

His head settled on my back as we both fought for breath. "Fuck, babe." He panted before he undid my robe belt from my wrists and picked me up again, then gently set us on the bed.

He lay alongside me, on his side, gazing at me as his hand lifted and his fingers tenderly brushed my hair off my face. "Come with me, babe?" he repeated his earlier question and I frowned in bewilderment.

"I don't think I understand you, Jax."

"America." His expression was casual as though he'd just asked what I wanted for lunch and I looked at him in astonishment.

"Jax. I... I can't just drop everything and leave."

His brows lifted towards his hairline and his head tilted. "Why?"

"My God, Jax. It's not that simple. I have a career, a family, my band, my charity... It's impossible." I sighed heavily as he looked hurt.

"You were willing two years ago, E."

I shook my head and scoffed. "Yeah, Jax. And you promised to come back two years ago, but that didn't happen either."

"You know why, babe." He looked angry now and I clicked my tongue.

"Do you know what I can't understand, Jax? If our relationship had meant that much to you, when you saw that photo why didn't you fight for me? Why didn't you ring and demand to know what was going on?" I asked. I noticed a flicker in his eyes. A flicker that made my stomach clench.

Rearing back, I glared at him, "You went out and fucked someone. Didn't you?"

His expression said it all and I bit my lower lip. "Well fuck me. You saw a photo of me hugging someone then went and had a revenge fuck, eh? Just thought 'Fuck her' I can do one better."

He rolled onto his back and huffed. "You been fuckin' Sed, babe" he said stiffly as though that condoned his actions.

"What the hell, Jax? I've been sleeping with Sed for three weeks. That's it," I stated angrily.

He turned to look at me with wide eyes. "You're telling me you didn't sleep with anyone until Sed?" I could hear the scepticism in his tone and I glared heatedly.

"Eighteen fucking months, Jax. The first time I fucked after you! Eighteen long fucking months and it still felt like betrayal even then!" I shouted at him. "Don't you dare twist this round to me to make yourself feel better!"

He looked sad for a moment, his top teeth nibbling furiously on his bottom lip. "You waited that long for me, babe?"

"Yes Jax," I said quietly. "And now I... I don't think I can just up and leave everything here because of that. You moved on too quickly, Jax" I said sadly. "And... to me, our relationship was everything. My life, my whole soul, I only breathed for you Jax, but you... you just gave up on us way too soon."

He scrunched up his face as though deep in thought and I watched the many emotions cross his face. "Wasn't like that, E. I never got over you, never forgot you, and never pushed you out of my heart. Just cos' I fucked someone doesn't mean I didn't love you, babe."

"Yet, you were willing to think that of me Jax," I posed softly.

The sadness in his eyes gripped my heart but I had to be strong. I had to make him realise what he had done. "Yeah," he said, nodding faintly.

Now it was sinking in, the pain on his face broke me in two but there was nothing I could do or say to change it.

Our relationship was doomed, unobtainable and just impossible.

"Don't think I can do it again, babe," he whispered softly as his eyes pierced mine and I frowned at him.

"Do what?" I asked quietly as I took his hand in mine, attempting to alleviate some of his ache.

"Leave you, babe."

I closed my eyes and sighed heavily. "I know baby but we have to. You can't let the guy's down and I can't do that to my boy's," I said sadly.

The anguish on his face mirrored mine as we both accepted the inevitable. Our minds recognising we couldn't be together but our hearts rebelling against the truth.

Monday morning we would finally have to accept the death of our relationship, once and for all.

CHAPTER 44

Jax, Boss and I were on our way to see Bruce. I was driving but my phone wouldn't stop ringing so I eventually switched it to Bluetooth when Leah had been trying to contact me incessantly for ten minutes.

When her call came through again, I managed to connect and her voice filled the car. "E. God damn. I've been trying all bloody morning!" she grumbled and I rolled my eyes.

"Ten minutes, Leah. You have been ringing for ten minutes."

"Yes well, it seemed like all morning to me. Anyway I need to confirm for the MTV interview tomorrow and Saturdays performance, oh and Elizabeth wants to meet. Sed Tyler's been ringing constantly and Halo's manager has approached you about doing a single with them..." she raved on.

"Righ...." I tried but she spoke over me.

"Barney Graves has been after a meet with you and Wesley wants lunch next Wednesday."

She finally took a breath and I opened my mouth to speak but I wasn't quick enough. "Oh and some weird guy has been hammering your personal line. Tried to take a message and really didn't like the sound of him, E but he wouldn't leave one. Before I forget, I've stocked your fridge and picked up your dry cleaning. Oh and don't forget you've got that photo shoot for Grey's magazine Monday..."

"Christ woman. Shut - Up!" Jax declared loudly and I smirked at him.

Boss, who was seated in the rear, growled out, "I agree. Do you breathe or just absorb oxygen through your tongue?"

I chuckled quietly at her gasp. "Excuse me. Who are you?" she barked out horrified.

"The men with the bleeding ears," Boss shouted. I snorted but butted in before she got too upset.

"Leah, everything's fine but I need you to decline with Wesley and Halo. Barney, I can do in a couple of weeks and arrange Elizabeth for probably end of next week?" I finished with a query.

She huffed and puffed as she went over my diary and I rolled my eyes again. "Nope, E. Thursday you've got the Scottish morning TV performance and then you've got the talk show with Keith Kershaw don't forget and Friday you've got to travel back, so it'll have to be the beginning of the week after."

Blowing out a huge breath I confirmed with her and 'accidently' disconnected the call.

Jax was staring at me and I glanced at him, "Everything okay, Jax?"

His eyebrows went high as he scoffed. "Babe. Do you have a private life?"

I laughed bitterly at that and shook my head as my phone rang again. Groaning I hit accept on the dash. "Christ, Leah. What now?"

"Well, well, well. Eve fucking Hudson," the male voice growled. I knew instinctively who it was. *Shit!*

I shot a sideways glance at Jax and cringed. "I'm on Bluetooth and I have company. Can you give me ten minutes to pull over?" I asked nervously.

"Five. Be ready," he ordered as he disconnected.

"Babe?" Jax asked suspiciously.

"Just a private call I need to take, Jax." I told him as I pulled over into a layby and wrenched my phone off the holder as I opened my door. "I won't be long."

Exiting the car, my legs wobbled and I cursed myself for showing my nervousness in front of Jax and Boss.

I walked to the curb and waited.

I wasn't quite sure how I was going to handle this and I nearly dropped my phone when it rang.

"I'm here," I told him.

"It's 'bout fucking time," he snarled and I turned away from Jax and Boss's inquisitive looks.

"It's the first time you've rang," I argued as I endeavoured to keep my voice calm.

"But you were supposed to ring me weren't you?"

I sighed loudly. "What do you want?"

He laughed loudly, it was the kind of laugh that sent chills down your spine and through your blood "You know what we want, Eve."

"Look. I've had the damn thing for seven years and I haven't shown it to anybody. I can promise you that I won't," I offered but he laughed again.

"Well you won't need to keep it then will you," he jeered and I bit my lip anxiously.

"You know I'm not going to give it you so... how we gonna resolve this?" I closed my eyes as if to hide from him even though I knew he couldn't see me anyway.

He barked out another laugh. "We gonna resolve it by you giving it to us."

Running my fingers through my hair, I rotated my neck sideways and shifted my eyes around to make sure I wasn't being watched... or targeted.

"I can't do that," I said quietly.

He tutted mockingly, "Now you see, that's not a very wise decision, Eve. You're gonna make my boss a very unhappy man." He warned and I swallowed heavily. "Such a shame when you have such a beautiful voice." He finished and the line went dead.

Oh crap!

I stared at my phone for a few minutes as though I expected it to count down and blow up, then I made my way back to the car.

The guys were silent as they watched me buckle in and pull off. "Clue us in, babe." Jax ordered with narrow eyes but I put on a smile and turned to him.

"Everything's fine. Just something I had to sort out for somebody." Christ! Even the most gullible person wouldn't have fallen for that.

The car was silent for a few moments and I set my attention on the road, repetitively checking my mirrors to divert my attention from the thick atmosphere around me.

"Bullshit, babe," Jax said eventually but I ignored him.

The silence grew even thicker and it was becoming difficult to breathe so I opened my window a little, frantically striving to pull some air into my tight lungs.

I thanked god silently when we pulled into the vet's car park. I was out of the car before the guy's, my legs practically running across the tarmac but I could still feel Jax's glare through the space between us.

Bill smiled widely as we entered and I grinned back. "Just in time, Eve. He's just woken up and so far he looks good," he divulged with a beaming face.

"Bill. I owe you big." I sighed as I hugged him tight.

He rubbed my arm and gestured to the back room with his chin. "Go on through."

I bounced excitely as I peeked my face around the corner of the door. I could hear the thud of his tail on the wall of his cage before I heard his yap.

"My beautiful boy," I whispered as tears pooled in my eyes and I settled on the floor in front of him.

He tried to drag himself onto my knee as I opened the door but I held him back. "Oh no, you don't. Stay there big man, I'll come to you," I told him sternly as I snaked my arm in and scratched behind his backside.

"Hey, dude," Boss said from behind me as he settled a hand on my shoulder. "See, hot stuff. I told you he'd be fine." I nodded and smiled back up at him.

Bruce whined a tune, I knew what he wanted. "What do you want today then?" I asked him. He answered with a low howl, it was all he could manage but I was so proud of him.

I treat him to Guns N' Roses 'Sweet Child o' Mine' as his tail tapped in rhythm before Bill came in. "Don't wear him out, Eve. He won't sleep while you're here and he needs to rest." I nodded again.

My phone was ringing nonstop in my bag and I grit my teeth against it. I was spending a precious moment with my boy, some people needed to learn the act of respect. Even though they didn't know what I was doing at that moment but I still thought it rude.

I leaned in and kissed Bruce as did Boss and we walked back into the reception. "I have to go back down to London tomorrow but Aaron will be in. Just send the bill to Leah and she'll sort it but I'll be back up Sunday if he's out by then," I informed Bill.

He smiled softly. "He should be out for Saturday so I'll deal with Aaron."

I smiled tightly as my phone rang again, just as Jax's and Boss's rang. We all eyed each other warily, knowing something was wrong when all of them went together.

As I pulled mine from my bag, I frowned when I saw Romeo on the screen. "Hey," I answered. My skin prickled when I heard sirens in the distance, "Romeo?" I asked hesitantly.

"FUCK!" Jax yelled beside me as he spoke to someone on his phone and I grew even more worried.

"Romeo?" I asked again.

"Jax will fill you in, I gotta go," he said before he disconnected.

Jax was staring at me, his face full of anguish and my heart stuttered. "Just tell me," I barked out.

"Babe…" he choked out.

"God damn it! Tell me!" I demanded.

"Your house, babe."

I opened my hands in a 'What?' gesture as I glanced at Boss's white face. "What the hell is wrong with my house?" I was seriously getting pissed off now as they both stared at me.

"It's gone!" Jax informed me and I frowned dubiously at him.

"What the hell do you mean?"

Boss shot Jax a look before Jax took my hand and led me over to one of the waiting room chairs. "It's just blown up, babe" he said quietly.

I barked out a laugh and scowled at him. "Jax. I'm not that stupid. Try again."

Boss crouched in front of me and settled a hand on my thigh. "He's not joking, baby."

My eyes shot from one to the other as it sank in. "Oh my God. That was quick," I breathed to myself.

"What was quick, babe?" Jax asked suspiciously.

"What?" I frowned.

"Babe. Serious shit, E. Clue me in," he insisted sternly but I continued to stare at him in shock.

"The guys!" I cried as it occurred to me that they were in the house.

"They're fine, E." Boss assured me quickly.

"Babe. Need to hear you," Jax pursued urgently.

I shook my head at him. "I... I... Oh God!" I was suddenly struggling to breathe and I grabbed at my chest as my lungs screamed in agony.

"Breathe, babe." Jax instructed softly. "Look at me, E." His hands cupped my face gently as he turned me to look at him.

He mimicked pulling in a breath. "Hold!" Then he blew out and I copied. He repeated for a few times, his eyes fixed on mine softly as I followed his every move.

"Good girl," he nodded as he replicated one last breathing technique.

Bill appeared beside me with a glass tumbler containing a shot of whisky and I downed it as I eyed him sceptically. "I keep it in for Bruce," he winked. I snorted and nodded slyly.

My phone was ringing again and I groaned, knowing it would be Leah as the alarm system would have notified her to its activation.

Jax pulled it from my bag and answered it. "She knows," was all he said before he disconnected. Boss scoffed at Jax's bluntness but Jax just shrugged.

It rang again and he glowered at me. "Is it always like this for you?" he asked and I nodded.

"That's my life," I told him nonchalantly.

"The fuck, babe! Even Room 103 don't put up with this kind of shit!" he chided but I shrugged again.

"Need to slow the fuck down, E" he told me before he answered my phone again.

Turning his back to me, he walked over to the other side of the room. I flinched when I noticed his shoulders stiffen. The anger radiating off him soon became drowning and I swallowed desperately against it.

Boss glanced at me and then back to Jax as Jax turned around.

He was furious as he glared at me and I knew immediately it was '*them*' informing me of what they had done.

He dropped the phone from his ear and stalked across the room to me, his raging eyes never letting mine free as his jaw tensed tightly and his teeth bit his lip vehemently.

"Words, babe. Now!" he growled as he loomed over me and I shrank back into the chair.

Boss regarded Jax cautiously and Bill took a step away from the wrath of Jax.

"It doesn't involve you, Jax." I stated more confidently than I felt.

"The fuck, babe!" he hissed and I blinked against his anger. "You either tell me E, or I'll ring the fucker back and sort it myself!" he warned and I cringed.

"You really don't wanna do that, Jax. They're not nice people," I warned him quietly.

He started laughing then; indignantly, loudly and sarcastically. "Ya' think?" he scoffed.

I removed my gaze from his and just looked at the floor; anywhere would do as long as I wasn't looking at his furious face.

"The fuck, babe. You should've clued me in," he chastised and I shrugged at him.

"And what ya' gonna do, Jax? Go beat 'em up. Put a couple of bullets in their heads. Tie 'em to the train tracks?" I mocked.

You can guess what happened can't you?

You'd be correct... he was pulling me through the vet's front door within seconds, straight across the car park and then I was bundled into the back of the car, him following me into the cramped space.

"Don't fuck me off, E" he growled. I pushed against his chest, striving for space between us.

"You're fucking *me* off right now, Jax. Move!"

His chest rose heavily as he sucked in a few deep breaths, trying to calm himself down before he looked back at me. I ignored the worry and anguish on his face and stared straight back at him.

There was nothing he could do to help.

It was that simple.

"Look, babe. I know you loved your dad and I know he loved you but..."

I snorted loudly at that line and Jax narrowed his eyes on me. "E?"

I cursed myself for my lack of control and shook my head at him.

He inhaled deeply and grasped my chin. "Babe. You're trapping those words again and I really need to hear 'em now. I wanna help you."

"Christ, Jax. Why bother? Eh? You're fuckin' off back to America Monday. I'll be right at the back of your mind while you fuck some other girl so... so just fuck off and leave me alone!" I shouted at him, finally snapping at his persistent interrogating.

His growl was loud in the confines of the car and I flinched against it, "The fuck, babe!" His fist smashed into the headrest beside me before he flung himself out of the car and took off.

I sat in the car, watching his body shrink further into the distance, his long legs carrying him briskly down the road and before he turned the corner, his fist smashed into the wall forcefully.

The tears came then. Tears for our doomed relationship, tears for my house, tears for the worry of the mob I was dealing with and finally, tears for me, for my fucked up life.

I had fought so hard in the last two years to make something of myself, my final promise to my mother, but if I was honest with myself, was it everything I wanted?

When I glanced in the direction of where Jax had disappeared I was suddenly wondering if my career was as important as other things?

CHAPTER 45

Boss glanced through the car window before he climbed in beside me. I had moved into the driver's seat but I had just sat staring at nothing for a long while.

"Jax?" Boss asked as he belted up.

I shrugged at him then smashed my hand against the steering wheel, just for the hell of it. Boss squeezed my thigh and I smiled woefully at him. "Why us, Boss?"

He shook his head, sadness covering his face. "I dunno, hot stuff. You two were born to be together but sometimes fates a bit of a bastard and tends to rip everything apart." He sighed as if talking from experience.

I nodded firmly, completely agreeing with him. "I just... I love him *too* much, ya' know," I told him openly. "It always hurts so fucking much with Jax. Two years and I still couldn't forget him."

We both sat in silence for a while until Boss spoke. "He told me he'd asked you to come with us."

I smiled and nodded at him. "Yeah but... life tends to get in the way." I sighed as I turned my face to the window, hiding the pain in my face.

"Life is what you make it, E. Yours alone; yours to control, yours to fight for and yours to take. Fucking take it, E. Take what you can, cos' no-one out there will give it you."

I frowned at him then smiled, "When did you get so smart?"

He shrugged. "I had four Weetabix this morning," he told me, nodding with respect for himself. "With a banana," he added seriously, very impressed with himself now.

I stared at him for a while, and then we both burst out into laughter, huge rolling fits of giggles that brought tears to my eyes. My God I loved this man!

"You're gonna need to book into a hotel Boss, I've got something I need to do first." I told him as we settled down and he eyed me sceptically.

"If you think I'm leaving you alone hot stuff, you can think again." He smiled meaningfully and I rolled my eyes.

"Boss, I'm not gonna give in to it after eighteen months. I just need to..."

He held up his hand. "Don't care, baby. I'm with you," he said casually then turned away from me to end the discussion.

Sighing heavily I started the engine. "Fine but you stay in the car."

He turned back to me and nodded happily as he began to skim through my iPod.

"Do you need a wee cos' it's a bit of a drive?" I asked him sarcastically.

He scoffed loudly. "Bushes, hot stuff!" he declared without casting me a glance.

Men!

***

I cut the engine as I pulled up alongside the cemetery and Boss snorted loudly. "If you think I'm waiting in here alone you can think again, hot stuff," he told me with a stern shake of his head. I regarded him in bewilderment and realised he wasn't joking.

"Boss, I think you're safe in a car *outside* the cemetery." I chuckled. He glared at my humour.

I sucked on my lips to bite back the giggle, but he was as white as a sheet and my eyes widened in astonishment. A big brute like him and he was frightened of being alone in a graveyard.

"Fine," I huffed.

He nodded frantically and clambered out of the car, eyeing the churchyard warily. "You wanna hold my hand, Boss?" I mocked but he nodded again and grabbed for my hand.

It was getting really difficult to bite down the laughter so I just walked towards where I needed to be.

"Your Mom?" Boss asked as he felt the falter in my step when we approached a gravestone.

I nodded solemnly, "And my Dad."

I squeezed Boss's hand and he dropped mine. "I just need a moment," I asked. He nodded and took a few steps back but I noticed not too far.

I smirked when I saw his fearful eyes flitting from gravestone to gravestone with horror. "You'll be fine," I told him as I took a step nearer to my parents.

"Hey, Mom." I started as I traced her name on the stone. "You'll be pleased to know that thanks to you, I now have a gang of merciless bastards blowing up things around me," I told her sardonically.

I half expected the backhander at my cheek but all was quiet so I carried on. "Jax is back. He wants me to move across the world with him but... well, you understand. You're the one that would understand but you're not here to tell me so..." I sat down at the edge of the grave and started uprooting all the weeds and tidying the spot.

"I shouldn't have put you in here with him. I'm sorry, I just didn't think at the time. I've been trying to find my father's resting place Mom, but no luck so far. It's pretty hard when all I have is a name and 'Gerry Smith' is pretty common... who knew?"

Taking a deep breath, I moved on to the other person sharing the spot in the ground with my mother.

"Dad."

The words seemed to be struggling to come out and I stared at his name for a while.

"I loved you, Dad. Hell, I idolised you but..."

I blew out long deep breaths as the tingle in my veins started itching and my brain released the usual jolts of electricity.

"How could you…?" I whispered as a tear rolled down my cheek. "Thirteen years of trusting you, thirteen years of worshipping the very ground you walked on. You ruined her life, took everything from her, which in turn ruined mine, Dad. You… You took my father from me, took my mother's love but what hurts the most is… you took my life when you sent those men into me… you turned me into something I don't… I don't really like."

I felt Boss sit beside me and I realised I was crying louder than I thought. He didn't speak, or even look at me, just took my hand in his for support.

I swallowed loudly and stared at the etching on the gravestone. "I… I… don't know what to do Dad? Do you want me to give in and give it them? Do you want me to hang on to it? I… just…"

It was such a mess, and all I needed was some direction, but I knew I would get none here today. "Is it worth it?" I finished quietly. Boss squeezed my hand tightly and I returned the gesture.

"I think I forgive you Dad, but I'll never forget what you did to my Mom or my father… never. But I'm the one that has to live with that, not you. I'm the one left behind to deal with your betrayal, your selfishness and all the lies, all the damn secrets that changed my life forever."

Plucking the last weed from the ground, I ran my fingers over both their names. "Anyway, I'm here to say goodbye. I won't be back. You're in my head and my heart, not here, under the soil, under the weeds and dirt. My heart." I whispered.

I stood, blew them a kiss each and walked away. Boss's hand held mine tightly as he guided me back to the car.

He took the keys from me before we both climbed in and after scrolling through his iPod he played *Amy Grant's, 'I will remember'* as we pulled away.

✳✳✳

I groaned as I saw all the paparazzi camped outside our hotel but Boss circled round to the backstreet and pulled into the underground car park.

Luckily my car had tinted windows, so the small group that had resided here didn't know who we were as we drove straight past them.

I frowned when I saw Jack waiting beside the elevator and Boss shrugged at me. "What are you doing here?" I asked him as I climbed out.

"Heard what happened so thought I'd come up."

I smiled appreciatively at him, "I'm back down tomorrow though."

He nodded in acknowledgement. "Yeah, I know but I've come up to sort everything out with the police and insurance people. After what happened, you need me here, E."

I sighed and nodded as we entered the elevator and rose to the main foyer.

The receptionist smiled widely at me as I approached. "Oh my, Eve Hudson," she gushed and I grinned at her.

"Hey."

She leaned forward. "I know you're probably sick of this, but could you sign something for my daughter, she adores you?"

I nodded and signed a slip of paper, adding a personal message for her daughter, before she handed me my key card. "Mr Cooper and his friends have already arrived and are currently in residence," she told me.

I nodded. "Thank you."

Jack escorted me into the elevator, his hand placed at the bottom of my spine protectively. "Hold on," he said as he checked out the lift before we entered.

Rolling my eyes, I followed him in. "E, bloody hell, you need to be more alert now," he scolded. I nodded dutifully. "I'm driving you back down to London tomorrow so I'll send someone for your car. Leah has had some clothes and basic necessities sent to your room here." He told me and I smiled at my PA's initiative.

She was sometimes a bloody nuisance but I knew I wouldn't survive day to day living without her. "God bless, Leah." Jack nodded then turned to Boss.

"She also had some things delivered for you guys."

Boss reared back and regarded him. "Wow. I've changed my mind about your PA, E." He chuckled and I nodded slyly at him.

"I'll give her that, she's damn efficient," I agreed.

Boss hugged me tight as we stopped at his door on the way to mine. "I'm leaving about 4am tomorrow, so I'll see you down there," I told him. He nodded at me before I made my way to my room.

Jack entered before me and scoped out my room before he left me alone, but before I relaxed, I phoned everybody I needed to, then kicked off my shoes and after ordering coffee, I slumped on the sofa.

After my coffee was delivered, I pulled off my clothes and stepped in the shower, relishing the beat of the water on my back.

I sighed in relaxation as the stream massaged my aching back and legs. Before I knew what I was doing, I was sinking to the floor, my body heaving in heart-wrenching sobs, as everything came to a head in my frazzled mind.

I knew the main reason was the thought of having to say goodbye to Jax and the guy's once again. My heart was hurting already and I hoped my mini breakdown now would stop it from happening when they actually left.

Don't lie, E. You knew damn well that wasn't gonna happen!

I was suddenly lifted and pulled onto Jax's naked lap. I stared at him in surprise for a while, then gave in and wept uncontrollably into him as he took all my sorrow and pain.

"How did you get in?" I hiccupped eventually.

He smiled softly as his thumbs swept under my eyes and removed my tears. "We're sharing babe," he stated bluntly.

Oh okay.

His fingers started massaging my scalp as he turned me around so my back was to him and I moaned in delight. "That's nice," I breathed.

He chuckled softly and I smiled slyly as I felt his erection grow beneath me. "You like it too, Jax?" I smirked.

He growled playfully as he reached up to the shelf for the shampoo. My groans got louder as he continued to wash my hair, then he lifted me and sank me down onto his firm cock.

"Oooh, that's even better." I sighed as he groaned when he reached the tip of me.

We didn't move, just stayed like that, him inside me, as he finished my hair. "I feel ya' babe," he whispered in my ear as he took my lobe between his teeth and bit down gently.

"I feel ya' too, baby," I replied.

His hands swept up my back and then over my shoulders and down until he reached my breasts. "God, I love your tits, E."

I groaned and shifted on his lap when he took my nipples between his fingers and teased them, the same time his mouth encouraged my arousal by grazing over the tender skin on my neck.

"I hear ya', babe" he whispered into my ear as my moans got louder and I started to move on him more.

"Need to see you, E." He lifted me, turned me to face him then lowered me back down onto him.

His mouth found mine as he kissed me in his unique way, his tongue governing everything mine did. I palmed his face as I drove us higher into oblivion, my body instinctively taking control as it rose and plunged back down, faster and harder with each stroke.

My thighs clenched him tighter as he took one of my nipples in his mouth and savoured it with his tongue and teeth. "I love you, Eve Hudson," he rumbled as his eyes penetrated mine.

His words brought my climax and I fell to pieces around him, crying out his name as he did the same and spewed into me. His ejaculation seemed to last forever, as he continued to pump into me. "Fuck. Christ!" he growled as he jerked wildly into me.

"Can feel your heart beating through your chest, babe." He wheezed as he rested his mouth against my breastbone and held my eyes with his own as he peered up at me.

"I love you too, Jaxon Cooper" I whispered. He groaned and closed his eyes as if relishing my words and engraving them to memory. "I'll always love you, Jax. Right until my soul shrivels and dies."

Which would probably be Monday, when he boarded the plane back to America.

He sighed heavily and cupped my cheek with his hand. "Babe... I need you. I need all of you, with me, E. I can't... it hurts too damn much..."

I nodded and pressed my lips to his, "I know, baby."

He rubbed his nose around the tip of mine, "You mine, babe?"

I smiled softly, "Lock, stock and barrel, baby. Always and forever."

CHAPTER 46

Thursday afternoon I was stood behind the closed door to the room that contained the band members of Hell's Eden in the MTV studios.

Leah was staring at me irritably as my hand hovered over the door handle. "E. What the hell is wrong with you?" she hissed before I took a huge breath and walked in.

They were sat around a small table drinking coffee. My temper rose when I spotted Mad, laughing and joking with them.

They each turned to me and smiled as I entered but my eyes glued to Mad. "Get out. You're fired!" I said simply.

Angel and Hunter laughed and prodded Mad but Mad knew from my face that I wasn't joking.

"Can you do that, E?" he smirked and I smiled slyly.

"Well it's either you or me Mad and I think Brent will find it easier to replace a drummer," I spat.

Angel and Hunter squinted at us both, wondering what the hell was going off, but Mad and I locked on each other.

"Well?" I provoked. My breath hitched when I saw the members of Room 103 enter the room. Each one of them silently walked over to Mad and dragged him from the room. Not one word from any of them.

Angel stood up quickly, his chair flying behind him but I stood in front of him and shook my head. "Sit down, we need to talk." I informed him.

"What the hell is going on?" Hunter asked and I sighed as I sat before them.

"Mad tried to rape me then nearly killed Bruce," I told them frankly.

Both of their eyebrows hit their hairline but they just stared at me in shock. I filled them in as they were silent, both of them snarled when I told them what he had done to Bruce. Charming. No reaction for my part.

They both sighed when I finished but it was Leah who spoke from behind me. "I hope those guys kick the shit out of him," she said angrily and I nodded.

"What about the charity thing Saturday?" Angel asked.

"Boss is gonna fill in for him. But I've been onto Brent and he's already putting some feelers out for a new guy."

"So Brent already knew?"

I nodded. "I'm sorry I told him first but I needed to know if I had his backing, before I walked out on you all."

Hunter did a very rare thing then. He stood, hugged me and kissed me gently on the cheek, "With you all the way, E."

I smiled gratefully at him and Angel nodded, "Needs his balls cutting off. Knew he had a thing for you but..."

I nodded in agreement just as one of the studio men came to fetch us.

"Are we announcing his departure now?" Angel asked but I shook my head.

"No, Brent will deal with the press release."

"Holy fuck, E. Dunno how you're still alive after these last few days," Hunter scoffed.

It wasn't the last few days that would kill me.

It would be Monday.

***

Jack was waiting for me as I exited the studio and I frowned at him. "I thought I was going with Angel and Hunter?"

He shook his head. "Change of plan, E. Leah told me to pick you up and run you for an impromptu photo shoot. Angel and Hunter are done for the day," he told me as he held the back door open for me.

I groaned as Hunter and Angel laughed. They got into their waiting car in front of mine and I poked my tongue out at them before I climbed mine.

"Ooh gimme your phone a minute E, I've got a new number," Jack said as he turned to face me from the front seat.

I shrugged and handed it to him. "You could've just given me the number Jack and I would've done it," I told him as he fumbled about with my phone.

I stared out of the window for five minutes then looked back at Jack. "What are you doing? It's taking you ages." I moved to look over his shoulder.

He passed me my phone back and smiled. "Yours is a different phone to mine, I couldn't work out how to do it," he chuckled.

He pulled out into the traffic and I people watched through the window. "Who's the shoot for?" I asked but Jack shrugged his shoulders.

"Where is it then?" I tried but he shrugged again.

"Dunno, just got an address," he said simply.

I frowned. This wasn't like Jack; he usually knew everything down to the finest detail. "Everything okay, Jack?"

He just nodded again. I was starting to get a bit suspicious when he glanced at me through the mirror, but in the end I left him to it and settled back and closed my eyes, hoping to catch up on half an hours sleep before the shoot.

***

A beeping sound woke me from my sleep and I blinked a few times to clear my eyes so I could take a look at where we were.

A mansion greeted us as Jack pulled up a large circular drive and I frowned. "The shoots here?" I yawned, desperately trying to wake myself up.

The make-up artists would have a fit at me if I went in with bloodshot eyes, but they usually had some drops that cured it so I wasn't too bothered.

Jack didn't say anything but pulled up in front of the double doors and exited the car. I never waited for him so I opened my door and climbed out.

It was eerily quiet and I looked at Jack dubiously. "Are you sure you have the right place. There's nobody else here?" I said as I spun around and scanned the gardens.

"Yeah," he replied quietly and walked up to the doors.

Shrugging I followed him and entered a huge entrance hall after him. I whistled through my teeth as I took a quick inspection. The place screamed money; from its marble floors to its grand staircases and massive dripping chandeliers. You could tell from a quick glance that the furniture was expensive and the décor was as opulent as the rest of the place.

"Well if the shoots here, I hope people think it's my house," I chuckled to myself.

Jack scoffed and shook his head at me as a door opened at the end of the hall.

I stood in shock as I stared at a face I hadn't seen for a long time. "Hello Eve," he said.

My jaw dropped. "Oh my God! Evan!" I declared with a huge smile.

You remember Evan? He was the guy I met when I spent the few weeks in Cornwall.

He cocked his head and regarded me with an intimidating smile. All the hairs on the back of my neck prickled at the sight of him, he oozed contempt and malevolence as his eyes held a hatred that hadn't been there two years ago.

"Evan?" I asked warily as he started to walk towards me.

I backed up a little, the sight of him was frightening and my brain was instinctively telling me to run.

Jack stood behind me and I grabbed his forearm. "Jack. We need to get out of here," I whispered.

He seized the top of my arms with both hands and I turned my head to look at him. "What are you doing?" I hissed but he shook his head.

"You're a clever girl, E. Be bright," he smirked and I gasped.

"Oh God Jack. What have you done?"

He shrugged coolly as though he didn't care, "Bills to pay, E. Family to support. You know how it is." My stomach revolted at his heartless attitude.

Evan had reached us by now and I pressed my back into Jack, he was the least of the two evils.

"What do you want, Evan?"

His eyebrows rose and he barked out a humourless laugh. "E... you know what I want," he sneered and I looked at him questioningly.

"You want the film?"

I was utterly confused. Evan was my friend and the same age as me, he wasn't one of the men that came into my room. I couldn't comprehend his involvement in the whole thing.

"Of course I want the fucking film!" he spat in my face and I blinked rapidly against his fury.

"I don't understand?" I stuttered out.

He looked at me like I was stupid. Which I obviously was.

"My dad, you stupid bitch, the film is of my dad!"

My eyes widened and my anger surfaced. "You must be so proud of him," I ridiculed.

His fist cracked my cheekbone as it connected. I bit my lip at the pain as I glared at him. "Your Dad tried to rape a thirteen year old girl," I snapped.

His face came close to mine and the evil curl to his lips chilled my blood. "I wouldn't have failed." I shuddered against his malice and chose to ignore him as he perused my body with hungry eyes. "In fact, I might as well enjoy myself while you're here," he smirked.

I swallowed heavily and looked away from him as he grasped my chin harshly in his fingers. "Two choices, E and you know what they are."

I swung my eyes to his and smiled coldly. "You just shot yourself in the foot. You blew the fucking thing up with my home," I snarled at him.

His eyes narrowed then he laughed loudly before he punched me again. I stumbled back and Jack caught me. "Evan, steady on mate," he said in my defence but the iciness in Evan's eyes, saw Jack drop his hands away from me.

"You want paying, Jack?"

"Yeah." Jack conceded with a sigh and went to stand beside the front door.

Evan yanked my hair and dragged me across the floor towards the room from where he emerged from and I dug my feet into the floor. Stupid really as it was gleaming marble and my action went in Evan's favour, as my heels slipped along the ground.

Kicking the door shut behind us, he pushed me onto a huge plush sofa. He was on top of me before I knew what was happening, fumbling with my clothes and sinking his teeth into my bottom lip, demanding that I opened to him.

I pushed at him with all I had, but he was too strong and his hands ripped my shirt off me whilst his teeth now sunk deeply into my neck.

"Please, Evan." I cried out but he wouldn't relent and kept on at me, his hands now trying to remove my bra.

He suddenly lifted off me and was flying across the room before I could blink. I stared wide eyed as he hit an antique table and snapped it in half, both him and the table landing in a heap on the floor.

"Control yourself!" barked an older man.

My heart stopped as I stared at him. I quickly scrambled backwards and pushed myself against the arm of the sofa as he turned to look at me.

"W...w..What the... fuck!" I stammered as I shook my head in disbelief.

"Hello, Eve." He smiled softly.

My jaw trembled as each of my breaths became stunted. "You're... you're my...."

Everything went black.

Wasn't oblivion wonderful?

CHAPTER 47

It was dark when I came to and I shot upright when everything came hurtling into my brain at 200Mph.

I was on a large soft bed in a plush bedroom somewhere, my body clothed again but my shoes had been removed.

"Welcome back," someone said from the corner of the room behind me.

I turned rapidly to be met with a dark skinned man. He stood from a chair and walked towards me, the whites of his eyes glistening in the lamplight. I moved away from him the closer he got.

"Don't be afraid, Eve. I won't hurt you," he said gently and I eyed him cautiously. He settled himself lightly on the edge of the bed next to me and smiled. The tenderness in his eyes shocked me but I still regarded him with vigilance.

He sighed heavily and looked towards the window. "All I want is the recording Eve, then you can go home."

I remained silent and I noticed the softness slip from his eyes slightly. "You're making this really hard for yourself, Eve. What does it matter to you if I have it? It's not like it's of any use to you really, is it?"

"My... father?" I choked out.

He turned to me then, his eyes full of kindness again and smiled warmly, "Yeah. Bit of a shock, eh?"

I nodded faintly and sucked on my lips. "I don't understand," I said quietly.

He sighed and nodded. "Didn't expect you to really. It's all a bit complicated but that's your Dad's story not mine, Eve."

"But... but... he tried to kill me," I choked out, picturing my home in rubble.

The man scowled faintly and shook his head. "No, Eve. We knew no-one was home. It was just a warning." He explained then chuckled low. "You'd be no good to us dead, would you?" he added with humour.

Yeah, real funny!

"But, I've had it years and haven't done anything with it so why now?" I asked him and he pursed his lips.

"Well, I didn't know you had it until your wonderful mother got in touch and said she had some footage that was worth a lot to me." His face darkened for a second before he carried on. "She doesn't keep her promises, your mother, does she?"

He scowled at me as though my Mom's actions were directly linked to me. I shook my head at him. "But then again she did die so..." he shrugged and I looked at him in amazement.

"Yeah, that doesn't help. Selfish bitch!" I mocked sarcastically.

His hand spanned the width of my throat tightly. I tried to gulp at the pain and shock but his grip was too tight. "Don't fuck with me, Eve. I can cause you some real pain and we wouldn't want to ruin that pretty face, would we?"

I shook my head as much as I could and he released his hand. My own fingers came up to my neck to soothe away the soreness.

He stood up and walked towards the door but turned to me before he went through it. "Think about it a bit, Eve. I'll be back later, but I'll just let you know, this is your last chance to do the right thing," he said then narrowed his eyes on me and smirked. "Your niece is a real cute thing isn't she?"

My eyes widened at his warning but he winked and left.

Holy Shit. This was big trouble and I closed my eyes in distress. I knew what I had to do; I wouldn't risk Evie or any of my family, so the choice then became very easy.

My life was spinning out of control rapidly. Everything was happening at the same time. My poor addled brain was struggling to cope with the thousands of thoughts that were spinning through it.

The door opened again and my father stood in the frame. His face was difficult to read but his eyes were filled with something I didn't want to accept. Love.

I shook my head and refused to acknowledge him but he entered the room and quietly shut the door behind him.

"E..."

"Don't call me that! Only friends and family call me E. You can call me Eve... or Miss Hudson would be more appropriate!" I said with as much contempt as I could muster.

He hissed through his teeth and sighed at the same time. "Eve," he corrected. "We need to talk."

I snorted. "You are about twenty years too late I'm afraid. I don't wanna hear it. Just tell your boss I'll get the damn film for him and then I never want to see you again."

"Please. Just let me explain," he tried but I turned away.

"I met your mother twenty years ago...." He started but I covered my ears and closed my eyes as I started singing. Very adult, E.

His hands clasped mine and he pulled them away as he came close to my face. "Listen to me, Eve."

I turned away from him but stopped singing and remained quiet as he sat beside me on the bed and continued to hold my hands.

He was silent for a moment, and then he inhaled deeply. "Your mother was the most beautiful creature I had ever met, even her laugh was beautiful. I fell in love with her instantly. We had what you call a whirlwind romance but that woman... she was determined to self-destruct. I tried everything to help her, get her off the drugs but... well you know, Eve."

His gaze landed on the window, his eyes glazed as though he was physically in the past and my heart clenched a little at the raw pain on his face. "One day we were due to meet. We used to meet in a little coffee shop. I remember her order like it was yesterday; black coffee and cinnamon swirl, which she would cover with brown sugar out of one of those little paper packets." He chuckled, more to himself than me and I found myself smiling with him.

He sighed heavily and his eyes darkened. "She never turned up... but Robert did." I could hear the loathing in his tone when he said my Dad's name. "Can you believe the man held a gun to my stomach underneath the little table in a small rundown café," he scoffed. "Bear in mind this was twenty years ago, Eve and I was just a fucking pizza delivery guy. Nothing behind me, no money, and no education... fuck all!" he stated angrily as he gazed at me woefully.

"To cut it short, he told me if I didn't leave Lisa alone, he would finish me and make her pay painfully. And knowing what kind of man I was now dealing with," he shrugged and exhaled, "what would you have done?"

I didn't answer him; I don't think he expected me to.

He stood from the bed and walked over to the window, staring out into the darkness with a painful expression as though my mother was stood out there waiting for him.

"I never saw her again."

"I know all this," I told him blankly, still not giving him the satisfaction of putting any emotion into my words.

He nodded slowly then turned back to me. "I didn't even know she was pregnant, Eve. I never knew about you and Aaron until a few months ago when I was alerted to someone doing checks on me," he disclosed as he found my eyes again.

"My Mom only told me about you six months before she died, but she thought you were dead and... well I wanted to find your grave." I snorted loudly, "No wonder I never fucking found it."

Pain flashed across his face and I narrowed my eyes on him. "Don't pretend you care Gerry. You're in this whole mess too. You wrecked my house. My home that you blew up contained the only memory I have of my dead daughter. Do you even know how that feels?" I snapped with disgust.

"Oh God, Eve... I..."

I held up my hands to stop him. "Don't, just don't. Like I said, I'll give you what you need but then you leave me alone. I want nothing more to do with you. You disgust me!"

He nodded and exhaled wearily. "I'll tell Sal you've changed your mind," he said quietly as he walked towards the door but he turned when he reached it. "I *am* sorry Eve. This was all higher than me. Believe it or not, they were lenient with you because of me."

I snorted and shook my head in revulsion as he closed the door.

I lay down on the bed and curled up tightly, hiding myself from the whole shit that was happening. It all seemed too unbelievable and I still didn't understand how my father could do that to me.

What was it with my parents? Each one I'd had used me for their own tainted needs.

I gave myself up to the peacefulness of sleep, knowing I would need every bit of energy I had tomorrow but as I drifted, the only thing I dreamed of was Monday and a plane soaring high. A plane that contained everything my heart held dear.

Even after everything that had happened today, my heart still ached for my soul mate and I felt the tears wet the pillow before I sank deep.

***

I walked into the bank the next morning with Sal's hand pressed tight to my back and I rolled my eyes at him. "I'm not gonna do a runner. I just wanna get this over with," I hissed.

He chuckled and brought his mouth close to my ear. "You'll have to excuse me if I don't trust you, Eve." He sneered and I curled my lip in disgust.

"I'd like to view my safety deposit box, please," I told the woman behind the counter.

"Paperwork," she said methodically. I handed her the papers and my I.D before she disappeared into a room.

A moment later a miserable man came to escort me to my box. "Just you ma'am, I'm afraid you aren't allowed escorts in the deposit rooms," he told me and I looked at Sal.

He nodded once and went to sit on a chair whilst I was led into a plain room.

"Key," the guard barked at me and I jumped at his sudden voice.

I passed him the key and he disappeared and returned with a small metal box, before he left the room to give me some privacy.

I sighed as I unlocked the container and took the USB then removed the other item that was stored there.

Knocking on the door, I heard it unlock and I waited until the guard had returned my box and then walked back to Sal. He glanced at my hand as I came through the door and I huffed. "I told you to trust me. I just wanna get this over with."

He nodded and I passed him the USB. "Is this the only copy?" he asked and I sighed in frustration.

"Yes. I have no need for copies."

He nodded again and we walked outside to the waiting car. "You may go your way now, Eve. I'm really glad you saw sense. I like you." Sal grinned.

My eyebrows lifted in amazement but I handed him the item I had taken from the box. "Can you give these to my father and tell him if I ever see him again, then I *will* use the gun I have a licence for."

Sal stared at me then laughed loudly before he frowned at the bundle of letters I had given him. "They were what my Mom wrote for him. Even though he betrayed me, he still loved my mother and I know she loved him. They belong with him, for my mother's sake, not mine or his."

Sal sighed and gazed at me. "He's a good man Eve, but he works for me." He shrugged as though that explained everything. I pursed my lips but nodded.

"Do you want dropping anywhere?" he asked and I shook my head.

"Take care, Eve" he said as he passed me a business card. "If you ever need anything," he added and I laughed in astonishment but just nodded in resignation.

"Bye, Sal."

He smiled and winked, then clambered in his car and pulled away, leaving me staring at the rear of the car as it disappeared round the corner.

Pulling my phone from my bag I groaned when the display said *'Please insert Sim'*.

Thanks Jack!

A taxi pulled into the curb in front of me and I nearly died in shock at the first bit of luck I'd had in days.

"Oh My God, you're Eve Hudson," the taxi driver gushed as I settled on the back seat.

"I am," I smiled tightly.

He frowned through the mirror at me. "You okay, love?" He genuinely looked concerned and I had to fight back the tears at his sympathy. The last thing I needed was his story of how Eve Hudson had sobbed buckets in his back seat, plastered all over the Sunday newspapers. "Just a little ill," I lied. "I'll give you another twenty if you can get me home within fifteen minutes."

His sly grin said it all as he pulled into the traffic, bang in front of a bus, and I shut my eyes all the way home, wondering if I'd actually make it home in one piece.

CHAPTER 48

I walked straight into the kitchen, pulled the vodka from the freezer and poured myself a hefty amount before downing it in one and refilling.

Footsteps thundered on the stairs and Jax appeared in the doorway, his pale face held many emotions as his whole frame seemed to lean towards me. He didn't speak, just scanned me as if checking me for missing limbs or absent ears and eyes, but his face darkened when his eyes settled on my bruised cheekbone.

I took small steps across the room to him, his presence pulling me in. When I reached him, I fell against him, desperate just to feel him, for him to hold me and protect me.

He wrapped me up as I started to sob, uncontrollably and snottily. He carried me straight up the stairs and laid us on the bed, as he let me rid my demons and take all his comfort.

"Babe," he whispered as his nose settled in my hair. "Need to breathe you, babe," he choked out. I realised then just how much this man had worried for me, his own relief at my presence was palpable as we both drew solace from each other.

"My father's alive," I said bluntly between hiccups.

The hand that had been stroking my arm tenderly, stilled as my words sunk in. "Eh?"

I tilted my face to his. "My real father, not my Dad."

Jax continued to frown and I realised he still didn't have a clue what I was on about, so I brought him up to date, starting from the day in hospital with my mother.

"The fuck, babe!" he breathed out when I had finished.

I nodded slowly and sighed deeply. "Who gets parents like mine, eh?" I laughed bitterly and Jax's embrace tightened.

"Bastard!" he growled but I shook my head.

"It's done now, Jax. Over with. They'll leave me alone now and to be honest, I don't really care what they do with the film. My dad's betrayal hurts more than his death. That might be an awful thing to say but... well it's the truth!" I admitted.

Jax shuffled down the bed so he was level with my face and ran his finger down the bridge of my nose tenderly. "You're hurting right now, babe. You need time, and then get in touch again. He's your Dad, E."

I looked at him like he had three heads. "Do you forgive your dad for taking Mary Ann's life?" I scoffed.

His face darkened but he sighed gently, "Not a matter of forgiveness, babe. It's done. Nothing I can do about it, but I don't get the chance to make it right. You do!"

I gulped at his words as a part of me agreed with him but there was still a bigger portion that would never forgive what he did. "You hear me, babe?"

"I hear ya', Jax," I said softly as he leant towards me.

"Went through hell, E." He confessed as he swallowed deeply. "You just disappeared and I thought... I..."

I cupped his face and he nuzzled into me. "I'm okay, Jax" I whispered as I brushed my lips over his.

The pain and anguish that covered his face tore deep and we both just needed to feel.

He took me under his mouth in one of his exceptional kisses and I sighed deeply at the sensation of him. The soft structure of his lips as they welded to mine brought desire coursing through my veins and I moaned lightly into his mouth.

His hand settled around my throat gently. I pulled him closer to me and ran my tongue along his bottom lip. He opened to me immediately and I wrapped my tongue around his, caressing his muscle intimately as I drove our lust to the next level.

"Need to feel you, babe" he breathed against my mouth. "Need to take you, need to own you, just need to love you."

I moaned and grabbed the hem of his shirt, desperate to get it over his head so I could feel his skin. He lifted slightly, allowing me to do what I needed, and as my fingers settled on his bare chest he moaned faintly.

He shivered as I ran my fingers along his ink and then his own hands were pulling my shirt off. My bra went next and he flung it across the room with my shirt. "Fuck. Your tits always make me hard, babe." He growled before his mouth landed on one and he sucked at the soft flesh beside my nipple as his other hand massaged my other breast tenderly.

I moaned and arched my back, pushing myself into him as his mouth trailed over my piercing and took my other nipple. His tongue circled it relentlessly as his lips suckled and I grew heavy with need.

"Oh God, that's good. Bite me Jax," I whimpered. He groaned and then did as I asked, sinking his teeth gently against my hard nipple whilst his tongue soothed the ache.

My arousal surged at the pain in the pleasure and I was soon pulling at his jeans, frantically pulling them over his hips. "Fuck me, baby" I pleaded.

"I aint gonna fuck you, babe" he said as his fingers popped the button on my jeans and he drew them off my legs along with my knickers.

I frowned at him then groaned when his nose landed on my mound. "I'm gonna take you, gonna bury myself inside you and drive you fucking wild, babe." Wasn't that the same thing?

"I'm gonna love you, babe, not fuck you. I'm gonna love you so hard, that you forget to breathe. Gonna love you so deep that you feel the tip of me on your heart." He told me as his tongue now circled my clit.

His eyes looked up at me and he grinned wickedly when he parted my legs and rubbed the tip of his nose on my clit. "Oh God Jax, that's good. Just there, just a bit harder..." I garbled as he flicked my sensitive nub with the flat of his tongue.

"You hear me, babe?"

"I hear ya', baby. Please...fucking *love* me." I begged as I lifted my hips, pleading with him to bring me closer.

"Look at me, E. Watch me worship you," he breathed and I pushed myself up on my elbows to watch him attack me.

My eyes rolled as his tongue idolised every part of me, from my anus right up to my piercing and I jolted as his lips surrounded my clit and he sucked hard. "Oooh Yes Jax, Oh God, fuck! Baby I'm gonna...."

I groaned deeply and at length when I came around his face hard and intensely, my whole body juddering in ecstasy as he devoured me.

He was suddenly climbing up the bed on all fours over me but before he could enter me, I shuffled down underneath him until his magnificent cock was so gloriously resting at my face.

I flicked at the tip of him with my tongue, lapping up the cum that had beaded on the crown of him. He groaned and looked down at me from above and I grinned happily at him.

He chuckled and lowered his hand to my face to softly stroke my cheek, but it soon gripped my hair tightly when I completely demolished him. I worked him hard and fast as his breathing grew heavier and his groans grew louder and soon he was pulling away from me.

"Need to plant myself inside you babe," he whispered as he climbed back down, depositing little soft kisses as he descended.

We both exhaled loudly as he pushed into me. "Fuck, E! Feels so damn good." He hissed through his teeth as he started to move.

I met each of his thrusts with expertise as he sped up and banged me furiously. Small drops of sweat adorned his brow as he laboured into me and just as I caught the edge of my orgasm, he flipped me onto my stomach and pushed my knees up so I was on all fours.

I felt the tip of his nudge against my bottom and I gasped. "Need all of you, babe" he whispered in my ear as he leant over me.

I nodded and pushed back against him, allowing him entry as I forced myself to relax and let him in. We both panted as he inched in and soon the pleasure overtook the pain and I was rocking back onto him. "Harder, Jax" I begged but his hand settled on the nape of my neck.

"Not yet, babe. Just feel me first." Oh, I felt him alright. Very well!

He continued to love me slowly and tenderly, his pushes and pulls gentle and soft, before his own hunger took over and he sped up until he was eventually pounding me with so much force, I was bouncing up the bed.

Our orgasms hit together and we both screamed out in pleasure, as our bodies tightened around each other and we simultaneously shuddered violently with euphoria, both of us covered in sweat and panting hard.

"Oh Christ," he breathed as his mouth kissed its way up my back till it was at my ear. "I love you, Eve Hudson. Always babe, you're with me forever."

I swallowed harshly at his words, digging deep to hold back the tears that wanted to surface and I turned my face to his. "And I love you, Jaxon Cooper. You never left me and you never will. I'm yours baby, lock, stock and fuckin' barrel."

He rolled us over and kissed me with so much passion it took my breath and stole my soul.

Tenderly, he swept my hair from my face and kissed my nose. "You sure you can't come with me?" he asked but the expression on his face revealed he already knew my answer.

"I can't, Jax. You know I can't, baby. God, if my life were simpler I wouldn't even have to think about it, I'd jump on your back and ride across the fucking desert with you, Jax."

He nodded and sighed sadly but kissed my forehead softly in understanding, "Sunday. You and me, E. All fucking day. You don't leave my bed until I've loved you so many times you're screaming random quotes and beggin' for me to stop. You hear me, babe?"

I kind of just whimpered.

All through Saturday, Boss rehearsed our songs with us ready for the Animal Trust charity performance that night and Jax accompanied us, just to spend time with me.

I was due to sing two songs with Hell's Eden and the new single with Sed. I had yet to see him since that disastrous night after the Bafta's and I was apprehensive about how he would behave, especially around Jax.

I didn't have to wait long to find out.

He strolled in an hour before our performance, entourage in tow and an attitude the size of Canada. This should be fun.

He smirked at me widely as he stalked up to me, right in front of Jax, snaked his hand around the back of my neck and pulled my mouth to his.

I pulled back but he held me tighter and I struggled as I tried to push him off. "Don't do this, Sed" I warned against his mouth.

I had never seen Sed's fighting skills but I knew without a doubt that he was no match against Jax, especially an angry Jax.

"You ready for me, baby?" He smiled at me sinfully as Jax came hurtling across the room and before I could stop it, Jax had thrown Sed against the wall and had punched him with force.

"JAX!" I screamed and grabbed his arm before he could land another.

Sed smirked and pulled himself off the ground. "Well, well, well. If it aint Jax Cooper. Although I doubt Helen will be pleased you're guarding another bitch when you're marrying her in three months!"

Did you hear that? Because I was certain I had misunderstood what he just said?

Jax's jaw clenched tightly and I just stared at the small twitch in his cheek as my world crashed to the floor around me.

He turned to look at me and I could tell from the painful expression on his face that Sed wasn't lying. "Jax?" I choked out.

He closed his eyes in distress and lifted his hand to me but I stumbled back. Luckily Boss was behind me and lifted me into his arms, before I landed on my arse and made an even bigger fool of myself.

"I need to get out of here, Boss." I swallowed heavily.

"No problem, hot stuff," he whispered in my ear as he swept us out of the room and straight out of the building, into a waiting car.

He garbled an address to the driver, but in my mind fuck, I didn't hear where.

We were both silent and I just stared out of the window, people watching, as I refused to acknowledge the echo of Sed's words in my head.

How the hell had I missed it? He had even asked me to move out there with him. Did he think I would be the other woman? The woman who sat at home all day waiting to see if her married lover turned up that day?

I didn't even realise we were in a hotel suite until Boss passed me a glass containing a wedge of whisky.

"What the hell just happened, Boss?" I whispered in shock.

"It's not what it looks like, E. You've gotta give him chance to explain."

I snorted loudly, "Like hell, Boss!"

I swiped frantically at the stray tear that rolled down my cheek and shrugged. "Hey, it doesn't matter anyway. He goes back Monday and that's the end of us anyway."

Who the hell was I kidding?

The glass slipped out of my hand and shattered on the floor, along with my heart, and I quickly followed it as uncontrollable shudders racked my body.

"Shit, baby." Boss hissed as he picked me up out of the glass, and placed me on the sofa.

He crouched in front of me and took my hand. "E. Please, just let him explain."

"He should have explained before I slept with him, Boss. He always knew I wasn't one of those girls that fucked unavailable men. Hell, he told me he loved me. I mean... fuck!"

My phone was going wild and I knew it would be either Brent or Leah. I suddenly realised I'd walked out on a charity event. "Shit, Boss. I have to get back."

He nodded as I answered my phone. "Don't Leah, just don't. I'm on my way back. Sort it around me. I'll be thirty minutes." I ended the call before she could blast my hair off with her screech.

"You sure, E?" Boss asked as he huddled me through the door and back into the car.

It was like I was on a piece of elastic and I felt dizzy. "It's charity, Boss. I won't let them down. My own concert, yeah, but not these guys."

He sighed and paused before he regarded me with narrow eyes. "You ever think about yourself, hot stuff?"

I frowned at him and then thought about what I did for myself. Nothing! Okay, this was news and quite bitter news at that.

"I... well... I..." I sighed heavily then shrugged in resignation as Boss sucked air through his teeth.

"Baby. You're gonna have to slow it down before you drop, cos' you will E, fucking hard."

Pursing my lips I looked at him guiltily. "It helps."

He frowned at me and cocked his head. "It helps what?"

"Forget..." I turned away, embarrassed by my admission but Boss grabbed my chin and forced me to look at him.

His eyes bore into me and I'm sure he could read my soul. "It helps you forget Jax," He stated honestly.

I just nodded; it didn't need any words for him to understand.

"Shit, E. Has it been that bad?"

I shrugged and blushed furiously. I was mad at myself without Boss been mad at me too. "I tried Boss, honestly I did, but I just couldn't... it's like he's welded to the depths of my heart and as much as I try to rip him out, he sticks hard" I revealed, completely disgusted with my lack of restraint where Jax was concerned.

He nodded with a sad smile as we exited the car and fought through security to get back in. We were huddled immediately back stage and I didn't see Jax as I was trolleyed through the different parts of the building en-route to the stage.

It was the worst performance of my life but luckily the audience hadn't picked up on my mood and had still enjoyed the songs, but next came the big test... Sed!

I stormed into his dressing room, the door bashing against the wall as I flung myself at him and punched him hard in the chin. "You fucking twat!" I raged.

He reared back at the sight of my fury and his security guys had their hands around my arms before I could lay another one on him.

"What the Fuck, E?" he snarled as he rubbed at the sore spot on his chin. "I was just letting you know who you were fucking, baby."

I scoffed and shook my head in disgust. "Well it certainly isn't you. We do this performance Sed, and then it's strictly video only performances from now on."

I didn't give him chance to answer as I turned and stomped to my own dressing room.

I groaned inwardly when I was met with a room full of people wanting to tweak every inch of me.

My hair was pulled in every direction; my face was painted to within an inch of its life. I was adorned in sexy clothes and many exquisite pieces of jewellery. My feet were squeezed into five inch heels, but no-one actually bothered to look at *me*... not even just a quick look to see the *me* underneath it all.

If they had, they would have seen *me* dying a slow, torturous death. A death that I would never be resurrected from as my heart finally stopped beating and my soul once and for all, left for bluer skies.

The loneliness was back and the urge for the whip came with it.

CHAPTER 49

Sed was professional throughout our act and no-one would ever tell we had argued, never mind that I had just clocked him one.

As soon as we finished and we were escorted off the stage, my fingers were dialling the now unfamiliar number.

"William, Eve Hudson. You got anybody in for me tonight?" I asked as I closed my eyes in hunger whilst my hands shook and my pulse rate quickened.

"Eve, you sure about this?" William asked with concern.

"Just a quick session, William. I promise I won't go too far."

He sighed heavily but conceded. "Sure. Joel's in tonight."

I thanked him, then ended the call before I dialled a taxi and sneaked my way out of the building via the backdoor.

Everybody would be expecting me back in the dressing room to change so I didn't have long and I sighed in relief when I saw the taxi already waiting for me. I clambered in the back and gave the address just as Jax exited the shadows and as though he realised what I was doing he made a sprint for me.

"Move, quickly!" I shouted at the driver. He was a damn good driver! He squealed out of the alleyway and had rounded the corner before Jax had got within reach of us.

"Thank you," I breathed and the driver bobbed his head.

"No worries, love." He frowned then his face brightened as it dawned on him who I was.

I smiled timidly and cursed myself when I realised I'd given him my destination. "Look, I'll make it worth your while if you keep this our secret." I tried optimistically.

He grinned at me. "Sure, love."

I placed a hundred in his palm as I exited and kept my fingers crossed that my face wouldn't be splattered all over the newspapers tomorrow morning entering a sex club.

The Black Panther was heaving when I stepped into the bar area and I smiled widely when William approached me. He hugged me tight and held me back to inspect me but his face saddened. "E, you've done so well, sweetheart."

I nodded and bit my lower lip, "Just having a bad day, William."

He nodded in understanding before he led me up to one of the rooms. William always closed off the area for me due to my status, not risking photos from other clients making their way online. I always paid William heftily for his consideration and he only ever got his most loyal employees to deal with me.

My whole body trembled in anticipation as my veins itched ferociously and my brain ached. I bit down against the tremor that racked my bones. William glanced at me with unease. "Don't let it take you, E. Just let it ease it, I've already warned Joel not to go too far," he said gently.

I knew he didn't mean his words offensively; he was just looking out for me after what had happened before at his other club in Leeds.

I blew out a breath as I entered the room and my heart ached at my failure. Joel smiled widely at me, "Hey, E."

I nodded but didn't speak as I pulled my leather Basque off and William rubbed my shoulder tenderly. "Don't forget what I said, Joel," he stated before he closed the door behind him.

Joel gestured to the wooden frame with his chin and suddenly I couldn't make the journey across the room but when the jolt hit my brain, I found myself stumbling across to the structure eagerly.

I raised my hands and Joel strapped my wrists in and tied my hair back for me then placed the bunch over my shoulder so it was out of his way.

My breathing stuttered and my brow beaded with sweat as my body screamed out for him to hurry the hell up, but there was still something in my heart that was shouting at me to stop.

I took a deep breath and tried to ride the uncertainty. "The Bull or the Quirt, E?" Joel asked from behind me.

Pulling in a huge breath, I answered him. "The Quirt."

I hid myself away all of Sunday, refusing to acknowledge the constant ring of my phone or the relentless battering of the front door.

Eventually I turned off my phone and closed the curtains then watched old black and white movies as I ate pizza and ice-cream all day.

After the stream of Jax offensive died down, I frowned when after a few hours of peace I heard a key in the front door.

Clambering off the sofa hoping Jax hadn't magically cut a key, I was relieved to find Bruce come hobbling round the corner. The sight of his bandaged head brought forward my tears and I dropped to the floor to hug my poor broken boy.

Aaron followed him in with a stern expression. I gasped when he gripped my arms and yanked me upright. His hands grabbed the back of my vest and he spun me around before bunching it up. "What the..." he puffed and I turned and slapped at him.

"What the hell are you doing?" I snapped but he continued to look confused.

"Jax rang me and said you'd gone to the bloody club and he couldn't get to you on time." He divulged and I narrowed my eyes on him.

"Jax has no fucking right to phone you. Him and me are done, so what I do has nothing to do with him," I barked.

"But... but, there's nothing there, E," Aaron said in astonishment.

How bloody dare they!

"I didn't do it, that's why!" I shouted at him. He reared back in stunned silence at first, then his lips curled into a huge grin and I couldn't hold back my own smile at the sight of it.

"Fuck me! Fucking proud of you, E." He choked on a sob as he huddled me up tightly.

I gave in and embraced him back. "Don't ask what stopped me. It was just something there inside me that said 'No'... so I listened to it for a change." I smiled at his happy relieved face before I turned my attention back to my boy.

"Sing to me Brucey, baby" I beamed at him and he dove straight into song for me. I scrunched up my nose at him as Aaron and I joined him, happily blasting out *Train's, 'Bruises'* whilst I fed him treats.

"You gonna say goodbye before he goes, E?" Aaron asked when we settled down with a coffee and I shook my head.

"Nope. Too much pain Aaron. I can't... I..."

His hand settled over mine and he nodded. "I know but maybe you should hear him out..."

I shook my head. "It could be for a chuffing visa for all it matters Aaron, it's the fact that he's been home over a week, he's shared my bed and my body, and he still didn't think it important to tell me."

He turned to look through the window at Bruce digging up my gladiola and I snarled but left him to it.

That boy could have a gold plated biscuit for all I cared... he was alive and home and that was all that mattered.

"I just don't want to see you hurt like last time, E." He swallowed as if in pain and I clasped his hand.

"I have to get on with it, Aaron. Like my tat says 'If you're going through hell, keep going' and I intend to fucking run to get through it."

Aaron regarded me sceptically, "But the faster you run the harder you fall, E."

Monday morning came and went and I filled it with as much distracting things as I could. I bathed Bruce which was always fun, then I cleared out my wardrobe and the cupboard under the stairs, which wasn't fun. Then I baked some muffins, much to Bruce's disgust when I tried to force one on him and before long the time had passed and his plane had flown.

Then I sat and cried, hating myself for missing the opportunity to say goodbye once and for all.

Monday afternoon saw me in the studio interviewing new drummers, most were impressive but none were Boss. We eventually picked out a guy called Kirk, whom we nicknamed Blade because he had a thing about knives. Don't ask!

Monday night saw me sobbing into my pillow with a concerned Bruce whimpering beside me as I wept until I was sick.

I relented and pulled on Jax's old G N' R t-shirt from years ago. I had never parted with it and had refused to take it off my back for about three weeks the last time he left.

He continued to phone and text for the rest of the week but I never answered or read any and after a couple of weeks I was flagging.

The boy's grew concerned at my gaunt appearance and my mood swings, and the following Monday they called a meeting.

They all eyed me with both concern and anger as I entered the room and plonked myself wearily into a chair.

"Gotta sort this out now, E." Hunter spoke first and the others just stared at me.

"I'm fine," I barked back and Angel scoffed loudly.

"Have you seen the state of yourself, E? You're fucking dropping as you stand and you're breaking us with you."

I bit my lip and looked away from them. "E. We love you girl and this isn't working. You are brewing one hell of a storm and I don't wanna drown under you," Hunter added and I flung myself upright.

"Then buy a fucking umbrella!" I hissed as I attempted to leave the room but Leah grinned mischievously as she waggled the key at me when I pulled at the door.

"Just let me out, Leah." I demanded but she shook her head slowly.

The large screen on the wall flickered to life and Brent's face appeared before us. "Sit the fuck down, E" he snarled at me. I narrowed my eyes at my manager, forgetting that he could see me as much as I could see him.

I huffed and sat, digging my nails into the palm of my hand to control my temper.

"You're dragging, E and we need to sort it out now. I wanna know what you want?" he asked openly and I shrugged.

"Nothing Brent, there is nothing you can give me what I want, believe me."

Brent pursed his lips and nodded slowly. "So Red Music wouldn't have what you want either?" He smirked and my eyes flicked up to his.

"What..." I breathed out with a puff.

Angel smiled and nodded. "It's ours if you wanna do it, E."

I looked from guy to guy to Leah and they all smiled and nodded. "America is ours, E but do you want it?"

My heart soared but my brain sent a warning to my mind. He was getting married, would he still want me? Would I be able to settle over there? It was a complete different way of life.

"E." Brent said and I looked up at him. "You never fail until you stop trying." He smiled as he recited the tattoo that ran across the nape of my neck.

CHAPTER 50

Bruce licked my face as I sat on the mound in the park and threw his stick for him again. He bounded down the hill after it, then I knew I had lost him when his girlfriend, a Red Setter by the name of Ruby, came flirting up to him.

He was a typical boy; his tongue hung out of his mouth eagerly as his nose attached to her arse. The motion reminded me of Jax.

Amanda, Ruby's owner, came and sat beside me. "Morning, E." She smiled sweetly and I beamed back at her, and then cringed in horror when Bruce decided he wanted more than friendship with Ruby.

"Bruce!" I shouted but Amanda laughed.

"Leave him, Ruby's a tart. I wouldn't be surprised if she had offered him a biscuit for a quickie." She chuckled.

I stared at her then burst out laughing. "Sex and food. My boy is in heaven," I smirked.

"How are you, E?" Amanda asked and I shrugged. Amanda had been my bounce board for the last few weeks as we had met every morning on the mound.

"I have the opportunity to move to America," I told her frankly.

She nodded once, "Okayyy and…"

"And…" I shrugged then looked into the distance. "He's getting married, Amanda. Watching that happen will finally kill me."

She settled her hand on my knee and squeezed. We both grimaced when Bruce managed to manipulate Ruby into a position that looked kind of painful. Both our heads tipped sideways as our expressions showed the same amazement. "Wow," Amanda breathed and my jaw dropped.

We both shook off and diverted our eyes as a shudder racked through both of us. "What does your heart say, E?" she asked softly.

I frowned and tipped my head. "It says go for it." She shrugged as if that's all that mattered. "But my head says 'Fuck girl, don't do it to yourself again'."

She scoffed. "E. If none of us took a risk once in a while, the whole earth's population would die off. Men come with their own code, a code so difficult to crack, God even gave up when he created them and just left them as they were."

I nodded seriously in agreement.

"But we women have something unique."

I glanced at her questioningly and she smirked at me. "Tits and an intimate relationship with the oven, darling."

I looked at her in astonishment, and then laughed loudly and heartily, until we were both crying at her humour. "Are you sure you never met, Jax?" I asked. She seemed to know what ruled him intimately.

She laughed then regarded me sincerely. "Seriously though E, there's only you that can decide what to do with your life but you really need to sit down with Bruce and discuss your options."

"Well that's another thing... Bruce," I fretted.

She frowned at me with confusion "Bruce will settle wherever he is, E."

"Yeah, but there's all the laws on travel and stuff," I said worryingly.

"It's just straightforward paperwork now, E. Most countries accept animals with simple documentation from your vets, as long as they're up to date with vaccine's and stuff, then it's full steam ahead," she informed me and I pursed my lips in surprise, expecting quarantines and all that mess.

My phone rang in my bag and I frowned when I didn't recognise the number. "Hello?" I asked hesitantly.

"Hello is that Eve?" a woman's soft voice came over the line.

"Yes," I acknowledged slowly.

"This is a little difficult really so I'm just gonna come out with it. My name is Helen Jenkins and I'm Jax's fiancé," she disclosed and my stomach clenched.

Amanda frowned at me and I mouthed to her who it was before I put it on loud speaker so she could hear.

"Right, okay." I murmured and she sighed.

"I'm really sorry for ringing like this but... but, well I'm a little worried about Jax since he came home," she said quietly. I looked at Amanda in bewilderment. She shrugged and we waited for Helen to continue.

"He told me about you, Eve and he said you know about us but you don't know the story."

My hackles rose a little at this but I remained silent.

"We're not in love Eve, hell, we haven't even kissed." She disclosed. Amanda looked at me with raised eyebrows but mine were puckered in confusion.

"We're just friends and Jax is doing me a huge favour. There is no wedding Eve, it's all a farce and I feel really bad that it's come between you two. Jax is a great guy and he's hurting so much right now, Eve." I scoffed loudly and I heard her inhalation. "Please just listen," she urged and I sighed heavily.

"Go on," I conceded.

"Jax and I met when he first came to America. He looked a little lost so I helped him settle in, showed him the sights and taught him the lingo, you know, that type of thing and anyway we became good friends, absolutely platonic, Eve."

I picked at my nails while she carried on and my heart started to melt a little.

"Well at the same time I started seeing this guy..." She took a huge breath before she continued and I could sense her anguish through the line.

"After a while we progressed to living together, sharing bills, that sort of stuff, you know how it goes. But anyway after a few months he kind of... well he started to get aggressive."

I pursed my lips and sighed as she became silent. "You okay?" I asked softly.

"Yeah, sorry... Jax started to notice the bruises. He didn't say anything at first but after a few months it got worse but I couldn't get out of the relationship. He was one of those bastards that thought he owned you as soon as you moved in with him."

Amanda and I nodded to ourselves in complete understanding with Helen.

"I found out I was pregnant..." She added and I cringed for her. "So of course Sed..."

"Whoa...." I halted her there. "Is this Sed Tyler we're talking about?"

"Yes," she answered bluntly. All the air stored in my lungs erupted in one single gust.

"Holy shit."

"Yeah. Jax told me you got involved with him, that's another reason I rang you, just to warn you, Eve."

"Don't worry Helen. Sed and me are completely over, have been for a while."

She blew out a huge breath in relief. "Oh thank god. He's bad Eve, so bad. He wouldn't let me go and when he found out I was pregnant he got worse. Anyway one day I eventually opened up to Jax," she revealed with a bit of a hiccup.

"Jax went ballistic and stormed round, beat the shit out of him but even then Sed didn't get the message and wouldn't leave me alone so... so Jax told him we were in love and getting married and that it was his baby," she finished with a huff.

Well this was different. Amanda's face showed as much shock as mine. I didn't quite know how to digest this and I paused for a long moment. "Did it work?" I asked finally.

"Yes," she said bluntly. "But please don't tell Sed it's not real," she added desperately and I promised her I wouldn't. "He loves you so much, Eve. He's a mess and I honestly don't know what to do with him."

"Then I need a favour, Helen."

CHAPTER 51

2 WEEKS LATER

"Jesus Christ E." Harry, one of Room 103's tech guys hugged me tight. "Fuck me girl, it's been years," he shouted in my ear as the crowd at Madison Square Garden's went wild when Room 103 kicked into one of their most popular songs.

My soul pulsed violently at the sound of Jax's tones through the air. "He doesn't know I'm here?" I asked Harry who shook his head and led me side stage to where the rest of the crew were.

They all beamed widely and each one hugged me, even the new guys who I hadn't seen before.

The sound guy approached me. "You ready, Eve? Boss knows what to do," he divulged as he handed me a mic and led me to the steps beside the stage.

My heart stuttered wildly as I caught sight of him. He had lost weight and his face was paler but he was still my gorgeous rock God and my heart exploded inside my chest.

My hands shook and my legs trembled as they finished their current song. Boss approached Jax and said something in his ear, Jax shrugged and spoke back, but Boss shook his head and lifted his hands in a 'don't ask me' gesture.

I could make out Jax say 'I don't know if I can Boss' but Boss nodded sternly before he walked back to his drums.

"MSG," Jax addressed to the crowd which roared in acknowledgement. "Gotta bit of a change. Someone wants us to perform "Shocking Heaven'." He said to his fans whom cheered and whooped loudly.

"You'll have to bear with me cos' I gotta sing... I gotta sing E's part," he choked out. I gulped in much needed air as hastily as I could.

The mass clapped in approval before he turned and signalled to Romeo.

Romeo came in with his slow riff and the crowd were already swaying along with him as Jax choked out the first line but then seemed to go with the flow of our song, his eyes distant and glazed.

"You're there, seen from the stars
Peaceful dignity with so much quiet misery
Trying to hold on, to breathe
Just don't ever leave
I'm beggin ya', ya' need to believe"

I took a calming breath then as Jax started to sing the chorus, I stepped onto the stage from the side. The spotlight hit me as I joined him in the chorus. His face was classic as his jaw dropped and his knees wobbled. His whole face showed shock, merged with disbelief, mixed with elation and exhilaration.

The crowd roared and thundered and chanted and screamed as I smiled and sang with all my heart to my man.

"But if you're going through hell, keep going
Cos' you're just shocking heaven
Shocking heaven
And shaming angels
Cos' you're just screaming in silence
Bringing me to my knees"

I had reached him by now and he stood in amazement, his eyes skimming me and absorbing every single inch of me as I went into my verse.

"You're near, touching my mind
Forever seeing with so much abandon
Trying to take back, to live
I've not much more to give
But I'm beggin', make me believe"

He managed to join me in the next chorus, just barely, as his eyes searched my face for an explanation of what was happening and if I was actually real; and then, finally, a huge grin erupted over his face as he sang his next verse with so much emotion, a tear slid from both of us.

"You're here, inside my soul
Brutal caress with so much tender slaughter
Trying to break free, to run
Don't leave me when you're done

I'm beggin' ya, don't fire the damn gun"

He took my hand and kissed the back of it before we joined together for the next section, both of us singing with so much passion and feeling, our voices rasped and choked out the words.

"But we're trying to carry on and love
Gently fighting against each other for the passion
Linking together as one, no more lonely souls
And now we're shocking heaven, just shocking
heaven"

Then Jax belted out the outro, as he pulled me tight against his hard body and held onto me for dear life as his whole body trembled.

"If you're going through hell, keep going
Keep going, keep going
Don't ever stop, never stop
Keep going, keep going"

"The fuck, babe?" he shouted over the rumble of the fans appreciation. I smiled widely and palmed his cheek.

"You mine, baby?" I whispered against his lips as I told him how much I adored and loved him with just my eyes.

He gasped as both of his hands slid around each side of my head and he breathed me as I inhaled him.

"Lock, stock and barrel, babe."

EPILOGUE

JAX

E turned and looked at me with those damn beautiful big eyes of hers and I grabbed her hand, linking her long thin fingers with my own. "Chill, babe" I told her but her eyes communicated everything she was feeling.

"But Jax, what if..."

I placed a finger against her soft pink lips and shushed her. "No ifs, babe." She was starting to panic and it hurt my heart to see her this way. "E, they won't be here for another two hours. Breathe, babe."

She nodded at me frantically and I watched her pull one of those delicious plump lips in between her teeth.

My cock twitched at the sight of it and I couldn't tear my eyes away. "Fuck, E." I whispered as I growled and nipped that lip with my own teeth then pulled it into my mouth.

She moaned faintly and her hands slipped into my hair as she grabbed a handful. That simple action always had my dick pressing into the zip of my jeans and I returned her groan with one of my own.

"I need you, Jax" she breathed against my mouth. I leant down and scooped her up.

She continued to kiss me in the way only she could kiss; soft, pliable and so damn erotically that I could never resist her after she dominated me with her lips.

She tasted like heaven and Angels but with so much delicious sin, the inspiration for the song I wrote for her. She never knew it was her kiss that had inspired me and she never would, but she realised what her kisses did to me and I knew she used them whenever she wanted her own way.

I just couldn't say no to her... ever. But then again, I never wanted to.

I laid her down gently on the bed and slowly peeled every single piece of her clothing off her, displaying that stunning little body of hers to me. She was so damn beautiful, every single inch of her. I just stood back and took in all of her.

The sight of her fucking exquisite tits brought the blood pumping to my cock potently, they were just so perfect; small but absolutely succulent and those nipples, God those nipples. I had never seen nipples like E's; so pink and plump, my mouth drooled every time she exposed them to me.

I bent into her and took one in my mouth to idolise, circling it with my tongue as I suckled on it. I knew this drove her wild and she arched into me.

"Ooh Jax, that's so... oh wow so nice baby, yes, bite me Jax..."

It always made me chuckle inwardly when she started gibbering, I knew I had her wet and ready for me when she got like this.

"Fucking ace tits, babe" I told her. It always helped to compliment her, and a bit of romance never hurt anyone, so I did it as often as I could, just to see that god damn stunning smile of hers.

Her fingers started fumbling with my belt and I helped her along and stripped down for her before I positioned my throbbing dick at the entrance to her delicious pussy.

She lifted her hips. Begging me to take her and I grinned as I pushed in.

She always felt so fucking incredible and we both moaned in satisfaction as we fused together. "Fuck, babe. Always so fuckin' amazing."

She nodded in agreement but I wondered if she had actually heard me as her eyes rolled back and her bottom lip quivered. Fuck me, that always drove me wild and I started to move inside her.

She clenched around me as I hit the very tip of her and rebounded back. "Fuck Jax... that's it baby... love me..."

Oh, I loved her alright. All of her; every single, fucking, fragment of her. Her heart, her soul, her skin, her brain, her mind, hell, even her breath was fucking sent from god.

She lifted her hips into me as I gave her what she needed and banged her hard. She cried out loudly and I could feel her orgasm approach as her pussy tightened so much it threatened to choke my cock.

"Baby...." She cried as she came around my dick and I followed her over the edge, spurting almost painfully into her as I shouted her name.

She always made me come wild and hard, always had, from the first day I claimed her, and loving her just seemed to get better each time.

She was fucking awesome and I had sworn that she would never be out of my sight ever again, and had taken her as my wife two years ago.

She was utterly angelic that day on the beach. Her soft hair flowing in the breeze, her hot little body wrapped in a simple white gown as Boss had escorted her along the trail of cherry blossom towards me.

She had blown me away at the sight of her and my heart had literally stunted when I saw her beam at me happily.

"Jax..." she whispered in my ear and I looked down into her soft eyes.

I pulled out and ran my nose along the length of hers. "Babe, stop worrying. Promise you, they'll be here," I told her confidently. She nodded at the sincerity in my words.

She sat on the edge of the bed beside me and fiddled with her nails, a habit she had when she was nervous.

I sat behind her and flanked her legs with my own. "You need to hear me, babe."

"I do baby, I hear ya'. I'm just nervous, Jax."

I nodded, that was understandable. Hell, even I was nervous but I knew this would complete her, would complete us.

She pushed off the bed and started to dress. I sat and watched each of her moves as she stripped backwards and I engrained her body to memory until next time I could get her underneath me.

I followed her moves and dressed before we went back down and waited impatiently.

"Do we have everything ready?" she flustered as she scratched behind Bruce's ears. I rolled my eyes and nodded in response to that question for the twentieth time that day.

The doorbell rang. I watched her lithe little body shoot towards the ceiling and I bit back a chuckle. I didn't think she would appreciate me laughing at her at that time.

She blew out a big breath and looked at me so nervously that I took her hand and led her to the front door.

Her hand trembled as she palmed the handle and pulled the door open.

I heard her breath skip as a small choked sob rumbled through her chest.

Rowena beamed at E and handed the precious cargo over. "Mr and Mrs Cooper, welcome to parenthood," she said as E cradled our two week old adopted daughter, Lily.

I swiped E's tears from her face and whispered in her ear, "You both mine, babe?"

She turned to me and stole my heart all over again with the smile that adorned her beautiful face.

"Lock, stock and both barrels, baby."

THE END

Thrilling Heaven
Boss's Story

Book 2 in the Room 103 series
By D H Sidebottom

Available now

<u>Prologue</u>

<u>Jen</u>

You know that moment in your life when someone turns to you and says 'If you could go back to a point in your life and change one thing, what would it be?'

And then everyone sits there, for like ten minutes, deliberating what moment they would choose? Well, mine wouldn't even take a tenth of a second to determine.

It was nine years ago; nine years, eight months to be exact; September 16th 2003 at exactly 11:20pm.

Precise, you say?

Hell, yes. I'll never forget it because it was the moment that my soul died.

The moment when Kyle told me to choose. The moment when Ethan walked away and left my now husband to say to me, "You choose him and I'll hunt him down, Jen. Hunt him to the ends of the earth and make him pay, painfully, viciously and fucking mercilessly for taking you from me."

Nice, isn't he? Kyle, that is.
He was; when I first met him, when I was a fourteen year old schoolgirl with an arrogance and smugness that the schools hottest boy wanted me.

I was blinded and amazed by his determination to date me; me, a plain, brown haired, grey eye ordinary girl, and him, a tall hard muscled sixteen year old, biker/ footballer that all my friends and every other girl in the school drooled over.

He had done everything to make me his, and to be honest at the time I had relished in it, baked in his relentless pursuit to have me, and believe me, I had made it as difficult as possible for him. I had purposely ignored him, refused to even spare him a glance and waved him off whenever he would get close as he continued to fight for my attention.

In the end, all it had taken for him to get me was for him to stick up for my best friend Maisie, who was a stick thin, black frizzy haired girl, with cheap NHS glasses and those metal braces that were glued to her teeth.

Some boys had been throwing her bag around the yard and as much as Maisie and I had tried to retrieve it, they just threw it even more, until along came Kyle, caught the bag and handed it back to Maisie before he kicked the shit out of the three fifteen year old boy's.

Swoon! I was his. Any boy that stuck up for my best friend deserved my upmost attention, and that's what he got.

Me! Lock, stock and barrel and within six months we were in love and inseparable.

And, yes, I'll admit, we were the happiest couple around. Everyone was jealous of our easy, happy relationship and it grew even stronger until on my sixteenth birthday, I gave Kyle my virginity. And yes, it was wonderful and orgasmic.

And that was where my first mistake occurred.

He had all of me now; there was no going back on my part. Kyle knew this, knew that as soon as I gave him that part of me then he was mine and I would always be his.

That was just me. I didn't sleep around. I purposefully waited until my sixteenth birthday to have sex for the first time.

Sex to me was something important, at the time anyway, and should be shared between two people in love who were going to be together forever and you wanted to give them your all.

Instantly after that night, Kyle changed, right in front of my eyes.

His cockiness and irritability with me came through to the forefront of his personality. It was like now he had me, he didn't need to try to keep me.

His moods were dark and sometimes volatile but even then, there was still some of the old Kyle left in there; the Kyle who would open doors for me, the Kyle who would bring me a latte and an apple muffin when he picked me up for college every morning and still the gentle Kyle in the bedroom.

But this is also when the arguments started; loud, volatile and sometimes frightening arguments that would often see Kyle storming off for hours, sometimes whole nights before he would come back, tail between his legs with flowers and chocolates.

This is where Ethan came in. He was always the one to pick up my broken heart and fix it back together with his strong arms and his sweet smiles and gentle words as he slowly patched me up and brought back my smile.

He was the most charming, cutest and adorable boy I'd ever known. His patience and gentleness found me slowly falling in love with him and it soon emerged that he was falling for me too.

The sexual attraction between us was the most intense feeling I had ever felt. His naughty little innuendo's and suggestions had an arousal so fierce surging through me that I knew it was inevitable that we would soon give in to the desire.

Even though we both fought it hard and for so long, it was just too strong to deny and the night I gave myself to him was the same night he told me he loved me, just as he brought an orgasm so extreme I couldn't breathe.

The way he told me he loved me will forever stay with me, until I'm old, grey and toothless and my grandchildren cook my tea whilst I watch Countdown.

We were making love for the first time and he was inside me, so deep inside me as he suddenly stopped moving, cupped my cheeks and said, "By the way, Jen...", he then thrust once more and came inside me as he whispered "...I love you."

As soon as it had happened we were both riddled with guilt for what we had done to Kyle and we tried desperately to stay away from each other but it was too strong, our feelings, our love and very soon we were doing everything we could to sneak away and meet up.

Our special place was the field behind Mr Tarney's garage.

Every single time I bounded through the tall grass, looking for the long stick with the small white piece of material attached to it showing me Ethan's location in our own secluded world, my heart would thump so rapidly I could feel the beat in my toes, my soul danced excitedly like a pink aura that would swirl around me and my smile would cheer up the devil himself.

*Because Ethan **was** the beat of my heart, he **was** the aura my soul danced with and he **was** the sun that lit my smile.*

*He **was** my everything.*

But it all slammed to a halt that night, September 16th 2003, when at exactly 11:20pm a drunken Ethan told Kyle, "I've been fucking your girlfriend for two years, Kyle and I love her and she loves me."

Bang! Just like that my whole world collapsed.

Ethan announced it to Kyle, Kyle went ballistic and ordered me to choose, Ethan walked out and then Kyle uttered those infamous words.

Two days later, at the age of eighteen, I was sat beside a dark and simmering Kyle, in the front of his clapped out Corsa to start a new life in London and I never saw Ethan again.

16399882R00266

Printed in Great Britain
by Amazon